The GREAT RESTORATION

A Tale of the Verin Empire

~

\- WILLIAM RAY -

The Great Restoration is a work of fiction. Any resemblance to actual events, locales, or persons living or dead is coincidental.

Cover by Ramona & Adrian Marc

In memory of my Great Aunt Thelma.
She was always more of a sci-fi gal,
but I like to think Fifi would enjoy this anyway.

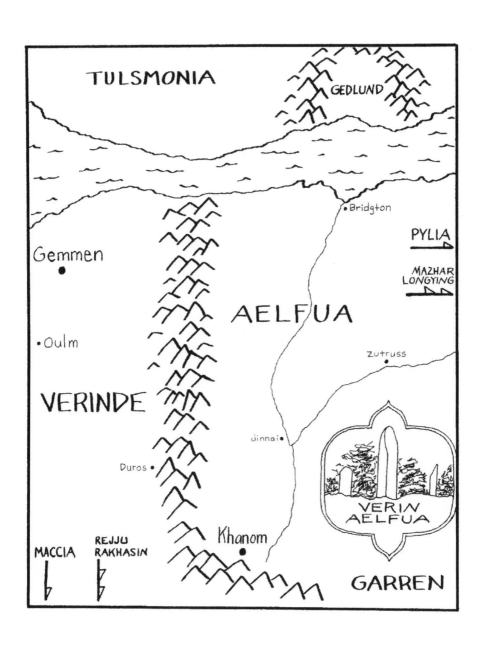

The City of Khanom

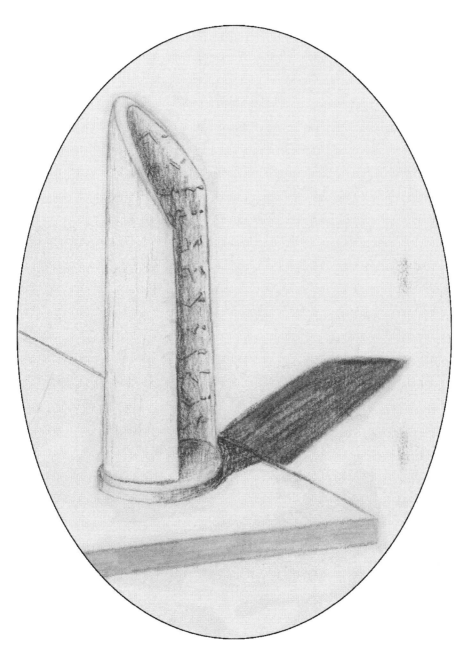

One of the many Elven obelisks that remained in Khanom.

~

"Queen of Tulsmonia Found"

Refugees from the purges in Tulsmonia continue to escape from the ongoing chaos in that once proud kingdom. As mindful readers will no doubt have observed, several women have already emerged claiming to be the widow of the deposed magnar, Hamul Berengar. While the Workers' Revolutionary Committee has repeatedly asserted their extinguishment of the Tuls' royal lineage, rumors of her survival persist throughout the world, and a likely new claimant has emerged in Sakloch.

Doctor Gleb Nichols, formerly the magnar's royal physician, has interviewed the woman at length and firmly asserts she is indeed the rightful queen of Tulsmonia. Even with the destruction of their kingdom, many loyal members of Tulsmonia's deposed aristocracy will no doubt flock to her as the magnar's legal inheritor. The Berengars' fantastic personal wealth also extended well beyond Tulsmonia's borders, and with sufficient political support, many believe she may be able to restore peace and stability to Tulsmonia.

– *Khanom Daily Converser*, 22 Ozr. 389

~

- CHAPTER 1 -

Dorna knelt patiently on the cold stone floor as the other Wardens entered the room and took places upon their knees alongside her. Each was wrapped in the identical green robes of their movement, with veiled hoods pulled over their heads, and only their eyes were visible; each seemed nothing more than an anonymous portion of the whole. Elsewhere, they were ordinary men and women of varying social rank, but here they shared a common devotion to a cause greater than any division raised between them by the world beyond.

With her hood drawn forward, and her face obediently downcast, Dorna could not see much more than the polished marble floor, but in the lair of the Malik Verdun, the Master of Wardens, she knew she was always surrounded by wonders of the ancient world. This meeting chamber held her favorite: a pair of tapestries depicting the ancient Elven court, embroidered in silks so fine that individual strands were nearly invisible to the naked eye.

An immortal Elven artist had used their centuries of practiced skill to painstakingly create images that were sharper and more alive than any photograph Dorna had ever seen. Whenever she looked at the tapestries, it was as if the windowless meeting room was somehow set amid the court of the Elven queen. The soft hiss of the room's gas lamps would seem to fade away as the interplay of colors made her feel the gentle warmth of late spring and smell the sweet scent of the flowering trees just beyond the frame of the embroidery.

She had sometimes snuck here as a young girl to stare up at the image of the Elven queen, who had eyes of soft jade that seemed to hold measureless wisdom and a slight upturn of her lips that promised gentle compassion. In the tapestry, the queen was surrounded by attendants—the Master had named them her advisors. As a child, Dorna could not imagine what sort of advice they could possibly add to the perfection of their immortal queen, but now she wished they had warned her of the encroaching danger of humanity.

The tapestry across from it showed a panoply of Elves in elegant dress—the nobles of the realm, awaiting their turn to address the queen. The walls of that embroidered throne room were lined with knights resplendent in gleaming golden armor of polished elfsteel. The impudent armies of Dorna's ancestors had never faced the Queen's Guard, who no doubt still stood vigil over her, wherever she had gone.

The two tapestries, the Master had explained, were to remind the Wardens of the grandeur of those they served and of the beautiful perfection they hoped to restore. As the Wardens filled the room behind her, she could almost feel the queen's approving gaze, overseeing the proceedings as if they truly knelt in her presence.

She suspected that nearly everyone must be in attendance tonight since perhaps forty or more knelt in fellowship, although Dorna was never sure of their true numbers. They rarely gathered so many together at one time, lest their passage here draw the attention of what lurked in the Oblivion, but the Master had warned that dramatic events were drawing to a head and that he would have assignments for them all.

Something imperceptible signaled the Wardens to silence. Dorna felt the call for it clearly, as she always did, though she never knew how. With the room stilled, she could hear the soft whisper of his slippers on the stone floor as he stepped into their presence.

Though she did not look up, she knew her Elven lord smiled down at her as he passed, and she felt a familiar shiver at his recognition. Despite their veiled hoods, he somehow always knew which one she was and always shared that secret smile of approval. As a little girl, she had occasionally peeked up to confirm it, but now she simply felt it and had faith in that presence.

After he passed her, she slowly raised her head, watching that movement echoed in turn by each row ahead of her, as the Master walked to the front of the room. Once there, he slowly turned to face the gathering as two Wardens from the first row pushed quickly to their feet and hurried by. Two large pieces of seemingly random jumbles of natural wood were pressed together by the Wardens behind him, interlocking like a puzzle to form his elegant throne, and the Master sat down without looking back, showing his complete faith in those who served him.

It was an honor shared by them all in rotation, but Dorna always felt a small sting of jealousy whenever it was not her turn. As always, she also felt a bit of pride for them as well—she did not know who they were outside of this company, but she was a woman of low birth and little money, and in a world ruled by mortal men, such honors would always be beyond her ilk. Here, Wardens were judged only by devotion and ability.

Seated, the Master smiled down at them, and raising his hands, he spoke. As always, he began with an invocation of the proceedings in classical Elven, the words of which none of them understood, but despite that, Dorna knew every syllable. His voice was melodious, perfect, and his words sang out in their hearts. It was a melancholy tune, but she felt it flow through her and felt a sense of deep communion in sharing the experience with the other Wardens.

Dorna's whole body felt an electric shiver as she listened to the invocation, and she had to fight the urge to close her eyes and simply let the experience wash over her. The words were important, even if she didn't know the language, so she moved her lips in time, silently mouthing each syllable to keep her focus upon them.

The movement of her lips was hidden by the veil covering her face, but she always bit her lower lip in embarrassment once the invocation ended, worried somehow the Master might notice what she was doing and take it as a sign of disrespect. By ancient tradition, Wardens were to remain completely still as they focused upon the words, and her silent mimicry was inappropriate. It was a solemn, holy moment, not to be disturbed by anything, but she worried letting her mind wander could be the greater sin.

The Master took a moment to smile benevolently down upon the rows of cloaked Wardens kneeling before him, but Dorna knew him well enough to see the sadness behind that gaze. He spoke next in melodic Verin, his voice as perfect and musical in the human tongue as it was in his own. "Loyal Wardens, you have served well, and we draw ever nearer the Great Restoration. The imbalance brought about by wayward men can yet be undone. Glory and salvation await us all once the rightful sovereign of all peoples returns."

Dorna resisted the impulse to look over at the image of the Elven queen, once the ruler of a nation at peace with the magical world, who had guided her realm with the accumulated wisdom only immortality could earn. Without that balance between the material and spiritual worlds that the queen had protected, crops were blighted, disease ran rampant, and people suffered. The Elves had ruled in a kinder age, and a comfortably prosperous one, until mankind's greed destroyed the balance and forced the Elves into war.

The Master's smile faded, and Dorna tensed for the news he had summoned them to deliver. "Alas, once again we face a blasphemy that must be resisted. Despite our efforts, loyal agents tell me that once again men conspire to raise their tower in celebration of the banishment of the elder race. Given their way, it will rise upon the very site of the queen's palace."

Around the room, there were hisses of anger from many of her gathered fellows, and Dorna was forced to clench her jaw to hold her own silence. With another speaker, they might even have broken into angry rumbles, but Dorna knew none of them wanted to risk missing even a moment of his honeyed voice.

The Wardens had worked time and again to prevent the desecration of what had once been the heart of Elven civilization. Their Master's plans in that regard had been subtle and multifarious, disrupting attempts both high and low. For years, his will had shaped the human city's relentless growth, carefully directing it around the most sacred sites to preserve them for the return of his people.

Dorna had performed several assignments for the Master to stop this very project, and though her last mission to do so had been a personal failure, the Master had stepped in to make things right. She had hoped it was finally settled.

After giving them all a moment to quiet themselves, the Master continued. "The city around us is no less offensive. Typically, another tower to human arrogance would be merely another expression of mortal folly."

Dorna nodded sadly in agreement, and saw Wardens in the rows ahead of her doing the same. Unlike the Wardens of human myth, she had no hatred for her own kind, but she had seen the limits of mortal wisdom and the price of their impatience. As a young girl, her father had been worked to death by a callous foreman in the employ of an uncaring mine owner.

If the Master had not seen her promise and taken her in, the limited vision of human mercy would have seen her cast out into the street. It was that sort of benevolence that had won her to his cause, and she did not doubt the loyalty of many fellow Wardens had been earned by similar acts.

"This is worse, however, and not just for where it sits. At great personal risk, our agents have obtained the latest designs." Their Master paused, as if pained by the import of his next words, and then said, "The twisted monstrosity they seek to raise there is a tower of iron."

There were rumblings of outrage throughout the room. Even though she already knew of the tower's design, hearing it again made Dorna's blood boil with anger at the audacious effrontery of it. For all that men trumpeted their victory over the Elves, the Wardens knew it was not force of arms that had ultimately driven away their immortal lords, but the treacherous web of iron rails that had disrupted the mystic ley lines upon which Elven civilization had been built.

In ancient times, when rebellious men had first sought her overthrow, the Elven queen had mercifully banished them from her lands and forced them to fend for themselves. Men lacked the magical wisdom of the Elves, but over generations they learned to compensate. Dorna suspected they had known enough to purposefully lay railways across key points of the ley lines in a sinister effort to doom their former rulers.

With the flow of magic stifled, the Elves had been forced to withdraw from the world, and without their wise leadership, mankind continued to throw the natural order further and further out of balance. The Master was all that remained of that elder civilization, but he could not save the world alone. Each Warden was here because they knew everything now hung upon a precipice and had sworn an oath to help restore what had been lost.

For years they had secretly disrupted rail lines and other building projects the Master deemed dangerous to the Great Restoration. Dorna was no thaumaturgist, but if scattered railways were a problem, then an iron spire in such a key location was more than just an insult—it could well mean the end of the world. Even as she thought it, the Master spoke again and confirmed her fears.

"Your secret guardianship has nearly paved the way for the Great Restoration, but this tower places all your work in jeopardy."

Across the room, a woman began to weep, and, whoever she was, Dorna hated her. Now was not the time for lament, and if Dorna had her way, that day would never come. They had sworn their oaths as Wardens, and in the face of such an affront as this, she felt no sense of defeat—only outrage and the urge to fight.

He spoke again, his voice soothing as he reassured them, "When foul spirits ruled the world, the Elves brought order and made the world safe for their vassals. When men embraced the gods of darkness, Elves and Wardens stood firm against it for centuries. Our queen aided Caerleon in his hours of need and defended him as he scaled the temple for Maladriel's mirror. Throughout history, we have faced these challenges together. Together, we will thwart this tower. Nothing will stop the Great Restoration."

A lesser speaker might have received an ovation, but feeling the honeyed grandeur of the Master's words wash over them, the room fell silent. Dorna was pleased that no one interrupted him with their trivial gestures of approval. His majestic presence did not require their approval.

"You have passed through darkness to aid us, and loyalty is rewarded with service. All of you will have a role to play, but I have chosen three of you for a special errand that must begin immediately. The rest of you should return to your tasks and be ready for my instruction."

The Wardens murmured the Elven chant he had taught them and then bowed low, their heads touching the floor. As the Master stood, the two Wardens at the front rushed forward and pulled apart the throne. They led the way out of the room, and as they passed each row, the Wardens kneeling there stood and filed after them in quiet order. In the hall beyond, they would no doubt quickly shed their cloaks and begin displays of merry camaraderie that Dorna always felt were absurd in the context of their collective mission.

Dorna remained kneeling, along with two others. She had not been told to remain, but somehow, she knew she was one of the three chosen. Her master could do many amazing things—appearing as a mortal man or woman, speaking without words, or swaying the thoughts of lesser minds—so when she simply knew a truth, she had learned to embrace it as his touch upon her.

The door to the hallway closed, muting the growing babble from those who had left. The Master smiled down at her again. She could not see it, with her face pressed to the floor, but she felt it in the shiver that passed down her spine. Somehow, just as she had known she was chosen, she knew it was time to rise to her feet.

In the hooded robes, she could not be certain, but judging by the bulky frame on one of them, she suspected it was Dougal. He was a dangerous man, if a bit indelicate, and was usually only called upon for important tasks. He was reserved for tasks in which the cause must sometimes override common moral restraint, and she worried his presence meant the Master did not trust her to go as far as was needed. That sign of doubt wounded her, but she resolved to embrace it. However dire their task, she would not flinch.

Nothing could be permitted to stop the Great Restoration.

~

Advertisement for the Augustus P. Offer Publishing Company:

Give the Boy a Chance!

That boy who has been working and could not start with the fall class – he has no time to waste on impractical theories, superfluous verbiage, useless technicalities, and unnecessary restrictions. He is entitled to the most practical approach. Place in his hands Offer's Brief Course in either Robb-Michaels or Weaver SHORTHAND and see him gain on the class which has the advantage of a four months' handicap.

Learn why at our expense! Paper-bound copy free to shorthand teachers. Give name of school and specify Robb-Michaels or Weaver. No time to lose, so write to-day!

– *Gemmen Standard*, 6 Tal. 389

~

- CHAPTER 2 -

The sharp jostle of his shoulder shook him from dreamless haze into semiconsciousness, and was followed by an exasperated, "Gus, wake up!"

At first it was too bright to open his eyes, but the woman's voice sounded urgent, so he pushed through the instinct to lay his head back down. Gradually, the world resolved into a brownish blur with light streaming in from behind him. He was seated, and a slight movement of his leg bounced his knee against the desk in front of him, pulling him even further from slumber. If the brownish blur was his desk, then this was probably his office.

Gus leaned forward in his chair, bracing his fingers against his forehead and setting his elbows on his desk to provide additional support when his head proved too heavy to hold upright. Emily would give him no peace, however, and pushed him back in his chair, saying something that did not at first resolve into any sort of coherent message.

The night prior was difficult to recall, and ignoring Emily for the moment, he tried to sort out how he got here. They had been paid a few days earlier, and the client's promissory note had finally been negotiated into cash. With pockets full and having soundly embarrassed Detecting-Inspector Clarke once more, Gus had resolved to go out drinking and perhaps pick up a girl or two.

Head swimming, he squinted up at his office; the pale walls caught the light, although they were broken by the occasional framed something or other. Looking down was no better, with his dark wooden desk surrounded by that hideous orange carpet he had somehow been talked into. Emily thrust a glass of water at him, and with a grateful grunt, he tossed it back.

Between his thirst, his headache, and what seemed to have been a night of blessedly dreamless sleep, it was clear last night's drinking had been accomplished. Apparently, he had failed to pick up any girls. If he had been successful at the latter, then he probably would have taken them home and awoken there, rather than at his desk. It was a little disappointing, but at least a hangover didn't usually want money from him in the morning.

"Oh, you're a mess," Emily complained as she brushed at something on his sleeve, "Try to pull yourself together; she'll be here any moment, and you need to look the part." He scowled up at her, but she just watched him expectantly. She was worse than an army sergeant—or at least worse than he had been as one. Surely he had never kicked awake tired, hungover men and demanded they 'look the part'.

With a defeated sigh, he pushed to his feet and grimaced at both the familiar pain in his left calf and the realization that as a sergeant he had, in fact, done that exact thing several times. He had at least always shown them the courtesy of drinking with them the night before though, and thus shared their morning lament. He assumed he had offered Emily a place in his revels last night, but she was too prim these days.

The entire situation seemed grossly unfair, as he was long since out of the army, and she was his employee, not the other way around.

"Sure enough," she replied, making him realize he had spoken at least some of that aloud, "but not if you don't make any money."

A retort bubbled up from the back of his mind—that maybe she should just settle down and get married. It was the sort of thing people said often enough amid the recent surge of women seeking office employment, but in his more wakeful moments, her actually doing so was an inevitability he dreaded. Fortunately, he had recovered just enough presence of mind to keep his mouth shut.

Emily swept her hands over his jacket, trying to smooth it out, then sighed and said, "Your pants are rumpled too—no, don't take them off! Missus Phand will be here any moment."

Gus rubbed at his eyes, searching his memory for any appointments he had made for today, but could not think of any. Usually he immediately stopped looking for more work once he had been paid for the last job—there didn't seem to be much point in working until after he had spent the money from their last bout of employment. Emily clearly expected he should know who Missus Phand was, however, and was just waiting for him to embarrass himself.

Finally, although he hated giving her the satisfaction, he asked, "Who is Missus Phand?"

Emily gave an exasperated sigh, possibly having already explained this, moments earlier when he was paying less attention. "Alice Phand. She's the wife of that famous engineer. The one who made that bridge near Oulm? It was in all the papers last year."

He dimly recalled the bridge being in the papers but not why. His family was from Oulm, so he had carefully avoided it in the past twenty years. In his childhood memories, Oulm was a sleepy industrial city that completely lacked Gemmen's vibrant night scene. At least, he assumed it was still vibrant, based on what little he remembered of the night he had just spent enjoying it. On the other hand, given that he had awoken in his office instead of his flat, he wondered if perhaps the Verin capital's late-night charms had finally begun growing stale.

Even if it had though, the haze of alcohol always did wonders for blurring out his memories of the army, particularly the war against Gedlund's armies of grasping dead and the chilling laughter of its

Everlords as they descended from the sky. His faculties were returning now, which did him no favors, so he did his best to push those memories behind his throbbing headache.

The glass of water Emily had given him had been mysteriously refilled, and he sipped at it again. Eventually that would start to address the headache, at which point he supposed he'd need more alcohol.

"I don't remember meeting her before. Is this something you set up?" he asked with a scowl, not appreciating the imposition of Emily's client selections. Occasionally she would decide they were not making enough money and bring in clients herself when his business tapered off. He found those efforts on his behalf vaguely insulting and, in this case, inconvenient; he had enough to drink away another week, perhaps two if he didn't hire female companionship as often as usual.

He groaned at the burst of sunlight when she opened the drapes wider, which had not only kept out the worst of the sun, but also pleasantly muffled the sounds of traffic on the street below. Judging by both, it was still quite early in the day, and he wondered what sort of horrid client would schedule an appointment at a time like this.

Squinting at Emily, he grumbled, "This is another one of those you met at the temples, isn't it?"

Her newfound piety was a nuisance, and the clients she brought by from it tended to be boring small cases that pulled in very little money individually, which meant he needed to do more of them. Gus's own clients offered a much bigger return for his troubles. After his testimony before Parliament about the war in Gedlund, Gus had won a brief moment of celebrity and had managed to rub elbows with more of the right sort. They, seldom meeting trustworthy men of low character, had found him quite useful.

It turned out the upper echelons often needed someone to discreetly investigate things that they could not manage themselves for various social reasons, and they paid well for the favor. A titled gentleman could hardly stroll down to meet the local fences in his effort to recover a stolen heirloom or spend the afternoon watching a business rival in the hopes of finding some bit of leverage upon him. Satisfied patrons had told their friends, who had told their friends, and thus his career as a private inquiry agent had begun.

Gus's pension from the army was enough to live on, if not comfortably, so the extra money he earned mostly impacted how much he could drink. Emily's income, however, now depended entirely on his continued employment. Perhaps those finances were the real source of her newfound temperance—she probably spent far less on tithes than he did on alcohol.

Emily sighed, waited for his eyes to refocus, then shook her head and said, "No. She came looking last night, just before I closed up. I told her you were on a case. Her husband is famous, and the papers were saying he's starting another big project soon, so it's probably good money."

With an unseemly familiarity he had long since grown accustomed to, she tucked his shirt back in and tugged his collar straight. She was treating him like a child, and he had to fight off the temptation to sulk like one.

He really wanted a strong thick coffee to help clear his head, but some charlatan had recently convinced her that coffee was somehow sinful or perhaps just unhealthy. Before that, he hadn't cared which drink he took in the morning, but now the forbidden beverage seemed infinitely more desirable. Without that, in his current state he felt he shouldn't be expected to remember anything about famous engineers.

"Why is she coming here, though? Why me and not Drake's?"

Emily shrugged, apparently without an answer for once.

For the past two years, Drake's had been slowly stealing away his clientele, or he never would have let Emily bring in clients in the first place. Drake's Detectives were from out east and huge and organized and worst of all had presented a menu of standard rates for their services.

Until Drake's came along, rates were fluid, based on an agent's ability to guess how much the client could pay and balanced on the back end by the bonus of anything they found that made suitable blackmail material. Most of his competitors held on to particularly lush discoveries as plans to finance their eventual retirement, but Drake's was too big and too prominent to pull off that sort of thing. He'd yet to come across something like that of his own but didn't consider himself above the usual approach if an opportunity presented itself.

Word would get around if one of Drake's ever stooped to it, and since word hadn't gotten around, their services were beginning to seem almost genteel compared to unfranchised inquiry agents like Gus.

Emily grabbed at the sleeve of his jacket, batting at his arm as she tried to clean away something that had gotten caked there. Her ministrations ceased a moment so that she could pull back and eye him critically, and Gus took that moment to pull open a desk drawer where he kept a small mirror, hoping to straighten his mussed hair. As he did, there was a glint of gold as the morning light reflected off the elfsteel blade carelessly left stuffed in that drawer, and he quickly replaced the mirror, willing to let his hair be a little mussed rather than sink into another melancholy recollection of friends lost.

Seeing he was awake enough to start tending himself, Emily looked him over in one last critical review and then headed through the door back towards her desk in the foyer to await Alice Phand.

When he set up here, the room between the hall and his office had been entirely superfluous—having a receptionist to greet clients had really boosted his professional image, even if that receptionist was just a woman. The wall between his office and the foyer was pointless since anyone sitting outside could hear everything within, but closing the door seemed to reassure clients of their privacy.

Gus scratched absently at the stubble on his jaw but knew there wasn't time to shave. His light brown hair usually let him skip a day or two, but it had been at least two days, so he just hoped Missus Phand wouldn't notice. He slicked back his hair and tried to straighten his jacket. Women of the upper crust often disdained the very idea of women in offices, so he might already be on shaky ground with Missus Phand and wanted to look his best.

At the sound of footsteps in the hall, he knew time was up, and with a wince at the stiffness in his injured leg, he walked over to the framed medals on the wall; Adelaide had done that for him before he broke her heart, or perhaps it was the other way around. Either way, he fixed his attention on the framed collection, hoping his melancholy study would seem more like grim reflections on an exemplary military career rather than a middle-aged man's musings on romantic failures.

In the front room, the two women exchanged cool, professional greetings, and with a light rap of unnecessary warning, the door to his office slowly swung open. Emily looked relieved to see him standing and looking the part as he turned to welcome their new client and said, "Missus Phand, please come in. Have a seat. Can we get you something? Coffee perhaps?"

Emily ushered the tall blonde woman inside and then said, "I'll bring in a pot of tea," giving him a parting glare for offering coffee he knew they didn't have.

Looking over his shoulder at the framed medals, Missus Phand ignored his question and asked, "Is that the Queen's Stars? You fought the Lich King in Gedlund?"

Gus grinned and said, "Well, it wasn't much of a fight—he was already dead when we got there."

In the years since his return from the army, that line had earned him many drinks, although by now it was long since stale from overuse as every veteran of Gedlund made the same crack. Missus Phand was unamused.

For her part, Missus Phand was a remarkable looking woman. She was younger than he had expected, perhaps even still in her twenties. She was handsome enough, if a bit too sporty for Gus's taste—most women of her class were willowy in youth and plumped quickly with age, but Missus Phand was unusually athletic of build.

Her slippers were flat-heeled, but she still stood several inches taller than he. An unbustled frock of blue, in the modern cut, did little to flatter her fit physique, although Gus could not object to the curves it did manage to emphasize. The black fur around her shoulders said she had money though, and there were few things Gus found more attractive than that.

Beneath a broad-brimmed, flower-strewn, yellow hat, her eyes were cold slate, and despite the inquiry about his medals, she regarded him with the barely disguised contempt that women of her class often held for the working man. She glanced at his unlit fireplace with a frown and pulled her fur stole out of the way as she took a seat in one of the chairs across from his desk.

"Mister Baston, I require services of a discreet nature," she began. He walked across to his own chair, trying to disguise his limp, but Missus Phand's eyes darted down, and she seemed to take it in as another distasteful element of his character. War heroes were to return unscathed or not at all—no one wanted the injured lingering about disrupting visions of the Empire's martial glory. With a chiding tone, as if he'd had the poor taste to interrupt her with a burp, she continued, "I've had some friends ask about, and they say you might meet my requirements."

Gus nodded and did his best to emulate the professional seriousness that often comforted her sort, replying, "Of course, Missus Phand. We pride ourselves on our discretion. I take it this is not something you care to trust to Drake's?"

The competition were actually surprisingly discreet, but hinting the worst about them in front of potential customers often helped when it came time to haggle over prices. Given her initial reaction to his limp, he stood by his chair, rather than further embarrass himself with the awkward display required of easing into it.

She regarded him suspiciously for a moment, then slowly nodded and said, "My husband is Edward Phand, the well-known engineer, and I could not afford this going to the papers before things are settled." Missus Phand hesitated again before going farther, "As you might imagine by our age difference, I am not satisfied in our current situation."

It began to grow clearer, and Gus gave her what he hoped was an understanding smile. The law-and-order types that Drake's pompously referred to as their 'detectives' were sometimes less than zealous in these sorts of cases. Sanctity of marriage and all that. "You'd like out."

The woman frowned at him but nodded and said, "We've been married for many years, but now a younger fellow has caught my interest." Gus had no idea how old the engineer was but doubted that was a career where wealth and fame quickly accrued. Hard work had probably kept him from seriously courting until he was more settled, so she was probably quite a bit his junior.

If Phand had an eye for younger women, it would be easy enough to find, or manufacture, the evidence Missus Phand would need for a good accounting in the dissociation. His earlier distress at being interrupted mid-binge was entirely washed away by the potential of easy money.

Emily entered the room bearing a tray with a pot of tea and some sweetened biscuits she only ever produced for clients. Gus loved the biscuits and resolved for the umpteenth time to figure out where she hid them; even with all the other mysteries he had resolved, the answer to that one continued to elude him.

Missus Phand glanced back and frowned at the secretary, confirming Gus's expectation of her reaction. With Emily's dark hair bound into a simple bun, her plain white blouse, and simple dark blue skirt, she was the very image of the modern career-minded woman, but such women were little respected in proper society. Missus Phand's elaborate blonde coiffure and expensive clothes marked her as Emily's complete opposite, and he supposed antagonism between the two was only natural.

Gus grinned and waved his hand as if to fan away Missus Phand's concern for the case. He leaned casually against his desk and said, "Of course, of course. This happens all the time, and I completely understand. We can set something up." He plucked a biscuit from the tray as Emily frowned at him from behind Missus Phand, clearly having taken a dislike to the woman, and he took a quick bite as he ignored Emily's concerns and smiled down to his client.

Gesturing to Emily, he said, "Miss Loch is quite charming when she dresses the part, and we've done this sort of thing before. It's important that you have some reliable witnesses to accompany you when you catch them in the act."

The stately blonde looked over at Emily, then back to him in obvious disgust, and shook her head. Gus took a breath, ready to explain his experience in such cases and how common these sorts of arrangements really were, but she held up her hand to forestall him. "That is not necessary. He's been cheating on me for years, Mister Baston."

Gus did his best to look sympathetic, although Emily quite outdid him in that regard—she laid a comforting hand on Missus Phand's shoulder. Missus Phand brushed away that comforting hand with a look of distaste, and Emily frowned at the reproach, immediately suspicious. Gus trusted her instincts on other matters, but Emily always seemed that way with clients seeking to escape the banns.

A wealthy woman who wanted to leave her husband for a younger man but keep the wealth of the one she had—it seemed completely understandable to him. The announcement that Phand was already cheating was disappointing since that news seemed to render Gus's more expensive services somewhat superfluous. She would probably pay less if she just wanted him to find more details about something she already knew.

"What makes you think he's cheating?"

"Women can tell these things, Mister Baston. Time is important to me, but I do not wish too big of a scene. Find me someplace he is taking her but nothing too crowded—some place out on the street where my witnesses and I might surprise him."

Gus smiled confidently and said, "I believe we can help you. Miss Loch, will you get the paper for Missus Phand to sign?" Producing a pen, he smiled at Missus Phand and asked, "He lives and works here in town? That being the case, our expenses should be low, and you will only need to cover that plus the usual rate of … uh …." He paused for Emily to call back the amount since usually she was better at guessing how much a female client would pay, but Missus Phand would not wait.

She stood, imperiously tossing her fur back around her shoulders and announcing, "Yes, yes. I will pay you two hundred and fifty peis. Half now and half when you report back. Flat. I don't care about your expenses." She slapped down a handful of gold peis on his desk and looked to Gus as if daring him to refuse. Startled by the gesture, he glanced at Emily, who stood in the doorway still looking suspicious about the whole arrangement.

On his own, Gus would have asked much less up front and then pressed her for more in expenses on the back end, dickering back and forth and, if she were any good, ending up at less than two hundred for the whole affair. He doubted Emily would have done much better. Restraining himself from acting giddy at his windfall from Missus Phand's impatience, Gus smiled pleasantly and replied, "I think that should be acceptable, under the circumstances."

Missus Phand nodded once and spun on her heel, marching out of the room in a manner he would have admired as a colour sergeant. As Missus Phand pushed past her, Emily gave a few awkward goodbyes that were totally ignored, then looked back and frowned at the money on the table. She hurried across the room, quickly scooped up the cash, and counted it a few times, murmuring petulantly, "She didn't sign the contract."

"It's fine. Woman like that? She'll pay the rest. If she doesn't we just won't tell her what we find, and we'll still have the first hundred."

"'Women can tell.' Ha. Not as often as they think, or I'd have been in a lot more trouble." Emily cleared away the untouched tea, which Gus had no doubt was another strike against Missus Phand in her book. "She was putting on airs. I don't trust her."

Gus shrugged and looked around for his coat, saying, "Well, you don't have to. It's a quick tail and report, and I won't need you to do anything. Besides, you weren't expecting me to do any work this week, and yet we're already well paid up front!"

"You were the one not expecting to do any work! I was still hoping you would! Do you even know where you're going?"

He grinned at her and said, "Phand and someone, right?"

Emily looked surprised and replied, "Saucier. I didn't think you'd remember them."

"I didn't, but if he's a prominent engineer, he's part of some firm with his name and someone else's, right? I'm sure Louis will know where they are." Somehow his coat had ended up crumpled beneath his desk, and Gus kept his left leg stiff as he awkwardly bent down to retrieve it. "I'm surprised you remember it though. That must be some bridge."

She shook her head, looking baffled at his ignorance. "It is. I can't believe you don't know it; you're from Oulm!" He just shrugged; he supposed he had lost whatever vestiges of civic pride he might have had after joining the army. She frowned at him in frustration and added, "They even mentioned it in the paper again this week! Apparently Doctor Phand has some new big building under consideration for the upcoming exposition in Khanom, but people are protesting it."

"What for?"

She shrugged and said, "They think it's ugly, I guess."

"No, I mean why are they building things like that for an exposition in Khanom?" Expositions were usually a Garren thing, an excuse to demand everyone come to some distant city to see their latest display of national pride as if they hadn't needed Verin to save them in Aelfua. Khanom was in Verin's section of Aelfua, which seemed remote enough that Gus had a hard time imagining what they could be so proud of.

Emily stared at him a long moment as if trying to decide if he were serious, then said, "The Aelfua Exposition? It's to celebrate forty years since we defeated the Elves."

"Forty? Aren't these things usually at fives?"

"I suppose they didn't feel like waiting another decade. They've been discussing it for the past year—as the biggest city in Verin Aelfua, Khanom is going to host it. Don't you ever read the paper?"

"Of course I do, just not every section." Emily rolled her eyes at that, and Gus limped towards the door, slowly working some of the stiffness out of his leg. He stepped out into the foyer and plucked his hat from the rack, somewhat relieved to discover it had made it here through his evening's revels. He turned back to Emily, tried to conjure his most charming smile even though that seldom seemed to work on her, and said, "Relax. This will be easy money."

~

"Tuls Ship Found Adrift"

Garren sailors aboard the OMV Fuquare have reported sighting a Tuls ship adrift along the western waters of the Aelfuan Strait. The vessel's name remains unknown as none aboard were able to read Tuls, but all witnesses agree it was an older mercantile vessel. Although the ship was under sail when sighted, no crew was visible abovedeck.

With reports that spreading disease is being left unchecked by the newly empowered Workers' Revolutionary Committee and foul health running rampant in Tulsmonia, fear of contamination prevented further investigation by the Fuquare's crew. Sailors interviewed claimed no warning flags were flown by the Tuls vessel to indicate plague aboard, but the second mate speculated that inexperienced sailors fleeing the chaos in that country might not have thought to raise one.

– *Gemmen Herald*, 6 Tal. 389

~

- CHAPTER 3 -

The chill of winter had been slow to fade into the pleasant cool of spring, but the warmth of the morning sun and the leavings of traffic had already thawed much of Gemmen's stench. The war in Gedlund had taught Gus to hate snow, but in Gemmen a light dusting worked wonders for the nose. Unfortunately, that seasonal mercy had already been replaced by a continuous cold drizzle that only worked half so well. Come summer, that would dry up a bit, forcing anyone with means to leave the city and escape the fetid mix of horse, horse droppings, soot, and whatever refuse lay rotting nearby.

Gus made his way from the office towards the nearest taxi stand and paused at the corner to toss down a couple of bits, so he could take a paper from the boy stationed there. It was usually the *Gemmen Standard*, but some days the boy from the *Gemmen Herald* managed to seize control of the corner.

One paper was as good as another as far as Gus was concerned, and he didn't pay attention to which it was. As he scooped up the latest edition, however, he relished in proving her wrong once again. Of course he read the paper. Half of his job was standing around and holding up a newspaper, so he would look inconspicuous. That didn't mean he should be expected to remember every article.

Paper in hand, Gus decided to cut through an alleyway running parallel, rather than risk his pants to a splatter of muck from the roads. The alleyway was full of garbage, including a slowly decaying mutt that had died there sometime last month, but in the shadows between the buildings, frost still clung through morning, muting the usual reek. In summer, the alley was untenable, but in spring, it was the only route safe from the foul slurry tossed up by passing traffic.

Keeping to shallow breaths, he made his way behind the buildings and then back onto the street at the end of the block where the taxis usually loitered. He approached the nearby taxi stand but bypassed the first two hacks, ignoring the drivers as they touted their services. Their rates were regulated, and passengers were supposed to go with the first cab in line, but fares here weren't so plentiful as to let that stifle competition.

In this part of the city, taxis were required to charge based on the number of intersections passed through along the way, so they competed to lure passengers from each other by shouting out popular landmarks and claiming how few intersections it would take them to get there. In practice, the intersection count was often conveniently forgotten, and then they would dicker with passengers over the proper rate at the other end.

Louis sat in the third spot in line, ignoring the competition and reading a paper of his own, although he set it aside and grinned down as Gus approached. The other two cabs were open top, but Louis had an enclosed taxi with windows, which on a tail made it a little less likely Gus would be spotted and recognized while following. It was also one of the nicer cabs in this district, which meant it could blend in with those in more upscale neighborhoods, but it wasn't so nice that it would seem out of place here either.

The drivers ahead in line shouted angrily as Gus hopped into Louis's hack instead of theirs, spitting out colorful curses that Louis merely waved off with his coachwhip as he urged his horses out into traffic.

Albeit a few months late, the city had finally cast more sand over the roadway, which made it safer for the horses, but in the weeks that followed new sand, vehicles rolling over the granular slurry made an awful grinding sound. The presence of the new noise required drivers to shout their imprecations at one another more loudly, and the horses, picking up on the commotion, seemed to adjust their various musings to match.

Over the clatter of the streets, Louis called back through the small open window behind the driver's perch, "What are we after today, sir?"

"An engineer. You ever heard of Phand & Saucier?" It was an absurd question, really; Gemmen held thousands of businesses, most of which were firms named someone and someone else.

The cabbie thought for a moment as he drove forwards, then called back, "That's downtown, isn't it? Same building where George Lupo's got his firm."

Gus laughed and shook his head ruefully as if Louis had beaten him at another attempt to stump him. Truthfully, he had no idea who George Lupo was, much less where his office sat, but it helped for an inquiry agent to have a knowledgeable mystique. Taking the laugh as his answer, Louis nodded to himself and begun to whistle a bright little ditty as they rolled along.

With any other cabbie, Gus would have had to look up more information before hopping in, but besides owning a hack and a pair of horses to pull it, Louis was notable for never forgetting a song and being able to find just about any place in town. On numerous occasions, Gus had tried to stump him on both counts, and had yet to be successful at either.

Emily criticized him for spending too much on the cabbie, but if Louis hadn't been here waiting for a fare, Gus would have had to taxi all the way to the library or else drop by the Register of Deeds and been out the cost of a bribe for a peek at the index. Even better, Louis would usually work on credit, only making Gus pay up once the client paid him for the job.

As much as he wanted to listen in, to try and guess at whatever song the cabbie was whistling, Gus imagined the famous husband of a plummy younger woman like Alice Phand would likely work in a nicer part of town, so he sank away from the cab's front window as they neared the rail bridge. Various rail lines divided the city into sections, and since the tracks were kept elevated to avoid disruption to traffic, passage from one section of the city to the next meant braving a rain of soot falling from overhead.

As the soot fell past the windows, Gus laughed, suddenly realizing that Louis's tune was 'White Parasol', a popular club ditty from last season. It was about a man trying to court a girl above his station, who was so rich that she never had to step beyond the nicest parts of town, thus her perfectly unsullied white parasol. Amused by the cabbie's choice of selection as they passed below the tracks, Gus hummed it for a bit himself.

Louis drove them towards the richer districts of the city's center, where the girl of White Parasol supposedly lived. Massive digging was underway there. In a few years, the city's rail systems would be underground to reduce congestion and free up valuable real estate. Hurtling through dark tunnels choked with smog didn't strike Gus as much of an improvement, but he imagined the White Parasol girl would never be pressed into crowded trains anyway. Once completed, the train tunnels would probably be like the hidden passages for the servants in her home—there for her benefit, but not a place she need ever deign visit herself.

As they drew into the heart of downtown, the buildings were a pristine white, although most had a band of brown occasionally visible through the bustle of the sidewalk, stained where legions of job seekers habitually leaned against the buildings while they idled the day away. Some could find work on the train tunnels, but those who weren't chosen that day would linger, standing about in the hope that some wealthy benefactor native to these districts might need an errand run.

After the war in Gedlund, there had been a temporary burst of
prosperity when passage through the Aelfuan Strait was finally open to
commercial traffic. Trade with the distant east had brought new goods
and new money, but only briefly, leaving the city crowded with
hopefuls seeking opportunities that had quickly evaporated. Somehow
either the eastern merchants were getting the better of their Verin
counterparts, or the people at the top were keeping it all.

The initial flourish of trade had managed to mint many new
millionaires, but when the money never quite materialized, the ensuing
market panic impoverished the whole nation. Most of those now
leaning against the buildings hadn't even been playing at stocks, but
somehow they were all now paying for it. For an inquiry agent trailing
a mark, however, rampant unemployment had been a great boon; men
loitering around and looking through the paper were now such a
common sight that he was practically invisible.

Louis eventually pulled to a stop in front of an unassuming
building near the center of town. The streets here were always a bustle
of activity during the day, with busy people hurrying about on various
errands. Hopping out of the cab, Gus gestured towards the entrance,
and Louis nodded to confirm that was the place.

The roads in this part of town had been widened for traffic by
cutting down the width of the sidewalks. There was enough room for
two people to pass one another, but with the usual assortment of
loiterers leaning up against the wall reading a paper, having a smoke,
or just staring with dismal hopelessness out at passing traffic, there
was barely enough room for a single-file of foot traffic. Gus
shouldered his way into the crowd and made towards the nearest
entrance.

The building did not seem like the sort of grand edifice that
would contain a firm famous for engineering marvelous things, but
Gus supposed they had to buy their office space before they could start

making designs of their own. Seeing he was a bit better dressed than
the loitering workmen, a bored looking footman swung open the door
for Gus as he approached. He stepped into a palatial foyer of white
marble and glittering gilt, a bit startled by the ostentatious display
inside a building with such drab exterior.

Gus looked around for some sort of directory at the entrance,
but apparently no one had considered that here. Without any other
clues as to which office would be theirs, he eventually had to accost a
well-dressed young man descending the stairwell from the levels
above. Putting on a sheepish grin, Gus asked, "Excuse me sir, but I'm
looking for Edward Phand. Is he in this building?"

The young man smiled warmly, "Oh, yes! We're up on
twelve!" Gus murmured his thanks and started past, but then the
gentleman called after, "If you're seeking Doctor Phand, however, I'm
afraid he's on his way out just now." The helpful stranger gestured
towards a heavyset older man with curly black hair and a distinctive
square-cut beard who was making his way out the doors. Gus called
his thanks back and hurried out after his quarry.

In front of the building, Louis was engaged in an argument
with some Gemmen businessman who was apparently vigorously
haggling over the cost of a ride. Judging by his clothes, as cheap as he
was about the cost of a cab, the man probably had more money than
Gus and Louis put together. Seeing Gus's approach, Louis reached
down with his foot and gave the businessman a shove to the shoulder,
"Off! My fare's here. Beat it!"

From the look of annoyance on Louis's face, Gus wondered if
he'd have given the man a ride even if they weren't already engaged.
Fortunately, Louis was loyal enough to keep his end of the bargain
rather than go after higher-paying fares; otherwise, a flashier offer
might leave Gus without means to follow Phand. A good cabbie was
an important tool for any inquiry agent. Gus climbed up into the cab,

scanning the street and trying to figure out where the engineer could have gone in the brief moment he was out of sight.

There were a few cabs on the road, but none were just now pulling out, and Gus doubted the tubby, well-dressed older man had stepped into the filth of the roadway to hop into a cab amid traffic. Turning his eyes back towards the sidewalks, Gus quickly scanned past the shabby loiterers and spotted Doctor Phand as he emerged out of an alleyway, pushing along a safety bicycle of all things.

After making a comically awkward climb aboard the contraption, he began to wobble out into the street. Bicycles were all the rage when he made it back from Gedlund, and Adelaide had even talked him into trying one out. But balancing precariously atop a giant wheel had proven awkward when his leg wasn't bothering him and disastrous when it did. The fad had died down, but the papers claimed the new safety bicycles like Phand rode were rapidly gaining popularity.

With both wheels the same size, and the whole contraption much closer to the ground than the earlier model Gus had repeatedly fallen down from, messenger companies had adopted the new bicycles almost immediately. Apparently, they were popular with overweight engineers as well. Watching Phand wobble along lanes crowded with horses that towered over him, Gus found the sight of the man dodging his two-wheeled conveyance around the larger piles of manure left in the road entirely hilarious.

The engineer hadn't even dressed for the exercise and was wearing the sort of dark suit and clean bowler he would put on for a day at the office. Doctor Phand's shoes and pants would be liberally splattered with muck by the time he got anyplace, and every time he swerved around a pothole or pile of dung, he had to grab his hat to keep it from falling askew.

Phand's uneven pedaling might have been moving him faster than he could have managed on foot, but the overweight engineer still couldn't keep pace with the horses trotting past. Gus let him work out a slight lead and then leaned up to Louis and called out, "Follow that fat man on the bicycle!"

This job was not only easy money, but also turning out to be fun. He worried they were making a spectacle of themselves as the other hack drivers cursed over at Louis for moving so slowly, but they had to avoid overtaking their man as he made his way down towards the nearest train hub. Huffing away as he furiously pedaled his way down the lane, Phand seemed not to notice them.

The hub ahead was no minor stop off, but a center of much of the city's urban congress. A recent arrival was unloading streams of foot traffic, with men and the occasional woman filling the platform and spilling out into the sidewalks. The men wore suits of dark khakis to hide the stains of travel, and the women were either accompanying them in frilly dresses or else traveling alone in the white blouses and straight dark blue skirts of the modern career girl.

The women drew glares from some of the men lining the streets; newcomers to the job market, single women often took jobs as low paid typists and receptionists, stealing the work from men who would presumably want more money to support their families. Very few of those loitering would likely have been well suited to that sort of work regardless, but that fact did little to stem their resentment of losing the position to a woman. Of course, many of those women were likely similarly unemployed and were just in this part of town to knock on doors, asking for work, but that wouldn't make them any more welcome among the fellows leaning.

Phand dismounted his bicycle, laid it aside in a nearby alley, and pushed through the crowd to the platform beyond. Slipping from the cab, Gus made his way through the press to follow him towards the track. As soon as they stopped, Louis was once again set upon by passengers making bids for rides in his cheaper looking cab, and as he walked away, Gus grinned as he heard his married driver chatting with a woman trying to flirt her way into a cheap fare.

A fat man going against traffic was easy to follow, and Gus found himself merrily humming 'White Parasol' and wondering how he should spend the money Missus Phand was paying. He briefly worried that Phand would hop aboard the train, but then it occurred to him that Phand likely wouldn't have left the bicycle like that unless he planned on returning to it soon.

Phand stopped as he sighted two gentlemen awaiting him on the platform, and distracted by fantasies of easy success, Gus very nearly ran into him. The engineer called out a hearty greeting that was less breathless than Gus would have imagined the man capable of after his ride here, and Gus hovered back, conspicuously reading from the latest fare postings as he surreptitiously worked out what train the two men had arrived on.

There was a cheerful man in his middle-thirties and a scowling old vulture who walked with a cane. Both gentlemen were accompanied by suitcases, borne along by liveried railway men. From the luggage, Gus knew they must have come from farther off than just across town, but if they lived here and were simply returning, it would be odd to greet them on the platform like this, rather than letting them settle in at home first.

The one near Gus's age was fashionable enough, but the older wore a stiff black suit that looked thirty or forty years out of style. Their train was westbound, but from their initial words of greeting back to Phand, their accents seemed Verin, so they weren't foreigners. Gus could tell they must be very well-to-do and generous tippers, given how attentively the railway men were looking after them. They could be wealthy landed gentry, but he couldn't imagine why two country lords would be visiting an engineer.

All the major cities in Verinde proper were west of Gemmen, and remembering his own long trips to the colonies in Rakhasin, he knew they didn't have enough luggage to last the voyage from the colonies. From all that, Gus guessed they were arriving from somewhere in Aelfua—Khanom perhaps, given what Emily had said about the exposition.

He was briefly proud of himself for working that out and had half composed a smug speech about the encounter he could deliver to Emily when he returned, but then it occurred to him that the meeting almost certainly had nothing to do with Doctor Phand's affair.

Gus considered the outside chance one of the two men might be Phand's lover, but then dismissed it. He had been around a few of that particular persuasion when untangling a blackmail case a few years back—the younger one seemed too relaxed for someone arriving to a secret tryst of that sort, and the vulture looked entirely too unhappy to be here.

If they were here about the tower Phand was supposed to building out east, then that might be useful to Missus Phand. It probably meant a lot of new money for Doctor Phand, and Gus wondered if that sort of intelligence about incoming wealth would be worth something to his client. He wasn't sure how that would work with divorce proceedings, but with a tidbit like that, he might impress her enough to tell her friends about him, which could bring in more work like this later.

After a round of handshaking and enthusiastic welcomes, Phand led them out to the street, and Gus left his study of the rate board and blended with the thinning crowd working its way towards the street as he followed the trio out. He ventured as close as he dared, hoping to hear whatever the three were discussing, but couldn't catch much. It looked like they were just sharing the usual sort of remarks on rail travel—suits rumpled, things passed by, food endured, that sort of thing.

When they reached the curb, they looked over at Louis's taxi, and Gus had a moment of panic. Phand wouldn't leave his bicycle, so he probably wasn't taking the cab with them, which would stick Gus with trying to explain to some center town cabbie how to discretely follow someone. If Louis made a show of waving them off, it would make him memorable and thus conspicuous if Phand spotted the cab behind him later in the day.

After a moment's reflection and a slight pucker of distaste from the younger man, they passed it up for a cleaner, newer carriage parked just behind. The differences seemed negligible to Gus, but Phand's associates seemed to find it an acceptable improvement. The engineer made a show of helping them with their luggage, although he did little more than direct the railway men to do the obvious, and then packed the two visitors into the black carriage with a friendly smile.

Leaning from the cab, the younger man said a few more words Gus couldn't quite hear, and the older just scowled down at Phand and then wrapped himself more tightly in his coat. Once their cab rolled away, Doctor Phand gave a relieved looking sigh and then went to retrieve his bicycle. Gus hurried to hop back into Louis's cab, and when the engineer emerged with his bicycle, a simple nod to the cabbie's questioning glance set them on his trail once more.

Weaving through the streets on his safety bicycle, Phand swerved around pedestrians, street garbage, and manure as he wobbled down the lane. Louis had no trouble keeping up, but Gus was still impressed to see an out-of-shape businessman make such good time on the thing and briefly wondered if he should try one of these new models himself. He laughed as he tried to imagine returning home on it in his usual drunken stupor and decided to stick with cabs.

Four blocks later, Phand pulled up to a fancy gentleman's club, and Louis pulled to a stop half a block back while Gus peered out the window of the cab. A valet stepped forward to take the bicycle with a distasteful frown, and the engineer began to lecture him on its proper disposition. Unable to hear their discussion from across the street, Gus supplied his own dialogue for them.

"It's important you keep my bi-cycle-mobile someplace warm and dry," he said, giving Phand a deeper voice than his own and giving it an effected warble he felt sounded particularly snooty. The valet looked skeptically down at the contraption but took the bicycle from Phand and responded. Gus gave the valet a nasally snivel that went, "Very good, sir. Right away, sir. I know just the place, sir, if you would be so kind as to bend ov—"

The valet's reply fell far short of Gus's hopes for his improvised little play. Both men stepped through into the club proper. Phand took a moment to remove his hat, fanning himself with it as he glanced around the street, almost as if expecting he were followed. His eyes passed over Louis's cab without any spark of recognition. Finally seeming to catch his breath, Phand settled the hat back on his head and stepped inside.

Gus thought he might be able to slip in, posing as a guest or perhaps even a prospectus, but something wasn't quite right, and he watched the club door pensively while he tried to figure out what it was. Finally, Louis asked, "You going in, or are we sitting out here a bit? I could park closer to the door."

As soon as Doctor Phand pressed inside, the valet stepped back out with the bicycle, presumably to store it someplace other than inside the club as requested. Then the details clicked, and Gus called up, "No! Go around! Get around to the other side of the building, fast!"

Louis shrugged and whistled at his horses, eliciting several curses as he wedged them over through the bustling lane of traffic to circle the block. Sure enough, as they reached the other side, Phand was exiting from an alley behind his club, looking around the building suspiciously as he stepped out onto the sidewalk and hailed a cab.

"Clever, sir! How'd you work that one out?"

Gus grinned at his driver and replied, "When he went inside, he kept on his hat. Keep following!"

Phand climbed into an expensive-looking downtown remise – a posh leather-lined cart of the sort that only worked the nicer parts of town. With one horse and only one axle, it could weave in and out of traffic with greater ease than the traditional four-wheeled cabs, and worse still, the passengers faced rear, which made following them a riskier proposition.

With the change to that sort of cab after passing through the club and now the rear-facing ride, Gus began to worry Phand might be a trickier tail than he had first imagined. He was a little heartened that at least it was all the sort of thing a man might do to avoid being followed; someone only did that if there was something interesting to be seen doing.

The agility of the dog-cart proved little use in the late morning's traffic, so Louis had no problem staying behind them, but Gus nervously leaned back in his seat, hoping the shadow of the overhang would make him less conspicuous. Trusting in Louis's expertise, Gus held up the paper, scanning the top story over and over as he pretended to read between uneasy glances over the top edge.

Phand watched the road behind him, but his attention didn't seem fixed on Louis's trailing cab. Despite the blatantly clandestine nature of his rendezvous, Doctor Phand did not lead them into seedier districts but merely transitioned from the opulent centers of commerce to the equally opulent neighboring Palace District, which was usually occupied by more idle wealth, although ironically not the Imperial Palace itself. The lack of mercantile bustle, not to mention the presence of a much more diligent police force, meant that once they passed under the rail bridge that divided this district from the next, the loitering masses were gone.

Near the boundary to the Government District, where the Imperial palace actually stood, Phand's cab pulled up to the Hotel Harrison. Stopping a bit before they reached the elegant covered porch that marked the hotel's entrance, Gus hopped out of Louis's cab and hurried forward to see where Phand went next. The famous engineer dismounted, paid his cabbie, and then took a moment to straighten his suit and fuss with his clothes.

The muck on Phand's pants proved stubborn, and Gus did not doubt the smell of it would linger until he changed, but the engineer took so long in his grooming that Gus had to slow down or risk catching up with him. He worried a moment that perhaps that was Doctor Phand's plan, so when the engineer finished and took another glance around, Gus approached one of the nearby cabs as if he were only there to hail down a ride. Looking nervous, Doctor Phand stepped through the decorated portico into the luxurious lobby beyond.

Offering an apologetic smile to the hopeful cabbie he'd begun to approach, Gus waited a moment, then turned and slipped through the door shortly after Doctor Phand. Attentive stewards rushed to his service the moment as he stepped inside, and Gus waved them off and murmured something about being there to meet an associate. The chief concierge overseeing the stewards frowned at him from across the room but did not intervene as Gus joined a handful of others waiting in the lobby.

There were chairs scattered about, divided in a few separate sitting areas set atop expensive Mazhal rugs. The seating areas surrounded a wide staircase that led to the floors above, letting guests descend in regal majesty to whoever happened to be waiting upon them below. The men waiting in the lobby were dressed in nicer suits, more like Doctor Phand, and while Gus's plainer attire might not be quite up to the chief concierge's standards, it was nice enough to let him keep their company without seeming too out of place.

Pulling out his paper, Gus found a chair set against the wall and sat there as he peered over its pages, observing his quarry. Doctor Phand paced awkwardly between faux-marble columns near the foot of a sweeping staircase with gilded rails. When he suddenly froze, Gus knew the man's appointment had arrived, and looking up, he could see why Phand had been so anxious.

Her black curls were bound back but loosely enough to give the illusion of the intimacy of naked tresses. She wore a form-fitting silken dress in the far-eastern style, black but patterned with a silver serpent design that wrapped around her, highlighting the woman's sinuous curves. The serpent's scales glittered in the light as she descended the stair into the lobby, and she gracefully extended a long-gloved arm, directing the older, overweight engineer towards a curtained alcove.

Both of them slipped inside, and the lobby instantly resumed its former bustle as if embarrassed by their collective distraction. It was no wonder his wife knew about the affair—even with all the sneaking around to get here, the woman he was meeting was far too ostentatious to keep secret for long. Still, it meant Gus was likely to wrap this job up even more quickly than he had hoped.

Grinning as he resumed the pretense of reading the paper, Gus murmured, "Well done, old boy. Quite impressed." A gentleman nearby chuckled in agreement, and they sat there amiably for a while, occasionally interrupted by a lobby steward asking if there were anything they might need. All Gus needed was to sort out when and where they might be meeting again, and then to collect his money.

As he waited, Gus peered discreetly over the top of his paper, trying to catch a glimpse of whatever was going on behind the curtain across the lobby. He doubted they would be waving around a social calendar, but he did not consider himself above enjoying a lascivious glance at the goings on behind the curtain, if such a thing was made available. Unfortunately, the curtain hung still, and nothing interesting was revealed.

Eventually, Doctor Phand slipped out again, grinning and cheerful as he made his way outside again. Gus was tempted to check on the engineer's companion but after a moment's hesitation decided to stick with his quarry.

Phand did not hail another cab at the entrance and instead leisurely strolled down along the avenue, humming cheerfully, and smiling to all passersby. Gus trailed along behind, trying to look inconspicuous, but Phand never glanced back. Eventually, Phand made his way to a theater situated down the street and approached the box office.

Gus queued up behind him.

"Two tickets for the opener this weekend, good sir," Phand requested, smiling brightly at the man behind the counter.

"Is it a good show?" Gus piped in from behind. It was a risk if the engineer recognized him from earlier in the day, but he hoped the good mood would make his target chatty, and it did.

"Oh, I've no idea, but I'd planned dinner at Marley's down the block, and we've just enough time for a leisurely stroll here before the curtain." Collecting his tickets, Doctor Phand tipped his hat and then moved to the street to hail another cab. Close enough to hear the directions, Gus knew Phand was headed back to his office and decided not to further risk exposure by hurrying to follow. Ignoring the polite inquiries of the ticket seller, Gus walked back to the Harrison.

Welcomed inside once more, he saw that the curtain before the alcove of Doctor Phand's rendezvous had already been pulled back, and the alcove was now empty; he had missed the paramour's grand exit. Approaching one of the idle stewards, he murmured with a lascivious edge, "Who was that woman in the snake dress?"

The man by the door grinned and replied, "That was Miss Aliyah Gale, sir. She's—" Whatever revelation was to come never happened; there was a harsh click of shoes on the marble floor as the chief concierge saw their chatter and quickly made his way over. Seeing his boss's approach, the steward stiffened and fell silent.

Under the chief concierge's suspicious gaze, Gus declined any further offer of aid and made some lame excuse about having apparently missed his party. He stepped back out and returned to Louis's cab, which amidst this high-class crowd was having no trouble at all discouraging additional fare.

Unless it turned out she was being invited to the theater, Gus felt like he had enough information for Missus Phand to act upon, but having resolved this in one morning for an exceptionally generous flat fee, he felt it would be rude to send Louis off so soon. He hated to appear charitable, but he figured if they followed Doctor Phand around a bit more, then Louis could collect a full day's fee. Besides, an early return would just encourage Emily to find more work for them.

Their quarry already gone, Gus invited Louis to join him for a quick bite before returning to haunt the front of Phand & Saucier's building. Gemmen's newest culinary fad was street vendors who fried potted sausages over a portable stove, sometimes with onions or a bit of bread.

Canned meat had been the usual fare in his military service, and while Gus had not appreciated it at the time, he had developed a discerning palate for the stuff. There were a few competing varieties, but his favorites were Thomas's, followed by Pittman's, with the distant third place difficult to assign.

Early in their association, he and Louis had bonded over their shared appreciation of the stuff, so whenever they were on a job together, Gus tried to work out a way to get them. There was no regular place to get a cheap lunch in White Parasol's part of town, but Louis knew a Thomas's sausage cart that traveled through a nearby district, and they found it in short order.

Eventually, the police always came to chase off unlicensed vendors like this one, typically insisting they were securing the public health, although Gus had noticed they generally preferred such concerns addressed with a quick bribe. The police's collection attempts gave rise to rumors that those health concerns might even be real, but this particular cart's brisk custom and the trail of discarded cans around it was a comforting confirmation that it wasn't serving them rat or something worse.

With his paper having long since worn out its entertainment value, Gus found himself chatting with Louis as they lunched by the side of the street. Louis's little girl was now old enough for suitors, apparently, and it bothered the poor man to no end. He had already forced her to switch bedrooms in their flat, in an attempt to catch one late-night window-rapper at his game. Gus supposed that if the girl took after her mother, then her looks would fade soon enough, so it seemed to him that getting her hitched now might be a blessing. But still he did his best to console his friend and advise him on where to pick up a reliable pistol.

Making their way back to Phand & Saucier, Gus took up his paper and found a spot along the wall across the street where he could make conversation with the loiterers and pretend to read the paper. The top article was something about the deposed queen of Tulsmonia, attempting to rally followers from her exile in Mazhar. The author seemed very concerned about the dangerous possibility of Revolutionary Committee assassins trying to finish the job, by which Gus determined he was reading the *Standard*, since at the *Herald* they were probably cheering the assassins on.

Late in the afternoon, the good doctor finally made his way outside, hopping upon his safety bicycle once more and wending off into traffic. Most of the loiterers had given up for the day and moved on already, so Gus folded his paper and pretended to join them as he moved to rejoin Louis. He was confident after this morning's jaunt that Phand wouldn't manage to lose them, but did wonder if he'd had the bicycle delivered from the club or just kept several scattered around the city.

Doctor Phand led them into the neighboring Market District, not quite to the standards of White Parasol, where he stopped at a well-to-do brownstone. Once he climbed off his safety bicycle, Phand tossed it amid the flowers in front with a casual disdain that told Gus that this had to be the man's own home—and he clearly wasn't the one who tended to that small plot of green out front.

Apparently too cheap to hire a proper valet, Phand was met at the door by a housekeeper in drab dress and long apron. They exchanged a few words, and after a quick glance around to make sure the neighbors weren't looking, Phand leaned down to give her cheek a kiss before they both slipped inside.

A bit shocked, having seen the man entertaining the likes of Miss Aliyah Gale earlier that day, Gus guffawed and slapped the paper against his knee. "Oh, you dog! Will you look at that! I'm actually starting to admire the man now. I almost feel bad about having to turn him in."

"I still get paid though, right sir?" asked Louis pointedly, provoking another laugh from his passenger.

"Absolutely. Emily would have my head if I dropped a client for something like that. Let's go back." He relaxed, looking down at the paper he'd spent so much of the day pretending to read, and wondered if he should actually glance through it on the way home. Instead, he settled on taking a moment to rest his eyes.

Gus was careful not to let himself fall asleep, which would risk alarming Louis on the trip back. He'd need a bit of sauce before he could handle a proper nap, but with all the new money coming in, he'd need plenty of energy to properly celebrate his success.

~

"Assassins Faced in Mazhar"

A bold attempt was made upon the life of Andra Berengar, the deposed queen of Tulsmonia. Late last week, several assassins scaled the walls of her refuge within the Sultan's palace in Mazhar. By all reports, their climb up the sheer walls of the palace should have been humanly impossible, yet they did so while evading notice until they reached the parapet of the queen's domicile there. Bodyguards hired by her loyal retainer, Doctor Gleb Nichols, bravely leapt to her defense, and by their extraordinary efforts, the great lady emerged unharmed.

Speculation of the Sultan's involvement in the attempt has been angrily denied, and indeed there are rumors of a thaumaturgic investigation being undertaken by his government to ascertain whether the Workers' Revolutionary Committee assassins used any unnatural methods to facilitate their attempt. Rumors persist of both witchcraft and wyrding being practiced among the Committee's hooligans, and this latest outrage certainly lends new credence to such claims.

– *Gemmen Standard*, 6 Tal. 389

~

- CHAPTER 4 -

Baston was an idiot. As an inquiry agent, he was clever enough to get her what she needed, but Dorna could barely conceal her contempt as he reported Edward Phand's upcoming night out and then tried to pressure her for more money with the promise of news on his business arrangements with the tower.

Whatever Edward Phand's latest plans for the tower were would be mooted soon enough, and whatever he had learned had no part in the Master's plan. She assured Baston that the evening's plans were not with her, that his work was done, and then placed the remaining payment directly into his hand—six gold coins and five silver, with not one penny more.

The agent's simple-minded greed blinded him to the possibility that she might not really be Alice Phand, and she now understood why the Master had instructed her to go with an independent agent rather than a larger firm. A fellow Warden working in the Khanom constabulary had heard of Baston through his counterparts in Gemmen, and she felt she could now confirm their opinions of the man.

Fortunately, some bit of upper-class aloofness was part of the role, so she was not required to hide her overwhelming disdain for either him, the frowning slattern he kept by the door, nor the false sympathy they offered in their clumsy attempts at comfort for the sorrow she was supposed to feel at the alleged adultery.

Waving her borrowed fur around like a badge of office, she pushed her way out of Baston's office and marched down the stairs again. Taking a deep breath in the dim gas-lit foyer of the building, she pushed once more into the stinking city outside, glaring around at the orthogonal irregularity of the cityscape.

All that was left of the Elven cities now were the paintings showing their elegantly sweeping curves and the delicate spires rising into clear air with graceful harmony; humanity had spoiled all that and replaced it with cruder stuff. By comparison to those lost marvels, the Verin capital was nothing but a series of unevenly spaced boxes.

Dorna hated Gemmen. It stank, and ever since she had arrived, she could feel the unpleasant grime that layered on everything in the city, even on her own skin. The air was thick with soot, and even a glass of purest water would soon have a film atop it if left uncovered for more than a moment.

The walls of the buildings had been stained by the smoke of passing engines, and the only green visible was in the moldy hay left out for the milk cows at an urban farm just down the street. Steam travel let vegetables be grown remotely, but milk and eggs still had to come from little operations wedged into the heart of the city, and Dorna never trusted the produce of animals trapped in places like that.

Gemmen was a city of pestilence and filth and an icon of all that had gone wrong with the world in the absence of its caretakers.

The carriage they had bought for the mission was waiting down the street, and Dougal was at the reins. She waited as he directed it up to the curb and then climbed inside without waiting for him to lower the step.

Dorna closed the door, watched carefully to make sure they were not followed as they pulled away from the building, and then cast off the wretched animal corpse wrapped around her neck and unpinned that hideous hat she'd been forced to wear. Terry, the other Warden sent with them, had picked those out for her, insisting they were necessary elements of the disguise.

He'd also worried when they bought the carriage that it looked too cheap, but Baston had never even caught sight of her in it. Terry had been named her second on this mission, though she suspected he was only here to provide money, legal advice, or social influence if things went wrong. So far, he had mostly seemed useless. Seated across from her, he gave her a moment to settle in before finally venturing, "Did he find out what we needed?"

"He did. They're going to the theatre tomorrow night. We even know where they're walking from to get there."

Terry gave a thoughtful nod and then said, "So we just have to pull up, grab the man, and head back home?"

He never remembered instructions, and Dorna wondered again if someone less devoted with half a brain would have been a better choice. She had helped the Master approach him years ago, and he had seemed bright enough then, but having spent more time with him on the trip to Gemmen, she had found him irritatingly obtuse. He couldn't understand why they didn't just grab the man at home or in front of his office or why they couldn't just follow him themselves, asking again and again as if Dorna were making up the plan rather than simply following it.

She took a moment to fight back the several harsh responses that bubbled to mind, then marshaled her patience and said, "No. We hire another cab and driver first and do the snatching in that, so they don't come looking for our carriage on the way out."

It was, she knew, a plan of seemingly excessive complexity, but the Master's mind was far sharper than theirs. If his genius and experience told them all this was necessary, then it would be foolish for mere humans to second guess that. Clearly, for the Master's purpose it needed to be public yet also completely untraceable, and his purpose was their purpose.

Terry nodded again with a faint gleam of recognition accompanied still by a flicker of doubt. People like him ran the world now—short-sighted, dull men who saw only the immediate profit and no further. The Master assured her this would help bring an end to all that. They needed guidance. They needed wisdom.

Once the Great Restoration came, mankind would have that again.

From the front, Dougal called back, "I found us a driver with a cab to hire."

He was even more of an idiot than Terry, but at least she had a better idea of what his uses were.

"Good! If that's done, then our work today is done. You can drive us back to the shop." Dorna was eager to get out of the ill-fitting, upper-class finery, but from the corner of her eye, she saw Terry was working up the courage to say something, so she turned to look at him. Often the look sufficed to quell whatever nonsense would be forthcoming.

"So, uh, since you're dressed up and all, there's an art gallery I wanted to look in on, and I thought you might like to accompany me?" Terry offered in another of his awkward attempts to charm her.

He was a petitioner, or clerk, or something, and socially stationed well above her in most circles, although among the Wardens, she greatly outranked him. Whether he thought she was pretty or was just interested in her influence in their society, she could never quite ascertain, but he was too short for her tastes and lacked any other charms to mitigate that physical inadequacy.

She gave him a cool, disinterested look, the sort that usually shut him up, but he determinedly continued. "They have a lot of Modernist pieces, so I thought you might enjoy it."

Despite the annoyance she felt from his cloyingly hopeful tone, the gallery did intrigue her. Their expenses had been minimal, and with the extra money in her control, she'd entertained the notion of returning with some gift for the Master. Ideally, she would have liked to restore some true Elven trinket to him, but yesterday she had allowed Terry to escort her to an auction that included a few and had discovered that the prices on such things were astronomical.

Modernism, however, was an attempt by men aping some of the lost styles of the Elves, adopting their love of natural subjects and contrasting intricate detail with flowing abstract shapes. Despite her initial disdain at the idea, some of it was quite good, although nothing approached the true artistry she had seen in the Master's collections. Certain she would regret it, but with little else to do until tomorrow night, Dorna sighed and acquiesced to a tour of the galleries.

As embarrassed as she was when Terry announced their destination to Dougal, the worst part was the big man's wink back at her and knowing chuckle as if this were a development in their relationship he'd been expecting. She almost countered Terry's instruction then and there, but then remembered her goal. She wanted to find something for the Master, so she simply sulked the rest of the way in the vain hope it would diminish both Dougal's amusement and Terry's expectations.

When they arrived, she was impressed by the size of the place. The capital's Central District held not just one gallery but many. Most of the shops were connected by arcades of polished marble into a palace of commerce that Dorna suspected would exceed even the dwelling of the Verin king.

The Modernist movement was popular this season, and many of the shops were devoted to it. A few Easternist pieces were mixed in here or there, either of actual foreign origin or artists who simply copied Longying's styles, as the Modernists did with the Elves.

The Easternist pieces were an overabundance of draconic themes and splotchy paintings of insects and were often overly abstract in a way that struck her as distasteful. The Elves had included abstract shapes to depict wind, water, and other real things, even if they were not always strictly as they appeared to mortal eyes, but Easternist notions, like the series of ink-blobs arranged to look like a scorpion, only struck her as crudely childish.

Fortunately, the Modernist pieces were predominant at the place Terry had selected, and some were very similar to the authentic Elven ones in the Master's collections. Gold and gems wrought crude earth into living shapes that glittered and gleamed in the late afternoon light that filtered through the windows. Much of the show was dedicated to flowing depictions of nude women that would have been illegal only a few years ago, but many such social strictures had eased when Queen Muirne had stepped down.

The young Verin king was considered quite liberal and had become an advocate for vague notions of freedom, although Dorna suspected it was only an attempt to save himself from the fate that had so recently befallen the magnar of the Tuls. His censors might allow more images like these, but even with his supposed enthusiasm for the Women Question, he had never advocated for more than that his Parliament should 'consider' it.

When she was younger, the Master had laughed when she asked if the Elves allowed women to vote. The Elves had ruled by merit—why would there be elections when the same person had centuries of expertise in their role? Muirne had been little more than a figurehead, but the Elven queen ruled because she was the best suited for her role. Her people had never considered their queen's gender something that diminished her.

She ignored the more scandalous pieces, and Terry's attempts at conversation, and focused upon her goal. It was close to sunset when she found something that seemed appropriate, a small wooden box of curling organic shapes that twisted together like intertwined branches, making it impossible to see how it opened. It reminded her of his throne, and she felt the Master would appreciate it, even if it was of human design.

Noting her interest, Terry waved over the gallery's shopkeep, who eagerly explained to her how it opened and closed. Once she was sure she knew how it worked so that she could demonstrate the gift when she presented it, she agreed to the ridiculous sum the man was asking.

Terry handled the money, so he counted it out for the shopkeep and then tucked the box under his arm—his sense of chivalry apparently required him to carry the thing on her behalf. As they stepped back out into the chilly arcade, he paused and said, "I've heard there's a lovely dinner club just down the avenue. We could stroll over that way and celebrate your find."

She frowned and said, "We've spent too much now. We've got to be careful with expenses going forward. I'm not going to waste it on fancy dinners."

With a hopeful smile, Terry shook his head and replied, "No, he gave us far more than we needed for the mission—he obviously expected you to buy a gift like this with it! If we stick to the plan, everything will work perfectly."

Dorna was taken aback by the idea that her gift had been anticipated. Was Terry's faith so much greater than hers that he even considered such a thing? She had never been to Gemmen before, but the Master had. Surely he knew what things cost, but what if that money was for something he expected that they did not yet see?

While she hesitated, Terry smiled and offered, "I'll pay for it out of my own pocket. How often do we visit Gemmen?"

Looking around at the chilly opulence, set amid a city filled with the desperately poor, Dorna felt this first visit was already far too often for her taste. She had lived alongside the Master's veil of opulence for most of her life now. For him, it was an easy deception for a greater cause, but merely human, she was faced with daily temptation to leave behind her austerity and share in ready comforts so close at hand.

Now worried that purchasing the Master's gift was a test she had failed, Dorna let that bitterness creep into her voice as she replied, "And what about Dougal? They wouldn't let him in unless you brought along a spare dinner jacket that would fit him. You expect him to just sit out on the street while we eat?"

To Dorna's relief, Terry's smile faded a bit, and so she pressed on, her voice lowered to a hiss lest some passerby overhear, "We are not here for the fancy dinners of the corrupt upper echelons of the crumbling human state."

After the uprisings in Tulsmonia, that sort of talk tended to unnerve those of Terry's ilk. When they first met only a year ago, he would have shrugged it off and tried to persuade her that there was no harm in indulging a bit, but now he just meekly surrendered.

Terry seemed dimmer now, like so many others of his kind who had joined their ranks over the years. So many men came to the Wardens, thinking themselves great, and then lost their edge in the face of the Master's truths.

Since he had nothing left to say, Dorna simply nodded and led the way back to the street, where Dougal waited with the carriage. Unlike Terry, Dougal had not seemed to dim in his time with the Master, either because of his humbler devotion or perhaps simply because he had never been that bright to begin with.

Given how much money she had spent on the Master's gift, Dorna insisted on a simple stew at one of the pubs nearer the empty storefront the Master had arranged for them in the Tanner District. Dougal seemed friendly enough in social situations but said little and, thankfully, drank little. Whenever the big man did drink, a dangerous glint grew in his eyes, and Dorna always worried what Dougal might do with but a bit more liquor in him.

Just a few beers were enough to send Terry reeling, however. She had to endure his declarations of devoted friendship as she helped Dougal carry him back to their headquarters. They dumped Terry unceremoniously atop the pallet he had been sleeping on for the past week, and Dorna went back to her own alcove in the shop.

It was to be their last night sleeping here, and she would not miss the place. It had been empty for some time and somehow smelled of both dust and mold. The economic decay that left so many shops empty was symbolic of the cultural malaise that afflicted her race— there were always an arrogant few with too much wealth and power but lacking patience and wisdom. The human vanity of that privileged handful had carelessly ruined so many others in one foolish greedy gambit after another.

After their brief journey back to the shop, the dangerous glimmer had faded from behind Dougal's eyes, and he was quietly tending to some bit of maintenance with his luggage. In truth, she wondered if he ever slept. Though his demeanor was generally placid, he was seldom idle. He seldom read, but could often be found meticulously cleaning his knives or carefully checking over the carriage they kept behind the shop as he did at the moment. If it was his way of dealing with the same nervous energy Dorna felt the night before their mission, Dougal's bland expression gave no hint of it.

With little else to do and unable to sleep, Dorna stripped out of her upper-class finery and into a more utilitarian outfit. In Khanom, women who found themselves trapped in work at the factories or the mines often wore baggy pants and kept their skirts rolled up around their waist. It was originally intended to be rolled back down when away from their labors, but few bothered with that now.

The women in Gemmen's factories maintained their city's conservative style, and if they wore something more practical at their labors, they changed out of it before emerging back onto the streets. Even with a notional skirt, pants would attract too much attention here, and Dorna was too practical to risk that attention just to make a petty point, so she dressed in something plain that she knew wouldn't draw any attention.

Their deception would be done soon, and she accepted that it was luxury enough to be able to wear her familiar work boots—they were all she had left of her father, and wearing them always made her feel more resolute. Feeling their weight as she stepped out into the alley behind the shop soothed her nerves, not yet enough that she could sleep, but she thought perhaps a stroll might settle things.

Dougal stared at her as she emerged, a bit of grin across his broad face that she guessed was the result of some lascivious imagining, and she worried he might be less sober than she had thought. She pointedly ignored him at first as her rank in their secret society afforded her some degree of safety from whatever predations he might otherwise consider. None had ever dared defy the Master by assaulting a fellow Warden, and despite her recent failure, she was still one of his favorites.

Dorna took a moment to look up and down the alleyway, as if she had not yet noticed him, and then looked back in his direction. She narrowed her eyes and frowned, letting him know she knew exactly what he was thinking. He shrank back a little from that glare and tried to recover his manners by focusing again on his maintenance of their carriage. Satisfied with his reaction, Dorna pronounced, "I'm going out for a walk."

Dougal bobbed his head and muttered some servile acquiescence as she wandered out into the evening alone. It was dangerously uncouth for a woman to wander off alone after dark— even more so in Gemmen than in other places. The revolutionaries among the Tuls loudly promised to reform all sorts of things, but with their government in the fumbling hands of uneducated peasantry, Dorna doubted freeing women locked up in the terems had even crossed their minds.

A nighttime stroll alone was considered the sort of brazen behavior that encouraged urban predators and the type of thing never done by the type of women who wore the sort of finery Terry had picked out for her. Dorna was dressed more plainly now though, and something about her often made people uneasy; she felt the combination of those two things would make her an unappealing target for even Gemmen's notorious criminal underbelly.

There was a small park a few blocks away, and she hoped a bit of greenery would help her relax enough to get some sleep. At home, the mountains were always on the horizon and the forests always in view, even if distant. Here though, the Verin capital left her only with views of ugly buildings, which in this part of town were all in bleak disrepair—their paint faded and cracking, their wood rotting, their metal rusting, and even their brickwork crumbling away.

She had spied the park through their carriage window a few times in passing, but seen up close, it was a disappointment. It was trimmed but seemed otherwise ill-tended, even for the season. There were trees and other plants, some of which might bloom in a few months' time, but they were all planted in neat rows, boxed in, squared off, and rather than being sheltered to grow proudly amidst urban blight, they were instead cut down to conform to the city's crudely blunt aesthetic.

In truth, it was a crudely human aesthetic—the Master had once sadly confessed to her that even with humanity's advances in architecture, to more cultured eyes their boldest efforts in concrete and steel were still nothing more than sturdy huts. As disappointing as she found all this, surely he would find it offensive. Elves had ceded these lands to humanity thousands of years ago, but no doubt the sight of what had become of them was still shocking to immortal eyes.

Within the park, far enough back from the confining walls, she could see the stepped peak of the RFTB. It was Gemmen's newest and tallest building, dedicated to the exploitation of far-off colonies, and it loomed over the rest of the city rather than lifting all of it upward. It was a utilitarian sentinel tower from which the city's distant masters could oversee the toiling below. It was a perch from which to watch the destruction they wrought without being soiled by stepping through it themselves.

Rather than help her relax, the sights from the park just made her angry and even more restless. She left and began walking through the city instead, staring out at the towering factory chimneys across the river, stilled for the night. She stepped over homeless children sleeping in the streets and was propositioned by several men staggering out of pubs along the avenue. One of them had to be warded off with her knife, but for the rest a stern glance was enough.

The filth of the city clung to her boots, and she scraped them off on the curb. Looking up, she realized she had been making her way down the infamous Nettle Lane. They had been staying in their shop in the Tanner District, and she had known Nettle Lane was there as well, but she had never before ventured there.

It was everything the papers had described in such lurid detail last summer when the dismembered bodies began washing ashore. There were rows of grimy pubs split by the darkness of unlit alleyways, and prostitutes plied on every corner. Dorna supposed the women who still sold themselves in this district must be particularly desperate, for the police had never found the culprit, and many worried that the horror of Nettle Lane was only hibernating for the winter.

The prostitutes scowled at Dorna as she passed through their territories, not welcoming any potential competitors on whatever marketplace they had staked out as their own. They called out to the other passersby since, at this time of night, nearly all were men, and their huckstering mixed with the raucous sounds spilling from the pubs to spoil the evening's quiet.

Ahead of her, she saw the olive and gold uniform of a stiffly starched policeman as he ambled onto the street along his nightly rounds. Dorna watched as the women fell into dutiful silence as he passed by, his beat pausing only to collect money from a few men and women along the way.

A group of suspiciously well-dressed partiers spilled out of one of the pubs. Their clothes seemed too fine for the neighborhood but also for those wearing them. There were two men in overlarge dinner jackets and a young woman wrapped in an elegant fur and wearing jewels ill-matched to a wearied face that spoke of a life of common toils. Thieves most likely, and though Dorna understood they must be driven to crime by the failings of the human system enslaving them, she also noted that the excess of their masters was being put to no better use once stolen away.

The policeman, seeing the trio flaunt their obvious lucre, trundled over, pointed his truncheon, and asked pointed questions. One of the tuxedoed men, looking somewhat less drunk than the other two, smiled and handed the officer something. After taking a moment to count it, the corrupt policeman smiled, tipped his hat to them, and resumed his rounds.

Eventually Dorna reached a small temple set in amidst the city's corruption. It shared Gemmen's architectural theme of orthogonal decay, but hoping some solace of the gods might settle her nerves, she decided to step in to offer them their due respect. Despite its boxy exterior, the inside was still traditionally round, with a dais at the front from which a devotee might deliver sermons and rows of pews for their listeners. The walls were dark wood, but the ceiling arching above them was once mostly white, now faded to a yellowish brown.

Painted across the faux dome of the ceiling, Caerleon's Trinity of Light shone symbolically down upon the faithful who bowed at prayer. Most of those gathered here were ragged, desperate wretches— likely people who had found no luck in begging on the streets tonight and now sought divine aid to ease their hunger, their sickness, and their weakness. The human world had failed to succor them, and with no one else to turn to, they were forced to appeal to the gods directly.

Alcoves lined the walls, holding small shrines where followers of the Trinity could pay homage to the other gods. Circling the edge of the temple, she found the shrine dedicated to the Holy Mother, goddess of the Elves. At home, the Master's own shrine had beautiful and elaborate depictions of her, but Nettle Lane's temple bore only abstract symbols and a scattering of dried flower petals someone had left in respectful offering.

Bowing her head, Dorna murmured the prayer the Master had taught her. Even in this horrible place, she felt the warmth of it settle over her. The love of the goddess was a power undimmed by the filth of mortal men. The disruption of the ley lines, the world wrapped in iron, and the horrifying carelessness and greed that threatened to consume everything and plunge them into a new age of darkness—all those outrages faded at the sweet touch of grace. Dorna closed her eyes, breathing deeply as she felt the Holy Mother's love wrapped around her.

The cheap incense of the temple gradually pulled her from her reverie, and she felt better. Reaffirmed. Reinvigorated. The Master's plan would go perfectly, and she had faith in his wisdom and judgment. She merely had to play her part in it as he had already decided she could and would.

Stepping outside, Dorna hailed a cab, which were ubiquitous even here, and returned to the empty shop, wandering around the block to enter from the back. Dougal was softly snoring, and she went to the alcove that had served as her bed since they came to Gemmen. Whatever goods had once sat upon its shelves were long gone, and now it was just another dusty corner in another empty storefront.

And yet men and women still slept rough on the streets tonight. That was the way of the human world. She murmured the Elven words once more, wrapping them around herself like another blanket as she thought of how the Great Restoration would soon set things right.

She lay awake a while longer, pondering her part in their venture in the next night to come. She had to be flawless. All Wardens hoped their efforts now would earn their place in the new Elven-led society after the Great Restoration, but Dorna felt few of them had done so. If she did this with near-Elven perfection, the Master would be proud of her, and when the Elven queen strode the world once more, Dorna intended to be recognized as someone whose loyalty had made a difference.

Morning came, and their cabbie rolled into the alleyway behind their empty storefront. He'd brought the clothes and necessaries he might need to remain here with them for the next week, as instructed. He'd been paid half up front, and Dorna hoped he had left the money with his family.

Dougal smiled and welcomed him in a chummy accord that neither Dorna nor Terry had the heart to emulate. The cabbie knew the route to their destination well enough, but the Master's instructions were to practice the route a few times, so Dougal and the cabman would spend the day riding through the city from their empty store to the Palace District and back again several times.

As soon as they were gone, Dorna wrapped the rich green cloak of the Wardens around her, leaving the hood off for now. It was a too early to dress for the evening's events, but she was eager to move on. At home, she kept it in a trunk of cedar, and that rich woody smell clung to the green fabric. She breathed deep, eager for any smell other than the rotten stench of Gemmen's decay. Closing her eyes, she thought of the high mountains outside Khanom.

The Master's description of the world that was, before mankind brought everything to ruin, rang in her thoughts as she remembered their long walks into the mountains together when she was a girl. Aelfua was the last to fall, but before humanity turned on its leaders, the world had been full of beautiful palaces, lives lived in harmony with nature. He had seen it, and through his stories, so had she. Their world had equality in government, civility among the people, prosperity for all, and none hungry. No more abandoned children left to starve.

Dorna and Terry spent their morning cleaning up the store, removing all trace of who had been here. The stove had been needed for warmth, and the Master had told them there was little use in trying to disguise that. She marveled at his foresight in knowing that they would need it, that it would be difficult to clean, yet those spent ashes would be unimportant to their task.

Their instructions were full of minute details like that, and she felt reassured that the Master had indeed thought of everything. When they were finished, someone looking carefully for such signs might notice that people had been living here, but Dorna felt confident they would have no trail to tell them who, how many were here, or for how long.

With that done, she and Terry had little else to do but check and recheck their supplies. She packed her belongings into their carriage and made sure the Master's concoctions were carefully stored. Terry lazed about reading through an old copy of the *Standard* and raised his hands in humble submission when she reminded him they could leave nothing behind that might suggest when they were here.

Dougal and their driver finally returned in the afternoon and brought in a mix of sausages fried with onions and bread. It was not a dish she was familiar with, but it was hearty, filling, and thankfully plain. It would be their last dinner together as a group, but any reflections on their trip together so far were muted by the presence of the cabbie. They had only been traveling together for two weeks, but it felt infinitely longer.

Dougal chatted amiably with the man, discussing the driver's family and his plans for after their job was done. Terry made a few half-hearted attempts at geniality but faltered into stretches of awkward silence that Dougal was forced to fill. Dorna kept silent, too uncomfortable at dining with the cabbie to worry if the man found her rude.

 Her stomach roiled with stress as she worried about the evening ahead, but Dorna forced herself to methodically eat as much as she could handle—the Master had instructed them to get their fill before their mission, in case something went wrong and they could not risk stopping for food after. When she finished, Dorna demanded the cabman show her their vehicle, so she could inspect whether the door had been properly oiled. It was a ruse—Dougal had purchased two roundtrip train tickets to Khanom and handed one to Terry while Dorna occupied the driver.

True to his genius, the Master thought of everything. His plans were perfect, and Dorna knew if anything went wrong tonight, it would be her failure. For this mission, the timing of their meals, the clothes they would wear beneath their robes, and at critical times like these, even the schedule of their leavings had been set out by him. Sometimes when she had not seen him in a while, she began to question the necessity of such minute control.

She had no doubt much of her anxiety over their mission stemmed from her absence from his presence. For thoughts like that, she repeated the words she had been taught and felt it strengthen her resolve. She spent much of the afternoon pacing back and forth while the boys played cards with the cabman, happy to finally have a third to join their usual games.

The street lamps hissed to life across the city, and they filed out, cloaked in their Warden robes. The cabbie chuckled quietly at the sight of them but did not seem surprised, which made Dorna wondered what Dougal had told him they would be doing. All three wore their hoods, but they kept the face-covering veil lifted back as they rode and simply lowered the shades to prevent anyone from seeing them inside.

Terry and Dougal took the back-facing bench, leaving Dorna with the other side to herself. She peeked out through a sliver of window and watched as they pushed through the city's night-time bustle, so many people blithely unaware of the important errand their cab was on. All the horribles of the night before were gathering again as the sun set, loitering alongside the streets the cab passed on their way out of the district.

As they moved into wealthier precincts, streets had been swept clear and were brilliantly illuminated by expensive limelights instead of simple gas. Marley's restaurant was too exclusive to call much attention to itself and was housed in an unassuming building identified only by a tiny plaque by the door with type too small to be read from the street.

Their cab pulled to the curb a bit short of the restaurant, and the cabman pulled out his own dinner, pretending to take a break as his hack sat idle. A few eager customers tried to hail him, but he would simply raise up his flask and a piece of bread, and they would move on to seek other transport.

Terry fidgeted like a child, and Dorna suspected if his robes did not conceal it, she would see him trembling. Dougal sat in a seemingly peaceful contemplation that would have been the very image of serenity if not for the malevolent smirk he wore. Without the Wardens,

Terry would no doubt have still had some career of middling success, but Dougal—seeing him staring blankly ahead in sadistic daydream, Dorna was sure he would have been a criminal of the worst sort. She worried for their cause if the Master was forced to rely on the likes of Dougal.

Most of the buildings here were empty this time of night, and as the play finished, a multitude of well-dressed attendees queued up to pile into the taxis lined at the door. Their own cab was far enough back to stay out of that, and Dougal pushed the shade slightly aside to watch the crowd.

Eventually, the famous engineer emerged. Laughing, Edward Phand and his wife strolled down the streets. In this brightly lit part of town, there were few places for an ambusher to hide, and the police were less cheaply corrupt. Normally the two of them would have had every right to their illusions of safety here.

Dougal called ahead to the cabman, identifying their target, and the horses began to stroll casually forward as they moved past the line of cabs waiting to pick up exiting theater patrons. Apparently, Dougal and the cabman had settled on the proper spot earlier on, and they pulled ahead of the happy couple and halted there.

As the cab creaked to a stop, Dorna pulled down her veil, and the other two followed suit, the three Wardens now facelessly cloaked in green, only distinguishable by their eyes and what little of their body shape the robes left hints of. Even in the robes, Terry's thin figure was easy to tell from Dougal's ape-like physique, but Dorna felt there were few hints she was even a woman. The anonymity made her feel powerful, and Dorna tensed in anticipation as she peered out at the sliver of the empty lane she could see around the drawn shade.

As they neared the door, the cabman gave them his signal, "Looking for a ride, sir?" At that, the three of them rushed out of the hack, spilling into the street, knives drawn. Terry circled behind Edward Phand, holding up his knife in silent threat, and as the engineer's attention was on the blade, Dorna rushed forward with her ether. As the Master had promised, the engineer quickly collapsed once the rag was pressed to his face, and Terry caught him under the arms as he fell.

Dorna took the knife from her partner as he began dragging their quarry into the cab; she would have thought Dougal better for the heavy lifting, but the Master's plan was quite clear on their roles. Only as that was done did she notice the man's wife was shrieking. Turning to look, she saw Dougal threatening her with the knife as he pressed her up against the wall of a building.

His demands for silence were completely ignored, and in his struggle to muffle Alice Phand, had not noticed they had already seized their target. Whistles sounded from down the block as a pair of constables on their rounds began sprinting over, truncheons in hand. Against the Master's instruction for her to remain silent, Dorna ran over and grabbed at Dougal's arm, hissing out, "We've got him. Come on!"

Dougal nodded and started to back away but paused with a strange glaze to his eyes as if he felt he had forgotten something. The look cleared, and he jerked himself from Dorna's grip. His free hand darted forward as the big man clutched at the pearls and tried to yank them free, but the clasp held stubbornly closed.

Yanking at the pearls just tugged the woman awkwardly forward as she continued to scream, and charging constables were already halfway down the block. He pulled again, and although the clasp held, the string gave way, sending large pearls spilling across the sidewalk and bouncing into the street.

Dougal looked down at the gems scattered across the pavement, and his knees began to bend as if he felt the need to pick them up. Grabbing at his arm again, Dorna tried to pull Dougal back to the cab, shouting, "Leave it! We have to go!"

He shook his head, cursed, and then sprang into the cab without any further hesitation. The panicked cabman slapped the reins as soon as Dorna leapt inside, and the hack jolted into motion, flying through the streets.

One of the policemen chased their cab down the street, but he could not keep up with the cabman's horses. Dorna was glad they only carried clubs here—in some less settled areas of Aelfua, men of the law often bore pistols. The other constable had stopped, and shortly after they rounded the corner, they heard the loud cranking of the police rattle, sounding a general alarm through the area. Once out of sight, however, their cab simply blended in with all the others in the city and slowed to a more measured pace as they drove back to Tanner.

Terry began to laugh, semihysterical as they fled the scene of their abduction, and Dorna collapsed into her seat. Her heart was racing, and she felt like she could barely breathe under her hood, so she pushed the veil back up out of her face. In less than an hour, they arrived in the alley behind the shop, exactly as planned.

Dorna had half-expected the sound of police rattles again and to see hundreds of olive and gold uniformed officers descending upon them the moment they arrived, but to her relief, all was quiet. For several moments after the wheels stopped, they all just sat in the hack, everyone catching their breath. Edward Phand lay completely limp but was still breathing when she checked. With Terry's help, she pulled the engineer from the hack and then up into the private carriage they had kept in the small stable behind the shop.

The cabman seemed understandably nervous; it had looked very little like some club's playful hazing or whatever Dougal had claimed he was involved in. He had to know that if the constables or Alice Phand had caught the number on his cab, he would soon be arrested.

Dougal pushed back his hood and climbed up next the driver. He put on a reassuring smile that made Dorna's stomach turn and then helped guide the hack back into the stables as he promised the man that everything would be fine.

Wincing in anticipation, Dorna looked away but still heard the strangled gasp and then the wet coughs that followed as the cabman died. She murmured another Elven prayer, unsure of the meaning of the words but drawing strength from them. The world must be healed. Nothing could be allowed to stand in the way of the Great Restoration.

~

"Week in Sport"

In the match between Oulm and Whitby, the former team spiked an epic 521 before the game was called. Lord Brex (176), Lord Gimley (82), Mr. S. Opple (64), and Mr. A. Pendelton (not barred, 62) were the chief contributors to this gigantic total, and though the Hon. J. Blackacre (107) threw exceedingly well, he had little assistance from the other Whitby men, who were eventually defeated by the third, with the final roundings called off as untenable. Also this week, Garelsby has beaten Derphon by 47 over. Alston has won the Inter-University bracket by seven.

– *Gemmen Standard*, 8 Tal. 389

~

- CHAPTER 5 -

Having successfully located his flat the night before, Gus was in a good mood as he strolled down the lane towards his office. The sun was shining, and it was nice enough to walk the half-mile between. He had no plans to do any work, of course, but Emily would be upset if he didn't put in an appearance. Despite the previous night's libations, he had awoken very nearly on time and was looking forward to astonishing Emily with his relative punctuality.

The bustle of morning traffic was mostly over, but newsboys still stood at the corners, the morning editions not yet all sold, but they were already promising extra news for just a few bits more. Whistling to himself, Gus tipped his hat to the woman who ran the restaurant on his block.

As usual for this time of day, she stood out front smoking a cigarette as she tried to hawk her services. In more polite neighborhoods, a woman would never smoke in public, and Gus half suspected she only smoked on the street here to catch more attention from passersby. She glanced him over as he walked by but quickly dismissed him from her consideration when it was obvious he was not a customer.

A gang of young boys darted out of the alley, and Gus lowered one hand, preparing to guard his wallet, but they were laughing and throwing garbage at one another, apparently having as upbeat a morning as he was. He paused a moment to avoid the flying detritus of their passage and then slipped into his building.

He bounced up the stairs to his office two at a time and grinned at Emily as he stepped inside. Her reaction had an entirely unsatisfying lack of surprise. Looking up at him, she simply gestured to a pot on her desk and asked, "Would you like some tea?"

Gus's first impulse was to playfully insist upon coffee, but she was clearly not in the mood, so he nodded and let her pour him small cup of the stuff as he shed his coat and hat. It was every bit as bitter as expected, so he tossed in a bit of the sugar she kept on her tray. As he stirred that in, she stared at him pointedly until finally he asked, "What?"

"Should I take it from your good mood that you have a plan for this mess?" she asked, one eyebrow arched.

Gus shrugged as he took another sip, but she continued to stare until he finally asked, "Which mess?"

With a roll of her eyes, Emily handed him the paper. The top left article was another report on a plague in Tulsmonia and a warning that ships full of sick refugees had been seen sailing for Verinde.

Rampant disease in Tulsmonia seemed to be the top article every few days, and Gus felt a little insulted that they still felt it merited as news. Either the Tuls weren't sailing here, they weren't sick, or they were always turned back. He gave Emily a quizzical look, and she jerked the paper out of his hands, folded it so only the top right article was visible, and then handed it back.

'Prominent Architect Kidnapped By Wardens', proclaimed a histrionic, smaller headline next to the one about the Tuls. It didn't seem relevant to him as he didn't know any architects, but he supposed maybe she thought it was a mess they could make money from. Francis Parland was obsessed with Elven stuff, so maybe it was something the petitioner might be interested in. A potential distraction to get Parland off his back hardly seemed like a 'mess'.

Looking over the body of the article, he saw the architect was kidnapped after leaving the theater by a masked trio cloaked as Wardens. It made for a good headline, and he was sure everyone over fifty would be in a tizzy over it.

The Wardens were a bogeyman of his parents' generation rather than his own. A thousand years ago, they had fielded armies against their fellow men who were fighting for independence from the Elves. A few centuries back, those accused of being elf-worshipping Wardens were periodically put to death by the religious orthodoxies of the day. They had cropped up for the last time during humanity's final war with the Elves.

By the time of that war, no sane man could have seen the horrors wrought against humans and imagined that the rulers of Aelfua wanted anything but their extinction. The deluded few that had remained served as spies and saboteurs working in isolation against their own kind until the Elves all suddenly vanished. Those who had stuck it out to the end either surrendered or killed themselves once they realized that their 'living gods' had abandoned them.

There were no Elves left to warden for, so Gus supposed that particular wrinkle just added a bit of tastelessness to their crimes. It was a bold choice of disguise.

The architect's wife was offering a reward for his return, a full thousand peis, but a substantial sum like that also immediately struck him as an opportunity rather than a mess. It was probably an opportunity for someone else though, since Gus hadn't managed to drink away the profits from their most recent venture. It seemed odd though—if she was offering a reward, why not just pay the kidnappers and be done with it?

Reading more carefully, he saw no demands had been made yet, which explained the reward on offer. A chance to show up the Chandler's Crossing inspectors to be sure, but Gus didn't understand Emily's urgency until he glanced back up to the first sentence for the name of this prominent architect; despite the headline, he was not an architect at all but a famous engineer named Doctor Edward Phand.

He felt a chill wind blow away the vestiges of his good mood. Suddenly, his leg ached from the morning's stroll, and he wished he had slept in a bit longer. He wondered if perhaps he was more hungover from the night before than he had realized. "Oh. Well, that is a mess."

"Exactly. And you know we'll be suspects. We were hired by the wife, and they always blame the wife first," groused Emily, moving around to hover over his shoulder as he read the paper again.

Gus nodded absently, glancing through the story a third time, hoping some new detail might pop out at him and make things better. "If it was her, why would she offer so large a reward, though? Seems a risky prospect with at least four accomplices who might try to claim the cash by saying where he was."

"Murder, then? You think she came to us to find the best place to set him up?"

"No, if the point was murder, he'd just be dead. If they'd simply stabbed him and snatched her purse, she'd have an alibi with plenty of witnesses and far less police attention than a kidnapping. A sham kidnapping doesn't make sense if their aim was murder; the possibility of effecting rescue just makes search efforts for the culprits more intense."

Emily nodded, then said, "And why was the wife there at all, instead of the mistress?"

Reading the details again he added, "It says they grabbed for her pearls in the attack though, which doesn't make any sense for a kidnapping. Why mug her and then toss him into a cab? The public spectacle, the robes, the half-hearted robbery—it's too strange, almost like they wanted to make headlines and keep us guessing."

Emily stepped back and paced for a bit, an annoying habit of hers when she was trying to work things out. Pausing and looking back at him, she said, "The man downstairs said it was probably some secret society."

Benbow, in the office below theirs, was an accountant or maybe a petitioner or perhaps a petitioner's accountant. It was something dull that left him eager to share his very dull opinions, so Gus immediately discounted the idea and then worked backwards to figure out why.

As near as he could tell, secret societies were a game the wealthy played amongst themselves, where the moderately influential would pretend at vast importance. They were cliques that thrived on an aura of mystery, and usually some claim of mysticism that was obvious hokum. They were nothing but an excuse to drink among friends and socialize, for those who felt they needed such excuses, although sometimes they did get carried away with their premise.

Though loathe to agree with Benbow, Gus still thought it made more sense than an elaborately staged mugging. "It's too high profile to just be a membership hazing. Was he already a member but with past dues? An enemy of the club?"

He tossed the paper onto his desk and took another sip of tea; terrible stuff, but he was feeling a bit more awake. Looking down at his cup, Gus wondered if he should buy something of better quality since Emily was proving more fixedly against coffee than he had anticipated.

Emily didn't offer any other ideas though, so Gus continued along his own train of thought. "Dressing up like Wardens doesn't make sense if they wanted to make a point about their own club by going after someone. It's probably just a blind to keep us looking in the wrong places."

That made her grin at him, which seemed totally out of place until he realized he'd just implicitly agreed to look into the case. He sighed in defeat at the sight of her already counting the reward money. For a mere employee, Emily proved to be a relentless taskmaster.

Trying to pluck his deflated spirits back up, he said, "It should be easy, right? We know it can't really be Elves, and we already have a few leads from earlier. I'll check around. Since the wife was about to be rid of him, it's probably not her or the boyfriend; it might be a business rival or one of his girls on the side."

"What about the police? Won't the Crossing suspect us as being involved?" She paused then added, "You think Missus Phand mentioned us to them?"

Rising to fetch his coat, Gus shrugged and said, "Maybe. Detecting-Inspector Clarke would love an excuse to kick down our door, but his first move will be to find that cab. All the cabs are numbered, so it's a terrible choice for the kidnappers to use, right? But these guys are smart enough to think up a blind like the Warden robes, so finding the cab probably won't help Clarke find the kidnappers anyway."

He nodded to himself, gradually resigned to the job even though he felt a few more days insensate between jobs would have been nice. Reward money, getting himself out of trouble, and making Ollie Clarke look foolish were each, on their own, perfectly good reasons to take on a case, so he could hardly afford to skip an opportunity that offered all three at once.

Emily was still staring at him quizzically, so he explained, "It's too obvious. Someone with the guts for a scandalous distraction like being Wardens would cover their tracks, maybe a false cab number covering the real one or something like that. With the police chasing down a false lead, I can probably stay a step or two ahead and get to Phand before the police."

That made her smile, and she rose to help him into his coat, brushing at his suit a little to make sure he looked his best before handing him his hat. "I'll ask around as well," she said, "Maybe I could get a little more detail out of the witnesses."

"Don't bother. The police and the papers will have gotten all that from their own interviews already," he said. She gave him a smirk that told him she thought he was wrong and would do it no matter what he had to say on the matter. "Anything they saw is probably a false trail anyway. I'll follow up about the mistress; in cases like this, it's always about either women or money."

Gus dashed down the last of the tea, immediately regretted doing so, and handed the cup back to Emily. He nodded his farewell and made his way out of the office once more.

Approaching the stand, he scanned the line of waiting cabs for Louis. Not spotting him, he supposed Louis was apparently already engaged and hailed the first cab in line instead. Climbing inside, he directed the driver to take him to the Hotel Harrison.

No longer needing stealth, he had the driver pull right up to the entrance. Given the part of town they came from, the cabbie seemed only marginally disappointed in the lack of tip, but the stewards looked more crestfallen when a decidedly unfashionable passenger emerged with no luggage whatsoever.

Projecting all the bluster he could conjure up, Gus strode purposefully past them and to the front desk and was relieved when the manager who stepped forward to greet him was a different man than the concierge who had chased him off a few days prior. Nodding dismissively at the usual recitation of greetings welcoming him to the hotel, Gus said, "I'm here to meet Miss Aliyah Gale. Could you ring her room and let her know to come down?"

The manager looked a bit stricken at his request, and in a voice of meek apology he said, "I'm afraid she left earlier than expected, sir. She settled her bill yesterday and took the first train out this morning."

Well, that was inconvenient. Putting on a scowl as if terribly affronted by the news, Gus replied, "What? But we were to meet here this morning! Did she say where she was headed?"

Sounding genuinely sympathetic, the manager said, "I'm terribly sorry, sir, but I believe she said she had to return home right away, so she caught the 8:30." The man's eyes lit up a little, apparently seeing an opportunity to make money, and he coyly added, "We do, however, have our own wire service if you'd care to send a message ahead to her."

Unfortunately, Gus had no idea what sort of message to send her, much less where to send it, and he worried a telegraph form would give his ignorance away to the manager. "I should probably just go after her. Do you happen to have a copy of Martin's?"

Of course they did. Eager to be of service, the manager quickly produced their well-thumbed railway guide with a ribbon tucked away to mark the day's schedule of departures from nearby Imperial Hub. Gus flipped the book open as if looking for the next train out, but scanned backwards to find what had left at 8:30—*points east, including Aelfua.* Flipping through the book, he found a list of stops along that route, and sure enough the particular train she took passed over the mountains to the southeast through Khanom.

Deciding to test his hunch, he glanced through the schedule again and then groused, "Looks like the next direct to Khanom isn't until the overnight."

The manager nodded sympathetically and said, "I'm terribly sorry about your meeting, sir. Are you sure you wouldn't like to cable ahead and let her know you're coming?" He looked sincere enough, so Gus felt the hunch confirmed. Khanom was a long way to go for a slim lead, however, even if it did look like she might be fleeing the scene.

Maybe Phand staged his own kidnapping, so he could run off with his mistress? A splashy kidnapping would make the papers in Khanom, complicating that sort of marital escape plan if any of

Phand's business associates there saw him. And why dress like Wardens, which was sure to attract even more widespread attention?

"No thanks," he said, disappointing the manager's ambitions for making a few pennies off of him with the wire service. "I still haven't decided whether it's worth following her out or not." He grinned amiably at the man, tipped his hat, and then stepped back outside the hotel.

The liveried stewards all stiffened and made ready to attend their clientele, but then slumped back to their resting positions once they saw who emerged. Stewards, he had found, had a remarkable memory of who were the best tippers. Pausing by the door, Gus looked over at them and said, "I don't suppose any of you helped Miss Aliyah Gale to the station yesterday?"

They grinned at each other, chuckling a little at some mutual recollection, but one stepped forward and said, "I won the toss on that, sir. Helped her into the hotel's coach and back out again."

Knowing a handful of pennies wouldn't impress here, Gus fished around in his pocket for a few full peis instead. Gus pulled out a couple of the coins, letting the man catch a glimpse of the silver in his hand as he asked, "Did you take her luggage all the way to the platform?" When the man nodded, Gus followed up with, "Did she meet up with anyone for the trip? Maybe a hefty older gentleman?"

Another hack rolled up, and the steward's colleagues darted off in search of tips. The one talking to Gus shook his head in answer, but his eyes anxiously strayed to the new patrons disembarking as he said, "No, sir. Didn't seem right, a woman like that traveling alone, but she was in a palace car and had the whole bit to herself, so I reckon she was safe enough."

Gus nodded seriously as if the idea of a personal palace car was entirely the sort of thing one expected. With murmured thanks, Gus slipped the steward some dosh, which was quickly pocketed as the man rushed away to join in the aid of the hotel's new guest.

Gus strolled along the street for a time, pondering the situation. If Phand kidnapped himself, and they didn't meet on the train, chances were they traveled separately. If he was smart enough to think of that, he probably traveled under a pseudonym as well—all of which assumed he had the forethought to hide his tracks so well, which seemed a bit beyond the usual criminal education of an upper-class engineer of fancy bridges. Certainly no such skill had been on display when Gus had tailed him a few days ago.

He meandered towards the site of the kidnapping and recalled the steward's comment about Miss Aliyah Gale's travel arrangements. A palace car to herself on a busy line like that? A cabin was one thing, but the manager had said she left earlier than expected, and to buy out the entire car without a reservation must have cost a fortune. If she was a lover after Phand's bridge money, somehow she was already spending it.

Other than His Majesty, Gus wasn't sure who would have the sort of cash on hand to casually roll about buying up entire palace cars and suspected if Phand even had that sort of capital, he would live in a far nicer house. Whoever she was, it meant she probably had far more money than Edward Phand, which made her part in this even murkier.

He supposed it was possible that things might be turned around, and Phand might want to run off with her to get her money. Phand was older, not particularly handsome, and the paper had mentioned no titled relations affected by the scandalous kidnapping, so if Miss Aliyah Gale were wealthier to boot, then surely she would have better prospects.

She was from Khanom, in Aelfua, the former home of the Elves—perhaps that could account for the kidnappers' tasteless choice of disguise. Chasing her to Khanom to find out would cost money, however, and he was not yet willing to invest that much on so insubstantial a lead; other possibilities for finding Phand existed in town.

Phand was a hardworking man of business, which meant he probably spent nearly as much time with his employees as his wife. An interview with them could turn up something useful. His course of action decided, Gus whistled an old marching song to himself as he waved his hand to a passing cab.

~

"Lord Mayor's Ball"

The ball given last week by the Lord Mayor of Gemmen and the Lady Mayoress at Courthill in Palace was a very successful affair. The interior of that interesting old building, with the adjoining Courthill Library, was skillfully and tastefully decorated for this festive occasion by the Lord Ellis, and Francis A. Casey, a prominent member of the RFTB. The covered entrances of Courthill were adorned with banners and shields bearing armorial devices, and the front was draped in azure. Promenades and refreshment rooms were established in all the corridors and official apartments, in the Greatchamber, and in the Crypt beneath.

– *Gemmen Standard*, 8 Tal. 389

~

- CHAPTER 6 -

The Earl of Wending stood upon a landing between the stairs that descended into his elegant manor's marble-tiled foyer. Judging by the stiff and artless smile he greeted her with as he stood upon the stair, she suspected he was well aware of her current employment.

There was a thin and oft-crossed line between inquiry agent and blackmailer, and in her usual financial straits, she could hardly blame him for the nagging doubt that she might be ready to cross it. The clothes and jewelry he had once bought for her were all sold long ago, save the dress she wore for this visit, and she wondered if he remembered buying it.

It was reddish-brown trimmed in lace, and with a few decorative combs in her hair, she looked like a well-to-do woman from out of town rather than someone from the wrong side of it. She had dressed herself up for the visit much as she once had, although she no longer felt the need to cinch her corset beneath it quite as tightly.

The Earl of Wending had been a regular customer of hers, back when he was merely Mister Roderick Sloe and she still indulging in another profession altogether. Emily had always thought of him as a handsome man, but it seemed his appearance had finally begun to journey from distinguished into simply old.

In their previous transactions, he had always been courteous and had paid well enough to secure careful discretion. Further, anything she knew of politics had first been learned from that association, and she was just patriotic enough to worry over what havoc the loss of his influence might cause the nation.

Roderick had even bid a touchingly apologetic farewell upon hearing of his elevation, which made the risk of scandal too great for their association to continue. At the time, Emily had not really considered their relationship anything beyond a simple transaction and found the entire display a bit overwrought. She was surprised to feel a twinge of sadness upon seeing his look of relief when the footman led her through the foyer and into the drawing room beyond to meet with the Lady Wending.

Their drawing room was daubed in white, which caught sunlight from their large windows, bathing the room in an unflattering brightness. Despite that brightness, the gas lamps had been lit, banishing whatever few shadows might remain and gradually staining the walls behind them a dull yellow that the Lady Wending no doubt tasked someone to routinely whitewash over.

Paintings of Earls past hung along the walls in elaborately carved gilt frames, but the white and gold of the walls was starkly contrasted by the dark brown woods and deeply red plush velvets. A few flowers were arranged in various styles of vases on little side tables in a wide enough variety of flora to obviously be expensive purchases rather than the results of the Earl's own gardens. It was ostentatious to the point of tackiness, but in a way, that was the point.

Long before she was Lady Wending, Missus Sloe was a notorious gossip, and the room was decorated to facilitate the impression that she was both important and reliably tactless. That reputation was one she had worked hard to cultivate, and it had paid handsome dividends—for ladies of the upper classes, she was a critical hub of social information. Emily had always detested the woman, but fortunately that bit of gossip had eluded Missus Sloe.

Now known as the Lady Wending, she sat in a high-backed chair at the center of the room with two other ladies sitting at one of the facing couches to her left. The visitors wore dresses that billowed everywhere but at the tight-fitting waists, one in yellow, one in light-blue, and both edged in white lace. Lady Wending wore much the same in a dark blue, although her own dress billowed more and carried far more elaborate flourishes of lace.

Both guests were around Emily's age, younger than Lady Wending by a decade or more. When they had first met, Emily had envied Missus Sloe's lustrous black curls, but over the years they had faded to steel grey. Now she just envied the woman's money.

Seeing Emily, the Lady raised a hand to her guests, instantly silencing their conversation. She rose to her feet and crossed over with an enthusiastic smile, touching her shoulders and leaning in to kiss at her cheek. The other ladies were compelled to their feet as well, and Emily suspected the display of affection was mostly to toy with the other guests.

Although not formally divided, women of Lady Wending's class kept themselves decidedly apart from anyone not in service. Aside from their husbands, even the men of their class were only met in formal situations. Their resulting social sphere was small, tightly entwined, and bitterly petty. Emily hated mixing with them, but in the past, they had proven a valuable resource to Gus's inquiries, and he could hardly meet with them himself.

Lady Wending smiled at Emily, saying, "Oh, it's so lovely to see you again, dear! Ladies, this is Miss Emily Vonnut, my husband's cousin. She's third from the Earl!" That was a clever bit of extemporization on Roderick's part when Missus Sloe and Emily had first met, many years ago now. If she had learned or even suspected otherwise, Missus Sloe, now the Lady Wending, had never given any indication.

"Emily, this is Missus Graishe," said Lady Wending, looking to the woman in yellow. "I'm sure you must know her already. And this is her lovely friend Missus Casey. Her husband is some sort of successful financier." The last part was offered in an apologetic tone, since in Lady Wending's circles, winning enormous wealth through a shuffling of papers was barely a step above shoveling coal.

Emily sat at Lady Wending's right, seated across from Missus Graishe. There was a teapot and a tray of tiny biscuits, and the Lady Wending poured and offered Emily a share. Missus Graishe complimented Emily's dress, but Missus Casey echoed the sentiment with far more sincerity.

Normally with a visiting relative, the Lady Wending might inquire about the Earl's various relations, of whom Emily knew absolutely nothing. On the few occasions she had visited, Emily had always managed to catch the Lady's attention with some other subject before the Earl's old lie could be exposed. This time, she came armed with a specific one in mind. Looking to Lady Wending, she asked, "Did you hear about poor Doctor Phand?"

A wolfish grin came to the Lady's lips, and she glanced at Missus Graishe before answering, "We were just discussing that very thing!"

If Emily had any doubt that was the case, she would never have come, but with a fantastic crime like that happening in Palace District, she felt sure Lady Wending was doing all in her power to have something interesting to say about it to her visitors.

Missus Graishe nodded and said, "My dear friend Missus Casey was there! She and her husband were outside the very theater as it happened!"

She spoke as if her 'dear friend' was not sitting immediately beside her, and Missus Casey looked like she might blush at Missus Graishe's excitement in delivering that news. It was a bold attempt to claim some of the social credit for bringing Missus Casey's story into their social circles, but Emily doubted it would result in anything other than mild resentment from the Lady Wending.

Emily had expected Lady Wending would be making calls all night to find a witness suitable for her drawing room, but she was still impressed the Lady had managed to snag one so early in the day. No doubt as the word spread, there would soon be a number of callers to hear the tale; this late in the winter season, it was undoubtedly a triumphant convergence of events for Lady Wending.

Looking to Missus Casey, Emily felt a pang of sympathy—neither of them really belonged in Lady Wending's company, but at least Emily knew she was an impostor. She opened with the question Missus Casey would no doubt hear many more times before the day was out, "Were they really Wardens?"

Missus Casey nodded, her eyes wide as she repeated her story, "Oh, yes. We had just come outside and were waiting for our cab when it happened! A black coach sped down the lane, and three jumped out, all dressed in the same green robes, waving the same wicked heathen knives. It was terrible!"

With a grave nod, Lady Wending said, "You ladies are too young to remember them, but when I was a little girl, they were a constant menace. A gang of them brazenly rode down my very street, carrying powder to the central hub!"

She seemed horrified by the recollection, and Missus Graishe laid a comforting hand on the Lady's shoulder. Lady Wending would have been quite young at the time of that famous attempt to destroy the city's largest rail hub.

Emily knew from that morning's article on the kidnapping that the last major effort of the Wardens in Gemmen had been before the end of the war and was carried out by a lone radical operating under cover of darkness. She gave a sympathetic nod to acknowledge Lady Wending's own traumatic, if somewhat imaginary, experience and then asked, "The same green? So their robes all matched?"

Missus Casey nodded again and said, "Certainly—no motley leftovers or cheap costumes, they were quite real. All the exact same green as," she paused, looking around the room and then pointing to a flower in a vase on the side table, "that third leaf down, each just like the other, like proper Warden uniforms. Their knives were curled and everything."

"Curled?"

Missus Casey traced the shape of the curved blade in the air with her finger and then said, "They weren't gold though. I told my husband to tell that to the police, but he never did."

Emily knew the Elves had some problem with iron, so elfsteel was golden hued. They were a rare prize after the Elves vanished from the world, and she might never have seen any had Gus not kept one as an overpriced souvenir. When money was tighter, she had been tempted to ask him to sell it off to pay her salary, but the sadness in his eyes whenever he stared at it had warned her off. Instead, she just pretended not to notice it.

Since they were human, she didn't know if the real Wardens had used elfsteel or not, but she supposed the exotic shape of their knives might be useful information. She wondered if any of the other men interviewed by the police had reported that. Anything she could get that put them ahead of the Crossing might mean the difference between beating them to the culprit and collecting the reward.

"Three of them leapt out of their coach, waving those around. Two of them went after the man, Doctor Phand. They bashed him on the head," continued Missus Casey, pantomiming the bash, "then carried him into the coach while a third one tried to pull Missus Phand in as well!"

Lady Wending waved her hand impatiently at Missus Casey, saying, "You haven't told the most scandalous part yet! Go on!"

With a smile that told Emily she was hesitating for dramatic effect, Missus Casey took a deep breath and then said, "One of these Wardens was a woman!"

Missus Graishe gave a scandalized gasp despite the fact that she had undoubtedly heard the story already, and Lady Wending nodded sagely as if this confirmed some theory she would claim to have held all along.

Seeming pleased with Emily's own look of shock and buffeted by the dramatics of her companions, Missus Casey leaned forward, lowering her voice to an appropriate volume for discussing a scandal as she said, "At least one! Only one spoke, but I'm sure it was a woman. She said, 'We have got the man,' and when the other one had trouble pushing Missus Phand into their coach, the same one said, 'Leave her. We have to go.'"

"You think the other Wardens were women?"

Missus Casey smiled and shrugged, saying, "Who could say, in those robes?"

"Did your husband tell that to the police, at least?"

Missus Casey laughed and said, "Heavens no! The poor dear can barely hear the whistle on a passing train. Besides, what man would ever admit to seeing a gang of women haul off another fellow?"

At that, Lady Wending gave a disgusted frown and said, "The Elves were always mixed up about such things anyway. They're as bad as those Committee types in Tulsmonia!" Emily laughed softly at the thought of Lady Wending's reaction should she ever come by Gus's office and see her there, but she covered it with a nod of agreement, hoping it would seem she was merely laughing at the Elves.

Emily had heard the Lady's disdain and horror at the idea of women working in business offices before. Women in service were

acceptable, and the poor souls toiling away in the factories were easy
to overlook, but women with office jobs peripherally impinged in a
way that Lady Wending's sort found peculiarly offensive.

At the mention of Tulsmonia, however, Missus Graishe perked
up again and changed to the next subject. "Did you hear there was an
assassination attempt on That Woman in Mazhar?" When Lady
Wending shook her head, Missus Graishe added, "I think it means
she's real. Why else would someone try to kill her?"

Lady Wending harrumphed and said, "Because the Committee
are murderous barbarians, if it even was the Committee—Mazhar has
always been dangerous, dear."

They continued to discuss rumors about the fallen Tuls
aristocracy and the dangers of similar worker revolts in Verinde. With
little to add and not much interest in the latest theories of Committee
conspiracy, Emily pondered Missus Casey's story while waiting for an
opportunity to politely excuse herself.

When her moment finally came, Emily paused to compliment
Lady Wending's floral arrangements. Leaning down, she sniffed at the
flower Missus Casey had pointed towards and discretely plucked away
the third leaf down.

Quickly tucking it into her chatelaine, Emily thanked the Lady
for their hospitality and slipped away, leaving behind the sound of
whispers and muffled gasps of scandal. At Emily's age and supposed
rank, Lady Wending was sure to have many titillating speculations
upon her marital status. Emily had no doubt those scandalous theories
would be shared as soon as Lady Wending thought she was beyond
hearing.

Roderick was standing outside the house as she departed, and
Emily gave him the sort of secret smile that had never failed to charm
him, back when they were both a bit younger. His bashful reaction was
everything she remembered and for a moment, made him look just as
he had when they first met.

His footman hailed her a taxi and echoed the district of her supposed destination to the driver. Once the driver had rounded the block, Emily leaned forward and corrected him. Unfortunately, the imaginary Miss Emily Vonnut spent time in far nicer places than Miss Emily Loch.

Reaching down to the purse tucked under her top skirt, Emily jangled it, wondering exactly how much money she had left in it and wishing she had been less habitually parsimonious with how much she chose to carry that morning. She grimaced at the two extra intersections rounding the block would add to her fare and tried to think of a closer address from which she could walk to her next destination.

~

"Tuls Burglars Once Again!"

Once again, the city has been struck by a crime of audacious magnitude and success, witnessed by many, yet Chandler's Crossing has been entirely unable to collar the culprits. Mister Gelmont Freer's home was struck by daring rooftop robbers in the middling hours of last night as he conducted a private entertainment for his closest acquaintance on the floor below.

It was by fortune alone that Missus Freer stumbled upon the burglary in progress, and her hue and cry summoned party guests to the upper level and neighbors to their windows. Upon hearing the alarm, the burglars leapt through the upper windows and ascended to the rooftop above. Mister Freer and several of his guests attempted to give chase, but the burglars leapt across neighboring rooves with elf-like grace and quickly vanished into the night.

By all accounts, and by their garb, the burglars were said to be Tuls. As the police have proven useless in this affair, your editor has joined in with Mister Freer in submitting a formal request to the government to halt all further immigration of refugees from that country until our native safety from such predations can be assured.

– *Gemmen Standard*, 8 Tal. 389

~

- CHAPTER 7 -

Gus rode the elevator up to the floor that housed the reception for Phand & Saucier, ignoring the discomfort in his leg and standing straight in an effort to seem professional as the operator shuttled him up. It was important in places like this, he had found, to look like he belonged.

Slouching or chatting with the elevator operator would be noticed by the receptionist when the doors opened, and the receptionist's reaction would be noted by their boss, earning Gus a completely different sort of welcome. When the gate was opened on the twelfth floor, Gus held his left leg stiff and stepped out into a surprisingly bustling center of enterprise.

He had expected that, with one of the principal partners abducted, the various employees would be at something of a standstill. When he was in the army, soldiers seldom found tasks of their own if there were no officers around, but Phand's subordinates hurried about as if nothing were amiss in their operation. If they worked this hard while Phand was gone, perhaps it was Saucier who signed the paychecks.

The reception area beyond the elevator was a large open space with a high ceiling, and at the center of it stood a strange spike of twisted metal. To Gus, it most resembled an abstract artist's rendering of a lace-draped fir tree—small crisscrossing strips of steel arranged on a triangular base rising to a narrow point at the top. It reminded him of when Adelaide had dragged him to art shows with modern pieces, before she gave up endeavoring to explain their appeal.

Gus supposed the intricate structure might have some appeal only understood by bridge makers. The metal column was at least five feet tall and supported nothing at all but was seated prominently upon a table at the center of the reception area. He stared at it for several moments, trying to figure out what it was for, when a voice at his elbow surprised him by saying, "Magnificent, isn't it?"

The young man standing there seemed familiar, but Gus couldn't place him at first, so he replied amiably, "Oh, yes. Quite. Your work?"

The man laughed and shook his head, "No, sir, I'm afraid all I contributed was rivet counting; but then, any part in it will be something to be proud of forever." Still not sure what the big deal was, Gus just nodded as he pretended to admire the thing. "Were you ever able to catch up to Doctor Phand? Obviously, any meetings he had will have to be handled by someone else until he…"

The young man was obviously unsettled by recent events. Gus didn't really recall the man's face, but he did remember getting directions from someone that afternoon. Looking over at him, Gus said, "We met the other day, didn't we?"

The man smiled faintly in affirmation. People loved to be remembered, and Gus had found they would often give even the most casual acquaintance far more information than they would share with some curious stranger, so with a friendly smile, Gus grabbed the young man's hand and shook it enthusiastically as he said, "I never caught you name, though! Have you been with Doctor Phand very long?"

"Norville, sir. Norville James. I was lucky enough to catch the doctor's attention right out of school, so I've been working here for almost a year now."

"James, you say? Any relation to the famous soldier?" At the blank look, Gus replied, "First to kill an Everlord in Gedlund? It was in all the papers. There was a parade in his honor." It was a stretch—it was hardly an unusual surname, and Gus had only ever seen the famous man in passing, but claiming a shared acquaintance never hurt.

Norville shook his head, "Sorry, sir. I was still in primary school at the time and didn't really follow all the war news. I had some uncles who were naval officers, but certainly no soldiers in the family."

The very idea seemed repellent to Norville, and Gus supposed it was with good reason—upstanding people didn't serve as common soldiers, so no one of Norville's class would ever acknowledge a relation who did, no matter how heroic their career. In retrospect, it had been a risky gambit, and Gus just hoped he hadn't alienated the man by suggesting it.

Gus's own family was never so lofty as to produce officers and engineers, but they had still disowned him when he took the Queen's Coin. He had won medals and enjoyed some brief renown upon his return, but that wouldn't redeem him in their eyes. Being severed from his family had never bothered him much, truth be told, so he'd made little attempt to reconnect. It bothered him less, in fact, than being reminded he was old enough that he had been off fighting monsters while Norville here was still learning his letters.

In the back of the office, past reception, Gus caught a glimpse of the men Phand had met at the rail hub and gestured vaguely towards them as he said, "Seems he had a few important meetings planned too. Or is everything all settled now?"

Following his gaze back, Norville replied, "With the Exposition Council? Oh, no, sir. I'm afraid that's a bit of a mess still. We were hoping to have the papers signed this week, so we could begin arranging our construction contracts, but obviously we'd need Doctor Phand to sign the agreement, and well…"

Gus nodded sadly, "What about Saucier? His name's on the door; surely he could sign?"

The young engineer sighed and said, "Well, that's part of the problem. He's been out of touch for weeks. There was some art collection he was keen to see, so he took vacation while we were waiting to see how the Exposition's finance hearings came out. We've wired all the hotels again, trying to locate him, but so far no response."

"Really? That seems rather inconvenient for you," he replied while suspecting that it seemed rather all-too convenient for each partner to have disappeared just in advance of some stage in this deal.

The two men from the train began to work their way out of the offices, the younger pausing to greet each of Phand's employees as he passed. At first, he just seemed excessively gregarious, but then Gus realized the man's older companion, limping stubbornly along with a cane, was just barely keeping up with his colleague, and the pauses were a discreet way of letting him catch up.

As the younger one approached, he smiled warmly in their direction and said, "Mister James! My apologies for disrupting the order of the interviews this morning, but Mister Thomas and I would miss our train back if we waited until this afternoon."

Norville flushed a bit as if embarrassed to even be addressed and shook his head, "Oh, no, think nothing of it, Mister Sylvester. I'm glad we could shuffle things around to let you keep your schedule."

Sylvester smiled pleasantly as Mister Thomas caught up to them, the older man frowning petulantly as if he felt the need to counterbalance Mister Sylvester's positivity. They stared at Norville expectantly a moment, and then the young engineer finally caught on and looked to Gus, "Oh! Yes, may I present Maurice Sylvester and Rain Thomas, representatives from the Council for the Aelfuan Exposition. Sirs, this is one of Doctor Phand's associates, Mister—" The young engineer paused as he suddenly realized he had never quite gotten Gus's name, and his cheeks flushed even redder at the misstep. They had seemed likely to be prominent gentlemen when Gus first laid eyes on them at the rail hub, but Norville's reaction certainly confirmed their status here.

With a smile, Gus stepped forward to shake their hands, "Gus Baston."

Both men shook his hand. Sylvester's grip was friendly enough, but Thomas's was surprisingly strong and stiff, squeezing tightly as Thomas's steely eyes searched his, silently daring him to show any sign of weakness. Gus gritted his teeth in a forced smile as he endured it.

Eventually, the older man released his hand and gave a grim nod as if satisfied with whatever he had discovered in that test. Thomas leaned heavily upon his cane once more and asked, "What is it you do, Mister Baston?"

Gus smiled at the question as he pondered the best answer, but ultimately decided there was no need to dissemble under the circumstances. "Actually, I'm an investigator, sir, hoping to find out more about Doctor Phand's abduction."

Of course, he left out who he was investigating on behalf of, hopefully letting them draw their own conclusions without needing him to extemporize an employer they would cooperate with. Even still, Norville looked over at Gus as if he had suddenly sprouted horns.

Reminded of something by that, Sylvester lit up and said, "Oh, Mister James, I believe I'm supposed to send in the next interview." He paused and looked to Gus, then said, "Unless you've already handled it?"

Uncertain what these interviews were all about, Gus just shook his head and gestured Norville onwards. The young engineer gave an awkward farewell, still looking troubled by the revelation of Gus's purpose here. Looking back to the Exposition Council members, Gus said, "I'm afraid I only just arrived, sirs. Who is conducting the interviews?"

Sylvester glanced over at Thomas, looking thoughtful a moment, which made Gus worry he might have tipped his hand as a private inquiry agent, but then Sylvester said, "I believe he introduced himself as Detecting-Inspector Clarke."

Mister Thomas nodded, scowling as if that were a stupid thing to waste his time discussing, and Gus hoped neither had noticed him wince when they mentioned Clarke's name. The older businessman reminded Gus of someone, but he couldn't quite place it. He somehow seemed even less congenial now than he had for the handshake, so the last thing Gus wanted to do was give any sign of his unease at the presence of his governmental nemesis.

Hoping an informal conversation would draw a bit more out of them than Ollie Clarke would have managed, Gus asked, "So you gentlemen are headed back to Khanom now?"

Sylvester grinned and jovially replied, "Oh, yes, holes to dig and slaughter to be done, so we must away home."

It sounded like a quote or paraphrase of something, but Gus hadn't the foggiest idea of what, so he just smiled as if he had caught whatever reference was being made and then asked, "So what is it you gentlemen do, when you're not running the fair?"

Thomas scowled, but Sylvester laughed merrily, "Oh my, what must you think of us then? Slaughtering and digging holes? We're honest entrepreneurs, Inspector Baston. I run the Khanom Mineral Company, and Mister Thomas is, of course, the largest supplier of meats in the Empire."

"Oh! Of course," he replied, laughing with Sylvester. Pretending to be an official of the crown was a crime, of course, but being mistaken for one wasn't, so Gus let Sylvester's error in his title slide. He doubted the detecting-inspector down the hall would see much of a distinction between that and flashing a faked badge, but Gus wouldn't be paid if the police found Phand before he did. "I imagine this whole kidnapping business is rather inconvenient for both of you. Will you just finalize the deal with Mister Saucier once you return home?"

A look passed between the two businessmen, and Mister Thomas shook his head and said, "Saucier lives here in Gemmen. I've no meetings scheduled with him either way."

Sylvester nodded and said, "The same for me, I'm afraid. It was odd he didn't arrange an appearance during our visit. He's not missing as well, is he? Do you suppose he was somehow involved in all this?" Sylvester frowned slightly, his merriment seeming dimmed at the prospect of some sordid complication between the partners.

Gus smiled, raised his hands and said, "Oh, no, someone had merely mentioned to me that Mister Saucier was traveling, so I thought he might be meeting with you. With Doctor Phand missing, you'll need his partner to sign off on the thing, won't you?"

Thomas harrumphed as if he thought that were a stupid thing to say. Sylvester looked to the tower model, then shook his head sadly and said, "I'm afraid it won't work that way, Inspector. The design is under patent in the name of Doctor Phand. Without his signature, it just can't proceed." He paused, looked at his companion, and added, "Not that everyone will object to that outcome."

Mister Thomas looked uncomfortable at the suggestion as if directly accused in front of the law officer he thought Gus was. Thomas gave a Sylvester fierce look that Gus would have blanched under, but the younger entrepreneur merely responded with a bland and patient smile until the old vulture finally replied, "I've always said it should be a park and not this ugly metal thing. I've made no secret of it."

As he said it, Thomas gestured back towards the model at the center of the room, and Gus realized the metal frame Norville James was so proud to be part of must be the tower planned for Khanom. Gus glanced back at it but still couldn't quite see what was so significant about the thing, and he was inclined to agree with Thomas that it seemed a rather ugly monument.

Sylvester gave a placating smile and then looked back to Gus, "They nearly killed it on the financing, but with that straightened out we were supposed to sign the final agreement this week. It was the whole point of our trip."

Gus nodded, although he wondered who 'they' were who had nearly stopped the financing. "So what will go in that thing's place if the agreement can't be signed in time?"

Sylvester shrugged and said, "That tower was the only thing we were able to get enough of the committee behind. Without it, I suppose we'd be stuck with Mister Thomas's park. That tower would be the pride of the nation, and if we can't have it, then I'm not sure there's much point to any lesser structure."

Thomas harrumphed again and gestured at the model with his cane, "There likely isn't enough time to pull together the committee's ambitious monstrosity as it is. Certainly won't be if they miss the start of the season."

"Season?" Gus asked, hoping to draw more out of them. Fashion had seasons, and hunting and fishing he supposed, but towers would seem to be a year-round sort of commodity; but if Phand's abduction was related to the tower, a time limit on the deal might well be a time limit on the abduction too. "They're not planning on growing the thing, are they?"

Mister Sylvester laughed merrily and went so far as to slap Gus on the shoulder, reminding him of the rough camaraderie of his army days. "Grow it! Ha! No, Inspector, but they'll have to deal with the weather. Since Khanom is in the mountains, it gets colder than it does here, so the ground is too hard in winter to start anything. All the digging would need to be done by the end of spring to leave enough time for the foundation to dry, and then they'll need the entire year to build it. As it is, we're already being generous, hoping against foul weather and other possible delays."

"When is the deadline?"

"The eighteenth. Ten days from now," grumped the older man, "Although we're headed back to Khanom, so if Doctor Phand turns up, he'll have to meet us there."

Gus looked back at the model in the center of the room, trying to figure out why they all seemed so taken with the ugly metal jumble, but the significance of the design eluded him. He supposed he could see why someone would be opposed to erecting it in a park, but not so strongly that they would kidnap at least one of the men responsible for it.

Turning back to the two Exposition councilors, he asked, "I'm sure Ollie asked you already, but did either of you know Doctor Phand apart from the fair? See him at social gatherings, that sort of thing?"

Mister Thomas's disapproving scowl seemed answer enough. Apparently, Doctor Phand was good enough to build towers and bridges but not quite up to the level of society they occupied. Gus was somewhat surprised by that given the more egalitarian reputation of the Aelfuan settlers. Without families of rank though, Khanom was known as a bit of a plutocracy, so perhaps Phand just didn't have enough money to socialize in Thomas's circles.

Sylvester took the question more in stride, but his answer was the same, "I'm afraid not, Inspector. We only met him last year as a result of his proposed tower. I'd imagine his social circle was here in Gemmen rather than out east. We are, unfortunately, still a bit on the outskirts as far as that sort of thing goes."

Thomas harrumphed again and growled out, "That'll change."

Sylvester grinned and gave an enthusiastic nod, "The Empire will see what we've built out east, Inspector. The Exposition is going to amaze the world, I promise. Khanom will take her place among the great cities soon enough."

Gus smiled and nodded, amused by Sylvester's enthusiasm. It would take more than a fair for the settlements to win respect from the well-heeled traditionalists in Gemmen. Not wanting to encourage a sales pitch for their Exposition, Gus decided to turn the conversation directly to the abduction of Doctor Phand by asking, "What about the green robes? Any chance the kidnappers dressing as Wardens struck either of you as familiar? Secret societies, that sort of thing?"

The elder councilor gave a derisive snort and said, "Secret societies are an obsession of bored and jaded souls back west, Inspector. In the east, we keep too busy to indulge in that sort of nonsense. Besides, we live in the heart of the old elf lands; if there were still Wardens, they would want us dead most of all. Hardly the guise we'd tolerate for sport."

Sylvester nodded in agreement and added, "The whole thing is most inappropriate."

"So I guess that's a no, then," he said, and looking up, he saw the Chandler's Crossing inspector was peering out at him. Gus decided it might be better to slip away before Clarke decided to question him as well. Ollie Clarke had held some grudge against Gus from the moment they met and was always hunting for some excuse to drag him in.

Now that Gus actually had a connection to the case through his earlier employment by Alice Phand, it seemed a particularly inopportune moment to risk that sort of harassment. Eager to depart, Gus smiled at the two Exposition men and said, "Well, gentlemen, I'll be in touch if I have any further questions. Have a nice trip home."

Mister Thomas grunted his dismissal, but Sylvester reached forward, enthusiastically pumping Gus's hand, "Of course, of course. Best of luck to you in your investigation. If there's any news, please do let us know. I'm sure the whole council will be following this case with bated breath."

Detecting-Inspector Clarke's head popped out from one of the doors down the hall from reception and peered over towards them, spotting Gus right away. Clarke bore a bushy military-style mustache, the sort designed to emphasize an officer's stern frown of disapproval, which Clarke emulated quite well for a civilian.

Gus hurriedly promised Sylvester to keep in touch and then moved quickly towards the front desk. Clarke marched down the hall towards the two Exposition men, no doubt intending to ask what Gus had been up to. Even in a dark suit that bore no sign of rank, Clarke's officious demeanor left no question as to his commission.

While Clarke paused to speak with Thomas and Sylvester, Gus approached the reception desk and explained that he needed to drop a letter off at Saucier's home. Gus refused an initial offer to pass the letter along, insisting the letter was of a personal nature, which seemed to strike a chord with the man at reception. The receptionist obligingly produced Saucier's personal calling card, which listed the partner's address here in town.

Clarke was nodding gravely at whatever Sylvester was telling him and kept glancing back towards Gus as he did. Offering his thanks to the receptionist, Gus dashed off without looking back. He couldn't risk a wait for the elevator with Clarke right on his heels, so Gus tucked the card into his pocket and went down the stairs as quickly as his bad leg would allow.

~

"Sortilege Conviction"

Amanda Moil of Lower Market has been sentenced to six weeks' imprisonment for sortilege. She had assured a young domestic servant that she could thaumaturgically restore to her the love of a certain young man and then took a full gold coin in payment without awaiting the resolution.

– Gemmen Herald, 8 Tal. 389

~

- CHAPTER 8 -

The old grinder critically eyed the knife Emily handed him and then looked back to her, slightly concerned. He was an old man, clearly foreign and a fair sight older than the usual fellows who spent their days pushing carts through the street to hawk their services.

His small cap did nothing to disguise his balding pate, nor did the long, curly, white and silver fringe of hair around it. The curls were bound back in a loose tail that hung almost to his waist as if it intended to balance against the long beard he kept tucked into the belt around his thick leather apron.

The grinder brushed the knife off against the apron and held it up, peering at the edge again. His wistful frown as he checked the knife again told her that though he wanted to take her money to grind it down, he was having trouble with his conscience. Finally, his accent giving him away as Tuls, he said, "This knife, it look already sharp."

Emily smiled at him and reached out to reclaim her knife, somewhat relieved that his honesty would save her the cost of a perfectly good edge. Slipping the blade back into the chatelaine under the decorative apron atop her skirt, she said, "Well, perhaps you could help me with something else then? I have a question about knives."

He chuckled at that and looked up and down the street, clearly wondering if he could take the time from his rounds to answer. Other grinders worked these streets, and Emily had only picked him to question because he was the first one she came across. Not wanting to go in search of another, she added, "I'll pay for an edge, and you'll just have to talk rather than work the pedals."

The old man grinned and glanced down at the treadle below his cart. He was old enough to be her father, and as much as Emily's father had complained about his knees the last time she saw him, she suspected the old Tul was happy to turn a few pennies while resting. "Knives, I know!" he replied, tapping the side of his cart. He had several bits of twine along the side of it, each bearing worn-down blades that jangled together when he moved his cart to help draw the attention of customers. "What is question?"

"Have you ever seen a knife with a curve like this?" she asked, her finger tracing across her palm the same arc Missus Casey had shown her earlier.

"I can put edge on curved knife," he said, but after a moment, he seemed to realize that wasn't her question. "Is not a kitchen knife. How big?"

Asking Missus Casey the size had not occurred to her, but hoping the banker's wife had more or less gotten the size right when she had traced out the shape at Lady Wending's, Emily held her hands apart the approximate distance. "This, maybe?"

"Fisherman use curved knife for nets but is small. Curved and so big, is foreign knife. Not for cutting. For decoration."

Emily smiled, thinking that was another question she could ask Madame Jande, which she had planned to make her next stop, regardless. Reaching beneath her apron, she produced a half-peis of pennies from the coin purse on her chatelaine and held them out.

The grinder laughed and shook his head, surprisingly nimble fingers plucking away only four of the copper coins. "Your small knife would only cost four. Is fair." He tucked the coins into a box on his cart and then winked at her and began pushing his cart down the lane, once again calling out, "Knives and scissors! Knives and scissors!"

Happily pocketing away the rest, Emily left the old Tul to his rounds and began her walk to the Sandelle Pavilion. Although technically within Market District, the Pavilion had been built along the edge of Potter, so those of more modest means attending some spectacle or another wouldn't be passing through the nicer parts of town on their way.

A fair bit of slush still lined the sides of the streets, but the spring thaw had at least left most of the walkways clear of ice. Having suffered through the recent water shortage that resulted from the unusually late freeze, Emily had been eagerly watching the thaw in hopes that the pipes in her flat would soon flow once more. Winter routinely broke some bit of plumbing, and none of it could be repaired until the thaw.

Although there was a covered walkway beneath the rail that passed between Market and Potter, the soot raining from above mixed with the melting ice to create a black slurry. She had worn black boots for precisely this crossing, but not having taken the time to change again after visiting Lady Wending, she was still in the dress she had worn there. Without money to replace the dress if it were ruined, Emily could only hope no one she knew would see her as she lifted the dress up to her knees and pressed on into Market.

Thirteen years ago, Crown Prince Augustus had been delighted by the circus leasing the space at Sandelle Pavilion and had declared his hope that they be allowed to remain longer. Eager to please the young man they thought would soon be king, the owners extended the lease at very generous terms.

When Augustus was famously assassinated, it hardly seemed the time to send them packing, and when Prince Oscar became King Dedrick, he paid a visit to that very circus in public remembrance of his brother. By that point, Emily was fairly certain the Pavilion's owners were eager to send the circus on, but they could hardly risk snubbing their new king, so the circus had lingered and become something of an institution despite the wishes of the landlords.

In a few places, wooden sandwich boards sat upon the ground, pointing towards the circus's side shows in the Pavilion's neighboring lot, including one advertising the otherworldly spectacle of the 'Mysterious! Magical! Mystifying! Madame Jande.' It had a painted depiction of a woman, who looked nothing like Madame Jande, gazing deeply into a crystal ball, below which it offered fortunes read, spirits contacted, and advice from the world beyond.

Emily had known of Madame Jande for many years but had only met her in person a year prior when Emily had begun making more regular observances at the temples. Despite the bombastic performances she put forth to earn a living, Madame Jande was a priestess of the Hidden Moon—the same order of Maladriel devotees from which Caerleon himself had arisen.

The side lot was full of large, colorful tents. She wandered down the lane between tents, enjoying the emptiness of the place in the middle of a working day. Most of the sideshows had not bothered to open, but without a crowd, the brightly colored aisles felt like some alien landscape rather than the heart of Gemmen.

Gus refused to go near the place, saying it reminded him too much of his time in the army, but Emily had trouble imaging how the rows of garish red and yellow canvas could seem anything like a military encampment. After she had visited her family two years ago, having avoided them for many years prior, Emily's sister suggested she move to Rakhasin to start over. Plenty of people did that, for all sorts of reasons, but it seemed like a terrifying place. Emily had asked Gus about it and had only discovered that he did not like to talk about his time in the army.

Madame Jande's tent was a peak-roofed square made of alternating red and yellow panels of canvas. The entrance to the tent was shaded by a dark blue awning dotted with yellow stars, and dark curtains blocked the opening. Instead of the muscular, dark-skinned Maccian man who usually stood by the entrance, there was a young boy dressed in the same sort of striped pantaloons and a baggy vest that hung to his knees. In his hands, he held the same small wooden bowl.

Generally, the Madame Jande was paid for her advice in advance, and the quality of her performance was determined by the 'donation' she received. Those wishing to meet her would put coins in the bowl, the boy would take the offering back to Madame Jande, and then he would return to invite them inside for whatever that donation was worth. A few pennies might get a simple fortune, a few peis a more elaborate advisement. For a twenty-peis gold coin, sometimes you could even get a full séance.

Those hoping for an audience with the Madame in her role as a priestess of the Hidden Moon were supposed to present a coin for each of the gods of the Trinity of Light: silver for Maladriel, goddess of the moon; copper for Rheena, goddess of hearth and forge; and gold for Phaeton, god of the sun. Emily considered it a large sum to part with, but Madame Jande usually returned it once she was inside.

She pulled open her purse for the three coins she needed but came up with only five silver peis and eight pennies. With a quiet curse that the young boy politely ignored, she sorted through the coins and found one of the coppers was of fairly new minting and still quite bright. Placing the silver at the bottom of the bowl, she rested a dull penny atop it, and then stacked the shiniest penny on top, in place of the gold.

It was a symbolic gesture, and she hoped it would be enough to get her inside, but she muttered a quick prayer of apology to Phaeton all the same. The young boy did not glance down at the coins in his bowl and simply took them inside with reverently mechanical movement probably trained into him as part of Madame Jande's act.

When he returned a few moments later, the boy gestured her inside with an intensely serious expression so adorable that she had to fight the inclination to reach out and tousle his hair. She wondered momentarily if he was Madame Jande's son or more likely a grandson, but then Emily's thoughts turned to her own son, whom she had never seen at that age. It was an unwelcome musing she tried to banish as she stepped into the tent.

Inside, dark fabrics of deep blue and maroon were draped from the ceiling, forming a path along the wall. It turned left, led her around the front corner, and then formed a small round room in the back. The room was lit in odd hues as sunlight filtered through the red and yellow canvas behind her. A small table was placed near the drapes, with a singular quartz crystal as thick as her arm as the centerpiece, catching odd colors from the room as Emily moved past it.

A small stool for the Madame sat behind the table with its back to the dark drapes. Three padded folding chairs sat across from the Madame's stool, and Emily stood in front of the center one while she waited on Madame Jande. Nervous about the copper substitute, she silently rehearsed an apology for not bringing the proper donation, just in case Madame Jande came out to read her fortune.

When Madame Jande finally emerged, she simply pressed between the drapes rather than dramatically casting them back, and she had not even bothered to put up her veil, leaving it hanging loose from her blue turban. It was an entrance bereft of the usual theatrics Madame Jande used for fortune telling, and Emily relaxed a bit. Clearly her donation had been understood.

As befit a priestess of a notoriously secretive order, Madame Jande was an older woman of indeterminate origin. Emily had heard her use no fewer than four different accents and was never sure which was really her own. The woman's skin was lighter than her usual Maccian doorman but certainly darker than typical in Verinde. Judging by the lines on her face, she looked older than Emily's mother, although perhaps that was just hard living.

Stepping into the room, the Madame dropped the bowl down on Emily's side of the table, the three coins still inside. She gestured for Emily to take them back and then said in what might have been a Pylian accent, "You're here for more of that tea?"

Emily sighed, shook her head, and said, "No, I'm afraid not. I can barely get him to take the stuff, and he still drinks as much as ever. Oh, and I'm sorry about the copper. It was all I had on me."

"It takes time! Keep trying and be patient." She settled down onto her stool and reached under the neck of her robes to produce a small silver medallion. Holding it forward to give Emily a better look, she said, "As for the copper! This was my predecessor's, passed down from hers, then from hers, and so on for well over three hundred years. See those bumps? It used to be a coin.

"In the age of darkness, symbols of Maladriel were forbidden, so those in our order would take an old silver coin and rub whatever king's face was on it down to nothing—a disc of the moon, a symbol for the faithful. Maladriel is light in the darkness, she is hope, and when the symbols of hope are taken, we make our own. Phaeton's priests might be more formal, but Maladriel has never complained when her people make do."

Emily smiled and mumbled her thanks as she took the coins and tucked them back into the purse on her chatelaine. In the age of darkness, worship of the gods of light had been forbidden nearly everywhere in the world. When Caerleon undid the Shadow Negus, and the Trinity cast the gods of darkness into hell, Maladriel's faith flourished in public. Madame Jande's secretive order was now merely a quaint oddity, but Emily often found the old woman's earthier approach to their faith comforting.

That wasn't why she had come, however. Emily slipped out the leaf Missus Casey had identified and asked, "Do you know anything about the Wardens? New ones, I mean."

Madame Jande frowned and shook her head, surely old enough to have bad memories from her youth of the real Wardens. If she didn't know of any, chances were they didn't operate as such here in town, but it was a big city. That sort of lead was more than Emily had hoped for though—she had really come to see Madame Jande about her other specialty.

Passing over the leaf, Emily said, "The three who abducted Doctor Phand all wore identical robes of this shade of green."

The Madame took the leaf and shifted in her seat, trying to get a good look at it in the strange light of the tent. "All the same shade?" she asked, and Emily nodded. When she wasn't telling fortunes or providing clandestine religious guidance, Madame Jande also served as the seamstress who made and maintained all of the circus's elaborate costumes. In Emily's former career, the Madame had also provided her a few of the fanciful underthings she had needed.

"Dark green like this is difficult," the old woman began, turning the leaf back and forth. "The Elves had a dark green dye that could be done in one bath by hand, but they took that secret with them. To make things green, we need two dyes—one in yellow and one in blue. If you do it by hand, you would need to match each perfectly, and twice, to make all three the same."

"So all three had to be done together?"

Madame Jande shook her head and said, "Not just together, at the same time. If you dip one and then the next and then the next, it would dilute the dye a little with each extra bit of yellow, so they would not match. If you did enough for all three all at the same time, you would need a very big bath because they would need to be spread out to make sure the same amount of dye gets in every piece without streaks."

Emily nodded, having had her own mishaps in dying, and said, "It had to be industrial, then. Who could I ask about fabrics of that color?"

"Me." The old woman chuckled, handed back the leaf, and said, "I watch the market for things, and there's been nothing of that color for at least the past year or two. If you want to mix it, the dark blue you would need for that color is expensive, which is why the police are that nasty pale olive.

"For something to be this shade, it was either a very expensive private run, or it was bought elsewhere. We use some exotic silks and things for a few of the acts and my side business, as you well remember. I've not seen anything large enough for three men in that exact color, though."

"Aelfua's full of people now—could someone have learned how the Elves used to do it?"

Madame Jande snorted and shook her head. "If they had, kidnapping would be a waste of time. They could sell that secret to the textile companies and be richer than Cornelius Zephyr."

The reference to Zephyr was lost on her. She was familiar with the names of most of the city's commercial magnates, so either he was from someplace else or just a reference from a previous generation. She smiled and nodded all the same and tried to think what Gus might ask next in this situation. He would probably just try to flirt a bit and see what else Madame Jande volunteered; Emily doubted that tactic would help.

"Do any of your acts use knives?" she asked, although she already knew the answer. She had seen posters for the circus's knife thrower on the way in. Madame Jande nodded, so Emily again traced out the curve Missus Casey had shown her. "I'm looking for knives shaped like this. Is that shape familiar?"

The Madame laughed and said, "A crescent? Yes, I believe I'm passingly familiar with the cycles of the moon by now. It's nothing used in any of our shows. It looks foreign; maybe you should ask a collector."

At that, Emily smiled, immediately thinking of just the collector she could ask. Bowing her head, she sketched the triangle of the Trinity before her face and leaned forward to give Madame Jande a kiss upon the cheek.

Madame Jande pished at her, swatting lightly at Emily's shoulder as if embarrassed by the display. Still, the older woman grinned as she waved her off and said, "Keep pushing the tea, and let me know when you need more."

Emily promised she would and bade farewell, taking the wooden bowl with her. She returned it to the boy out front, playfully tousling his hair, which earned her exactly the indignant scowl she had expected, although it did nothing to discourage her momentary amusement.

What did, however, was trying to guess at the taxi fare necessary to reach her next destination. She was not precisely sure where to find Francis Parland but knew how to find his address. The closest place to check would be the Potter District's Constabulary, but she dreaded passing back under the rail bridge on foot again. That left the Market District Courthouse on the opposite side of the district and slightly uphill the whole way. With a sigh, she began her hike.

~

"Fashionable Marriage"

The marriage of Mr. Augustus Froderick Gonlin, only son of Lord Claud Gonlin and Lady Margot Hedy-Loort, youngest daughter of the late Earl of Dountless, was celebrated on the 7th at the Shrine of Rheena in Old Park. The bride was attended by her little nephew, Viscount Martique, as her page. There were no bridesmaids. The bride wore a short dress of cream, figured satin with lace apron and ruffles and, over a wreath of orange-blossoms, a spotted lace veil. Her page was dressed in yellow satin brocade with stockings and shoes of the same colour and an old gold-coloured satin hat with yellow feather. The service was choral. The bride was given away by her mother, the Dowager Countess of Dountless.

– *Gemmen Standard*, 8 Tal. 389

~

- CHAPTER 9 -

Saucier's home was in the same district as Phand's but on a noticeably more upscale street than his partner's, and Gus wondered how that had come about. While both men kept homes far nicer than Gus's flat, Saucier's was clearly larger than Phand's and bore more fanciful architectural flourishes.

It was enough of a difference to make Gus suspect that it stemmed from more than just different spending priorities. Despite Saucier's prominence on their firm's signage, no one had been complimenting his engineering genius as they did Phand's, which Gus took to mean Saucier probably managed the financial side of their partnership's projects.

Although this neighborhood would usually have been far nicer than Phand's, at the moment it was cluttered with undesirables. One of the new underground rail hubs was being dug not far off, and men had gathered up and down the street, eager to offer their services at whatever labor might be required.

Railroad construction companies had quickly learned that for unskilled labor there were enough desperate souls willing to work for little more than a hot meal, and thus never doled out more than the handful of pennies the law required they pay. As a result, those not selected for that day's labors had nothing to do but loiter around in the neighborhood, hoping for other opportunities.

As his taxi slowed in front of Saucier's place, a shabby crowd coalesced around it. They swarmed the moment he stepped out of the cab, barely giving Gus room to pay his fare before they accosted him.

Most were looking for jobs, but several had lost enough dignity to simply plead passersby for money or food.

"Hey, hey, take it easy fellas. I'm just a working man!" The crowd slowly dispersed. Although some of them seemed suspicious of his credentials, most just looked disappointed.

There were several calling cards on the front door left behind to signify visitors who had stopped by and received no answer at the door. Glancing over the cards, Gus did not recognize any of the names, and they did not seem to bear any particular marks either, which was fine since he could never quite remember what the various creases or folded corners meant anyway.

Gus looked over the front of the place. The shutters had been left open, but this time of year, that was not too unlikely if the place were left briefly empty. They would only be shut to protect the glass if he expected to be gone through the stormy months of later spring. Studying the windows, however, he noticed the curtains were open in several places.

As a child, Gus had a cousin who had entered service as a footman and had once explained that, as the newest hire, his principal job was to open and close the curtains. A house like this would have expensive furnishings, carpets, paintings, and other pricy knick-knacks that would be gradually discolored if left exposed to the sun. To keep them looking nice, household staff would close the curtains when no one was using the room, so if they were open, then that meant someone was inside making use of the light, even if they weren't answering the door.

A stroll around the block bought him to a gap between houses that led to a utilitarian alley running behind them. With wrought iron or wooden fences creating a small private space behind each, the alley was barely big enough for a single cart but served as passage for servants and deliveries less suited to the more elegant front entrances.

Ducking down that alley, Gus wandered along the back side of the wealthy residences.

He smiled and tipped his hat in response to the suspicious glare from a man shaking out a heavy rug behind one of the neighboring houses. Maids and footmen moved about on various tasks, but most dismissed him from their attention after a brief glance. No doubt enterprising beggars out front made occasional attempts to storm these palaces from the back entrance, but Gus's carefully nondescript attire set him apart from those wretches, if not quite so high as the folk who lived here.

From the back, Saucier's home was much like the others. An unpainted wooden fence surrounded the back area and divided it off from the neighbors at eye level, but it was low enough for Gus to peek over with a little effort. An amusing statue of a goblin wearing livery was set out by Saucier's gate, holding a small metal dish that had apparently been appropriated as an ash tray.

It was clear the sculptor had never actually seen a goblin in person; the broad mouth and high-set eyes were accurate enough, but the body was proportioned like a child rather than having the broad-shouldered, long-armed silhouette Gus had grown accustomed to shooting at during his army days. Although stories of gobs stealing children's clothes had made it back to Verinde, few people here ever had the ridiculous sight of how poorly they fit.

What appeared to be most of Saucier's household staff, if not all of them, were gathered in the fenced-in yard behind the house. The five of them had a small table and six chairs that set back from the door and likely served as a place for them to take their meals. In the absence of other duties, it appeared to have become where they whiled away the hours in their master's absence.

As he approached, a plump young woman—Gus guessed by her apron that she worked in the kitchen—stepped beyond the fence with an unlit cigarette between her fingers. She was many years his junior and, if she took him for some hobbling vagrant, would no doubt call on her fellows to chase him off with a broom. He could be charming when seated or leaning, but women had no interest in flirting with a cripple.

Fortunately, she'd already given him an opening; cigarettes were usually considered an unsuitable pastime for the fairer sex, and over the years, Gus had found that nothing won over a young woman like supportive acceptance of her bad habits. Stiffening to hide his limp, Gus strolled towards her and fished in his pocket to produce a match.

He lit the match and held it forwards, and true to form, she smiled at him and extended her cigarette to allow him to light it. As he did, she said, "Not seen you before. You new? You're not just back here looking for work, are you?"

With a surge of relief that she had not seemed to notice his limp, Gus grinned and shook his head, saying, "No, no. Got a job. That's how I pay for all these matches." That earned him a laugh, and he briefly considered trying to arrange some sort of rendezvous, but a younger woman, particularly already gainfully in service, would expect someone with a better position even if he weren't injured and, worse, formerly a soldier. Still, it was nice to be smiled at, even if it was just for the moment.

He gestured to the house and said, "I'm supposed to talk with your boss, actually, but they haven't seen him at his office, and it doesn't look like he's been home for a while. Since the house is still open, I'm surprised you're not taking in the cards."

The cook rolled her eyes and then blew out a long plume of smoke before she replied, "Been gone for weeks now. The bell kept ringing, so we put a few cards out on the door so people don't think he's home yet."

Over her shoulder, a well-dressed man who was likely the household's manager loomed quietly just beyond the gate as if worried whom she might be talking with. Ignoring him for the moment, Gus asked, "He left the house open with no one home at all? Wife? Children?" He was about to keep going down the list of potential cohabitants, but the cook interrupted him with a derisive snort.

"Fat chance of those!" She giggled at the idea, which told him quite a bit about Mister Saucier. Gus chuckled as well, quite ready to play the amiable confidant, but that exchange seemed to be enough to incur the attention of the household's manager. The well-dressed man pressed his way out of the gate and positioned himself defensively between Gus and his employee.

"And who might you be, sir?" asked the newcomer in an imperious tone. His arched brow and turned-up nose pronounced quite clearly that he knew this stranger was up to no good and that he would brook none of it. Proper guests came to the front door, after all.

Mirroring the tone with a stiff professionalism of his own, an old army trick Gus had kept well practiced over the years, he replied, "I am Gus Baston, and I am investigating the disappearance of Mister Saucier. You will need to surrender to me any information you have on his whereabouts."

The manager tensed ready to fight this intrusion of his master's privacy, but Gus's tone and phrasing made him hesitate. Instead of demanding Gus's departure, the man nervously asked, "Are you with the Crossing?"

Gus gave an exasperated sigh, glancing at the cook as if sharing his frustration at her boss's stupidity. As expected, she was quite happy to see her manager derided by a supposed authority figure and tittered in amusement, which made the manager glare at her until she stifled her laugh and feigned a properly abashed expression.

With a stern frown, Gus said, "He's been gone for weeks. Has he sent any money for expenses and wages since his departure? If you're aware of any hints as to his location and conceal it from an official investigation—"

"No, no, we'd never do that," the man held up his hands in submission to Gus but then hissed back at the cook, "Get back to work. The staff meal will be soon!"

The young woman rolled her eyes behind his back, but she stubbed out her cigarette in the goblin's tray and pocketed the remainder of it. Gus gave her a saucy wink, and she giggled again before heading inside.

Once the cook was out of earshot, the manager sighed, looked down at the goblin statue, and said, "I hate that thing. Mister Saucier does too, but it was an ill-conceived gift from his mother, so he won't just throw it out. Instead, he put it back here, and now I must deal with it, and it just encourages them to smoke."

It was a familiar tactic—having failed with superior bluster, the manager was trying to restart their conversation on more equal footing now. If that failed, the manager would be reduced to interacting with the stiff formality used with someone approaching his master's social graces. It was an awkwardness inherent in service positions. Those in service had to exercise authority over their lessers and submission to their superiors, but not everyone came clearly labeled.

Having held, or at least pretended at, all sorts of positions on the social ladder, Gus knew that an equal had the best chance to get more conversation out of the manager's sort. He gave the man a sympathetic nod, then gestured for the manager to lead them inside. Buoyed by his successful flirtation with the cook, Gus did his best to exude confidence—he would play an equal but one backed by authority.

The manager hesitated. An inspector from the Crossing was really just a spy for the crown, and the man might get in trouble for admitting him without more of a challenge. Then again, if the manager were resistant, an inspector would just come back later with an unseemly host of uniformed officers, and then the manager would find himself in trouble for not allowing something more discreet. With a defeated exhalation, the man stiffened his back and made the conclusion Gus had hoped for.

They stepped past a housemaid and a footman who stood idle by the back door, and the manager led him through the servants' passages into the house proper. "My name is Garnick, by the way. I've been with Mister Saucier for over twenty years now, and, well, we've never been more worried for him."

They strolled through a wide hall lined with paintings and pedestaled objects of art. Everything was in the Modernist style, with flowing, surreal contours and images of nature in emulation of the lost works of the Elves. Some details were strikingly realistic but surrounded in complex abstract patterns and swirls. While he didn't find the fad as objectionable as traditionalists seemed to, Gus typically suspected Modernists were just including their fanciful flourishes to conceal mistakes.

Modernism was not the only theme present in Saucier's choice of décor. Nude and nearly-nude men with long flowing hair posed awkwardly in forest glades or amid strange swirls of color. Statuettes of similar style and subject matter were also highlighted, liberally scattered among decorative boxes. The columns they sat upon had over-wrought insect themes, which Adelaide had once explained was part of the movement's naturalist motif. Emily just called it creepy.

The abundance and intricacy of it all left the large house feeling cluttered and crowded. Remembering his conversation with

Norville James, Gus said, "I'd heard he told some people he was headed to an art show?"

Garnick nodded and replied, "Yes, sir. That was his plan. We packed a week and a half's worth of clothes for him, which he took to the station."

A week and a half worth of clothes narrowed down the list of likely destinations. An art show wouldn't be in some small town, and Verinde's next most likely location for such a thing would be Oulm, which was only a few hours away by train.

Outside of Verinde, Piago was only a few days south by train but was known more for its beaches than its art scene, and so close to Rejju, Gus suspected it was likely a socially uncomfortable place for a man of Saucier's apparent inclinations. There were several places in Garren, but that trip took several days by train each way, meaning that a trip of only a week and a half would leave him very little time at his destination.

"In Khanom?" Gus asked as if he knew and were only seeking confirmation, although it was only a guess.

Garnick nodded glumly. Khanom seemed to be where everyone was going these days. Gus had never been to that booming city on the southern edge of Aelfua, and though he knew that they had industry and money, he still always pictured it as a collection of the sort of ramshackle wooden buildings he had seen in other frontier towns while in the army. Clearly there was more to it.

Looking around the hall, Gus asked, "Is there a writing desk or something where he handles his correspondence? Or does he do all that from work?"

"Upstairs, sir. If you'll follow me?"

Desperation had probably made the man more gullible than usual, and Gus felt a twinge of sympathy. Unless Saucier left more cash on hand than most, the house's coffers must be nearly empty after such a long absence. Garnick no doubt needed his master to return soon, or else he and the other servants would not be paid. With the crowds on the street outside, they had daily reminders of how hard that next engagement would be to find. Gus wondered if Garnick would be in trouble for letting him in once Saucier returned.

Garnick led Gus up the main stair and into his master's private quarters. Within the master bedroom itself sat the writing desk, the top rolled up, and the surface strewn with various letters that his household staff were clearly forbidden to touch, given how orderly the rest of the room appeared.

One letter sat atop the rest at the center of the desk, and Gus stepped over to get a better look. It was a short, perfunctory note, despite its fancifully flowing script written in a dark green with an unusual metallic sheen to it:

Dear Mister Saucier,

It has been months since we met in Khanom, but I recalled with much fondness our discussions on art and your love of the Modernist styles. A friend is opening a new gallery and asked me to invite potential patrons. I will forward a sample of the works to be exhibited. The first showing will be on the 12th, which I fear will only be a few days after you get this letter. Please wire if you plan to attend, and someone will meet you at the hub.

Yours,

D.M.

"Any idea who D.M. is?" he asked, but Garnick shook his head.

A small box sat nearby, near enough to seem related, so Gus tipped back the lid. There atop the wood shavings in which it had been packed sat a shimmering golden token. From small loops extended the heads of two stags butting heads with their antlers intertwined.

Ignoring Garnick's indignant gasp, Gus reached down to pick it up. It wobbled in his fingers, and Gus quickly realized the thing had two pieces; the intertwined antlers formed a clasp connecting two sides of whatever went through those loops. A small belt, perhaps.

"Oh, please do be careful with that!" worried Saucier's man, but Gus ignored him and focused instead on the golden clasp. It was too light to be gold, and gently pressing at the intricately sculpted antlers, he discovered it was too stiff as well. Holding it closer to the window, he saw the color was slightly off, and just to tease Garnick, Gus lifted it up and gently bit onto the metal.

The man gasped in horror, so Gus laughed and held it out to show no harm had been done. "It's not gold; it's elfsteel. I'd need much better teeth if I wanted to bite through that."

Garnick gingerly took the buckle from him and inspected it, then sighed in relief to see that it appeared unblemished. "It looks like gold."

Gus chuckled, then nodded and said, "Well, in better light you can see the color is slightly more yellow, and of course it's much harder. Since the Elves couldn't touch iron, they figured out how to make this stuff instead. When they left, they took it with them too, except for those pieces that were already in someone else's hands. There weren't too many of those, so to the right collectors, it's worth far more than gold."

The house manager laid the buckle reverently back into the box and replaced the lid. Seeming surprised by Gus's ready expertise in the subject, Garnick said, "How do you know all that?"

"Friend of mine wanted to be a history professor," he said, leaving it at that. If this had been mailed from Khanom, or anywhere else in Aelfua, it was also a legally complicated piece to be in possession of. After the unexpected disappearance of the Elves, Elven treasures found in those lands had special rules. While Gus supposed there were ways around those laws, he also knew documentation was important, and he doubted D.M.'s letter would be sufficient.

Gus glanced over the other missives on the table but didn't see anything else in a matching hand and certainly nothing else with that shimmery green ink. The others he could read were fairly pedestrian invites to events here in town and what appeared to be some family correspondence concerning the health of an elderly uncle. "You've heard nothing from him since he left for his trip?"

"No, sir, not even a wire that he had arrived and been unpacked, which is unusual for him. He often leaves something behind at home—a letter or a particular ornament he neglected to have us pack. He almost always sends a request to have something forwarded to him on the next train." The poor man was fretting with his hands, and Gus suspected the man was beginning to reconsider having invited this stranger into the house.

Gus nodded and looked at the letter again, "Any idea what he was up to, the last time he was in Khanom? That might help me find this D.M. Did he talk with you about his trip?"

Garnick frowned as he pondered the question but eventually replied, "He only went on business before. Most recently he made a presentation to their Exposition Council and was confident he had won the Council over on financing. I recall no mention of any D.M., sir."

"If I were to guess, I'd say it was a woman's hand. Is it possible he met anyone over there of romantic interest?"

The manager fidgeted a bit, then in a pained voice replied, "Sir, he … is not the romantic sort. Strictly confidentially, we've always assumed he will, uh, remain a bachelor."

Grinning a bit at Garnick's discomfort, Gus considered at least one of his suspicions on Saucier confirmed. "I see. No chance he ever mentioned or ever did business with one Miss Aliyah Gale? Dark haired woman?"

"No, sir, that name is not familiar to me, I'm afraid. I would know it if she had ever come here, and I handle his private post and have never seen the name."

Gus glanced down at the table again, scanning for her name among the scattered letters across the top of the desk, but nothing caught his eye. He wanted to fish through them all for more hints but thought Garnick would draw the line at that without a more formal show of the authority Gus didn't actually have.

Gus nodded and to Garnick's apparent relief announced, "I think that's all I can get from here. If I get any notion of Mister Saucier's whereabouts, I'll be in touch."

Garnick nodded and led him out again and down the stairs towards the foyer, apparently discomfited enough by the entire situation that he absentmindedly led Gus towards the front door instead of the back. Or perhaps he just had a higher opinion of the social station of inspectors than Gus did.

Although he hated to give himself away, particularly with Clarke as the one working the Crossing's investigation, Garnick represented too good a resource to pass up. Gus dug into his coat pocket for a calling card; Emily would complain again about the pennies spent on cards, but it seemed worth the gamble. "If you hear anything before I get back to you or think of any additional details that might help, please send word to my office. Anything at all might help me locate your master and hopefully Doctor Phand as well."

Garnick took the card, studied it for a moment, and then paled as he read aloud, "Inquiry agent?" The man's face reddened in mounting outrage, his mouth moving as he struggled to formulate it into words. "You're not with Chandler's Crossing? I only told you all of that because I thought you were with the police! What's this all about?"

Gus smiled and held up his hands in surrender, trying a bit of disarming charm. He was better at that with women than men, but he wasn't sure what other approach to take, and anything new Garnick might find could be vital. In an apologetic tone, he said, "I'm sorry if that wasn't clear. Doctor Phand was kidnapped, and that someone may have Mister Saucier as well. I'm just here to help and make sure everyone's safe."

Garnick glared at him and down at the card, looking not the slightest bit mollified by Gus's explanation. Emily would definitely begrudge him the cost of that card. Whatever decision the man might have announced next was interrupted by a heavy rapping upon the door. Scowling, he muttered, "Can't they see all the cards out there already?"

A fist insistently hammered at the door as Garnick looked about for the footman who should be answering it. After one last accusatory glare at Gus, the manager stepped forward and started to open the door himself and was then pushed back as a familiar plain-clothed inspector stepped inside without further invitation.

Detecting-Inspector Clarke looked Garnick over a moment and then announced, far louder than necessary, "Sir, we are with Chandler's Crossing, investigating the disappearance of Doctor Edward Phand, and I have a judicial writ allowing us to search the premises. Is Mister Saucier at home?"

Garnick sputtered a bit, looking to Gus and then back to Clarke with a mixture of confusion and indignation. "What? Another? This gentleman just let me believe the very same thing! Do you have any sort of credentials?"

Clarke smiled, looking more than happy to demonstrate that he did as he reached into his pocket and produced a slip of paper, which he held before Garnick's face. As he did, the inspector gave a sharp whistle, and the door behind him was flung wide by a press of bodies dressed in the crisp olive and gold of the Gemmen police.

Without pausing, they swarmed past the startled manager and throughout the house. Shocked Clarke had caught up to his own investigation so quickly, Gus watched the police spreading into the house, and he wondered what they had been told to look for. It had to be something concrete; Ollie Clarke himself wasn't always the sharpest investigator, but the uniformed police he commanded were positively dense and useless without an obvious target.

Garnick looked entirely dumbfounded by the sudden invasion and stared blankly at the writ Detecting-Inspector Clarke held forth. There was no way for Gus to slip out this time, but as a matter of professional pride, he hated to let Clarke think he had the upper hand. Putting on a swaggering grin, an expression full of confidence he didn't feel, Gus called over, "Saucier's not here, Clarke. Been missing a while actually. You boys are slow as usual."

The inspector turned a baleful eye to Gus, and his mouth curled in an unpleasant smile. "*Mister* Baston," he intoned, emphasizing the 'mister' to Gus in that way Clarke always did, which Gus never quite understood. "You seem to be getting to all sorts of places early. Suspiciously early."

Gus forced his lips to maintain their cocky upturn. He had no idea what Clarke might know, but giving the inspector any sign of unease would doubtless make things worse. "Nothing suspicious about it, Inspector, it's just the sort of sharp investigatory talents my clients pay me for."

The grin that elicited from Clarke sent a chill down Gus's spine.

"See, now that's the kind of sloppy detection we expect from you freelancers. Investigating a crime two days before it happens is actually quite suspicious." Snapping his fingers at one of the boys in uniform, Clarke continued, "It's nice of you to save me a trip though.

Bind him up, Jerry. *Mister* Baston, you are under arrest. We'll arrange a ride for you down to the local constabulary, and *when I have time*, you and I will discuss this further from there."

The 'when I have time' seemed particularly ominous. Without formal charges, Gus would sit in a cell until Clarke decided he'd had enough or Emily managed to figure out he was being held by the law, find out where, and then send over a petitioner. That could take her days, depending on how loyally obstinate Clarke's men were.

Panicking at the thought of prolonged confinement, Gus blurted out, "What? No, I was hired by Missus Phand before the kidnapping! Now I'm just chasing the reward she offered!"

Clarke waved off his objections, and Constable Jerry DeRime, Clarke's usual gap-toothed crony, roughly bound Gus's hands together and shoved him out the door.

Outside, the vagrant crowd had gathered into a wide semicircle around the front of the house to watch the proceedings. Gus was sure nothing pleased them more than seeing the police rush into a well-to-do home and haul out someone in irons, and as they emerged Jerry received a round of applause for his capture. Had Gus known he was to be arrested, he'd have worn something shabbier, if only so the crowd would take him for a house-breaker rather than a bank swindler or other loathsome profiteer.

Playing it up for the crowd, Jerry gave Gus a kick towards the waiting carriage. The constable driving leaned down to give Gus a hand up, but Jerry would not wait and shoved him roughly inside where he tumbled to the floor between benches. Climbing over him, Jerry took a seat and slammed shut the carriage door.

Gus's leg ached from the rough handling, and he grimaced as he levered himself up onto the bench opposite. Seeing his discomfort, Jerry gave an almost-apologetic smile in response to Gus's glare, then shrugged as if to let him know there had been nothing else to be done under the circumstances. The crowd outside continued to cheer the arrest and only quieted down as the man up front cursed at them and drove his horses forward.

~

"Art Sale Concludes"

The sale of the second portion of the great collection of pictures and works of decorative art belonging to the Duke of Gonlin, and brought from Gonlin Palace in Oulm, was conducted by Messrs. Christie, Manson, and Woods at their rooms on Young Doe Blvd., Old Park, on the 5th, 6th & 7th. Many fine pictures by the Garren masters were sold; and six of these were bought for the National Gallery by Mr. Gilmot in his current role as acting director, and by two of the trustees, Mr. Pullman and Mr. Wilson, at very moderate prices. We shall give some further illustrations of this collection and of Gonlin Palace.

– Gemmen Standard, 8 Tal. 389

~

- CHAPTER 10 -

The Market District's Courthouse was one of the oldest in Gemmen, constructed in marble columns in the Pylian style two centuries back when the Elven architecture aped by Modernism would have been derided as too inhuman for the public's taste. Emily's principle concern with the architecture was the excess of stairs, that celebration of human independence seemed to require.

The narrow marble steps were pretty to look at, but after her hike through the slushy streets from the other side of the district, she wished the entrance were at ground level rather than two stories up a steep wall of tiny steps. A former client had once explained it had something to do with the way the ancient Pylians had heated their buildings, and as she neared the top, she found herself hoping the architects were now freezing in hell for using it as a decorative flourish so many centuries later.

A few stone benches were arrayed along the top landing, all currently occupied by others who had braved the stair and were now taking their rest. Judges and petitioners had their own more practical entrances, but the general public had to climb, and she supposed she should be grateful to whoever had thought to leave them a place to recover before heading inside.

She took a moment to make herself look a bit more orderly, adjusting the combs in her hair and brushing off her dress. There was little she could do about the muck on her shoes, but she managed to scrape some of that off onto the top few stairs, which seemed like fair recompense given the trouble they'd caused her.

Looking up, she saw the angry countenance of Taltek, the god of justice presiding over the courthouse doors that flanked him, and she reflected uncomfortably on her uncharitable thoughts towards the courthouse's long-dead architects. She uttered a soft prayer of apology.

Taltek was always depicted with a face on both sides—the outraged snarl that faced the damned at the gates of hell, keeping them trapped inside, and the stern gaze that faced away, judging the souls that might pass through the gate behind him. He bore a spear in each hand, the tip of the right spear always facing forwards, here sculpted with flames wreathing the stone tips.

The entire thing was lavishly painted and reminded Emily of a humbler wooden statue in her village temple growing up. As a child, she had always gone out of her way to pass it by on the stern side rather than the angry one. She laughed softly at her childhood superstition but still crossed to the other side of the landing, so she wouldn't have to pass under the angry half's ferocious gaze.

A gentleman, also on his way inside, held the door for her, and she stepped past Taltek and into the bustle of the courthouse's lobby. Numerous people gathered in various queues, most of which she could not begin to guess at the purpose of, although some of the lines looked markedly happier than others. Brown-robed petitioners marched purposefully about, breezing past the lines on whatever errands had brought them here.

With little experience of courthouses, Emily watched quietly for a bit, trying to figure out where best to ask after Francis Parland. As she waited, a pair of doors flung open revealing a crowded courtroom beyond. By tradition, the judges and petitioners must march past the gathered crowds after sentence was rendered, and she could see the white and red of the judge's dress between the quartet of petitioners packed tightly around him.

The group moved purposefully away from the courtroom, laughing in amiable discussion as they proceeded down the hall, and Emily quietly slipped after to see where they might go. After a short walk, they turned into one of the adjacent doors, which appeared to be the judge's chambers. Inside was a small reception, which the five breezed through into some office beyond.

Emily stepped into the reception and was immediately greeted by a young clerk seated at a desk there. He was surrounded by a tall stack of books and nearly buried in various slips of paper, but he apparently doubled as receptionist among his other duties. Despite looking tired and terribly overworked, he managed a friendly enough smile as he said, "Hello, madam. Is there something you need?"

Several lies that might motivate his sympathies sprang to mind, but she hesitated in choosing one. The clerk was around the same age as her own son, and something in that momentary resemblance made her want to be honest. Instead of the first few responses she had considered, she simply said, "I'm looking for Francis Parland's address. He's a petitioner, so I thought you might have it here?"

Her worries at any obstruction melted as the young man smiled, looking entirely pleased to be able to offer her something. Turning around, he pulled out a well-worn publication entitled *Guide to the Legal Practitioners and Practices of Gemmen*. The clerk flipped the book open but a few pages from the listing and then, with a smile, turned the book around and held it out for her.

It conveniently enough listed the firm with which he practiced, his professional address, home address, wife's name (Millie), and the number of their children (none). That last bit of data seemed sad, and she wondered if the publishers of the *Guide* had ever considered publishing such detail might embarrass their subjects. Emily silently recited the address a few times and then thanked the clerk.

As she was taking her leave, an officer in olive and gold pressed through the door, rudely shouldering her aside before pausing in recognition and giving her a gap-toothed smile. Jerry DeRime was an oaf, by nature and by trade, but he had married an old acquaintance of hers. Compelled to be civil, she gave a polite nod and wedged herself past him.

DeRime tossed a rumpled sheet of paper towards the clerk and said, "That's been served and signed." She was relieved she might avoid his conversation but had barely made it through the door when he turned his attention back to her. "Miss Loch! Saw your boss today. Tossed him in a cell myself. We won't go as easy this time, so you might finally have to find other employment; Jenny does well with her sewing."

The condescending sneer made her want to tell him Jenny couldn't sew worth a damn and was just slowly doling out money she'd earned on her back years earlier. DeRime thought he'd married a former Palace District chambermaid, and the truth would burn him. But she knew it would burn Jenny too. Emily bit back the words before she uttered them—courthouses were sacred to Taltek, consecrated to justice, and unpleasant truths were not the same thing.

Instead, she forced a smile and said, "Oh? Well then, I suppose I'll have to learn to sew."

* * *

Emily had expected Parland to live someplace swanky but was still surprised when the driver told her the address was all the way out in Old Park. In ancient times, that bit of land, adjacent to both the Palace District and the Government District, had been set aside for royal sport. Kings had stocked and stalked game there, just outside of the city.

King Randel, as part of the compact forced on him by the ironically titled 'Lesser Lords' had granted out the lands of his park, which were then made into relatively spacious estates. Most of those were still owned by the descendants of the Lesser Lords, although Roderick had once wistfully lamented that the title Earl of Wending had long since been separated from its original estates there.

From Market, the taxi had run about three and a half peis worth of intersections; that would leave her with just short of three peis in her purse. She might be able to make it most of the way home on that, but the trouble was, in this neighborhood no taxi would be around to be hailed on the way out again. Leaning forward, she said to the driver in her most convincing Palace District lilt, "I shan't be long. Would you mind terribly much just waiting here?"

The man shrugged and called back, "No, ma'am, but I'll have to charge for the wait, more if it passes the dinner hour."

Emily smiled sweetly, nodded her head, and then stepped outside, silently cursing the situation. For a self-employed taxi driver, the dinner hour was whenever the man chose to set it, so of course whatever time she spent here would go right through it. She supposed he had family and horses to feed and wondered if she could play on his sympathies when he realized she wasn't the rich Palace District sort she was pretending.

Of course, if she weren't pretending to be someone else, he'd rightly assume she didn't have the money to pay him to wait, dinner hour or not. She made plans to hash out that particular fee along the ride back, knowing there was no way she could pay the fare here from Market then near enough back to Potter plus whatever the man wanted to charge her for the wait.

It looked like rain, and foul weather often led to foul moods, which would make bargaining him down more difficult. Maybe she could talk him into waiting outside her flat while she ran in to get more money, but that might just set her up to be robbed later. Maybe if he dropped her off at the building behind hers, and she slipped through the alley, she could get his money without disclosing her own address.

Her train of thought on that transaction came to a halt as she approached the door, and it opened without the need for her to knock. A smiling footman stood there and gestured her into the foyer to wait while he took her name to Mister Parland.

The foyer was large, with a broad staircase from which a lord might make a grand entrance to greet his guests at a party. Looking around, Emily could not decide if this was the ancestral home of Parlands since the time of Randel's Compact, or if he was merely of sufficient wealth to have obtained it since.

The paint was not peeling, so it had been maintained, but there were still places where empty picture rails dangled none of the old family art along the walls. That art might have been sold in leaner times, but most families would recover it when they had money, and she knew from Gus that Francis Parland had plenty of that. She had not quite decided the answer when Mister Parland appeared on the floor above and descended the stair to meet her.

Parland's hair was mostly gone, and the wispy silver remains of it wrapped around the back of his head lent him an aura of respectable credibility, like some elder statesman, but that was contrasted by a sharply pointed beard of the sort only popular among Garren literati. He had been home long enough to shed the brown robes of his office, but the brown suit he wore was probably the same one he had been wearing all day beneath it.

He also wore a smirk she doubted was often seen in Taltek's halls. "Miss Loch. I don't suppose your employer has sent you all this way to finally complete the second half of our long-standing agreement?"

Feigning a fluster, Emily shook her head and replied, "I'm afraid I don't know anything about that, Mister Parland."

It was a lie; she knew perfectly well what he wanted, and Parland's derisive snort said he knew she was lying on that count as well. That golden knife in Gus's desk drawer pained him every time he saw it, and she could never understand why he wouldn't take whatever Parland offered just to be rid of it. If the petitioner knew Gus had it already, she was sure Parland would find some way to take it, regardless.

When she first discovered the thing, she'd even considered selling that information to him for a finder's fee, but the woman who might once have done that was long gone—as was her money. That reminded her of the taxi outside, which would be considered a serious eyesore in this part of town as its driver happily idled away the money he thought she could pay.

"Actually, Mister Parland, I came by to see your collection," she said and smiled at his look of surprise. With Gus locked away in the constabulary, she would need to beg for more than one favor, but that would be easier after she'd flattered his favorite hobby. There was a rumble of distant thunder, so she borrowed the drama that lent to add, "First though, I'm afraid I came by taxi, and he's waiting outside. Is there someplace he can shelter from the storm?"

Parland no doubt had shelter for his own horses, and Emily hoped if she could get the cabman out of the rain, it might make the bargaining over the fare easier later. Instead, apparently delighted by her interest in his collection, her host decided to be gallant.

Snapping his fingers, Parland called out to a footman, who appeared seemingly from nowhere, "Samwell? Can you go pay the gentleman outside and send him along? There's no need for him to wait in the rain since one of you can drive Miss Loch home when she's done."

With a smile of unfeigned gratitude, Emily stepped forward and looped her arm through Parland's to let him escort her on towards the collection she had come to see. The petitioner looked to be several years older than the current Earl of Wending, which made him just the right age to consider her young enough to still find that attention flattering. He smiled back at her and then led them on a leisurely stroll down a hallway that branched from the foyer.

There was nothing particularly Elven in either his foyer or the hallway he led her along, which made Emily suspect that Millie Parland shared none of her husband's interest in the stuff. Flattered or not, the petitioner still seemed somewhat skeptical as he asked, "So what brings about this interest in my collection, Miss Loch?"

"Well," she replied, "The news. The recent kidnapping, with the Wardens?" He gave a skeptical tsk at the mention of Wardens, clearly not convinced they could be real. She wanted to seem agreeable, so she nodded and went on, "I was speaking to people about that, and of course the subject of the Elves came up, and it struck me that, in all these years, I've never actually seen this collection you're always talking about!"

Parland laughed as he stopped in front of a closed door and said, "Well, not 'always'! I do have other interests, but you only ever see me when I'm pressing your employer to get to work completing our arrangement. I am quite proud of what I've gathered, however." With that, he pushed open the door.

Unlike the rest of the house, the room inside was brilliantly lit with patent lamps that bathed the room in a stark light more suited to the stage than any drawing room. It was an expensive option, and she wondered if their slow walk down the hall was for the benefit of some footman dashing along a side corridor to light them.

At the center of the room was a maze of unmatching glass cabinets that amplified the excessive brightness, but within them, she also saw the glittering pale gold of elfsteel. Stepping up to one of the cabinets, she looked over the dazzling array of golden knick-knacks stored within. Emily doubted the Imperial crown jewels could glitter more, although on reflection, she supposed they had the added allure of being actual gold.

"They're all whole, of course," Parland began, gesturing over the random ornaments she was admiring. "Elfsteel holds a better edge but isn't as durable against iron and is too stiff for forging. If broken, it quickly just crumbles apart and fades to a dull gray. I think everything here must have been originally cast from a molten form into its present shape, although no one really knows how it was done."

"Why didn't these pieces go with them, do you suppose?" The ornaments weren't why she was here, so Emily pulled herself away and began looking through the other cabinets.

"The Elves left with everything that was theirs. The pieces that were left were either traded away, back when the Elves allowed trade with men, taken by force, or recovered from ruins found before they vanished."

Pressing at her elbow, Parland guided her around the cabinets towards the back of the room as he lectured on, "And of course, that was a nasty bit of revenge on their part. The war was heavily financed on the prospect of seized Elven treasures, and there weren't any. The Elven Trove laws are still in effect, awarding any hidden treasures discovered in Aelfua to the crown, but aside from a few questionable trinkets, nothing was ever recovered."

As they rounded a row of tall cabinets, standing back between two large windows at the far side of the room was a dark figure cloaked in green. Emily was so startled by it that she nearly shrieked, and only restrained herself by clutching tighter upon her host's arm.

Parland chuckled and said, "This is my general. Don't worry; he's just a wooden mannequin. What he's wearing is entirely authentic, however. Poor fellow died at the battle of Mahnpaksipol, defending a city that vanished a few weeks later. A bit of cannon shell caught him in the thigh, and he bled right out. The pieces aren't all his originals, having been recovered from various places, but he fairly matches the descriptions we have of the war dress among Elven leaders."

The 'general' stood at about Parland's height, wearing a mask of buttery elfsteel that depicted an Elven face Emily suspected was a colder rendition of its original wearer's. The eyes were empty, with no one behind them, which greatly emphasized the face's inhumanly angular cast and narrow features. His head was wrapped in some sort of green turban, and he wore a quilted green suit that covered him head to toe. An elfsteel-tipped spear was held in one hand, and the broad belt he wore held two short scabbards behind his hips, one of which sat empty.

It was an impressive sight, and Emily could see why, even without guns, Elves like this might have inspired terror across the battlefield. What arrested her attention, however, was the knife diagonally tucked just behind his belt buckle. It was a smooth crescent, just as Missus Casey had drawn and even about the same size.

Slipping out the leaf she had stolen from Lady Wending's floral arrangements that morning, Emily held it up to the general's uniform, and even in the harsh light of the patent lamps, it was a nearly perfect match.

Emily supposed Parland must no doubt have thought she was mad, holding a small leaf up to the thing, but he waited for her to finish that comparison before asking, "What exactly is it you came to discover?"

Staging an abashed smile, she replied, "We've been working on that kidnapping case. Doctor Edward Phand? They say he was grabbed by Wardens." Parland harrumphed at the very idea, so Emily nodded agreeably then said, "They had knives though, much like the one your general has, and wore the same green he does. Their knives weren't elfsteel, however."

The petitioner shook his head and said, "It's a poorly considered joke, and nothing more. I do give them credit on their research; during the war, some Wardens did use those same ceremonial knives, made from iron or steel, since by then the Elves were forbidden to give any elfsteel to humans. It doesn't matter what they had though. There aren't any Wardens left because there's no one left to give them orders."

Emily nodded and was startled by a sudden flash of light from the window. The patter of rain was light against the window but reminded her that Gus always did poorly in storms. Another distant rumble of thunder prompted her to dispense with further niceties. She looked back up at Parland and said, "There is something else I need. Gus was arrested in Market this afternoon."

The petitioner sighed and looked out the window. The raindrop tempo increased, and although she didn't see the flash, she heard another rumble, nearer than the last.

~

"Health of Gemmen"

In Gemmen last week, 2398 births and 1387 deaths were registered. The deaths included 9 from redpox, 62 from solmuel, 36 from shakers fever, 19 from diphtheria, 85 from drop-cough, 1 from typhus fever, 7 from enteric fever, 2 from ill-defined forms of continued fever, 32 from diarrhoea and dysentery, and 2 from simple cholera. In Wider Gemmen, 3018 births and 1658 deaths were registered.

– *Gemmen Standard*, 9 Tal. 389

~

- CHAPTER 11 -

Gus shivered in the cold of his cell as the frigid rain of early spring leaked through the barred window at the back of the room and dribbled into a growing puddle on the floor. His cellmate lay in a bunk opposite Gus's own, fixing him with a territorial glare. A distant rumble made Gus close his eyes and pull the cheap prison blanket more tightly about his shoulders.

Bright light flared through the window in jagged bursts he could sense even with his eyes closed. His cellmate grumbled incoherently, his words lost to the pounding of rain and the rattling of the glass in their cell's high window. Each flash grew brighter than the last as lightning fell closer and closer, the thunder that followed growing louder and louder.

Clapping his hands over his ears, Gus began humming a song he'd learned in Aelfua. He'd picked up the tune from a ghastly fiddler there that had somehow mesmerized an entire village with it. Claude had made up words for the song, but the music was slippery, and hearing it dulled the mind into a gummy stupor—Claude's lyrics had always trailed off before he could finish the song.

They had discovered they could get a little further by focusing intently on the notes, but even still Gus never managed more than a few bars before his mind wandered off. In a pinch, that poisonous song had sometimes helped him get through a bad night when more reliable remedies were unavailable.

The room filled with light just as a blast of thunder rattled him from the fugue of his humming. Each crash felt too regular, too steady for a storm, and wrapped tightly in his blanket, Gus felt his heart beat as if he were running. The fiddler's tune eluded him, so he tried to remember Claude's lyrics, and eventually the melody came back to him.

Another blast struck, the report so powerful that it shook him from his reverie again. Through the high window, Gus heard a savage growl from just beyond the outside wall. He leapt from his bunk and ran to the barred door opposite. Despite his cellmate's grousing for him to lay down and be quiet, Gus shouted for help, for someone to come open the door. No one was there.

There was a bestial roar from the window, followed by a loud crash as the thing outside struck at the wall. The impact sent cracks through the plaster and revealed bricks buckling behind it. Gus pressed his back to the bars of the door, staring in horror as the outside wall began to crumble, and through the window, he caught a momentary glimpse of the giant's pale scarred flesh.

There was another crash of thunder, and the wall exploded, sending debris everywhere as the mortar between the bricks gave way, the strangely unbroken clay blocks scattered across the cement floor of the cell. The room was filled in unbearable light as another thunderbolt struck where the wall had just been.

In the fading electric brilliance, there stood the Sentinel, every bit as Gus remembered it: a hulking figure half again Gus's height but proportioned more like a great ape. Its grey flesh rippled with impossible muscle, the rain covering its skin highlighting a network of savage scars that covered its monstrous body.

It roared again, and a huge arm reached into the cell. It snatched the ankle of the poor cellmate who had not scrambled back in time, and the man shrieked as he was yanked from his bed and held aloft. The Sentinel flung the man down at its feet and roared again as it pummeled him, striking so hard that it cracked the concrete floor beneath as it beat the man into an unrecognizable mass of bloody meat and shards of bone.

Someone gripped Gus's elbow, tugging him back, and he was shocked to see Emily there, pulling him through the now open door of the cell. They ran.

They fled through twisting corridors and past the constables still casually loitering in the office beyond the cells. The Sentinel's unmistakable pursuit crashed behind them, thunder falling with every footstep. Looking back, Gus saw the thunderbolts that accompanied the Sentinel's every step were cracking open the building to the sky, tearing off the roof to let in the rain while simultaneously setting fire to everything below.

Charging past astonished constables, Gus and Emily dashed from the building and out into the street. Emily led the way, pulling him along through a labyrinth of narrow alleys as if they were chased by some ordinary pursuer who could be shaken off their trail by a confusing urban maze.

With a shock, Gus realized they were already in the alleyway across from his office, and he watched in horror as the bloated corpse of the dog that had lain there for weeks suddenly raised its head to snarl at them. Gus shouldered Emily to the opposite side of the alley, and they dashed on as it lumbered shakily to its feet, barking and gnashing its teeth. It stumbled forward on rotted legs, but then they rounded another corner, and Gus lost sight of it.

Emily pulled him onward, into a construction yard for the underground train. The mounds of earth there had been shifted and built into defensive walls, which were manned by Verin soldiers. The men on the wall worriedly scanned the horizon and paid no attention to the two stragglers clambering over the earthworks.

Beyond the wall were a series of trenches, just like he had fought from in Rakhasin. Whoever was giving orders must have expected an attack from both sides. Gus and Emily dove into the first trench, just within the wall, pushing past uniformed soldiers of the 37th regiment. He could not see the enemy yet, but whistles sounded, and the Verin soldiers began steadfastly loading their rifles and shooting into the rain-drenched blackness beyond.

They paused to catch their breath, and he was startled when someone thrust a rifle into Emily's waiting hands. For the first time Gus realized she was wearing the blue tunic and red sash of a soldier in the Verin military. He had once seen her in something similar at a burlesque, but that had been more a playful costume than what she had on now. Dumbfounded by the absurdity of seeing a woman in that uniform, Gus simply stared as she turned to join the ranks blazing along the trench.

All his questions bubbling up were dashed away as a hideous cackling came from overhead. Gus shouted at Emily, telling her to get down, but instead she looked up in confusion. A pale woman in a fluttering white dress descended from the sky, her face hideously disfigured by her huge fanged maw. It was the Lady Paasil, one of Gedlund's most horrifying Everlords, and somehow she had found him.

The flying woman swept in at incredible speed but veered aside before striking at Gus, instead grabbing Emily and yanking her skyward. Gus lunged to grab for Emily, but her wet hand slipped from his as she was pulled, screaming, up into the air, dropping her rifle somewhere beyond the wall.

"I need a rifle! Where's my rifle?" he shouted. Looking around, Gus saw several bodies in the trench; he had no idea how they had died, but all of their rifles were gone. He began to panic, but then someone thrust the weapon he sought into his hands. Gus was startled to see Glynn, looking exactly as he had last seen him before the corporal deserted in Gedlund and left Gus there on his own.

Together, they shot up at the retreating Everlord as it carried Emily off to certain doom, but the immortal shrugged off bullets with mocking indifference. Her wicked laughter floated down, echoing strangely, and yet somehow easily heard over the rain, the thunder, and the thunderous rumble of rifles blazing into darkness.

He started to climb from the trench and pursue, but Glynn yanked him back, yelling something and pointing towards the front line beyond the trenches. A marching line of undead soldiers emerged from the shadows; ashen parodies of the Verin lads he fought alongside. Though torn and tattered, the enemy wore the same uniforms, but their skin was gray and their bodies streaked in gleaming embers, like burning logs yanked from the fire. Gus took up his rifle, blazing repeatedly into the massed forces marching implacably towards the trench.

Seeing the spirits unslowed by their wounds, Gus took a deep breath, struggling to calm himself and aim carefully for the head. As he lined up another shot, sighting into the face of the enemy, he felt a chill of familiar dread when he realized the one at which he aimed was once his dearest friend in the world. It was Claude, just as Gus has last seen him: a man of ash, his face covered in a web of glowing embers as if he were being seen through a broken glass.

Gus trembled, fighting to hold steady but still unable to pull the trigger. He could not shoot his friend and turned to tell Glynn as much, but the corporal's rifle was already raised. Following his sights, Gus realized that Glynn was aiming right at the charging specter of Claude. Glynn wouldn't miss. Glynn never missed.

Gus looked back and forth between them, and finally shoved the corporal's rifle upwards, throwing off the shot to spare his long-dead friend. Time slowed, and Gus stared at the corporal, unable to tear his eyes away to look back at the specter of Claude that no doubt still marched towards them on behalf of the enemy. Glynn looked back to Gus, face twisted in fury. Teeth bared in a silent snarl, Glynn turned on him, bayonet thrusting toward Gus's chest.

Gus screamed and jerked upright, looking around the confines of his cell. The pale plaster walls were unbroken, despite the cold rain trickling in through the poorly framed windows and forming a puddle on the floor. His cellmate scowled groggily over at him as Gus gulped for air. Breathless and sore of throat, Gus wondered how many times he must have woken the poor fellow over the course of the night.

He hoped the man wasn't there for murder or something equally ill-suited in a disgruntled roommate.

Thunder crashed outside, but it was distant and presumably natural thunder. Their cell was frigid, and Gus wrapped himself again in the thin blanket they had provided him. Gedlund had been colder, but he'd been allowed to go out and warm himself by the fire there. No such luxuries were afforded in the local constable's prison.

He curled himself up as best he could, but his left leg couldn't tuck in as well as the other, so it sat outstretched, chilly and stiff. It always hurt at least a little, but for some reason it was worse in the cold.

Gus had fought goblins in Rakhasin and faced Everlords in Gedlund, with few scars to show for any of it. Instead, he was shot by an idiot private—a new man who had missed all the excitement and only joined them in Gedlund after Sikaardal. One dull afternoon as the new recruit was fooling around with his rifle, he somehow managed to shoot his sergeant in the leg.

The injury proved a small blessing in some ways, since it got him released early, with pension, but the daily pain of the thing often made Gus wonder if the remaining years had been worth the trade. With the Tuls looking likely to seize Gedlund for themselves, getting out had seemed rather fortuitous at the time. All his closest friends were gone by then, and Gedlund had seemed especially cold that winter in more ways than one.

Now, as he sat staring at cold toes he was unable to curl under the blanket, he thought a few more years on guard duty in Gedlund might have been the better fate.

Against all expectation, the Tuls had been too distracted with internal politics to come spilling over the mountains that year, and it would have been a quiet tour. With that winding down now, they might yet make a move on Verin holdings in Gedlund, but Gus would have been long gone by now either way.

Another crash of thunder came, still distant and irregular. He reassured himself that it was not Gedlund's Sentinel. The Sentinel lay buried under a mountain of rubble, and not even it was strong enough to shrug that off. It was a ritual reminder by now and one he had gone through in every thunderstorm since he saw the thing buried.

Usually he imagined that it still seethed under those tons of stone, but perhaps it was relieved to finally have shelter from the lightning. It was as close to defeat as that monstrosity was ever likely to come. It was gone.

The dreams were another thing. They were at their worst in storms but came almost every night, and the best treatment for them he had found was to drink into unconsciousness. He'd always been a bit of a tippler but as a matter of recreation rather than medication. Now, so long as he could afford it, each night he would drink until he passed out.

Whether that stopped the dreams or merely his recollection of them, it made the nights pass more quietly and left him better rested. Ever worried that he drank to an intolerable excess, Emily had tried convincing him to take the cure several times; she never understood that the trouble she hoped to cure was merely the cure that masked another trouble.

Eventually the storm subsided, and the cold rain seeping through the window slowed from a trickle to a drip and then to nothing as the morning sun rose over the city beyond the barred window. It melted away the last of the rainclouds and slowly warmed the room.

Gus's cellmate was still asleep when the constables came to roust them. They hauled the man off shortly after dawn, and he gave Gus one last angry glare before he departed as if trying to burn into memory the face of the man who had so badly disturbed his sleep.

The night of interrupted sleep left Gus feeling dazed and drained. The continual morning hangovers of his usual routine were far better; at least they felt like something he could struggle against. All he wanted to do now was lay quietly resting, but he was so tired that if he did, he might fall asleep again and just get more of the same.

He sat there shivering for a few hours before the constable came for him, clutching Gus's arm tightly as he led him out into the office just outside the jail, a large room with several desks shared by the various officers working here. It had a small kitchenette with a cistern for water to give any late-working officers all the comforts of home.

The entrance stood at the opposite side of the offices from the corridor with the jail cells, perhaps to force escapees to flee past the entire constabulary or perhaps just to conceal their conditions from visitors. Adjoining the main office were several smaller rooms where a constable could interrogate prisoners in discomforting privacy.

Gus's leg was painfully stiff, and it was a struggle to keep up as the constable pulled him onward at a punishing pace, not giving him a chance to stretch it out or any consideration for his condition. The constable guided him to one of the desks and shoved him down into the chair, grumbling some complaint about how Gus was being 'laggardly'. The hard, wooden chair was uncomfortable, but the room was thankfully warmer than the cells had been.

After taking a moment to stretch his calf, Gus tilted his hat back as he looked around. Detecting-Inspector Clarke was standing in the entrance accompanied by a familiar looking older woman. After a moment, Gus recognized her as Phand's housekeeper, but in his sleepless daze, he could not put together any plausible reason she should be there or what Ollie might be discussing with her.

Eventually, the inspector nodded, and the woman left while Clarke took a moment to flip through his little notebook. Frowning, the inspector made his way from the entrance back to the constable's desk, where Gus sat quietly staring up at him. Clarke pulled up a chair and sat across the desk from him. After taking a moment to look over his bedraggled prisoner, Clarke said, "Hmph. You look even worse than usual, *Mister* Baston. If I didn't know better, I'd have thought you spent the night out drinking."

"That was the plan, but I got a little sidetracked," he croaked out, suddenly realizing how desperately thirsty he was. It was clear in his voice, and with an irritable grimace, Clarke rose up and crossed the room to the cistern, filling a tin cup with water. His voice rasping a bit, Gus said, "You seem frustrated. Does that mean the kidnappers still haven't sent a ransom?"

"Was the plan to have sent one by now?" Clarke replied as he slapped the cup down upon the desk, heavily enough to splash a bit. Gus grabbed for the cup and thirstily tossed it back, gasping in relief and then laughing with a bit of embarrassment at his pathetic condition.

Clarke must have interpreted the laugh differently, since he just looked annoyed by Gus's reaction, and grumped, "You put on a fine show for Missus Phand just now, limping out here like that. She took pity, but despite that, wouldn't confirm your story. I asked her if she hired you, and she told me she had never seen you before in her life, so why don't you tell me again why you were following after Doctor Phand just before he was nabbed."

Gus shook his head wondering if Clarke's meeting with that woman were staged to trick him into a confession. "That woman you were just talking to? That's not her! Alice Phand came to my office— younger woman, blonde, very plummy. She said she wanted to catch him cheating, so she hired me to find when he'd be going out and ...."

He trailed off as he watched Clarke's thoughtful contemplation and fell silent when he realized it wasn't a trick. If the woman he had worked for wasn't the real Alice Phand, that left him as an unwitting accomplice to the crime. He wasn't sure what the legal consequence for that was, but he knew Clarke would never accept his innocence in that arrangement, regardless.

If something happened to Phand, Clarke would make sure Gus paid a conspirator's full penalty for it. Worse, once word got out that Gus had been, it would have unpleasant repercussions on the business, and Emily would never let him hear the end of it.

"So you tailed him to find out when they'd be best suited to conduct their snatch. Did you give up the cabbie too?" Clarke's harsh tone made Gus shrink back a little, feeling off his usual game with the inspector. Seeing Gus's hesitation, the inspector glanced down at his notebook and said, "Louis Siddel, driver of cab number 4669, an associate of yours if I'm not mistaken. And I'm not; I already followed up on it, so there's no point lying."

"Louis? Yeah, we," Gus began, then paused, the words seeping in, "Wait, what do you mean, 'gave him up'?"

Clarke sat back in his chair, frowning and looking critically into Gus's face as he weighed his suspect's reactions. After a heavy pause, Clarke said, "Last night, Mister Siddel was found dead in an alleyway. His cab was left there, but his horses were gone. His cab was the one used in the snatch. The coroner's jury hasn't been convened on it yet, but he was probably stabbed as part of Doctor Phand's capture. Not sure yet if he did the driving, or they just killed him for the hack."

"Louis? No. I mean, he's got a family, and he never ...." Gus shook his head, dizzy at the sudden rush of news. It seemed unreal, and he wasted several moments trying to puzzle out why Clarke would put forward that particular lie before finally coming to the conclusion that he wouldn't. The shock that came with that realization felt like a punch to the stomach; Gus thought if he'd eaten anything, he might well have vomited it up.

During his stint in the army, people had died around him all the time, and the consistent horror of losing friends had usually just left him numbly carrying on. With goblins or corpses charging after you in the dark, there wasn't usually time for grief. It had only hit during quieter moments or those terrible moments when dead friends came back.

Life had been better since. People left, but they usually just slipped away in broad daylight. Gus would imagine them the better for it, living happily elsewhere, and if they died after they'd left, he'd never know. "Are you sure?"

"I worked the Nettle Lane murders, Baston. We got good at identifying bodies, I promise." Clarke's words were gruff, but seeing the 37th's former colour sergeant paling, the inspector softened a bit. Clarke took off his bowler in a gesture of respect for the dead, then sat it on the table and brushed back his thinning hair as he contemplated Gus's reaction.

Eventually, in a more conciliatory tone, the detecting-inspector said, "Whatever they paid or promised to pay you, it can't be worth taking part in that sort of murder. Can't be worth seeing good men killed just to keep things quiet. Give us what you know, and maybe I can talk the Crown out of trying you for your part in it."

Gus shook his head, feeling stupid, but not stupid enough to give himself up as a witness. Doing that might make things easier for his petitioner if the Crown went after him as an unintentional accomplice, but being held as a witness would mean Gus's own investigation of the case would have to stop.

Since he worked for the Crown, Clarke couldn't even collect Missus Phand's reward, so if Gus were a witness working with him, he couldn't collect it either. While Gus could skate by with the money he had, Emily needed her share.

Worse, Louis's killer was probably long gone. Everything pointed to Khanom, which was in Aelfua and thus out of the Crossing's usual jurisdiction. By the time the detecting-inspector straightened that out, the trail would be completely cold.

Gus had passed through Aelfua while in the army, and from what he remembered, it was barely settled. By reputation, it was still a bit lawless in places, so he could get away with a lot there, and so long as he came back with at least fifty-one percent of Doctor Phand, he was probably entitled to the reward.

If Gus could just slip out somehow, he could clear his name, get the reward, and make sure something horrible happened to Louis's killer in the process. He just needed to slip out somehow.

Clarke watched him quietly but began to look suspicious when Gus didn't produce the gush of information he had clearly been hoping for. After a moment or two, the inspector shook his head, stood up, and said, "If you're not interested in talking, then we'll just have to discuss it again later."

He waved over the constable on duty and then jotted a few notes into his book as the constable roughly pulled Gus back up to his feet and back towards the cells.

With no plan for escape coming to mind, Gus cried out, "Wait a minute! I'm entitled to counsel or something! You can't just lock me up without letting me contact someone!" The constable did not relent and pulled Gus back towards the cold jail. Gus resisted as best he could, but his leg chose that moment to give out, and he stumbled, nearly knocking them both down.

Clarke snorted and looked up from his notebook, then called back, "You're only entitled to counsel if you're charged with something, and you haven't been charged. Don't worry; we only need to keep you locked up until the case is solved, so if you think of any more details, you just let the constable here know you need to talk to me."

The detecting-inspector gave a cruel smirk, then picked up his hat from the desk and made his way towards the exit. Gus called after Clarke several times, but the constable dragged Gus roughly back to the jail, tossed him into the same damp cell, and slammed the door.

Gus sat in the cold cell, wishing they hadn't taken his vengeful cellmate from the night before, so at least he would have some way to while away the hours. Emily probably wouldn't worry about his absence from the office until sometime in the afternoon. Even if he was lucky, it would probably be at least a day or so before she worked out which district he was held in and managed to arrange something. With a sigh, he settled in for a long wait.

He usually carried a pack of cards in his pocket but somehow had forgotten them the prior morning. The barred cell door faced only the pale plaster of the empty hall, so he sat against it and watched the window. The window was high on the wall, presumably to keep anyone outside from seeing in, but it left him with nothing to look at outside other than the top corner of the building across the street and a small sliver of sky beyond.

Judging by what little he could hear from down the hall, there only seemed to be two constables in the offices, and he stared out at the few clouds he could see through the window as he listened to their muffled interactions. With no other distractions, his thoughts focused on the tall blonde woman who had claimed to be Alice Phand. He felt like a fool and thought through his meetings with her again and again, trying to see what details should have revealed her deception.

She had dressed the part to the hilt; she had looked more like the wife of a wealthy businessman than the actual Missus Phand that Clarke had brought by. Why was a famous and wealthy engineer married to a plain woman who was at least as old as her husband? Men of title were stuck with their wives, but in Gus's experience, successful men of commerce like Phand frequently exchanged their originals for a jammier sort.

Was this kidnapping a scheme of Phand's to escape his wife? Running away with the blonde? Running away with Miss Aliyah Gale? What could the engineer be involved with that would be helped by such an elaborate deception and require a murder to conceal?

With the Warden robes, the dead cabbie, the very public kidnapping, and the nearly stolen necklace, the facts of the crime seemed to point in every direction. It seemed chaotic, but thinking through the facts, Gus realized the chaos was far too neatly orchestrated.

Someone had planned this carefully.

The engineer was well educated but busy and successful, and that left little room for an education in crime. Someone of his class would be unlikely to have worked out using a numbered cab as a blind, and he had too much to lose to risk a scheme that necessarily involved the police discovering a murder. If Phand were to later reappear with the blonde or Miss Aliyah Gale, he would be wanted for murder. No matter how skilled a builder of bridges he was, Gus doubted even Tulsmonia would take in a known murderer, and more diplomatic nations would simply turn him over to Verinde rather than risk an incident.

They involved an outside chump to keep the kidnappers out of sight until the snatch. The mastermind figured they would need an inconspicuous vehicle that could approach Phand for the deed, so they hired a taxi. It had to be one that could not be traced back to them, however, which meant murdering the cabbie.

Gus felt his gut twist at the thought of his friend murdered in some alley, just because Louis did what they had paid him to do. He pushed that down, trying to focus on the case as he watched the clouds drift across the slim corner of sky he could see. Whoever was behind this had gone to great lengths to hide all trace of themselves.

After pondering it a bit, Gus realized that as well hidden as the culprit probably was, trying to discover them through the facts here in Gemmen would never work. Clarke would be doing that with every agency the detecting-inspector could muster, and Gus was sure that whatever kidnapper had thought through this elaborate setup had plans to remain hidden from the Crossing's view. The choice of disguise, however, was alarming enough that the kidnapper must surely expect the Crossing to tear the city apart looking for them. The kidnappers would have to hide elsewhere.

When stymied on other cases, Gus had found that when he could work out the why, it would lead him back to the who and eventually the where. Knowing that a cheating wife had an eye for blondes or that a missing ring was useful for forgeries had helped him stop looking in the wrong places before. The best way to foil the plot was to figure out why Phand was kidnapped.

Out in the constables' office, voices were being raised, and Gus pushed to his feet, pressing his face to the door and vainly trying to see down the hall. He could not make out the words in the next room, but the two officers were arguing with someone and sounded a bit defensive. After a moment, he recognized the cadence of the other voice and felt a twinge of sympathy for those poor constables.

~

"Rakhasin Rampage Continues"

Several serious outrages are reported in Rakhasin as the recent spate of lawlessness north of Karhas continues unabated. A militia leader's home in Rileys was set ablaze while he was away in civic duty, and he returned to find his daughter had been attacked and left insensible; a rancher nearby was shot while returning from a fair, and while not very seriously injured, he was relieved of a prize-winning bull of great sentimental attachment to the family; a bailiff in charge of a farm was dragged out and shot in the legs; and a daring raid for arms is reported.

On the 24th, a band of men undisguised and carrying revolvers entered the home of Captain Castille of Muirnesville. After shooting a dog and tying the servants with ropes, the men carried off all the arms they could find. While reports remain conflicted, most agree this chaos is the work of the gang led by Elgin Ward, a notorious gunman and cattle rustler more widely known as 'Gentleman Jim'.

– *Gemmen Herald*, 12 Tal. 389

~

- CHAPTER 12 -

In ancient tradition, the robes of a petitioner were black to signify their allegiance to the goddess of truth, one of the Triumvirate of Darkness. Once the three gods of shadow were cast down, signs of devotion to them had fallen from fashion, and petitioners' robes became brown to make them look sufficiently humble as servants of justice rather than truth. In actual execution, petitioners seldom let that choice of color keep them from looking their best.

Francis Parland's robe was brown, but it was also made from a polished silk and done in an elegant cut that left no doubt he was a member of the aristocracy. As he strode down the hall of the jail, pushing past a flustered constable to stand before Gus's cell, the petitioner's robe flared dramatically with the commanding wave of his arm as Parland pronounced, "You will unlock my client and release him. Immediately."

Gus grinned, but Parland answered with a stern frown that indicated he felt this was no time for grins. The constable edged past the petitioner as if nervous to even brush against that flowing silk. Gus would have hated to be in the constable's place, on the receiving end of Parland's professional displeasure, but quite enjoyed seeing it exercised on his behalf.

The cell door was unlocked, and Gus gave the poor constable a pat on the arm and thanked him, which seemed to mollify Parland a bit as well. As soon as Gus stepped forth from the cell, the petitioner impatiently snapped, "A cab is waiting for us outside," and then spun on his heel and marched off with another dramatic flurry of expensive fabric.

The constable by the cell stood back to let Gus follow the petitioner outside. They swept past a second constable who looked disgruntled but cowed enough to stay out of Parland's way. When they reached the street, a cab was indeed waiting, the driver solicitous enough to hold the door open for them and offer a hand inside, although both passengers ignored him.

The door was shut behind them, and as soon as the driver climbed back to his perch, the hack began to roll forwards, apparently already having directions for their next stop. Slouching back in his seat, Parland loosened the knot on his tie and frowned, but Gus let him be the one to break the silence. "I assume you're not really involved in this kidnapping?"

"No, no, of course not," Gus said, then paused and added, "Well, not as a perpetrator, exactly." He supposed if Clarke set the Crown's prosecutor's sights fully upon him, Parland's intervention would go more smoothly if he had the facts. "The woman that I think did it hired me to do a bit of perfectly legal snoop work, which I did under the impression she was the man's wife. How did you even find me so quickly?"

"Your girl-receptionist came to see me—last night actually. I'd have been here first thing, but as I was filing a demand for your freedom, the Crown's prosecutor came in to request a writ to toss your office. I recognized the address and intervened on your behalf there as well." The petitioner frowned at him and grumped, "I'm usually paid quite handsomely for my services, and I don't like doing favors. It certainly doesn't help my reputation any, being associated with the likes of you."

Gus grinned and said, "Come on now. After all these years, aren't we friends?"

"No. We are not friends. I'm helping you because my collection has a glaring incompletion, and you promised you could address that. I assume you still claim you can, but I've heard nothing new from you on that front in ages. I doubt the other sword was lost somewhere here in town, and you've made no trips to Gedlund that I've heard." The man's steely eyes bored into his, and Gus wilted a bit under their intensity. "Where is my sword, Mister Baston?"

"It's close, I promise! There's no reason for me to go to Gedlund in person. I've still got friends out there, and it's very nearly in hand." That wasn't exactly a lie. On his discharge from the army, Gus realized the military pension he received for his injury would not leave him very comfortably set up, but luckily he and his friend Claude had literally stumbled across a retirement plan early in their careers while protecting settlers from goblins down in Rakhasin.

A goblin shaman had somehow obtained two elfsteel swords, which had probably served to mark him as leader of his band but had not rendered him bulletproof. Upon finding the gob's body, the two men had each taken one, planning to sell them as soon as their tours were over. When Gus returned from Gedlund, he had found someone to sell his sword, and it was auctioned off for a small fortune, with which Gus had bought his flat and his office. Parland had been the one to win that auction.

"My bid was only as generous as it was because you said you knew how to find the other sword. I finally talked the National Museum out of that benighted spear shaft, so my general is now missing only one thing, and you promised me you could find it. I promised you I'd match the price for the other, and that promise holds, but if you're holding out for more ...."

Technically, Gus had already found it and long before he ever met Parland. Claude had died in Gedlund, his sword lost in a farmer's field on a fool's errand. In the chaos after the war, Gus convinced his superiors to send him out on patrol, and with details from the only two survivors of that mad errand, he had found where Claude had fallen and there found the sword. Now it sat in his desk drawer, a lump of gleaming golden elfsteel that made him want to cry every time he laid eyes upon it.

Ironically, Parland's begrudging favor today had kept the sword hidden from him just a bit longer. Had the Crossing searched Gus's office, they would have found Claude's sword, which surely would have come to the petitioner's attention, and he would have found a way to claim it. Gus almost regretted that hadn't happened.

"I'm not. You'll have it soon." Gus hated himself for not having sold it ages ago. It made him miserable every time he opened that drawer.

"You've been saying that for years," snorted the Petitioner, clearly annoyed. "Well, the Crown's Prosecutor won't be tossing your office, and you're released for now, but they still consider you a suspect. Don't leave town, and if they call for you, be polite and responsive. Anything else, and they'll take that as a sign of your involvement, and back in you'll go until they find the real culprits. Assuming they can find the real culprits because if they can't and still think you're suspicious … well." He fluttered his hand, waving off the unpleasantness that would most certainly follow.

Gus thanked him, and they spent the rest of the way speculating on the recent escapades of Rakhasin's notorious Gentleman Jim. The *Standard* was of the firm opinion that Gentleman Jim's success could only be explained if he were some sort of foreign agent, and to Gus's mind, feeding a hidden army seemed like the perfect use for an uncatchable cattle rustler. Parland felt the whole idea was absurd and bet a full gold peis it would soon be proven otherwise.

When the cab pulled up outside of Gus's office, he stepped out and thanked Parland again for the ride, to which the petitioner only replied, "Find me that sword, Mister Baston!"

Gus grinned and promised, as always, that he was close, to which Parland gave a disbelieving wave of dismissal and knocked on the cab's side to tell the cabbie to go onwards. He knew Parland had already checked anyone he could find from Gus's regiment, but if any of them had any idea where Claude's sword had gone, they'd have sold that secret long ago. Only an idiot would keep a valuable treasure like that stashed in an unlocked desk drawer.

Upstairs, Emily was sitting at her desk, sipping tea and reading the paper. She hurriedly tried to put the paper away when she heard someone approach but gave up any attempt at pretense once she saw who it was. Gus tossed his hat onto the rack, grimacing at how battered it now looked after an evening of being pulled tightly down for warmth and then uneasily slept upon.

Emily looked him over a moment before announcing, "You look terrible." She poured him a cup of tea and held it out in offer, but he waved it off and stepped past into his office. "You're not sick, are you?"

"Just a bad night's sleep; they don't serve alcohol in jail," he replied, while opening the top drawer of the filing cabinet in his office to pull out the carpet bag he kept there, along with a small mandolin in its case and another hat, which was now the less battered of his two hats. Emily looked entirely sympathetic, but Gus ignored her as he hung up the second hat and set the mandolin down by the rack. He checked the contents of his bag, then went over to his desk to search for his revolver. "Thanks for sending Parland though. How did you find out so fast?"

"Just good luck really. I was looking into the case and happened to run into one of Clarke's men who boasted about arresting you."

Gus paused his search and frowned up at her, not liking the idea of having her do his job for him. People hated a snoop, and he'd been subject to violence more than once as a result. Emily could probably handle herself if something like that happened, but that 'probably' always gnawed at him. Rather than risk insulting her with that worry, he said, "What if someone had come by the office with work and no one was here?"

She snorted and replied, "If they were the sort that had any money to hire us, then they'd have left their card. Aren't you curious about what I found?"

Gus rolled his eyes and resumed his search, which she apparently took as an affirmative, since she said, "Well, a witness said one of them was a woman, so I think it's probably our false Alice Phand."

"Makes sense."

"And I asked around about the costume. Their robes were each a particular dark green that's hard to do in custom batches and wasn't sold in Gemmen any time recently. It was the same green the Elves used. They also had iron knives but in an Elven style that's not common." She paused a bit, then added, "I think they might have been real."

Gus chuckled and shook his head. "Emily, they're gone. Every elf in the world disappeared nearly forty years ago. I've been to Aelfua before; they even took their buildings with them. Cities, farms, crops, livestock, and Elves, all gone overnight. If any were left, someone would have noticed. Besides why would they go after an engineer? Somehow this is about money."

"How does dressing up like Wardens make anyone any money?"

"Well, if I had that figured out, you'd already be counting the reward."

Emily sighed and dropped the subject. Watching him a moment more, she said, "Are you looking for your pistol? It's on the left, in that second drawer. Did you get anything to eat?"

Gus snorted and replied, "I checked there first," but then checked again and pulled out the revolver and a handful of bullets. He dumped them all into his bag atop the rumpled clothes he had kept packed for just such an occasion.

He was pleased to discover a promisingly weighty flask in the bag as well and, after shaking it to make sure it still contained something, tucked it into his jacket. "They picked me up late, and you got me sprung fairly early; prisoners only get lunch. If it was anything like the sleeping arrangements they offered, missing out may have been a blessing. I'll eat on the train."

Ever the voice of reason, Emily sat the tea down on her desk and reached out to touch his arm, trying to make him stop and pay attention. "They arrested you for the kidnapping, right? That means you can't go anywhere! If they think you might be part of it, and you leave town, they'll think you're running away."

Gus shrugged and smiled at her as if that were a trivial concern, even though he had few doubts Clarke would find some way to get at him, even if he returned Phand alive and unharmed. Patting down his pocket, he realized he'd need more money, so he pulled up the strongbox he kept under his desk and unlocked it.

The false Alice Phand's two-fifty was still there, along with a bit under twenty in petty cash. With what he hoped was a charming smile, Gus looked up to Emily and said, "This will take a few days. I'll need to borrow from your share. Well, and I may need to cover his fare back too. How much do you have on you now?"

The first sentence earned him a look of indignation, but his question left her looking worried and somewhat alarmed. Gus upended their cash box into his carpet bag and looked pointedly down at the chatelaine that hung in front of Emily's skirt.

After a bit of hesitation, she reached in and produced two gold peis and a small stack of silver, which she began counting. Deciding the silver would probably be enough to get her through the day, he snatched the two gold coins and tossed them in with the others. She sputtered her outrage at his prodigious loan, but he just closed his bag and limped with it back towards the door.

Emily followed after and said, "Well, at least tell me where you're going!"

Standing beside the rack, Gus slapped the bottom of his second hat, sending it flipping into the air and catching it on his head. It landed at an awkward angle, but it was a gimmick that never failed to impress. Sure enough, Emily snickered a little at the trick, and he grinned at her with all the confident swagger he could muster. "The answers to this case are in Khanom, which means Phand probably is too. Just try to keep them from tossing the office while I'm gone, alright? You'll get all your money back and more when I claim the reward."

"Khanom? You don't know anything about Khanom! You'll be lucky if you don't lose all our money getting rolled right after you step off the train!"

"It's a frontier town! It'll be easy. Besides, I heard Dolly Dench ran out that way. If he's been able to make it out there, then I'll probably come back as their king."

Emily's nose wrinkled in disgust at that particular name. Gus had introduced them on a prior case, and she'd immediately disliked the man. Dolly was a snooty sort for a criminal and considered himself well enough above his fellow ne'er do wells that he was easy to persuade to turn on them. Until he'd been chased out of town, Dolly had been consistently useful but unpleasant, so it wasn't an acquaintance he was eager to resume.

Gus reached down to pick up his mandolin, then leaned over to give Emily a quick peck on the cheek. He'd hoped that gesture would startle her out of whatever objection she might offer next and was quite pleased to see it have the intended effect. Before she could recover from the surprise and try to talk sense into him, he hurried out the door. This wasn't the time for sensible suggestions.

She called after him as he bumped down the stairs as quickly as his bad leg would allow, but she didn't give chase.

From Gus's recollection of the train schedule that he'd looked at when asking after Miss Aliyah Gale, he had just enough time to get down to the hub to catch the next one rolling out east all the way to Khanom. If he missed it, the next direct wasn't until tomorrow, and he was too tired to try to work out the hub switches necessary to make an indirect trip.

If his guess was right and the kidnappers were headed to Khanom, then he was already days behind them. From Clarke's questioning, Gus was confident that they still hadn't made any ransom demands. They went to quite a bit of trouble to capture him alive, even down to meticulously dressing the part of Wardens; if it wasn't for ransom, what would a captured Phand do for them that a free one would not?

Gus hailed a cab, feeling a fresh twinge of angry sorrow over Louis's murder. The conspirators weren't above murder when it suited them, so it must be something a dead Phand was equally useless for.

If he left this up to Chandler's Crossing, they might get their men, or they might not. Despite their personal and professional antipathy, Clarke had an impressive record for catching lawbreakers, but the cold, careful, considered wheels of justice moved too slowly. Even if they hanged the one who wielded the knife, whatever the conspiracy had planned for Phand might still be accomplished. That didn't satisfy Gus's sense of personal outrage. Whatever they wanted, he would see it fail.

Winning the real Alice Phand's proffered reward wouldn't hurt his feelings either. He had to make a conscious effort not to cling conspicuously tight to his cash-heavy carpet bag. Travelers were always carrying plenty of cash, and he had worked enough cases to know they were prime targets for crime. Potter District's rail hub wasn't far, and Gus felt bad spending even some fractional portion of Emily's money on the trip, but after a cold night of poor sleep, he didn't trust his bad leg with the additional burden of his carpet bag.

As the cab rolled on, he wondered what things cost in Khanom; it was Aelfua's largest city, but he wasn't sure that would amount to much. The last time he had been there was eight years back, when he was still in the army and Aelfua still a barely settled frontier. A few monuments still stood here or there, abandoned for reasons known only to the Elves, but it had been a country of empty lanes connecting vacant lots.

The tiled roads of the Elves had made the land easy to settle, and from what he understood, Verin colonies there were developing at an incredible pace. The leading men of Khanom he had met at Phand's office had seemed quite proud of the place.

His cab pulled to a stop, and Gus paid the man, then lurched outside with his things. The train he was expecting had just arrived, so the rail hub was crowded with people pushing on and off of it all at once.

Plenty of others loitered around as well, and not all were passengers. As always, there were several begging alms for their fare, some even looking entirely genuine about it. Potter District was also just nice enough for people to make decent money lifting wallets off unwary travelers.

Gus spent the full sixty peis on a third-class roundtrip, although he left the return unreserved. Thinking back to Miss Aliyah Gale's departure, he looked over the board and saw that a palace car ran one hundred forty-five peis per compartment. Having never ridden that way, he wasn't sure how many compartments there were, but he was betting at least ten.

The train was mostly loaded by the time he limped his way carefully through the gauntlet of sticky fingers. Boarding his car, he forced himself to look unconcerned as he tossed his carpet bag up into the storage rack over the seats, then chose a seat just across the aisle from which he could discretely keep an eye on it.

As he sat down, a suspicious young man in a stiff black suit approached and said, "I'm sorry to bother you sir, but are you going to Khanom? We're asking passengers to Khanom to move back into the next car for ease of loading. Please come with me."

Gus looked him over and tried to remember if he'd seen him on the platform. The man wasn't wearing a steward's cap, so he wasn't working on the train. He could be a ticket agent, but why would they send a ticket agent from the booth to shuffle passengers on the train when that was the steward's job?

With a grin, Gus settled back in his seat and shook his head. Slipping the mandolin from its case, he plucked at the strings a little and said, "Nah, I already sat down. Sorry."

The young man shook his head as if to clear it and asked again, "Sir, if you'll please come with me. I'll carry your bag back for you, so all you need to do is just change seats. It'll only be a moment."

Gus just smiled at him. A man across the aisle interjected, however, and said, "I'm going to Khanom. Do I need to be in the next car too?"

Looking back at him, the young man hesitated and asked, "Can I see your ticket?" The fellow obligingly opened his jacket to pull it out, and there in his inside pocket, Gus could see the fat outline of his wallet bulge beneath the fabric. No doubt the young man saw it too, for he quickly glanced over the ticket and nodded. "Oh, yes, let's move you back one. Please come with me. Do you have a bag?"

The other passenger pointed it out, and the young man obligingly lifted it from the cart as he led the man out onto the platform and out of view. Gus knew what would come next: it would be crowded, and the young man would guide his mark through the press back onto the next car. Somewhere along the way, he would signal to his compatriots in the crowd, one of whom would bump into the man while another hooked out the wallet. The passenger would reach Khanom and wonder where on the trip he had lost it.

A minute or so after they left, the train jerked slightly as the engine began to engage. Setting the mandolin aside, Gus leaned back in his seat, pulled the flask from his jacket, and took a deep draught. He sighed as he felt the familiar burn of lahvu wash down his throat. It was sour, with a bitter grassy aftertaste; the original Elven recipe intended it as medicine rather than a recreational intoxicant. Unlike other liquors, somehow it grew fouler as it aged, and it had been awhile since he'd originally filled this flask.

Gus had often sworn that once he was out of the army, he would never take another sip of the foul stuff; but once he had his freedom, he found he occasionally still craved it. The Elven liquor seemed like an appropriate drink to lubricate a trip into Aelfua, so he quickly drained the remainder of the flask.

The train slowly accelerated from the hub, and a real steward came through, hat and all, shutting the doors and checking tickets. Despite Gus's fears for his bag, the lack of sleep worked with the lahvu, and the gentle rocking motion of the train to lull him asleep.

He woke again several hours later, and by the only passingly familiar landscape beyond the windows, he knew he had slept through several hubs along the way. His eyes darted towards his luggage, but the cheap carpet bag appeared undisturbed amid the pile of others on the rack. The money was not the only thing of importance in it: he expected to have a use for the revolver as well.

Looking outside, it was a dreary spring afternoon, with a light rain pattering across the countryside. The comforting walls of the big city had fallen away, and the train sped through wide open fields, racing past the scattered farm houses and towns along the track too small to stop for. With little else to do, he picked his mandolin back up and began quietly strumming whatever songs came to mind. The lingering bitter grassiness of the lahvu still on his tongue inspired his fingers to revisit a few of his old army drinking songs.

The landscape gradually changed as they travelled; rolling hills became steeper, the houses took on slightly different styles—more stone, less brick—and even the farms seemed to focus on different crops and animals.

Despite Adelaide's frequent insistence they take a trip south to visit the Maccian shores, Gus had not left the country since his days in the army. He had imagined he might feel a bit nervous to cross the mountains into the Aelfuan territories again, but as they drew closer, he found himself mostly just interested in the scenery, wondering about the lives of the people who lived out here, so far from everything he considered civilized.

He was on a different line than the one he once rode into northern Aelfua on the way to Gedlund. At the time, there had been black ribbons everywhere along the way—symbols of a nation in mourning for their fallen prince. Currently no such sentiment bound the nation together. Without gossip about the latest play in the theater or the same popular songs making the rounds through the pubs, he supposed the countryside was more of a foreign nation to him than a big city like Khanom would be.

In his army days, this rail didn't even go all the way to Khanom, which at the time was just one of many hopeful outposts in the emptied Elven nation. It was hard to believe anything in Aelfua was enough of a metropolis to justify anything as grandiose as an exposition. Thinking of Aelfua inspired him to play *Easiest War*, a favorite marching song of the 37th Regiment. None of his fellow passengers knew it, or at least, none chose to sing along.

Since they were mostly ignoring him, Gus studied his fellow passengers for a bit as he played. This car was the cheapest set of seats, and there were a few rough-looking men who were probably laborers of some sort, perhaps taking a rare holiday having visited distant family and now on the return. The rest were men of business; their cheaper suits and aura of uneasy impatience marking them as either up-and-comers or those who still struggled to win their fortune in the Empire's volatile markets.

A few of the businessmen were well past the usual age of retirement, which meant they had no family to support them into their dotage, or else their family fortunes had been so shattered by recent dips in the stock market that all hands had been called back into service. It was possible, he supposed, that they were a third type: men who were too stubborn to quit because they either enjoyed the hustle or saw themselves as building something with their commercial efforts and did not care to be stopped by old age.

Looking at one such down the aisle, he could see the telltale signs of finer craftsmanship on his suit and especially his shoes. If Gus were to guess, the man was a first-generation successful entrepreneur, with money for nicer things, but whose stinginess drove him to endure the cheaper seats rather than spend money on frivolities like comfort. It was a character Gus had an easy time recognizing, having endured it in his youth.

By sunset, they were speeding into the mountains, and the view was spectacular. The sky was a delicate pink with streaks of blue, and distant snow-capped peaks were tinted orange by the fading light. This was the way men had classically depicted the land of the Elves since for generations the Elven policy of isolation had meant the beautiful peaks at Aelfua's border were all most humans had been allowed to see of it.

At the base of the mountain, a newly built road wound slowly upwards, and Gus did not envy the unfortunate drivers who had to steer their wagons through the sharp switchbacks required to make it across the border into the Aelfuan territories. Far better to take the train and let someone else handle the driving.

~

"Country Living"

The picturesque joys of country living are always a joyful change for the urban dwellers blessed enough to share it with us here. What a merry jaunt it must be for them to leave behind brick valleys choking in soot and journey trails threading through cover and copse. Homely factories traded for lovely farmsteads that emerge from orchards and gardens of hawthorn. Rats and urchins replaced by rabbit and thrush. The noisy jangle of the grinder's cries fades away, replaced by gentle songbirds.

– Duros Examiner, 10 Tal. 389

~

- CHAPTER 13 -

Dorna watched as the train sped by, its thundering passage through the countryside scattering birds and spewing smoke into the wind. The Master had once told her the legend of a great dragon that, in the world's final days, would encircle everything, spewing forth smoke and fire as it constricted.

People had once taken that bit of prophecy to mean a literal fire-breathing serpent rather than a human-built monstrosity of iron. Dragons had died out long ago, so that ancient doom seem impossible, and eventually mankind entirely forgot about it. The relentlessness of mortal folly had overcome the steadiness of immortal wisdom.

Their network of iron rails was killing the world, but as she watched the passing train shrink into the distance, she greatly envied its speed. Her carriage plodded steadily on, but the two horses pulling it could never hope to keep pace. She had spent the past few days slowly navigating her way home with their prisoner, and it was fraying at her nerves.

Even at their present speed, she worried the carriage Terry had bought might not hold together as they passed from the well-worn thoroughfares of central Verinde into the rural counties closer to the border with Aelfua. He had worried the carriage was too dingy for her deception as Alice Phand, but as far as she knew, their inquiry agent had never laid eyes upon it.

At the time, she had felt what he wanted would be far too ostentatious out here, but now she worried over that decision as the springs creaked ominously below them. A woman personally ferrying her ailing father might attract too much attention if she looked wealthy, but a woman stranded with her ailing father due to a broken axel or something would be even worse.

Alongside her on the driver's bench of the carriage, Edward Phand gave a muffled groan. Nervous that someone on that passing train might recognize him, she had covered his face with a hat, but despite his drugged stupor, covering his face always made him shift and moan.

The Master had specifically instructed that she bring Edward Phand by the road instead of by train. Terry had speculated that the Master was concerned someone would be watching for rail travelers meeting Phand's description. It seemed likely Terry was right, but Dorna had still chided him for trying to second guess the Master's methods.

Edward Phand groaned again, so she pushed the hat back from his face. He shifted in his sleep and made a few more soft noises but mostly quieted. The prospect of leading the flabby engineer through the Oblivion made her uneasy for more reasons than just the difficulty of silencing him; as harrowing as it was, that was their place, their harrowing to share, not his.

Spittle dribbled down his chin, and Dorna sighed as she fished out a handkerchief to wipe it away—she was posing as the devoted daughter taking her ill father home to die and would hardly look the part if she left him a mess. That lie grated at her. She could barely remember her actual father, but from what she could recall, he had been nothing like Edward Phand.

Her father had died when she was terribly young, young enough that she struggled to remember his face. She knew he had been very thin—they had been too poor for him to grow fat. At the time, all adults had seemed like giants to her, but she remembered that her father's height was something people had remarked upon. What she remembered most clearly were his strong arms lifting her up and his rough, calloused hands.

Every part of Edward Phand looked soft. Even his beard was long enough to have lost the stiff bristling she recalled on her father's face. Her father had worked in the mines, digging deep into the earth for the scant pennies men like Edward Phand would pay for honest labor. When her father died in that effort, those men gave no thought to the young daughter he left behind. She had spent her days pleading in the street for food and her nights in their empty dormitory until management had cast her out to make room for her father's replacement.

Dorna prayed once again, to no god in particular, that the cab driver they had hired back in Gemmen had left their advance money with his family. He had mentioned a daughter, and Dorna hated the idea of taking the girl's father. The man's death had been part of their instructions, so it must be a necessity, but it still did not sit easily on her conscience. She worried that perhaps Dougal's main purpose on their mission had been that the Master did not believe she was sufficiently devoted to carry out that unpleasant detail.

The idea made her bristle with injured pride, so she took a deep breath and softly recited the Elven words again. The Master knew best; he always did. Her injured pride was replaced with shame and sadness—questioning him was inappropriate. If he thought her insufficient, then she would have been. Softly chanting the phrases that the Master had them memorize, she resolved to recommit herself to their cause.

As she looked up at the steep mountains they would cross tomorrow, Dorna took a deep breath of the cold air that blew down from them into this valley. It was stiff and harsh, but it kept her sharp as the day wore on.

For countless generations, these mountains had kept men from the kingdom of immortals beyond. For generations, jealousy had festered in the hearts of her people, and rather than learn from the experience of their long-lived neighbors, they had warred against them.

Despite their history of ignorant aggression, the Master still held out hope for the race of men. Perhaps that compassion was why he had been chosen to remain when his people left the world. After her father died, the Master had taken her in as a lost young girl and raised her beneath his own roof, and she knew he cared deeply for the good of the world.

The Master had told her how her father was an agitator among the workers and tried time and again to improve the lot of the common man in Khanom. Her father had struggled daily to improve the human systems of labor that treated its subjects so poorly.

The Master had hoped to show him that humanity's attempts at self-government had failed and that it was time to return the world to its natural order, with men and Elves each serving as they served best. Her father had not understood the need for such radical solutions.

With creditors to pay and a daughter to feed, Dorna's father had continued to work within the system until it killed him. Early in her life, the Master had taught her that she must forgive her true father's failure of vision. Humans were short lived and thus short-sighted.

It was petty human tyrants that made the world unlivable for the Elves, and the men who had profited from that continued onward, heedless of the consequences. It was only a matter of time until men like Edward Phand would make the world unlivable for themselves. Then they too would need to escape as the Elves had.

The Master would not tell any mere mortal where his people had gone, but even if he did, humanity lacked the magic to mimic their disappearance once things went further out of balance. Man was doomed by a great dragon they had created themselves.

With the benefit of his immortal patience, wisdom, and experience, the Master had easily risen to power and influence in human society. His magic let him take on mortal forms, and through those, he had built the wealth necessary to pave the way for the Great Restoration. It was the labor he had been set to since his people had vanished from the world.

Dorna was proud to be part of the new generation of Wardens—men and women who understood the precipice they all lived upon and were willing to do what was necessary. Despite their difference in species, the Master had more in common with her father than the drugged engineer did, and she doubted he would have left the cabbie's daughter to suffer destitution in their cause if it could be avoided.

If it could not, Dorna just had to reassure herself that the Great Restoration would make it right—for everyone.

Edward Phand groaned, and Dorna glanced down at him, wondering what sort of troubled dreams the Master's concoction trapped him in. Clearly, stopping this tower was important, but it was less clear why she needed to bring its designer to the Master. Perhaps the prisoner could be won over, or perhaps his mind would be bent to their cause? Perhaps there was some antithesis to his proposed tower that could be built instead, under the Master's direction.

Trying to second guess the Master was probably pointless—he was ancient and wise and so much more clever than a mere human could ever hope to be. It was foolish human arrogance to presume she could ever unravel his plans, much less better them. Pushing her doubts aside, she looked back at the clouds behind them and hoped she could stay ahead of the rain for a bit longer.

The chilly spring shower overtook them eventually, and they were slowed even further as the wheels of their carriage pushed through the mud-filled ruts. For all its claims of modern progress, Verinde had never matched the beautiful tiled roads of the Elves, and

Dorna looked forward to them when she finally returned home. Even what the Elves had left behind was better than what her own people built.

She was a few hours behind schedule when they finally rolled into the decaying town the Master's plan placed them in for the evening. Centuries ago, Duros had once been a center of great commerce, founded for trade between Elves and men at a time when the Elven queen allowed it. It had fallen on hard times when she closed the border, but brisk and illegal trade had continued despite the queen's wishes, and for generations the Verin authorities had happily looked the other way.

These days, Duros was little more than a waypoint for small-cargo haulers passing through from Aelfua to wealthier points back west as the ever-expanding rail system increasingly rendered such services obsolete. Grand edifices of past centuries gracelessly decayed and were boarded up, and the signs advertising that they were for let had faded from long exposure.

The Master had selected an inn for them that evening that he called the 'horse in green field'. Dorna had taken it for a clumsy name when he made her memorize the plan, but now she realized it was a description of the antique sign over the door, which depicted a horse's head upon a green shield. More recently, whitewashed in giant block letters across the brick face of the building was the name Nag's Head Inn.

Dorna wondered when the Master had last set eyes upon this town; perhaps it was in some bygone and less literate age, when businesses would simply identify themselves to their customers with symbols such as he had described. The building was certainly old enough. Had he traded with humans, centuries ago, on these very streets?

She pulled the carriage up to the door, unsure what to do about Edward Phand. There was no overhang to cover him, but thankfully the wet chill had reduced his noises to a pathetic whimper. Looking along the street she saw a man peeking up at them suspiciously as he trudged towards them, and uneasy with his furtive approach, Dorna pulled Edward Phand's hat forward again to hide his face. Despite the man's glances, he seemed to pay them little heed once he moved past and into the Nag's Head.

Dorna sighed in momentary relief, then looked down at Edward Phand again, contemplating how she might get him into the inn, per the Master's instructions. In phases where he was more awake, the heavy engineer could somnambulantly stumble along under her direction, but there were two more hours until the Master's potion wore off enough for that.

The doting daughter she posed as probably wouldn't leave her sick father out in the rain, but he was just too heavy for her to carry alone. With no other choice, she adjusted his hat again and then hurried inside.

There was a public house on the ground floor of the inn, with the likely proprietor manning the bar. The insides were dingy and drafty and seemed as much decayed as the outside. She suspected the rooms here would only be a little more comfortable than a night in the carriage.

Given the option, she would have looked for a barn or simply camped inside the carriage somewhere along the road, but she could not vary the plan.

The furtive man from the street was sitting at the back wall and looked up at her as she entered. Her heart skipped a beat at his momentarily expectant expression. She was not whomever he was expecting, and he looked away again. Scowling over at the bartender, she stomped about loudly on the pretext of shaking off her boots and rattled the rain from her long coat until he glanced up at her.

The bartender's face very nearly matched the one of a man standing at the same bar in the long-faded painting just over the bartender's shoulder, and she wondered how many generations his family had run Nag's Head Inn.

A small bogey statue stood next to the painting and was also depicted in it—a squat, bearded thing that superstitious mountain folk once regarded as a lucky spirit. Both the painted and modern incarnations of the bartender looked short and a bit portly, the latter of which probably marked them as successful in these parts, so perhaps the ugly thing had brought them good fortune after all.

When the man finally looked up to see his latest custom standing impatiently by the door, he quickly wiped his hands and hurried over. "You're here for a room, eh?"

The bartender smiled and looked her up and down, plainly assessing how much he could charge. Underneath her plain brown coat, she was still wearing one of the overpriced frocks Terry had chosen for her. It was a bit sullied around the hem now, and she had refused to match the shoes, opting instead to travel in her father's boots.

Taking all that in, the man said, "It's five peis a night."

Looking around the place with a critical air, Dorna wrinkled her nose and replied, "Surely it can't be a cent more than two." The man drew himself up, ready to haggle, but too tired to engage in her least favorite pastime, Dorna raised her hand to forestall him. "Four, and you help bring in my things."

The interruption seemed to startle him, but he settled back on his heels and produced a key from his jacket pocket with a smile. Apparently five was as outrageous a rate for this place as it had seemed.

Taking the key, Dorna nodded once and then said, "Good. Now come help me bring in my father." The bartender frowned, looking put-upon, and Dorna launched into her explanation, "He lived on his own in Oulm but has fallen ill. My husband and I live in the Aelfua territory and wanted to bring him home to live with us. The doctor has said locomotive acceleration would be inappropriate in his present …."

She trailed off as she saw the man's eyes glaze over with studied indifference—it was an expression no doubt intended to rebuff any additional request for favor she might be building towards, and perhaps that was the Master's plan in having her always offer explanation so freely.

She never felt herself a skilled actress, but so far, the story had been universally unquestioned. Dorna worried it would just attract attention and that someone might notice the lack of resemblance between she and her prisoner.

When he saw the girth of her 'father' waiting outside, the bartender frowned but kept to their bargain, and between them, they hauled Edward Phand down from the carriage and up the stairs. Only once Edward Phand was laid down in the bed upstairs did the man try to squeeze her for another peis and a half to stable the horses.

It was a scandalously timed effort, and she was half-inclined to respond by hurling him down the stairs, but the Master's plan demanded subtlety and constraint. She paid what he asked and clenched her fists at the man's look of smug satisfaction.

After being settled on the bed, her prisoner had begun to stir restlessly, so once the bartender left, Dorna slipped one of the Master's vials from her coat. She poured more of the Elven concoction past his lips and massaged his throat until he swallowed, just as she had been taught.

In moments, Edward Phand fell limp once more, and with hours to herself before he needed another draught, she felt she had earned a drink of her own. A woman dining alone might get a few extra glances, but a stranger in the public house wouldn't be too unusual for a way-stop town like this. After driving for hours in the chill, she decided a hot meal would be worth the risk.

It didn't seem like much time had passed, but apparently whatever tick of the clock signaled that the work day was over had been sounded. The inn's quiet pub had become noisome and full, and while she was not particularly in the mood for any society at all, it at least felt more like home to her than any of the places Terry had insisted they visit in Gemmen.

Most of the pub was occupied by travel-stained gentlemen she took to be lonesome cargo haulers, now all engaged in desperately loud conversation as if to make up for the long hours spent driving in silence. A few less-weathered men and even a pair of women she took to be locals were scattered about the room, sharing drinks and stories with the cargo haulers. The tables towards the back wall were quietest, so she selected one farther from the bar.

The furtive fellow she'd seen on the street still sat at a table in the back corner of the room, but he was no longer alone, and seeing him animatedly engaged in hushed conference with the fellows at his table reassured her that whatever his concern was, he wasn't a concern of hers. A few other men sat quietly by themselves at small tables there, and Dorna relaxed a bit, happy to have some buffer of likeminded unsociables making her feel less out of place in the now busy pub.

A young woman in an apron came by to describe their offerings and looked disappointed when Dorna only asked for a cheap wine and a bit of stew. The woman then asked one of the quiet fellows at a table nearby, but he just waved her off and looked annoyed at the interruption of his quiet reflection. The furtive man at the farthest table sent the girl away with a glare before she got too close, then returned to his hushed conversation.

Something about that suddenly sat uneasily, and Dorna took another look at the people around her. They were all well-dressed, certainly more neatly kept men than the bulk of the patronage in this place and of higher quality than the few at the bar she had taken for locals. She surreptitiously studied the man by himself who had just waved off the barmaid. As she did, he nodded, seemingly to himself, and reached into his pocket.

A stack of papers exchanged hands at the furtive man's corner table, and the man receiving them laid them out in front of him, examining them carefully while the furtive man from the street anxiously gauged his reaction.

"Hold it right there—you are under arrest!" said a man's voice from behind her, one of the quiet, well-dressed ones she'd barely paid attention to. Dorna froze, her hands clenching at the edge of her table. The man across from her leapt to his feet, producing handcuffs from his pocket, and in an instant, the better-dressed men from the tables all around her lurched to their feet in unison.

If she flipped the table over, she might make some space and have time to bolt to the door, but with Edward Phand abandoned upstairs, her mission ….

They roughly rousted up the furtive man from the corner table and clipped his hands together with the cuffs. One of the men making the arrest smiled and held some papers up over his head, waving them so that the whole room could see them, whatever they were. They weren't here for her at all.

Dorna shuddered at the sudden wave of relief, then slouched back in her chair, trembling. She felt suddenly out of breath and really wished the girl had been faster about bringing that wine she'd ordered. The man waving the papers was announcing something about certificates to the room, but Dorna's heart was pounding so hard she couldn't focus on it.

He suddenly turned to her and, holding the papers towards Dorna, the closest person still seated, he asked, "You saw that man pass these papers over to me, right?" The whole pub fell quiet, staring at the two of them.

She frowned and nodded, feeling every pair of eyes upon her and an icy fear of looming failure. More than anything, she wanted to recite her words but could hardly chant in Elven with the whole room watching.

"Perfect. I'll need your name and address, and we'll have you sign a quick statement to that effect."

The man seemed quite pleased with himself, holding his stack of what appeared to be rail certificates in various amounts. Taking a deep breath to calm herself, she stared him down and responded with a stiff and authoritative, "No."

Taken aback, he looked ready to argue a moment but instead hurried over to the next nearest table, making the same pronouncement. The men there all nodded, and Dorna sighed in relief.

She wasn't sure if these men could arrest her for refusing to be a witness, but with others able to step in, maybe it wouldn't be worth their time to do it. The bartender looked nearly as shaken as she was. While most eyes were elsewhere, he moved to the small bogey statue and filled the small cup at its feet with whatever alcohol he had on hand, an offering to the local mountain spirits. The Master had once confided in her that the custom was a foolish human superstition going back to ancient times when the Duer lived in these mountains.

Though a forgotten people now, the Master had shown her their ancient carvings, and she could see a vague resemblance in the small bearded spirit the innkeeper now plied with alcohol. It would do nothing for him, of course, but the police seemed to have little interest in arresting the man, so whatever his crimes, he would no doubt credit the bogeys for that forbearance and continue to spill booze on their behalf as needs arose.

Nervous about attracting any further attention, Dorna forced herself to wait for her dinner to arrive. Once it did, she found her appetite had totally vanished but methodically forced herself to finish it before heading back upstairs.

Edward Phand was still deeply asleep, so she took slow breaths to settle herself for the night, determined to wake early and leave at first light. She recited the Elven words again and again, feeling them slowly drain away her anxiety and replace it with faith. Perhaps the Master had foreseen even this.

Soothed by the words, she slept and woke in the early gray before dawn, with Edward Phand groaning softly as he struggled back towards consciousness. Groaning meant she had slept past the appointed morning dose, and he would be coming to more quickly than expected, so she hurriedly fetched the Elven flask and poured more of the thick syrup down his throat, sending him tumbling back into his artificial coma.

He was still breathing, but she checked for his heartbeat anyway, just as she had been taught, and then packed her things. She dressed again, looking forward to returning home and changing into the plainer clothes she normally wore and lamenting once again how they would have been far more suited to travel than the flimsy, lace-strewn stuff with which she had been provided.

Descending the stair, she found an older woman running things, probably the proprietor's wife, and the common room of the public house empty but for the two of them. The woman offered breakfast, but Dorna refused and instead enlisted her aid in dragging Edward Phand downstairs before she paid the amount agreed upon for the room and stables.

She wished she had time for breakfast, but if they were not down from the mountain by sundown, it would be very cold. Dorna had a heavier coat for herself, but Edward Phand still wore the clothes he had dressed in for the theater in Gemmen. As she set the horses in motion, it struck her as odd that the Master had not thought he might need one, and she wondered if Terry had been instructed to provide one and simply forgotten.

Outside the boarded-up buildings on Duros' main street, shabby merchants set up little stands along the streets, selling their goods from makeshift stalls while perfectly suitable empty buildings decayed behind them. She supposed the landlords, likely living in comfort in some far-off city, had apparently set the rents too high for anyone left in Duros to afford. Now, instead of the landlords making less money than they'd hoped, they made none and slowly strangled what little remained of a once vibrant border town. A few of the street merchants hawked their goods at her as she passed, but she would not stop for them.

The Great Restoration would help them more than the few coins from her custom.

Once free of Duros, she pulled out a hard bit of bread Terry had packed in case they were trapped in the mountains. It was difficult to chew, but it quieted her hunger for the moment. Per the Master's instructions, she checked Edward Phand's pulse again, and it was slow but steady. The timing of the next few doses was critical—she needed him to arrive just awake enough for her to guide him through the Oblivion.

Up they went, the horses slowly pulling them over the mountains, away from the ancestral lands of men and into Aelfua.

~

"Statue of Sir Cornell Tabble Unveiled"

Yesterday the Princess of Whitby unveiled the memorial statue of Sir Cornell Tabble at Bridgton, by the western edge of the Winged Bridge and overlooking the bustling port town he founded. Her Royal Highness was there met by the Mayor of Bridgton and the Marshall of Aelfua. An enormous public crowd was drawn, who journeyed there from throughout the region to witness the dedication.

An address was presented to Her Royal Highness reciting the benefits to the country that had resulted from the labours of Sir Cornell Tabble in compliance with the Mayor's request, after which Her Royal Highness pulled a cord that allowed the covering of the statue to fall—a proceeding which was greeted with cordial applause by all in attendance. The statue is bronze upon a granite pedestal. It depicts Sir Cornell Tabble in his military dress, a hand shading his eyes as he overlooks the bay below. The Marshall, who had accompanied Sir Cornell Tabble upon the occasion commemorated, remarked upon the expertise with which the likeness of the moment had been caught.

– *Khanom Daily Converser*, 12 Tal. 389

~

- CHAPTER 14 -

After passing over the mountains, the train wound through Aelfua's western forests, the view occasionally broken by farms or pastures and, once, several acres of stumps.

The first human settlements in Aelfua had been built where villages had stood for millennia until the Elves emptied their lands. The colonies replacing those ancient villages developed quickly, with white tiled roads already laid out and leading to lands already cleared. With that head start, the settlements had grown quickly beyond what the Elves had left them in the forested western half of Aelfua.

Gus could see why naturalists might look upon that wide swath of stumps as desolate and sad, but with their orderly alignment and scarce undergrowth, the Aelfuan forests had always looked decidedly unnatural to him. They seemed more like swept rows of trees awaiting the return of their immortal orchardists. Seeing them cleared away made the land feel more human. Occasionally that effect was spoiled by some stray monument the Elves had left behind, but those were few.

The rails turned south, and the mountains loomed in and out of view as the train wound over rolling hills and across wide valleys. Aelfua had always been known for its magnificent landscapes.

Eventually the train emerged from yet another forest into steeper hills, and Khanom rose above it all like a great citadel overseeing the lands below. Their path snaked along the hillsides, the train's route circuitous as it followed the land upwards towards the looming mountain range south of the city. In the shadow of Uhnjal

Peak, atop a wide plateau skirted in gray cloud, stood Gus's destination.

Khanom's residents always seemed intent on convincing everyone that they had built one of the greatest cities in the world, and laying eyes upon it, Gus began to agree. Though the city lacked Gemmen's endless sprawl, it fought to make up for it in modern grandeur. Gleaming towers of concrete and glass shone gold as they reflected the light of the waning sun. They stretched high atop the hill, many easily twenty stories tall, and four that were probably thirty.

Gemmen's tallest was the twenty-five story RFTB tower, which loomed ten stories above anything else in the city. Mansil, in Garren, supposedly had a temple dedicated to Phaeton with a spire nearly fifty stories high, but Gus had never seen it. Judging by the number of people on the train pressed to the windows and breathlessly ogling the view, he was clearly not the only one awed by it.

The locals feigned at disinterest or pretended to sleep, and not wanting to look like an easy mark, Gus sat back and did his best to look more blasé. He plucked out a catchy song about some town on the Pylian shore, whose words and title he could never quite recall, and turned his eyes from the spectacle of the city's center.

They rolled past huge pastures leading into the city's immense series of stockyards where animals were driven to be processed for sale and slaughter. Gus chuckled as he saw the familiar Thomas's logo painted atop one such building, welcoming visitors to Khanom with the promise of canned sausages.

The logo sped by quickly, hidden behind wave after wave of great factories positioned around the base of the plateau, their chimneys spewing smoke into the air. The visitors aboard the train gradually fell back from the windows as the gleaming towers were obscured by the gray foulness that filled the air just below the plateau.

Factory buildings abutted ancient Elven roads that had been laid out in gleaming white stone tiles that had now faded under an oppressive coat of soot fallen from smokestacks and passing trains. It was late in the day, and Gus caught glimpses of exhausted factory workers in shabby uniform as they marched slowly out in long lines. The early spring here was cooler than Gemmen's, but few of them had coats to wear atop their work suits, so they just hugged themselves as they walked, all apparently headed to some single destination.

The train wound up the steep side of the plateau and eventually rose above the gray that skirted the city, emerging dramatically at the base of Khanom's dazzling towers. Up close, they seemed little different than any other building unless one craned their neck upwards, as many of his fellow passengers did. Given the ubiquity of theft while traveling, Gus decided to keep his gaze a bit more level.

Here in the center of the city, the white tiled streets left behind by the Elves were clean, and people strolled about in finer clothes, catching cabs, or being picked up by liveried drivers in hacks of their own. The buildings were bedecked in signage at their base proudly cataloging the businesses within—architects, petitioners, various unspecified partnerships, and more banks than seemed necessary.

Occasionally a building would be dedicated to one company alone, and there would be some elaborate Modernist sculpture out front into which was worked its name and some symbolic indication of the business's function. The offices of Eastern Railways had a particularly ornate marble frontispiece of swirls that trailed behind flying women soaring over fields and forests that struck Gus as a better advertisement for witchcraft than rail travel, but then the last trial for witchcraft had been over a century ago.

People in Gemmen scoffed at the uncultured 'settlements' in Aelfua and Rakhasin, but here in Khanom the burgeoning wealth was palpable, and to Gus's eye, their finery looked no less elaborate or ostentatious than that back home.

The rail circled the northern edge of the plateau but did not venture inside the city itself. Khanom's main hub was the first stop, and as the train pulled to a halt there, it became quickly obvious it had been designed as a showpiece entrance for the city. Most hubs saved ostentation for the terminal buildings, but here even the platform was bedecked in elaborate white granite swirls in faux-Elven style and ringed in elegantly matched wrought iron fixtures that would have probably horrified the Elves had any remained to see it.

Gus rose from his seat and reclaimed his bag, somewhat surprised to see few others rising at this stop, but once he debarked, it became apparent that was because he had ridden in the cheaper car. Well-attired men and women emptied from the pricier rail stock in greater numbers, accompanied by servants bearing their things and quickly intercepted by an army of railway porters eager to share the burden in exchange for tips.

Looking down the track, Gus saw that it wound its way back down through the gray clouds into the factory districts only after making a few stops along the plateau. Apparently, the route had been designed to get Khanom's elite quickly to their destinations, forcing the lesser sort to pass twice through the sooty layer between, returned to the dingy town below only after they were shown the opulence of their 'betters'.

After two days on the train, having spent most of that time seated, Gus's injured leg was reluctant to cooperate at first. He struggled forward with his bag, apparently seen by astute railway porters as an unlikely source of gratuity. Limping after the crowd, he was able to find his way inside the equally gaudy terminal building of Khanom's opulent hub.

Amid the bustle inside, he saw a red-liveried ballyhoo employed by the city to welcome newcomers, complete with a tall shako designed to draw attention the man, just in case anyone might miss his vividly colored uniform.

Unlike a porter, a ballyhoo was employed to stand in one spot and be helpful, so he could not evade a poor tipper simply by rushing to the aide of someone who looked more generous. This one was an older man, his hair faded to gray, but he didn't look hard-lived enough to have been a miner or one of the early frontiersmen who settled the city. At a guess, Gus placed him as a failed speculator.

Hobbling over, Gus stopped in front of the man and let his bag fall to the floor, taking a moment to stand stork-like on his good leg while he bent the left back and forth to loosen it up. Finally, after the socially awkward delay while Gus grimaced and flexed, he looked to the ballyhoo and said, "I need a hotel. Nothing too pricey though."

The city's man looked thoughtful as he sized him up, and then replied, "There are a few cheap flophouses back down below, but if you want something here above, perhaps Rondel's on 3rd?"

When Gus looked at him quizzically, the ballyhoo hastened to add, "Everything up here is a bit … lavish, sir, but in preparation for the Exposition, they've opened numerous new hotels, so the market is very competitive. Push the clerk a bit, and you should be able to get a decent rate. It will probably still be expensive, but it's your least expensive option without going down below."

The way he said 'down below' had the ring of classist specificity to it, and Gus wondered which side of the city's murky gray divide the ballyhoo dwelt on. It wasn't the sort of advice one gave on hotel commission though, and ignoring the protests from Emily in the back of his mind, Gus decided the ballyhoo had earned a decent gratuity. Digging into his pockets, he found six pennies and gratefully slipped them to the man before picking up his bag and lumbering towards the exit.

Outside, a row of cabs waited, and as he drew nearer, Gus stared at the horses a moment, trying to understand the bizarre contraption they were attached with, and then laughed as he realized it was to catch their droppings. It seemed the white streets of Khanom were not to be sullied, although woe to the cabmen whose day-long perches would be continually perfumed by the equine offal.

He haggled a bit with the waiting drivers, but either he looked like a steady mark or they were just disinterested in indulging the spirit of capitalism, and none would back down from their standard fare despite Gus's insistence that it was a bit high for wherever 3rd Street was. Eventually he was obliged to submit to their recalcitrance and hire the foremost cab at what they insisted was the regulated fee.

The cab drove him through the center of town, passing along a large park at the city's center lined with odd deciduous trees whose new spring leaves were just beginning to emerge. Their strangeness was not in any natural twist of flora but rather their exceedingly unnatural one-sided shape. Towards the road, they branched out like any other trees, kept neatly trimmed by the city. Towards the park, the trees were completely flat. No branches extended inwards, and all of them seemed perfectly aligned as if an invisible wall constrained their growth.

The park itself was a grassy field with an array of shrubbery and unblossomed flower beds. A few people strolled through it, enjoying a bit of air in the early evening. New buildings were rising alongside the park, presumably less tall than some of the highest towers but tall enough to hide them from view at street level. Their heights were unfinished, and some of the frontispieces were covered in curtained scaffolds to hide the work in progress, but their crisply unfinished state was testimony of bustling expansion.

At the end of the block, as utterly incongruous amid a human city as the white roads, Gus saw an Elven obelisk. It stood eight or nine feet tall, a diagonally cut cylinder sculpted of a white stone that matched the tiled Elven streets. It was a sculpted crescent, smooth along the outside but with foreign sigils inscribed along the inner surface.

So far as he knew, no one had ever been able to explain why, when the Elves left, they took all their people, their possessions, and even all their buildings, yet left behind roads and random monuments such as these. As the hack drove onwards, they passed a few more such obelisks scattered along the way. The people of Khanom had apparently respected the obelisks enough not to tear them down; three were perched prominently along the main thoroughfare spaces in the park.

Further into the city, he noticed two others tucked away in back alleys; or rather, the buildings had simply been built around them, transforming whatever empty byway the obelisk had stood upon into an alley between two modern towers. When he started looking for them, he realized there seemed to be at least one on every block.

Rondel's sat several blocks southeast of the park, and the façade was an opulent affair that rivaled the Harrison in Gemmen, done in elaborate Modernist swirls around a colonnaded entrance. It looked far too expensive for the likes of a former army sergeant, but despite that there were no attendants at the door, and Gus made his way inside with his own bag.

When he stepped through the doors, he saw four employees in matched blue and yellow livery gathered around the front desk chatting casually with the clerk stationed there. A few patrons wandered through the spacious lobby but clearly nowhere near as many as had been planned for. At the sign of a new guest, the attendants were startled into action, and one hurried to relieve him of his bag while the rest scattered to other chores.

The attendant insisted on carrying Gus's bag for the six steps remaining between the entrance and the front desk. The clerk smiled, and per the rail hub attendant's advice, Gus haggled with them on the rate. Their promotional fliers, which the clerk was all too happy to refer Gus to, advertised it as a 'mere' twelve peis a night. After a bit of back and forth, they eventually arranged a second-floor room at a mere eight, of which Emily would begrudge him each penny.

Smiling with enough strained politeness that Gus felt he had won their engagement, the man at the desk handed him a key, and as Gus looked down at it, he saw a thin slot had been cut into the end of it. Apparently, the clerk had a way of making up for such shortfalls.

Gus pondered calling him out on the game, but then thought better of it—their scam could work in his favor. As he scooped back up his bag and turned to walk away, the clerk called after, "Do you have anything for the safe, sir?"

Gus grinned back at him and lifted up the bag, "Oh, no, I can't risk letting this slip out of my sight." The clerk nodded in understanding and failed to follow up with the usual comment about the hotel not being responsible for goods not in the safe. That meant management wasn't likely in on it, or there would be more concern for those legal niceties.

He took the bag with him over to the small bar area towards the back of the lobby and ordered several stiff drinks while he waited to spot the clerk's partner in crime. One of the hotel's attendants brought him some bread and cheese that were kept out for the patrons, and since there were so few others about, Gus shamelessly gorged himself on the stuff. He was halfway through his second drink before a fellow settled down next to him and ordered a tonic.

"Nice hotel, eh? Better deal than you'd get elsewhere, I think. At least until the Exposition opens," rambled the newcomer, and Gus glanced him over skeptically and sipped at his own drink. The man was unremarkably dressed and attired like a man of business rather than leisure. A lonely traveler might chat up a stranger, but the man wasn't rumpled from travel, which meant he had been around at least long enough to settle in and change clothes. If that were the case, why was he drinking here rather than at some proper club or public house?

"Yeah, got a deal on it," Gus gushed, leaning unsteadily towards him with a too-big grin as he spoke breathily to let the stranger get a whiff of the alcohol. Extending a hand, he said, "Baston. Here on business. You?"

"Oh, yes, business as well. My name's Sharpe," was the reply, accompanied by a firm handshake. A convincing performance, with the handshake and all, but a real man of commerce would also have gone for his card and immediately inquired about Gus's line. A rookie mistake, but not unexpected in a settlement town like Khanom, where the criminals would be less sophisticated.

Gus grinned at him, and they chatted about the weather and the town's scenery for a time. Any doubts he had that Sharpe was a local evaporated when the man raved over the city's latest architecture while seeming comparatively blasé about the odd trees in the park and the mysterious white obelisks scattered about. Sharpe even bought Gus another drink, to make sure his mark was good and sloshed.

After enjoying the free drink, Gus proclaimed himself too tired to continue, wobbled to his feet and collected his bag. Mister Sharpe rose with him and gripped Gus's elbow to help steady him. He gently pried the bag from Gus's grip before guiding him into the elevator and then on towards Gus's room.

Despite their amateurish obviousness, Gus admired that part of their setup—if confronted later, Sharpe could swear that, were he the thief, then surely he could have simply walked off with the bag while Gus was drunk. Instead, per the plan, Sharpe helped his mark into the room, set the bag down, and before he bid Gus goodnight, made a point of mentioning, several times, that he was leaving the bag right by the door.

As soon as Sharpe was gone, Gus pushed back to his feet, groaning a bit at the discomfort the inebriate act always gave his injured leg. In truth, he was only a bit tipsy, but as he had not had a good night's sleep in two days, he really was exhausted. He hoped Sharpe wouldn't take too long with the next step.

For eight peis a night, the room was quite nice, the gas lamps softly hissing and keeping it far more illumined than he would have ever been willing to pay for at his own flat back home. Had he known about all the lights earlier, Gus would have offered to put out about half of them to make a go at it for six peis a night.

Gus opened his bag and pulled out his pistol, checking over it carefully several times to make sure he would not fumble with it in his sleepy state. He locked the door with the slotted key, wondering if they had actually done this before or if this was the first real attempt. It was an old scam, but in a hotel so new, he might have the honor of being their inaugural.

With so much cash on hand, and so many distractions, travelers were ideal marks, and unless they were robbed on the way in, no one would ever have as much cash on hand as they did upon arrival. He'd handled a lot of these cases until Drake's swooped in with their price lists and name recognition among out-of-town visitors.

A well-stuffed chair was off to one side, and Gus pulled it over to face the door and settled down. He dozed off several times, on the last of which he was startled awake by the sound of the door's lock turning over.

Most people left their key in the door after locking it, to speed their exit in the event of fire. Not wanting to spoil Sharpe's plan, Gus had done the same. With a slotted key in the lock, the prospective thief could approach the marked room, slip an ordinary screwdriver into the lock, and use it to turn the key from the other side, engaging the tumblers and opening the door.

The poor saps asleep in the room would never know how they were robbed. The hotel manager would tut and remind them that they had been offered use of the hotel's safe.

The usual problem was that a person who already knew about that sort of scam would always check their key and refuse a slotted one. There, of course, that savvy traveler made a mistake since this only told the thieves to be more careful and gave them a chance come at their mark from another angle. With no crime yet committed, the traveler's only options were to complain to potentially complicit managers or else find alternate accommodations with an entirely new set of thieves.

If there were plenty of guests in residence, Sharpe might just strike other rooms, but with so few marks to be had, Gus needed to discourage them from any subsequent attempts. He'd purposefully kept everything out of the hotel safe to encourage them to act quickly and played at being tippled to make it as soon as possible tonight.

Mister Sharpe swung the door silently open, already half-crouched as he prepared to creep inside with a false beard in his left hand and the screwdriver in his right. Sharpe's eyes widened as he saw his mark markedly less insensate than hoped.

Gus grinned at him from his throne before the door and gestured with the pistol, "Hold it right there."

"Oh! I'm so sorry! I thought this was my room! Terribly sorry to wake you. Have a nice evening," Sharpe said as he quickly stuffed the false beard into his pocket.

At least he was smart enough for that. Some fools tried this with the false beard already on their faces as the door opened, which was as good as declaring yourself guilty of something from the outset. The beards might fool a sleepy mark who woke mid-robbery but were never good enough for direct scrutiny, and by wearing one in the doorway, you might as well mask yourself with a bandanna like one of Gentleman Jim's highwaymen.

Gus gave a sober chuckle and raised his pistol up. "I said hold it, Mister Sharpe. I've a message for you and your buddy at the front desk." He leaned back in the cushioned chair, making a show of getting comfortable as he waved the pistol about in the thief's direction.

Enjoying his control of the conversation, Gus reversed his earlier trick, now trying to play far less tipsy than he was. "The slotted key is a good trick, but you boys are out of your depth here, and I don't have much to steal. If I find anything missing, however, now I'll know where it's gone, won't I? I'll make it easy for you. This pistol's the most valuable thing I have with me, so if anything of mine goes missing, for your sake it better be this because otherwise I'm going to use it to shoot you and the clerk who gave me the key."

Sharpe paled at the threat, shaking his head. He edged backward as Gus rose to his feet and shut the door firmly in Sharpe's face, turning the lock again with a loud click. Behind the door, he could hear the man scuttling away, no doubt off to inform his confederate of their evening's failed robbery.

Sharpe's breed of criminal was very territorial by necessity since another thief operating in the same area would draw attention and make profitable marks more cautious. They would already be on the lookout for anyone else who might work the hotel and would now be particularly motivated to keep them away from Gus's room, which meant Gus could sleep in relative security.

Finally able to relax, he pulled out his flask of lahvu, draining the last of it and settling back in the bed as he felt the intensifying light-headed tingle blur his thoughts. If Sharpe were indicative of the quality of the local criminals Phand's abductor would need to conspire with, then a week might be plenty of time to find the kidnapped engineer. With a sigh, Gus set the gun on the nightstand and drifted off into the warm blackness of a sound, dreamless sleep.

~

"Rakhasin Explorers Convene"

At a meeting of the Royal Geographical Society in Gemmen, Lord Alderde presiding, a paper was read on the Geskhan Meadow by Commander Whitacre. The Commander described his excursions across the Meadow in the neighbourhood of Karhass, from Dessis, which serves as Muz'eraine's current capital, and along the Meryl. Journeying overland to the Upscot river, he visited the famed gemstone shores along its banks and observed the ever-expanding operations still being carried on there, even amidst the current difficulties.

Nathaniel Abiel, current Royal Governor of Rakhasin, and others took part in the discussion, and the Chairman announced that the Society had determined to send an expedition next year in order to further explore unclaimed lands south of Rejju's wall. On the motion of Lord Alderde, a vote of thanks to the lecturer was accorded, and the meeting adjourned to Bel. 19.

– Khanom Daily Converser, 13 Tal. 389

~

- CHAPTER 15 -

The peak loomed over Khanom and stretched morning's gloom several hours, which suited Gus just fine. Pleased he had slept the night through without being robbed, he wandered outside to watch the closing antics of the city's morning commute. It was far less pell-mell than he was accustomed to, but given the usual neighborhoods he occupied, he thought it might simply be a matter of being in a part of the city occupied by a wealthy elite that had little need to rush to and fro so early.

A pair of such met on the corner, exchanging greetings Gus could not hear, so he supplied their dialog himself: "Oh, I say, old chap, shall we put off work a bit longer and go get a coffee?" "A coffee? Don't be ridiculous. A man of my station could never fetch his own coffee!" They laughed right on cue.

Their imaginary discussion of coffee put Gus in the mind for some; Rondel's had managed to burn their coffee, and while it worked, it had tasted terrible. He hobbled past several cafés he had seen near the hotel, but not a one of them was open. Apparently, people in Khanom skipped breakfast or perhaps simply had it at home before coming into the heart of the city.

Looking around, he wondered if anyone might have hauled their bedroom furniture up all the flights of stairs necessary to dwell in these tall buildings. If not, then where did all these well-to-do up-toppers live when they weren't meandering casually in to work?

Given Phand's association with the Exposition, he supposed checking at their offices should be his first stop. Flagging down a cab, he tried to negotiate again but found the man as intractable on the price as his fellows at the hub the evening before.

Steering the argument towards how far it was, he managed to get the driver to argue that it was five, nearly six, blocks down Armistice Boulevard, which Gus remembered seeing along the way to Rondel's. Unfortunately, he realized the game when Gus tried to figure out if that was north or south along Armistice. Eventually they reached a mutually satisfying accord, and Gus strolled down the pristine streets to his destination having spent only a single cigarette for directions.

Emily would have been proud, although she would probably have been put out with him over the coffee on his breath this morning. He had also skipped breakfast, which some quack had convinced her was medically unsound, but Gus had learned never to admit to that particular omission.

That line of thought reminded him that he needed to wire in his arrival. After spotting a nearby office, he wrestled out a suitably legible abbreviation to update Emily for a mere sixteen pennies: *KHANOM RONDEL'S, G*

Khanom's civic center was only a few blocks beyond the telegraph office, and it was every bit as overstated as one might imagine for a young city desperately hoping to impress visitors. An elaborate frontispiece decorated the outside, depicting small men at work in mines and factories, and above them, towering captains of industry looked down like the gods in heaven, smiling beneficently as they directed the workings below, presumably with wisdom and compassion, although the fact that the city's labors was merely for the profit of their towering masters seemed to have been glossed over.

Gus supposed that with a change in facial expression, the same work could easily be a propaganda piece for revolutionaries like the ones in Tulsmonia. Perhaps if the workers in Khanom's factories ever came charging up through the gray, they might do just that. The destruction in the wake of the uprising in Tulsmonia hadn't been that carefully measured, but then, they were only Tuls, and Gus liked to imagine a Verin uprising would go more smoothly.

Once inside the civic building, a bored clerk at a desk in the lobby directed him to the Exposition's offices, which were tucked away a floor below street level. Even with all the excitement of the city's leaders Gus had witnessed in Gemmen, it seemed like none of the bureaucrats wanted to give up better office space to whoever had been assigned to work out the various particulars.

Making his way down the stairs, Gus was surprised to see that the basement actually made a serviceable showroom. Several gas lamps around the room were lit despite plenty of daylight coming in from narrow street-level windows overhead. There was a large central space where a handful of offices were set up along one wall, with a surprising clutter of old paintings hung over every available spot on the walls. The large central space was filled by two tables, each bearing a model city.

No one was present in the showroom when he arrived, although Gus could hear voices from one of the offices along the wall, which a placard labelled as belonging to Ryerson, Secretary. One was a deep-voiced man arguing something; he sounded rather musical, and from the dramatic rising and falling of his tone, Gus took him for some sort of an actor. The actor was arguing against someone offering what sounded like nasal-toned excuses—likely some sort of wheedling bureaucrat and presumably Secretary Ryerson.

The walls were thick enough that the substance of their debate was unclear, so Gus turned his attention to the huge models laid out in the center of the room.

A table on one side depicted Khanom's skyline as he had seen from the train. Model buildings were constructed of some beige material, set up atop a painted map of the streets and parks. At the center was a model of the park, complete with various benches and even its one-sided trees. A half-dozen oversized carts appeared to have been abandoned along the streets surrounding the park. Several of the buildings were depicted in full color, and looking at those, he realized they were the mostly complete structures that he had seen on his way in.

Most of the extravagant architectural flourishes worked out in miniature had been covered in tarpaulin and scaffolding, but judging from their depiction in miniature, they would no doubt be quite impressive once unveiled. Elaborate frontispieces featuring graceful arches covered in Modernist swirls and tiny figures that would no doubt be enormous once realized. The color models were clearly the Exposition buildings, huge display areas for the various fair exhibits. There were several blank spaces sketched around the park, presumably where more buildings would be added later.

The model on the other table was more confusing. It seemed to depict another city entirely with graceful spires that, for all their elegance, were of rather unassuming heights compared to the towers on the table just across the aisle. Rather than the beige of Khanom, all of its buildings were painted, primarily in bright reds and yellows.

As Gus studied the miniature buildings, the discussion in the next room wrapped up with a deep throated harrumph. The office door opened, and the nasally voiced bureaucrat called over, "It's marvelous, isn't it? It's the most elaborate reconstruction ever done, but then, there aren't any other cities where something so detailed would even be possible."

"Reconstruction?" Gus looked up and saw the bureaucrat the voice owned was very much what he'd pictured—thin, thinning hair, spectacles, and a suit that was probably quite fashionable when purchased years ago but was weathered enough that now it just spoke of failed expectations, the sort of thing worn by someone who loved rules and security.

The man nodded towards the model and smiled warmly as he continued proudly, "The Elven queen's summer palace was here, so there were many depictions of it to work from." Ryerson gestured about, and Gus took more notice of the artwork hanging from the walls.

The paintings were all classic Elven cityscapes, which had been popular centuries ago and were enjoying a bit of resurgence as antiques now that the Elves had taken the actual cities away. Seeing familiar peaks on the horizon in several of the paintings along the wall, Gus realized they must all be depictions of the original Khanom. "Both of these will be moved to a display in the main hall, and we imagine it will be one of the highlights of the show."

Looking back down at the models, Gus saw all the roads were laid out the same between the two cities, but the buildings were different. At the center of the city, where now there was only a park, had once stood the walled palace of the Elven queen. Although of modest height compared to modern Khanom, the palace's graceful minarets had once loomed high over the Elven city, with the only structure of comparable size being a pale gray, stepped pyramid directly across from it.

Nothing else in the miniature Elven city looked anything like it, making the pyramid a bizarre gray anomaly in the colorful ancient landscape. Gus glanced back at the park on the other model, then to the pyramid, and realized that the park encompassed the grounds of both the palace and the pyramid.

Ryerson grinned as he saw his visitor's attention drawn to it, clearly delighted to have a moment for pedantry, and walked over to gesture grandly at the model while pointing out the different angles as depicted in the various paintings surrounding it. "That was the Embassy Building; that's why that section of green on the other side of 10th Avenue is called Embassy Park. It's quite the historical curiosity, actually. Many people think it's just another part of Palace Park, but it's not."

"And this 'embassy' doesn't look anything like the rest of the town," Gus remarked, peering up at its depiction in the paintings; the structure's height made the rectangular gray peak visible in most of them. The colors had faded on many of them, but the bright paint splashed across the elegant facades of the palace and surrounding buildings made the pale stone pyramid seem stark and otherworldly in their midst.

The bureaucrat's head bobbed enthusiastically as he said, "Precisely! It's very mysterious. The name is translated from the Elven, and consistent across various sources, but Khanom was the home of the queen's summer palace, you see, her retreat from courtly life. She did not meet with any ambassadors or hold court out here. The building was not used as any sort of embassy as far as we can tell, so the name remains quite mysterious."

Gus just nodded, his interest rapidly waning; the Elves were long gone, and their naming conventions were not the mystery he was here to look into. Looking back to the model of the modern city, he saw someone else had quietly entered the room, presumably the deep-voiced theatrical, and was setting a painted building model down into one of the empty spots in the Exposition area.

Startled when he looked up at the newcomer, Gus remarked, "I didn't know there were gobs in Aelfua."

The goblin standing by the city model was typical of his kind, barely over four feet in height, with long arms but short legs and outsized hands and feet. His skin was deep olive, giving his broad mouth a distinct ranine aspect. The creature's yellow eyes narrowed behind strange blue colored-glass spectacles, and in a deep, melodic voice it rumbled out, "Not many, of course, but Rakhas travel well, I assure you."

Gus hadn't laid eyes on an actual goblin in years. Gemmen had travelers from all over the world and probably even a gob or two brought in as a curiosity, but he had yet to spot one there. He had fought savage gobs in Rakhasin, of course, and even known a few of their more civilized brethren among the local auxiliary forces, but those either wore their native costume or were cloaked in ill-fitting human clothes. This one wore a suit that had clearly been tailored to his oddly proportioned frame, and that, combined with the glasses, made Gus count him among the strangest things he had ever seen.

The bureaucrat moved between them with an apologetic smile, apparently concerned he might need to defuse any potential panic Gus might express upon seeing the dressed-up gob. "I'm sorry, sir. This is Mister Salk … salcot …."

That wide goblin mouth curled up in what Gus took for a smirk and then that deep voice rumbled in, "Salka'tok'tok'ton," to the obvious relief of the bureaucrat fumbling with the staccato Rakhasin syllables. "Most of my human associates simply call me Salka. At the Council's request, I've been consulting on the Rakhasin exhibit, although at the moment they're insisting an awning is an architectural feature that may not extend across the designated walkways." That last bit came with a bit of venom towards the bureaucrat.

They both looked at him expectantly until Gus got the point and supplied, "Gus Baston. I'm here about Phand."

"Oh!" exclaimed the bureaucrat in sudden delight, clasping his hands together. From that failure to introduce himself in turn, Gus decided the man must be Ryerson and that secretary must be a more important position than he'd guessed. "I had heard that was on hold, what with the kidnapping and all. You brought the model?" When Gus looked confused, Ryerson gave a petulant frown and said, "Everyone has to provide their own model for the Exhibition map. Doctor Phand was made well aware of that on his last visit."

Something about that tugged at the corners of his memory, and suddenly Gus recalled the wire framework everyone was gushing over in Phand's offices. Looking at the model of modern Khanom, he replied, "No, sorry, I don't have it with me. That's not why I came." He tried to imagine it sitting with the others, and from his recollection, it was easily three or four times the size of the tallest of the beige towers currently on the model city. "Where will it sit, exactly?"

The bureaucrat seemed a little baffled by that bit of ignorance from one of Phand's, but the deep voiced gob helpfully supplied, "Embassy Park. It would definitely be the centerpiece of the fair, if it can be built in time."

Looking over that green space on the city's landscape, Gus pictured the model from the offices in Gemmen. The base of that model would fit almost exactly to the corners of Embassy Park. It would tower over the city at a seemingly impossible scale, and Gus shook his head in disbelief. No wonder everyone had been so impressed by it.

Huffing indignantly, Ryerson said, "Oh, no. No, no, no. If that tower can't be built, and I've heard several engineers argue it isn't even possible, the Exposition hardly needs it to draw the world's eye. We've already started connecting most of the city in the greatest electrical exhibit in history! All the street lamps up here are being replaced with electrics, and we'll even have electrical trams to move people about the city."

The Secretary grinned proudly and moved to the far side of the table, which elicited a bit of a familiar eye-rolling from Salka. Flipping a switch on the other side, little points of light erupted all along the city's streets, and before Gus could ask what a 'tram' was, the tiny abandoned carts around the park whirred to life and began sliding along the model streets, following below tiny wires strung along the avenues, driven by some mechanism beneath the table. The carts toured the city in small circuits as stark electric lights provided unflickering illumination.

"Wow. Will it really have all these wires up though? I'm surprised that with all the experienced miners here to do the work, you didn't go with an underground system, like in Gemmen."

The bureaucrat shook his head, "No, it was considered of course, but Miss Aliyah Gale suggested that an electric tram system would be just as effective and more of a showpiece than a buried train. Others agreed that, as the city is already known as a prominent center for mineral extraction, putting ourselves forward as mere diggers of tunnels would be ... inappropriate to our modern image."

Her name perked Gus's ears, and he asked, "I didn't realize she was on the Exposition Council. Is she very involved on the tower too?"

The goblin snorted and rumbled, "Not much happens in this town without her involvement."

That suggestion seemed to miff Ryerson, who shook his head and said, "Actually, she was the original dissenter to the tower project, and she abstained entirely from the budget fight."

Salka's wide mouth curled up, and he remarked, "Not that she needed to do much, with Thomas and Ulm suddenly turning against it."

Ryerson shrugged and said, "And yet everything has been approved. It's all down to Doctor Phand now."

Gus nodded. Ryerson's words further solidified Gus's suspicion that this kidnapping was somehow about the Exposition's tower, even if he wasn't yet sure why anyone would be so invested in stopping the thing. "Who else is on the Council?"

A wary look crept into the bureaucrat's eyes again; this was all the sort of information someone sent here by Doctor Phand would know, and Gus was sure Ryerson had begun to sense something else was afoot. "Currently the Exposition Council consists of Misters Thomas, Ulm, Sylvester, Beck, and of course Miss Aliyah Gale."

"How did they turn against the tower later? I thought they had already voted it in?"

Salka chuckled, explaining in his melodic voice, "Oh, no, nothing is ever that easy. It was approved before the Exposition was even officially slated to move forward. It was one of the first things they considered, and then months later they had to settle the budget. Out of nowhere, Thomas announced he was now against Phand's project and put forward a proposal slashing the budget, to try and kill it."

Ryerson scowled over at the goblin's gossip, but Salka ignored him and went on. "Originally Beck and Ulm argued with Thomas, but then on the day of the vote, Ulm changed his mind too and sided with Thomas. Miss Aliyah Gale abstained, and without her, there weren't enough votes to approve the tower's full budget.

"They ended up settling on half the city's original contribution and making Phand put up the rest in exchange for giving him a share of ticket sales for going up in the thing. I imagine Thomas and Ulm felt that even with that concession on the tickets, it would kill the tower, given how much it must surely cost."

For an uneducated savage, Gus felt Salka showed an amazing grasp of politics. Every time the goblin rumbled something out in perfect Verin, Gus was bemused by the bizarre disconnect with the inhuman visage from which the sound emerged. "So he had the money?"

Ryerson's eyes widened at that question, and Gus realized that asking it had given away that he wasn't exactly working with Doctor Phand on the tower project.

Salka grinned, shook his head, and then said, "Oh, I doubt it; the rumor was it was a sum in the millions. He and his partner came to town after that to raise funds, and the word was they had fallen short and would miss the deadline; but then he wired back that he had the money, and Misters Thomas and Sylvester went out to Gemmen to sign the final agreement."

Secretary Ryerson drew himself up and said, "Sir, I'm not sure what this is all about, but if you're not actually here on Exposition business, then I'm afraid you will have to leave. Do you have any actual business here, or are you just some sort of … gossip? Are you with the papers?"

Salka seemed more amused by the secretary than threatened by his ire, so Gus replied, "Well, what's this about his awning?"

"No!" exclaimed Ryerson, waving his arms to shoo them towards the door. "The awning can't go across the walkway. Both of you, out. Go on!"

The goblin grinned as if this sort of ejection were a common enough occurrence and paused only to pick up an umbrella leaning by the door along with an oversized black hat. Gus tipped his own hat to the nervous bureaucrat, and then followed Salka outside.

Once beyond the building's entrance and standing beneath the steely gaze of Khanom's stone tyrants of commerce, Salka donned his hat and then opened the umbrella, shading himself with a lacey black parasol obviously designed for widows in mourning. Chuckling at the ridiculous sight, Gus said, "For a gob, you sure seem to have a firm grasp of the politics of urban planning."

With a wide-mouthed grin, Salka replied, "Oh not all, sir. Everything is so much more complicated with burrows, where you build above or below your neighbors instead of just to the sides. Compared to tribal politics on such things, this is easy!"

Gus laughed at the idea, finding it believable, although he had a hard time picturing it. "Well, maybe so. Seems like you do know a thing or two about the Council's politics. Could I stand you for an early lunch? No tree rat out for you here, but maybe we can find someplace with squirrel—that's got to be close, right?"

"It's past my bedtime, sir," Salka said and peered quizzically up at Gus, large yellow eyes squinting at the light, even behind tinted lenses. "What are you looking for, anyway?"

Gus weighed his options. He was sure Phand's kidnapping had something to do with the tower he was building. With millions of peis in the balance, it was the only thing in Phand's life where the stakes would be high enough to justify orchestrating the spectacle of his kidnapping. That also meant whomever it was probably had some interest in those millions.

Salka was like Gus, enough of an outsider that he probably had to have a foot in with more unsavory elements to get ahead, but even as well dressed as he was, Gus found it impossible to imagine even Khanom's criminal underworld taking orders from a gob. That meant Salka's money must come from something else, although Gus couldn't imagine what it might be.

If Salka were somehow connected, Gus would be giving away that he was looking for them here, but after a moment, he decided to lay out his cards. "Doctor Phand. I think whoever arranged his disappearance is in Khanom and probably connected to the Exposition somehow. Maybe I should chat with the Councilors."

Salka snorted, and for a brief instant, Gus was flooded with the memories of fighting along the frontier in Rakhasin. Thousands of gobs leaping from the tall grasses, spears flying, and the primitive magic of the gob shamans sparking through the air in a weak attempt to approximate the devastation of the cannons raining grapeshot down upon them.

They would snort and growl and sing their sibilant war songs. The gobs might have been primitives, but he'd seen many men fall in their barbaric assaults. After Gedlund, all of that had seemed like a holiday, but it seemed the memory of it could still give him a brief jolt of adrenaline. Gus's face went into a stiff smile as he pushed back the recollection, and Salka continued on.

"Well, Mister Beck's with the rail company, and he's always travelling; he winters in Ganbai though, so no luck there. Sylvester's usually easy to meet with if he's in town, but his offices are somewhere out near the mines—I've only ever met him here. Ulm's on 12th and Queen's."

Fortunately, the gob's voice was unlike the raspy, clumsy Verin Gus had encountered from the natives in Rakhasin, and turning his eyes to the street for a moment let Gus pull himself out of his recollections. "What about Miss Aliyah Gale?"

That wide lipless mouth curved into a deep frown as Salka rumbled out, "I wouldn't recommend just dropping by Miss Aliyah Gale. You could leave your card, I suppose. She has a place on Queen's and 3rd."

"And Thomas?"

Salka's frown deepened a moment, then broke into wide grin and deep musical laughter, "He works down below, at his yards. His name is plastered on the side of the building; you can't possibly miss it."

"Wait, is Rain Thomas the Thomas from Thomas's Canned Sausages?" Gus was shocked and felt like an idiot for not having made the connection. The product had been such a common everyday object for years, and the idea that they might be associated with an actual person of the same name had never crossed his mind.

The gob laughed again and nodded, carefully keeping the widow's parasol between himself and the sun. Gus shook his head, trying to shake off the foolishness he felt. "Thanks. That's all helpful. Do you know Doctor Phand?"

"I'd hoped for that honor once his tower was approved, but so far I've only interacted with his partner." Salka's expressions were tricky to read, but Gus had some experience in it from gambling with his sort in Rakhasin, and the well-dressed gob seemed legitimately friendly but tired.

"Any chance you've seen Saucier about lately? I'd heard he was out this way." Salka responded with just a shake of his head, and Gus suspected his window for extracting useful information was drawing to a close. "I probably owe you a drink or something at least. Where can I find you later?"

With a chuckle, the gob fished a calling card out of his pocket and handed it to Gus. It read *Salka'tok'tok'ton, Viridian Club, 6th and Blisan, Khanom, Aelfua.* "I'm here most evenings. I haven't seen him lately, but it's one of Richard Saucier's favorite haunts whenever he's in town. You should come by."

Saucier had met with someone who signed off as 'D.M.', and Gus supposed he might find them at the Viridian, but he could hardly ask the gob for the initials of everyone he might have met there. At least the false Alice Phand was distinctive, even if Gus didn't know her real name yet. "You have any tall blondes?" Gus asked, looking over the card.

Either the gob spent so much time at the club he'd had cards printed with it as his address, or he was the owner. A gob owning a fancy club seemed unlikely, but then so did the idea that the owner would let one just hang around long enough for one to print cards with it as his address. A waiter or other employee wouldn't usually have a need for calling cards.

The gob smiled in amusement, an expression so easy to read that Gus wondered if Salka had practiced at making more human expressions. "Not tonight, but we've got a new act I think you'll enjoy. Come by—you can stand me that drink."

Gus laughed and pocketed that card, "Yeah, I'll bet."

Salka tipped his hat and then strolled down the lane, leaving Gus to his thoughts. Miss Aliyah Gale had opposed the tower and was apparently a power of sorts here in Khanom, but if she had arranged the kidnapping to stop the tower, why didn't she just chime in on the vote against the tower's budget to stop it then? Why was she meeting with Phand apart from the other Councilors?

Thomas and Ulm both voted for the tower, but something changed their minds between the first vote and the second. Maybe the tower wasn't the issue at all, but if not, then why was Saucier still missing? Could he have disappeared to take out some grudge against his partner?

And why go to the bother to kidnap Doctor Phand? Kidnappers wanted something a dead victim wouldn't get them, and with no ransom demanded, it must be something Phand knew or could do for them while alive.

Tumbling through his thoughts, he looked up at the street signs. From what he remembered of the map, Miss Aliyah Gale's office was closest, but if she was as major a player as the discussion at the Exposition office indicated, then whatever ruse he could work to get a moment of her time would probably only work once. Once she knew him as an inquiry agent, he wouldn't be likely to get another chance to interview her.

He didn't know enough yet to ask her all the right questions, and tipping his suspicions early could make things go sideways if she was involved. A common criminal could only go so far underground, but someone like Miss Aliyah Gale, who could buy up entire rail cars on a whim, could easily disappear off to Mazhar and live like the queen of the Tuls.

Looking along the lane, he decided it might be easiest to start downhill and work his way up. For the first time, he noticed the double streetlights along Queen's—electrics going in to replace the old gas lamps. Men were hard at work bringing in the future, heedlessly building it atop the remains of the recent past. How much easier it would be if the past could simply vanish the way the Elves had.

~

Sara Calfaur, "A Response to Mr. Allison's Letter on Keat's Field"

To be sure, the rush of fortune hunters to Keat's Field would challenge anyone. Even if Sheriff Sorley cannot maintain the peace in the face of such difficulty, it is ill-becoming of Mister Allison to question the wisdom of the people's choice in selecting their champion.

Amid all the chaos and lawlessness surrounding it, that frontier village still stands, proud and prosperous. It would be a testament to the skill and suitability of any candidate holding the position of Sheriff under such trying circumstances, and the fact that he again questions Sheriff Sorley's qualifications shows his true concern is not the security of Keat's Field but rather his masculine insecurity here at home.

– Khanom Daily Converser, 13 Tal. 389
(Reprinted from the *Gemmen Herald*, 11 Tal. 389)

~

- CHAPTER 16 -

In search of a cab, Gus drifted down Queen's and ended up walking alongside Palace Park. Across the street, he could see the curious one-sided trees again, which he now realized once would have grown pressed against the walls of the queen's palace or at base of the mysterious Embassy Building.

Why the trees had not begun to fill out in the nearly four decades after those buildings vanished was another mystery in itself. Then again, he supposed with an entire civilization disappearing overnight, some residual strangeness was to be expected.

Ahead, a construction crew wrestled with a gigantic spool of wire. Following the wire as it extended into the distance, Gus wondered what they all connected to.

His understanding was that, somewhere, some great engine had to be running to generate the electricity. He suspected it was yet another of the many great engines adding to the bank of sooty clouds below the sparkling upper city. Those clouds of soot trapped below the plateau seemed likely to be more of that residual strangeness.

Gus crossed the street to avoid the construction and found himself outside the stern-faced façade of the First Bank of Khanom. He never understood why banks took such pleasure in pronouncing themselves 'first' in an area; it always seemed to indicate that they had bungled the job sufficiently to give rise to demand for a second bank. Lost in his musings on the city's financial systems, Gus paid little attention to the people outside until he nearly bumped into one he actually recognized.

"Dolly Dench!" he proclaimed in surprise, shocked to see the unmistakable scarecrow frame of his disgraced acquaintance loitering in a public place. After being shunned even in impolite society, Gus had expected to find Dolly hiding out someplace a bit skulkier.

For his part, Dolly looked horrified at the sound of his name as he spun to face his accuser. Dolly stared a moment, not recognizing Gus at first, the wheels spinning behind his eyes as he tried to place him. At last they clicked in recognition, and Dolly gave a nervous smile, clearly uncertain if Gus was on his trail or someone else's.

"Gus, old boy," he ventured, "It's been an age. I've been going by Adolphus here. Given the unpleasantness back west, I decided it best to use my full name for a spell."

Dolly seemed even thinner than Gus had last seen him and looked a fair bit older than he should for only being in his middle-thirties, but Gus supposed that was only natural, given the stresses of his misanthropy.

Gus smiled like they were old friends and said, "What're you doing here? I'd heard they had you down for a stretch for doing a kinchin lay."

That was a lie, of course. Gus knew the police had never been able to frame a trial to fit the exceedingly careful Dolly Dench, but their final attempt had ruined his reputation, which might have been Clarke's entire purpose in leveling the charges. Only the worst sort would work with a crook that had done the kinchin lay, and Dolly was snooty enough to quickly piss off that sort of criminal element.

Dolly's eyes narrowed, a scowl crossing his face as he lowered his voice and hissed out, "That was a false charge! Everyone knows I'm well above that sort of thing. Only the lowest of the low would ever—"

When Gus grinned with bemusement at the opening of his tirade, Dolly sighed and dropped it. Turning his eyes back towards his study of the bank, Dolly said, "I slipped the leash and made my way here. If word of that nonsense gets out around here, I'll be ruined again, and my Ogrian is still terrible."

'Ogrian' was the Garren word for Garren, and if Dolly was studying their language, then needing it was a possibility the man took very seriously. The thought of Dolly being chased out all the way to Garren was funny, but things weren't that bad for him yet. With his long coat and continued focus on the bank, it was quickly apparent to Gus that Dolly wasn't just here casing the place for later.

Watching people coming and going from the bank, Gus wasn't certain who the man's accomplices were, and unable to resist needling Dolly a little more, he asked, "So are you the stall?"

That offended scowl reappeared and Dolly replied, "Please. We just move slowly until the rush before lunch. We wait for a sloppy withdrawal, and it's a simple weed." Gus nodded, following Dolly's gaze until he was able to pick out the crew's stall loitering closer to the door.

As Gus watched, a man bustled out of the bank, conspicuously pausing at the door to adjust his hat, which immediately set the stall into motion towards a harried looking fellow who exited the bank shortly after, carrying the narrow folio that held his bank records and recent withdrawal.

"It's been a pleasure, so if you'll pardon me," Dolly murmured, slipping away to close in on the mark just a few steps further away than his stall.

To untrained eyes, the scene would seem perfectly innocent, one man pausing by the door as two others headed in to do business with the bank. The mark would be forced to weave around the man adjusting his hat as Dolly and his stall came towards the bank from opposite directions.

Usually the newly arriving customers would probably step aside for the poor mark, and everyone would just continue on. Today, if all went to plan, the stall would bump into the mark and then pause to offer his apologies, perhaps dusting off the man's coat as if somehow it had gotten dirty in the process.

Once that happened, Dolly would be the hook and reach in to quickly slip the cash out of the mark's bank folio. The mark would be on his way, not noticing his lightened load until much later. Even if he got wise, he would never notice Dolly slip by, and the stall, the only one of the three who caught the mark's attention, wouldn't have the cash if the police searched him.

Today was the poor mark's lucky day. As the stall drew close, Gus faked a cough as he called out, "Lam!"

Just as he suspected, Dolly's cues hadn't changed since he ran this routine in Gemmen, and with well-drilled nonchalance, the stall veered away, ducking past the mark without providing the crucial distraction the hook required for his weeding. The man adjusting his hat suddenly found its proper fit and made a show of heading down the street to go about his business. The mark, none the wiser, tucked his folio tightly beneath his arm and went on his way.

Dolly, of course, knew right away where that false call had come from and stomped indignantly back to Gus. "What in the hells was that for?"

Gus grinned impishly and replied, "I wasn't done talking to you! I'm looking for someone—tall blonde woman from Khanom, a few inches taller than me, handsome enough but big, muscle not fat, with either money or maybe just connections to money. Might be with a club that wears a lot of green, but that might just be a misdirect. She's part of a snatch job I need to track down."

Hands on his hips, Dolly looked particularly ridiculous in the oversized coat he wore for weeding. "What makes you think you can come here, ruin my business, and then start asking for favors?"

"Well, there's the classic approach, where I could tell the local police about you, but that's probably not good for my reputation, eh Dolly? You know all about the dangers of reputation by now, I'm sure." Gus gave the man a mild smile and let him work the true threat out for himself. After a beat, Gus added, "But we're old friends, and what good is a friend you can't call on for the occasional favor?"

After a moment of defiant glaring did not make Gus apologize and slink away, Dolly sighed. "Fine. Just this one thing though, then you're gone. Blonde girl, maybe wears green. I'll check, but that's not much to go on. With all the nonsense up north lately, there's plenty more blondes going around, you know."

With a grin and a pat on the shoulder, Gus added, "This one is tall and has connections to someone with big money and big plans. I'm sure you'll come up with something." He gave Dolly a parting wink then turned towards the corner to flag down a cab.

Lately Emily had been doing more and more of the necessary rumormongering, leaving him to the physical legwork like trailing people around the city. It wasn't exactly what he'd hired her for, but she seemed to know a lot of people and did it well. He was happy to see he wasn't losing his own touch for it.

She'd have been proud of him he thought, for handling that without having to resort to bribes or helping Dolly with some sort of scam, but then he realized she probably would have something religious against blackmail. He couldn't remember if Caerleon's book had anything specific to say on that topic, but it seemed like the sort of thing the Trinity was usually against.

The first cab he flagged flatly refused as soon as he asked the driver to take him to Thomas's office. For the second, Gus hopped inside before telling the man his destination. The driver asked for an outrageous fee, and when Gus objected, the man pointed out that it was down below, and he would have a hard time finding a decent fare for the trip back up.

Gus offered to hire him for the return trip, and the cabbie replied that there wasn't enough money to convince him to wait around the yards. It did not bode well for the return, but Gus agreed to the exorbitantly priced one-way trip, and the cabbie called the horses into motion.

The upper city was surprisingly flat for a metropolis built atop a hill, and Gus idly wondered if its shape was naturally occurring, if the Elves had smoothed the thing over with magic or just stamped it down with an army of slaves. When the cab reached the edge of the nicer parts of town, there was a noticeable jolt as it crested the steep angle to begin their descent.

They did not get far before hitting the layer of smoke that separated the city. First came a light breeze blowing across the slope, and then they plunged into a bank of foul smelling and gritty smoke that stank of ash and industry. Gus began coughing as soon as they passed inside, and looking ahead, he saw the cabbie had pulled a kerchief over his mouth, apparently well prepared for just this sort of occasion.

On the train, they had sped through this layer of airborne filth in the blink of an eye while safely tucked inside the closed train windows, but the horses did not move as quickly. They vigorously shook their heads as they passed through the gray, then snorted and bobbed in equine relief when they finally emerged on the other side. Able to breathe more deeply again, Gus quickly discovered that although the thick layer of smoky fog had been passed, the air below it still stank.

The strange belt of fouled air left the city's worst neighborhoods lining the gray bank, separated from its nicest districts by that intangible wall. The cloud extended overhead as the ground sloped away. Tenements, dive bars, and cheaper sorts of shops lined the upper slope, places now crumbling from poverty rather than actual age, all cloaked in perpetual gloom by the sooty exhalations of the businesses just below them.

The buildings they passed next were still relatively young, but all bore stripes of sooty discoloration along their sides, which Gus took as evidence that there must be some sort of tide to the wind above so that it occasionally drove the gray lower to the ground. Looking around, he realized that on the slopes there was not a brick to be seen—all the buildings were wooden, cheaply painted, with businesses frequently identified by names that were painted directly on the storefront, some barely legible beneath the soot.

Everything on the slope was packed so tightly that Gus wondered how they hadn't already all burned down. Khanom was much drier than Gemmen, as evidenced by the lack of lingering spring snow. Living in a tent city through Rakhasin's dry season had long ago taught him the dangers of fire in a dry climate.

Even the white roads of the Elves were stained gray here, and unlike the pristine avenues above, they were as thickly littered with a city's usual detritus as his own neighborhood in Gemmen. With the sun unable to grace them through the swirling ring of gray, the slopes were colder than the upper city, and ice clung to a few of the downspouts. A few people wandered up or down the hill on various errands, shabby coats pulled tight to ward off the chill.

Below the slope, Khanom was ringed by smokestacks sprouting from dozens of large factories. The ring of wind had to be something else the Elves had left behind; while some academics had spent their entire lives studying magical phenomena, humans had never mastered it. Some gob shamans claimed to be able to call rain, but that had always seemed like primitive flimflam.

Looking up at it swirling overhead, Gus wondered if the smoke ever escaped somehow, or if the cloud below the upper city would just grow thicker and thicker. Would it get closer to the ground as it grew or just spread out for miles around?

The grimy cloud thinned just beyond the factories, and though the smell still lingered, sunlight began to dapple through. Adjacent to the factories stood large brick buildings five or six stories tall, each painted with company insignias. Atop each of those adjacent structures was a forest of hanging laundry on improvised lines and hangars, and after a moment of contemplation, Gus realized they must be dormitories for the workers.

A few women wandered in and out on their own errands, as their other halves likely hewed within the adjacent factory. Children would occasionally sprint by, engaged in games amidst the grime of the streets with toys made from whatever garbage clever little hands could find. There was a definite flavor unique to the garbage of each dorm they passed, and Gus wondered if the children gathered to trade cast-offs from their specific factories, making treasure of the neighbors' unusual trash.

Beyond the factory dormitories was a scattered assortment of warehouses and small businesses—shops of the sort more successful factory workers might frequent, physicians and the like. Next was a major rail hub farther down the line than Gus had ridden and far more utilitarian in design—the sort of thing intended more for cargo than passengers. Just beyond that hub stood the yards.

As they drew nearer to the yards, the stench struck like a physical blow, and Gus understood why the cabbie had refused to linger here. Whether the sooty chemical smell of the factories had faded away or he had just gotten used to it, once at the yards a curling, visceral stink gradually mixed in and soon overpowered all else.

Gus's eyes watered, and his stomach struggled to hold on to its contents as every muscle in his body contracted in an urge to vomit.

The air was so fouled by the odor of rancid offal, he barely noticed the hack draw to a stop, and the cabbie had to shout back for his fee twice before Gus collected himself enough to fish out his wallet and pay the man.

Outside the cab, animal noises mixed with the loud whines and whinnies of the machines adjacent to them. Yardmen shouted back and forth, driving pigs and cows and other livestock into various fenced-in areas where they would await slaughter. As soon as Gus stepped out, the cabbie leaned back to slam the door closed behind him and immediately set his horses back into motion.

Away from the Elven road, only mud tracks passed between wooden fences, porcine snouts pressing between the slats for relief from the crowding within. Circling the edges a bit, Gus eventually found the only path a man could follow without ruining his pants and concluded the distant structure it led to must house the business office. Following the track of paving stones, Gus passed through dozens of separated pens, the rows of which extended at least a mile.

Stepping inside, Gus found the stench only slightly abated. He expected to see a reception area but was instead greeted by a sawdust-covered floor surrounded by narrow mazes navigated by fattened cattle. There were occasional shouts from men working the chutes, accompanied by bovine screams of panic that arose above the general clamor.

His only likely lead to any sort of office was a rough wooden staircase that led upwards to a door. Climbing up, Gus opened the door, stepped inside, and suddenly found himself in the reception area he had expected below. It looked the same as nearly any office he had ever seen, aside from the large window that oversaw the slaughter. Many factory owners had similar overlooks from their offices, but the scene below was hardly one of orderly manufacture.

The receptionist asked his business, the man's voice expertly raised above the muted din filtering through the windows. Gus gave a confident smile as he offered his name and told the man he needed a brief chat with Mister Thomas. He was asked to wait a moment, and the man rose from his desk and passed through a door that presumably led into Mister Thomas's private office.

Watching herds pushed into lines and driven towards the grim-faced men awaiting them reminded Gus all too much of his time in the army, so he instead turned his attention to the art along the walls. Thomas's collection in the reception area consisted entirely of maps. Railway maps sketched out the placement of tracks across Aelfua, with notations made for the distance to each point from Khanom. A broader map of the world stood alongside, also replete with cryptic abbreviations that likely only made sense to the meat-packing business.

Most engaging for Gus was an overview of the magnate's stockyards, which gave a more complete vision of Thomas's wealth than could be seen through the black wall that divided it from the city above. Apart from the yards, several of the adjacent factories were his as well, and his workers dwelt in the dormitories between. He seemed to own a small town of his own out here on the outskirts of Khanom, but nothing in the upper city was marked as his.

Judging by the map of his holdings in Khanom and the apparent commercial reach of his products, Gus suspected Thomas had to be one of the wealthiest men in the Empire.

Another round of shouts and lowing rattled the glass in the window and made Gus wonder why a man of Thomas's standing would choose to spend his days here, of all places. To run everything labeled on the map would take thousands, perhaps tens of thousands, of employees, most of whom must surely labor in more fragrant locales than this one.

After a few moments, the receptionist stepped back out and opened his mouth to speak but was cut off by Thomas's loud snarl from the next room, "Come on in, Inspector."

Thomas did not sound particularly happy to see him again, but as Gus recalled from their earlier encounter, he did not seem pleased with much. When Gus entered the man's office, Thomas was busy jotting on various sheets of papers, growling at a few of them as if the page itself had disappointed him.

Like the reception area outside, Thomas's office had a window from which its owner could look down over the action, and like the window in the room outside, it only slightly muted the awful din of it. The rest of the room was decorated only with corkboards covered in a fluttering array of paper. Thomas used some form of shorthand Gus did not recognize, so the notes may as well have been written in Tuls for all he could make of them.

Without looking up from his work, Thomas demanded, "What brings you out east, Inspector Baston?"

"Same case, I'm afraid. Still tracking down Doctor Phand. Haven't seen him, I suppose?"

Thomas frowned and looked up at him, peering over a pair of spectacles he hadn't worn in Gemmen. Removing them, he shook his head and replied, "No, of course not. I've barely been out of the office since I returned." The sausage magnate rose to his feet with a wince and unsteady tremor that Gus sympathized with.

The man paused to peer suspiciously out his window over the dozen or so workers he could see there as if he half-expected to spot them cheating him somehow. Catching them at nothing that required his intervention, Thomas limped out from behind his desk and said, "Can I offer you a drink, Inspector?"

"I seldom turn one down, sir," he replied with a grin, and Thomas moved towards a side table and poured out two glasses of something brown from a fancy crystal decanter that did not look to fit the man's practical tastes in the least. "I must say, when we met in Gemmen, I had no idea you were the man behind the canned sausages. I'm a great admirer of them, eat them all the time."

Thomas smirked and handed over a glass before downing his own in one quick toss. "Glad to hear it. Haven't had one in years, myself. Wife says they're bad for my digestion." He looked Gus over for a moment as if reassessing him in a more critical light, knowing more about his appetites. "So what brings you to me? It's a long trip just to tell me you like my product."

It was the first time Gus had observed the man being even remotely companionable, and he wondered if the usual unpleasant demeanor was the result of travel fatigue or just a habitual result of working in this noisome facility. It was something of a relief since a Thomas at ease would probably share more than an antagonistic one.

While detecting-inspectors of the Crossing were often consulted for their expertise all over the Empire, they were technically part of Gemmen's police force. They needed more extensive approval to operate outside the city proper, but Gus didn't know if Thomas knew that. Gus took a sip of whatever the drink was; it was surprisingly unfamiliar but definitely alcoholic, cloyingly sweet, and very rough.

Forcing a friendly chuckle, Gus tried to make himself sound casual as he said, "Just looking into Phand's business associates—the usual stuff in this sort of case." Thomas nodded, apparently buying into the idea of his second interview as proper procedure. "When the Exposition Council originally voted on Phand's tower, you approved it, but then you changed your mind and tried to stop it from being built with the finance vote. Can you tell me why?"

With a roll of his eyes, the potted-meat king gave a snort and pushed a stack of papers aside, so he could lift up a small frame he kept on his desk. Thomas turned it around, and Gus leaned in for a better look. The frame held an old daguerreotype of a smiling young woman wearing a wide floral bonnet.

"Missus Thomas. We would meet in that park when we were courting. There wasn't much else to see up there at the time, but we walked through it quite a bit. Haven't been there in years, but apparently, she's still fond of the idea of the place. When the tower was announced in the paper, she was livid." He poured himself another drink, "I've been trying to kill the thing ever since." Looking back to Gus, he caught himself on the phrasing and quickly amended, "The tower project, I mean. Nothing to do with Phand."

Gus gave an understanding nod. Despite the slightly unpleasant initial experience, he found Thomas's beverage of choice had a much nicer aftertaste and left him feeling pleasantly warm. He took another sip and asked, "Can you think of anyone else who might object to the tower?"

Mister Thomas shook his head, tossing back a second drink. "Plenty of people don't like it, artists and such, but no one serious, and you said you're looking into his business associates, right? Since you know how I voted, I assume you know Sandal Ulm switched his vote too. He fought me all the way to keep the project when I reversed but then suddenly threw his lot in with me when I thought up shorting the finances. Did you talk to him?"

"Not yet. Can you tell me about him? What's his line?" Gus asked as he drained the last of the unfamiliar beverage. By the finish he was quite enjoying it, and he'd have asked for the name if he imagined he could afford it. Thomas probably had to pay a stiff price to import it from wherever it originated.

"Furniture, maybe? He's inconstant—one of those aggressive up-and-coming types with fingers in everything. His kind never last long. He even has an office full of women, like a Sakloch harem." Thomas shook his head, pulling a silver-headed cane from where it leaned on the wall and hobbling towards the door. "Never told me what changed his mind, just flipped from praising the spectacle of it to claiming it was totally inappropriate for the heart of our city."

Gus envied the cane, but then Thomas was older, married, and far more successful, so could afford to be seen using one. Something about his remark struck a chord, and Gus asked, "It is the heart of the city, isn't it? Why hasn't anyone built there already?"

"Politics," was the heavy-breathed reply as the man hobbled towards the door. Clearly not a man with much fondness for politics, Thomas snarled out, "When we first settled here, it was all park. You've got to have permits to build up top, and it was such a good spot, people fought hard to keep each other from taking it, each imagining that they'd be the ones to build something there later.

"Plus, Miss Aliyah Gale's fought to keep them as parks for the past decade or so. Women love parks." He paused, taking a deep breath before attempting to open the door, so Gus quickly leaned over to open it for him.

"She's on the Council too, isn't she? And against the tower?"

Thomas nodded, and said, "Voted against it from the start. She's got deep roots in this city. Lot of power for a woman on her own, which is why she's so involved in politics. Always trouble, women in politics." He waved at his receptionist through the door, and the man dashed off down the stairs, apparently well acquainted with whatever Thomas wanted.

Gus grinned at the comment about women in politics and, thinking of a headline he had seen recently, he remarked, "It's a new age. There's even a lady sheriff down in Rakhasin now." That only elicited a derisive snort from Thomas, so Gus shrugged and then asked, "With so much influence, how did Miss Aliyah Gale lose the first vote?"

"Numbers," was the gruff reply. The receptionist came back up, hovering nearby with the air of a man impatient to interrupt them but one who had been growled at for that sort of thing before. Thomas looked up at him and pronounced, "I have things to attend, Inspector. If you need something more, either write it out, schedule an appointment, or talk with my petitioner."

Gus nodded and thanked him for his time, not wanting to wait to watch Mister Thomas awkwardly scale down the stair. Stepping outside, Gus saw that a private coach sat open, awaiting the slow descent of its owner. There were no cabs anywhere in sight, so Gus began his trudge out of the yards, grimly looking forward to exchanging the stench of the muck for the soot-choked air of the slums.

Louis would have waited for him, even here.

~

Advertisement for Ulm & Associates

Typists sought. Female applicants welcome.

Can you make sense of an educated man's dictation about something more than mere quantity? Nimble fingers alone are not enough, but at Ulm & Assoc. value is placed upon the enlightened mind, regardless of sex. Preference given for those fluent in both Robb-Michaels and Sepelak Universal. Typing speed is of the essence. Applications should be submitted in person to 1224 Queen's, Fl. 15.

– *Khanom Daily Converser*, 13 Tal. 389

~

- CHAPTER 17 -

After the Gedlund hearings, Gus had briefly travelled far enough up the social ladder to discover that established power felt little need to advertise. The fanciest dinner clubs had the smallest signs. Major players well settled in commerce would put their firms on a building's directory but never bother with a plaque outside.

Experience taught him that an influential up-and-comer like Ulm would want to plaster his name on the outside of a big tower, so Gus was surprised to find Ulm merely one of many tenants in the building on 12th and Queen's. The map of Thomas's vast holdings had made Gus imagine Khanom's real estate came cheaply, but if a city leader like Ulm lacked a building of his own, then it seemed possible Gus had just been overpaying for sausages.

Nevertheless, it was still an impressive building, and according to the directory by the door, Ulm's offices took up the fourteenth and fifteenth floors at the top. The outside of the building was decorated with a collection of strict geometries, but inside the lobby, there was a sculpted mural depicting faceless, angular brutes hard at work on abstract machinery. Gus wondered who it was that sculpted all this industrialist décor and if it paid well. Although he'd never tried his hand at sculpting, faceless people and gears seemed like a pretty easy bit to do.

The elevator attendant opened the gate on the fifteenth floor, and there was no question this was the place as they were immediately faced with an enormous sign that read ULM & ASSOC. Gus supposed he was trying to make up for its absence outside.

Despite Thomas's description of Ulm's operation, Gus was still surprised to discover a woman sitting at the front desk playing receptionist. Emily greeted people at the door to his own office, so it was perhaps a bit hypocritical, but it seemed to him that if Ulm could afford offices this fancy, he could have afforded a real receptionist to go with them.

Cheap labor might be good business sense, but it was hardly the sort of image one usually wanted to project to visitors. There was something pleasant about being greeted by the prim redhead when he stepped inside though, and as she sashayed away to inform her boss of the visitor, Gus could not help but wonder if perhaps he was underestimating her contribution to the establishment.

Moments later, Ulm came bursting into the reception area with the receptionist on his heels. He smiled broadly, grabbing Gus's hand in his and pumping it firmly, "Mister Baston! Welcome, welcome! Lana tells me you're from Phand & Saucier. What can I do for you?" Gus shook his hand in turn, having trouble matching Ulm's intense enthusiasm as his attention was drawn back to the receptionist returning to her desk.

"From? No, I'm just here *about* them, I'm afraid. Doctor Phand, actually. Do you have a moment to chat?"

Ulm's head bobbed up and down several times, his face going from a clownishly broad smile into an almost mocking look of deep concern as he replied, "Of course, of course. Back to my office then? Follow me." Gus studied the man's face carefully, but his exaggerated expressions were so artificial they would be of little help in reading the man's true reactions.

Ulm gave a decisive nod, then spun on his heel to return the way he came, pausing only for a quick wink to the receptionist, who replied with a gamely coy grin. As they passed deeper into the Ulm's operation, Gus couldn't help but notice the man had stationed his all-female typing pool on the upper floor outside his office.

Such utilitarian work would normally end up stationed on the floor below, leaving more space for Ulm's fellow corporate officers, but instead there were rows of desk machines operated by women. They all wore the usual long, dark blue skirts and white blouses, but here and there a few had flowers pinned to their tops. Some even had similar decorative little touches on their desks, giving the whole place a more feminine atmosphere.

The women looked up and smiled pleasantly as Ulm strode by with Gus in tow, and given the relaxed atmosphere of the office, Gus could see why a man like Thomas disapproved. Noticing his gaze, Ulm offered in a paternal tone, "I had the ladies stationed up here to reduce the chances of any unpleasantness with the gentlemen in my employ. This way, they always know I'm keeping an eye on things. Keeps everyone civil."

Gus didn't believe a word of it but nodded knowingly as if it were a wise move on the boss's part to think of such things. They stepped into Ulm's office, which provided a lovely vantage on the rest of the city, including a sliver of Embassy Park, which was visible just down the street. The room was nearly as elaborately cluttered as Richard Saucier's home had been, although the artwork on the walls had been restricted to more classical pieces suitable to an office—stern looking predecessors, bowls of fruit, that sort of thing.

Closing the door, Ulm stepped over towards the window and peered at the street below as he said, "Shame about Doctor Phand! I do hope he's alright. Did you have any news about him?"

Gus joined him by the window, glancing down and suddenly recalling he had never been inside a building this tall before. From this southern vantage, he could see over the closest buildings, picking out the edges of Khanom's sooty girdle, and even see past the seemingly endless rows of Thomas's stockyard to the broad river that meandered through the lowlands beyond and rolled out beyond the horizon.

Looking straight down at the gleaming white streets below, as Ulm did, made Gus's stomach roil. He goggled a moment at the vertiginous perspective and then stepped back, but Ulm remained there, staring down at the streets far below.

It occurred to Gus that as Ulm was surely used to this by now, the man's lack of eye contact was studied, rather than truly distracted. Not sure what that intentional remove meant, Gus simply said, "Not yet, but I'm sure he'll turn up. I'm looking into his business dealings here in town. You know him?"

Ulm hesitated, then replied, "We've met. I don't know him well, but I've been a great admirer of his work. I'd hoped to draw his firm in to do something here in town." As far as Gus knew, Ulm had no reason to think he was from the Crossing, like Thomas did, which made him wonder why such a busy man would indulge the interview.

"Something like that tower?" Gus asked, gesturing out towards the sliver of park visible below, where the tower would soar above the surroundings.

"Well, like it, perhaps, but not that, obviously. I've always opposed it." Ulm lied so smoothly that Gus was momentarily tempted to believe him. "So few cities have the blessing of much green at their heart, and I've long said we should keep those open. I really think it will lend an air of respectable civility as people pass between exhibit halls on the electric trams."

"Didn't you vote in favor of the tower at first?" Gus patted at his jacket as if looking for his notes. He had none, but people seldom waited for him to find them when it seemed like they were about to be caught in a lie.

"Oh, no! No, of course not. As I said, I'm a great admirer of Phand & Saucier's work in other cities, and admittedly I pushed to have them present something for our Exposition, but that tower was never suitable." He shook his head, looking out to where it would sit, "A hideous, industrial spike of iron, here of all places? Inappropriate."

Frowning, his eyes grew distant as if troubled by something he could not quite remember.

"So what did you want to bring him in to do? Seems like Khanom's already set for bridges and such." Gus had no idea if that was true but felt confident Ulm would quickly correct him if not, and if it was, Ulm would be forced to come up with some more complicated explanation. Ulm gave an eager grin at the question, and Gus briefly wondered which it would be, but then Ulm went to his desk, pulling out a map that he rolled out over the surface.

"Well, I've got several factories down below, but I just acquired this one here," he jabbed his finger at an intersection as if Gus should know it, "An old Knox works, where they made shotguns or something. Now, as you can see, it's not far from my new electrical plant, here, which offers a perfect opportunity to leverage my production there by using it to enhance the plant here."

"Electric shotguns?"

Ulm frowned at him and looked away as if to consider the idea, then shook his head. "No, just a factory with lights or maybe even running some of the machines electrically."

"What is it you do, exactly?"

Sandal Ulm seemed taken aback by the question and replied in a mystified tone, "I'm a businessman, Mister Baston. The company, you mean? It started as furniture making, but then to streamline it, I bought up a lot of the local logging operations and started investing in futures on—well, the point is, we do all sorts of things now. This new building I bought to turn into a factory for manufacturing matches. More uses for the wood our other operations produce that can't go into furniture."

"But you're putting in electric lights? There's a bit of irony, using the electric lights for making matches."

Ulm laughed and nodded. "Well, it will be a diminishing market, sure, but it's not as if everyone will switch to electric overnight. Besides, furnaces aren't electric, and people need heat. And of course, people will always smoke, and you can't light a cigarette with electricity."

They laughed at that together, and Gus let that brief moment of camaraderie linger while he tried to think of how to get more information from the man. Something was off with Ulm, and uncertain how to find it, he just went back to his question about the votes. "So from the beginning, it was just you and Miss Aliyah Gale opposing the tower, right?"

The change in topic seemed to startle Ulm, but he nodded and said, "Well, mostly just me. She abstained. The others were all for it though, so we would have lost the vote against even if she'd held firm."

"But that was on the second vote."

Ulm just ignored Gus's comment and looked back down at his map, his eyes sliding from down below towards the upper city, where the Exposition would be. His voice grew distant and he said, "It's not as if we'd need the tower, anyway. It would just be an eyesore. Inappropriate, here of all places."

He quickly shook off that distracted air, grinned up at Gus and said, "It will be a cultural touchstone for the world. We'll have artists and exhibits from every corner of the globe! Dancers, singers, even a complete goblin burrow people can visit!"

That last part threw Gus for a loop and momentarily distracted him from sorting through Ulm's odd demeanor about the tower. Salka had mentioned a Rakhasin exhibit, but Gus had just assumed he meant it related to the human colony on the surface. "Visit? Like, underground?"

In the army, Gus had spent several years fighting savage tribes of gobs in Rakhasin, even if now all anyone else remembered about his service was the year in Gedlund. With their diminutive height and keen eyesight, the gobs made their tunnels small and dark. The idea of tourists crawling through the darkness seemed absurd, and seeing his reaction, Ulm's face split into a keen grin.

"We have a tribe that will come in and dig out tunnels, making a whole burrow but with windows peeking in and a few dim lights inside so that people can see what goes on. The gobs will live there year-round and perform shows up top—staging, doing little tribal dances, that sort of thing."

"Singing creepy songs and killing the local farmers. Yeah, I'm familiar with 'em."

Ulm laughed and shook his head, "No, no, they'll be quite tame, I assure you. We've had one as a prominent entertainer in the community. The Honeyfugler. Amazing voice, which I'm sure he'll be lending to the Exposition as well. They're a very musical people, and not all their songs are about killing farmers. The Exposition will show that and so much more! It will amaze and educate the world."

Gus chuckled at the gob's nickname; he supposed that had to be the one he had met this morning. Something about the spark in Ulm's eyes when talking about the Exposition seemed more sincere than the rest. More honest. Hoping to leverage that sincerity, Gus tried to tie it back to his inquiry. "So you don't think you'll need Phand's tower to draw attention to it?"

"The tower? It would just be a hideous industrial spike of iron. Inappropriate. Especially here, of all places."

Gus narrowed his eyes at that response and studied Ulm's face, trying to make sense of the man. "Why is it inappropriate here, of all places?"

"A hideous, industrial spike of iron, rising from the heart of the city, where once the queen's palace stood?" He seemed incredulous that Gus could even ask such a thing, then frowned and said simply, "Inappropriate."

Ulm seemed on the edge of outrage at the very idea, and not wanting to incite him over it, Gus just nodded slowly and said, "I suppose so." That seemed to mollify Ulm a bit, so Gus changed the topic, saying, "We may be looking at the work of some sort of secret society. Are you familiar with any in town? Particularly one that wears green?"

Ulm frowned again, but then his face took to a more practiced-seeming stern expression, like a mask he put on to cover the frown. The man shook his head, then walked back from the map at his desk and gripped Gus by the shoulder. "No, Mister Baston. There are no secret societies in Khanom. That's something from back west, where people are idle enough for such pursuits. Now, if you'll excuse me, I have other appointments."

His words were firm, authoritative punctuations as he pressed Gus towards the door of his office, calling a definite end to the interview. It was such an odd change that Gus briefly considered changing his own tone to match—digging in his heels and demanding to know what was happening. That might lead to questions about his actual authority though, which wouldn't end well for him.

That tactic would likely just result in another trip to jail, and without Parland here to get him out again, he'd have trouble tracking down either Doctor Phand or Louis's killer, so instead he just smiled and said, "Of course, of course, I'm sure you're quite busy. Thanks for your time, sir."

Ulm stopped herding him forward once it seemed like Gus would see himself out, and free of his grasp, Gus slowed to a more comfortable gait and took a moment to smile down at the women in Ulm's typing pool as he passed. Their boss frowned at him from the doorway to his office and stood watch until his visitor had passed into the reception area.

Once out in the foyer, Gus put on an embarrassed smile, turned to the receptionist, and said, "Sorry, Lana, right? I'm supposed to meet up with Mister Ulm at an event, and I've already forgotten when it is. Do you keep his schedule?"

She nodded with such earnest sympathy that he even felt a glimmer of guilt for deceiving her. Pulling a book out from under her desk, she flipped it open and asked, "What was the event?"

"Club meeting. I thought it was this week." He leaned over to peer down at the schedule as she scanned down the list of appointments but found his eyes drifting to the neckline of her dress instead.

"Well, there's the Civic Alliance in a few days, and the KBBB this weekend. Oh, and a Wardens' dinner tomorrow night. That looks like all for this week though. Are you sure it was this week?"

Gus's smile froze at the name, absolutely shocked to hear it so bluntly delivered. She was young, perhaps a decade his junior, but that level of glib ignorance was astonishing. Perhaps Ulm had smoothed over the natural revulsion already.

That was the problem with involving prominent entrepreneurs in a secret society though—they couldn't handle simple things like scheduling appointments for themselves. Marshalling his reaction, Gus said, "Yeah, Wardens is the one. Did he tell you where we're meeting?"

She giggled a little at that question, and he nodded in faux approval. "Good, good. Can't let you know all our secrets." Leaving her with a wink and his most charming smile, he hurried out before Ulm came to make sure he'd really left.

Ringing for the elevator, he whistled a few bars of *Easiest War* until it arrived, he stepped in, and the doors closed. Once they had, he dropped the tune and said, "Gah!"

The elevator operator smirked at that but kept his eyes studiously ahead upon the controls, entirely too professional. Gus fought the urge to pace back and forth, not sure how that might impact things as they descended from over a dozen stories up. Pacing was never his style anyway, and what he really felt he needed was a drink.

Wardens. There it was. Ulm was almost certainly involved then, but thinking it over, Gus doubted he was the brains behind the kidnapping. The mind that thought up hiring Gus as a stalking horse would surely be a cannier liar than Ulm had been in discussing his vote. It felt like someone had fed Ulm the lines that he so faithfully kept repeating, but who?

With the Elves gone, who else would dare start a new group of Wardens? Anarchists and socialists held few charms for a successful businessman like Ulm. Colonial nationalists were a thing that came up in Rakhasin, but he'd never heard of any outcry for Aelfuan independence. It had to be a sham—or a bad joke.

There was no way to be sure without seeing for himself.

~

"Treason Charged!"

Welshie Bolmar, of 28 Bantham Street, NW Lower, was brought before the Hon. Augustus Ingram, at the Marjorie Street Police Court on Tuesday, charged with treason-felony, to which the original charge of feloniously dealing with Government rifles had been altered since the first hearing of the case last week at Cloudmill.

Evidence was given connecting the prisoner with the storage of the arms found in Southland Road, with treasonable intent, and also with having used a stable for similar purposes at a previous period in Hamesville. Sufficient evidence being held to move forward, a full trial will be arranged for the next circuit appearance in three months' time.

– *Khanom Daily Converser*, 13 Tal. 389

~

- CHAPTER 18 -

It was early in the afternoon still, and since he had already met Sylvester, that left only one of the Exposition councilors to meet. He had wanted to ask Ulm more about Miss Aliyah Gale, but he doubted Ulm would make himself available for further inquiries. When the elevator reached the ground, Gus gave the operator a friendly nod, made his way back to the street, and hailed a cab.

The slight incline as they drove south was barely noticeable, but the mountain loomed larger and larger over everything as they drew near, and for the first time he wondered what it was called, probably something unpronounceable in Elven.

Miss Aliyah Gale's building lay just a few blocks from the far end of the upper city, where the mountain loomed even more steeply. A plethora of large homes skirted the steeper slopes, apparently the dwellings of the sort of people whose faces were depicted in all those industrial murals. The only structures higher up the mountain than those appeared to be waypoints for the mines.

Her building overlooked the park more directly than Ulm's had, and Gus supposed she would have an excellent view of the Exposition once it started. The building looked a fair bit older than most of Khanom's towers as well, although if he had to guess, it wasn't much more than a decade old. Perhaps this was the tower that inspired the others.

Although the marble flooring and staid Pylian columns were perfectly elegant, they lacked the bombastic flair that seemed the favored style in Khanom. The lobby stood empty, and judging by the signage, most of the first floor was apparently taken up by Khanom Water Supply.

A directory was posted alongside the elevator doors, and upon looking it over, Gus saw that the building's tenants all had similarly uncreative names like Khanom Gas Works, Khanom Housing Design, Khanom Brickworks (sales), Khanom Cabinetry, and so forth.

Reviewing the list by floor, he realized their offices were all organized primarily by function: architects adjacent to engineers, construction companies next to related contractors, and so forth. To Gus, that convenient arrangement hinted that rather than being over a dozen separate entities, they were all simply branches of the same tree.

Judging by their names, all of the businesses here related to construction. With Miss Aliyah Gale so involved in construction, Gus wondered if perhaps she had objected to Phand's tower because some firm that wasn't hers had won the contract to build it.

Miss Aliyah Gale was listed as the sole occupant of the 12th floor, so Gus rang the bell for the elevator. The attendant was a man of similar cloth to the one in Ulm's building. He nodded politely and asked his floor but otherwise held a stiff dedication to duty that Gus imagined Saucier's man Garnick would have found refreshingly acceptable.

When the elevator doors opened on Miss Aliyah Gale's offices, it seemed for a moment that they had somehow taken him into a different building altogether. The blandly pragmatic lobby below gave no hint of the exotic opulence that lurked above it. Awash in deep reds and golds, it seemed the entire floor was one large room, filled with luxurious furnishings in polished woods and gilt.

Miss Aliyah Gale's office was furnished more like a private parlor than a place of business, and Easternist artwork layered the place in fantastic serpents and mist-covered scenes of strangely shaped mountains and unfamiliar animals that Gus found entirely unnatural looking. Several plush couches lounged about, and an enormous desk, intricately carved, sat back in one corner and was the only bit of furniture that seemed appropriate for an office. On the other hand, there was no bed or dresser or similar furniture in view that would mark this as a dwelling.

As he stared around in surprise, an older man in valet's livery approached and coughed softly, to loosen the Gus's attention from the surroundings. "I'm afraid you are not expected, sir, and Miss Aliyah Gale is not presently available."

Despite the inordinate wealth on display in the rest of the room, the valet looked out of place even in livery—his grimly weathered face seemed more suited to an aging brawler than a refined servant. He held out a small silver tray as if expecting a tip, and it took Gus several seconds to realize it was intended for his calling card.

Rummaging around in his pockets, Gus found a battered card with his name on it, and a bit more searching produced a pen, with which he jotted down *Rondel's,* so she would know where to find him.

The valet smiled placidly, although it looked like he was simply biding his time to punch Gus in the face. When Gus finally set the card down on the tray, the valet asked, "Any message, sir?" His tone certainly indicated he thought there should be no message.

Gus doubted Miss Aliyah Gale would meet with just any caller and particularly not an inquiry agent, but he didn't have any other card to offer and couldn't think of how else to find her. The Exhibition's deadline for the tower was looming, and he wasn't sure yet if it was worth his time to just sit outside her building in the hopes of spotting her.

"Just tell her I'm interested in discussing Doctor Phand, I suppose."

The valet nodded, setting the tray down on an extravagantly carved table near the elevator that seemed to exist just for that purpose.

Looking around again, Gus commented, "This is amazing stuff. She's obviously doing pretty well to have acquired it all. Must be nice to work among all this."

The valet nodded patiently, and when Gus continued to linger for a reply, the valet finally responded, "It is, sir. The décor was brought in by her predecessor, and Miss Aliyah Gale has felt no need to change it."

"Predecessor? To the business? I assumed she inherited it from family or something."

There was a distant rumbling, like a storm still miles out or perhaps a small earthquake.

"Yes, sir," came the valet's useless reply, and the man stood silent, clearly waiting on Gus to take the hint and politely depart. Whatever the rumble was, it was not unusual enough to spark comment or even a glimmer in the valet's eyes that he had heard something. Gus hadn't packed an umbrella, so he hoped it wouldn't rain.

The quickest way to the right answer was sometimes to give the wrong one, and faced with the valet's lack of specificity, Gus just picked a possibility and pressed on. Gus focused his gaze on the Easternist décor—in his experience people usually loved to talk about their art, and with that sort of in, sometimes they'd tell him more. "Then Mister Gale laid all this down, but now she's in charge. That's some great art. I'd love to know who picked it out. How long have you been with them?"

"Forty years, sir. I was hired by Cornelius Zephyr to this position, and he was the one whose collection you are currently admiring. For anything else, you would have to ask him, though he's unlikely to tell you much." He spoke with a sinister air that made Gus uneasy.

"Really? Why is that?"

"Dead, sir. Coming on twenty years now." The old valet's eyes met Gus's in a chilly stare that left no question he was unwelcome as he pronounced, "Will that be all, sir?"

Gus grinned sheepishly and gave a resigned nod of defeat. "Yes, quite. Please do convey my regards."

The valet nodded coolly, and Gus retreated to the elevator, stymied. That distant rumble sounded again, and Gus heard the valet mumble something to himself as the cage was closed and the elevator began its descent. He supposed he could use a newspaper to keep dry, but that would be useless if it got windy—and thinking about wind brought another thought.

Gale was a pseudonym. It had to be. Zephyr then Gale? One wind following another seemed too ridiculous to be anything else. She could have been Zephyr's mistress, inherited his wealth, and taken a similar name, but why do that rather than marry him? She would have been young back then, at least several decades his junior, but that sort of scandal was common enough.

She hardly looked to be much over thirty now, so perhaps Zephyr's tastes had run too young even for that. Zephyr certainly seemed to have had a younger man's taste in art—older men tended to go for more traditional things, and Easternism was a recent fad.

That thought made him pause and reconsider. Easternism was made popular by the opening of trade through the Aelfuan Strait a decade ago. Gus had been in just the right circles in Gemmen to watch it rise, but Zephyr was long dead by then.

Even twenty years ago, it would have been monstrously expensive and tackily exotic. Khanom at the time would have been nothing more than a scenic frontier trading post. The rails wouldn't even have run here yet, so each piece would have been carried through the wilderness by horse-drawn cart. As unlikely a pursuit as it seemed for an early frontiersman, no matter how wealthy, it seemed an even stranger thing for the valet to bother lying about. Why would someone wealthy enough to import art from the other side of the world settle so far from civilization?

There was also the issue of Miss Aliyah Gale's considerable influence in town. Suffragists were gaining ground, but men wouldn't easily accept a woman as a political equal. Gus wondered if he might not be considering things provincially enough. If all those construction companies were really hers, she probably ran at least half the crews in town.

When the Elves left, the roads were here, and the ground already flattened and cleared, but constructing all these towers on the plateau would still have been a monumental undertaking to the tune of millions of peis, and most of that would have been spent in the twenty years since Zephyr died. None of the other councilors were lord anything of anything, so all that money might be enough to give her political clout out here, even if she was a woman.

Foundations had to be dug, pipes for water and gas connected, cement poured, and so on. The business savvy to maintain all that might adapt to planning a kidnapping like the one in Gemmen. Perhaps she was a front these new Wardens used for their above-board dealings, or perhaps they were a front for her illegal ones.

If she ran the city's construction rackets, it could also explain her private meeting with Doctor Phand. That made more sense to Gus than the wealthy and beautiful Miss Aliyah Gale having a secret affair with a tubby engineer. The man hadn't seemed upset when he left that rendezvous though as he probably would have if he were being leveraged somehow by Khanom's queen of crime. Whatever it was though, it put her in the city as the crime happened and beating a hasty retreat the next morning.

The elevator reached the ground floor, and Gus paused in the lobby, peering out the door. From the earlier rumbling, he had expected to find it raining, but happily, there was no storm outside. He emerged from the building and couldn't see a single cloud on the horizon, so he decided to walk back to Rondel's to change for dinner. It was several blocks to Rondel's from Miss Aliyah Gale's building, but his leg wasn't bothering him too much, so he decided it wasn't worth the fare.

Dressing for dinner was not a custom he had grown up with, but during his brief celebrity in Gemmen after his testimony in Parliament, Gus had quickly learned that people of a certain class considered it quite uncouth to just show up for the evening with whatever it was you wore during the day. To have any chance at talking with someone at the Viridian who knew Richard Saucier, he needed to look like he belonged there.

The walk gave him a chance to look around the upper city a bit more, and he found its polished glamour grew quickly repetitive, leaving him stuck thinking about the case.

As mad as it seemed, there really was a society in Khanom that called itself 'the Wardens'. It was tempting to assume they must be the culprits, but having met Ulm, Gus was far from certain. For one thing, he was skeptical that any club that claimed Ulm as a member was possessed of the criminal experience that seemed evident in their plan.

Using Gus to trail their victim, rather than doing it themselves, was farsighted for someone unpracticed in masked ambush since the witnesses to that tailing might call out Gus but wouldn't be able to recognize whoever had hired him. They hired him under a false name, and even if he were so inclined, the best he could offer the Crossing was that there was a tall blonde woman involved.

The kidnappers had known to offer him just enough money that he wouldn't think about it too hard until it was too late. If not for Louis's murder, he might even have let it go and just given Ollie

Clarke's goons what little information he had. That murder pointed even more strongly to something more sinister than a social club for wealthy gentlemen with poor taste in costume.

Louis had been charismatic yet tight-lipped. He would have shrugged off false Wardens and wouldn't have ventured to argue with them over the kidnapping once they'd convinced him to do the job in the first place. Even had he thought they were real Wardens, he wasn't the sort to confront them himself.

Arriving at Rondel's, Gus saw the familiar desk clerk on duty, winked at him, and was satisfied with how unsettled the clerk seemed to be by the gesture. Apparently, his threat to the clerk's partner was working. Gus went upstairs and shook out his dinner clothes. They were rumpled from travel, but maybe the Viridian would be dark enough that no one would notice.

Gus was pretty sure viridian was a color, and it meant either red or green, but he wasn't sure which. His guess was that a red club would probably be brighter lit than a green one, and since there wasn't time to get his suit pressed, he hoped for green. After dressing, he went back down and asked the Rondel's doorman how far Blisan was down 6th and was pleased to learn it was only a few blocks more.

That seemed sufficiently close enough to regale Emily with how he had cleverly selected a hotel right in the middle of all the important things and thus saved them untold coin in taxi fare. The downside was that the moment his feet hit the sidewalk, his thoughts returned right back to the dismal reflections he'd left off of it with—Louis's murder.

If there hadn't been any argument from Louis to set things off, that meant the murder was planned. Not only that, it meant whoever planned it sent along someone who could spend however much time they needed to with Louis and then murder him in cold blood. Such men were thankfully rare and seldom travelled in the same circles as men like Sandal Ulm. Perhaps the social club was just being set up to take the fall.

Gus still expected he might find something useful by following Ulm to his 'Wardens' meeting the following night but knew the best bet to find Phand was to figure out why he'd been kidnapped. The kidnappers had already planned to stoop to murder, so it wasn't just a symptom of moral apprehensions.

With no ransom, why did they need Phand alive? Extortion would do no good because anything they made him sign to while kidnapped, he could just refute afterwards. What could a living but unavailable Doctor Phand get the kidnappers that a dead one could not?

All anyone was talking about with Phand was his tower. It was an enormous project, worth millions of peis, and that was just the sort of financial speculation that could drive a complex crime. The problem was, no one else seemed to be in line to get that money if something happened to Phand.

The tower would draw more people to the Exposition, which meant more money for everyone involved. According to the council, without the tower, it would just stay a park. People like Thomas might prefer a park for some reason, but those sorts of preferences probably wouldn't inspire the kidnapping, especially when another, bigger park already sat just across the street.

Had the kidnappers seized Phand's partner too? Since so much of the kidnapping had seemed carefully planned, and being mysteriously absent while his partner was kidnapped was not the sort of thing calculated to look innocent, Gus doubted Saucier was behind everything. The tower's opponents had gone after it financially once it had been approved, and Saucier seemed likely to be the moneyed half of Phand's firm.

Perhaps there would be some additional reward to be had in finding him too. Once he found Saucier, Gus supposed he could wire Emily to ask after it. If Saucier had been out of touch for weeks though, where had Phand gotten the money to promise Thomas and Sylvester that he could complete construction?

Thousands of tons of steel and the labor to erect it would be an enormous undertaking to pay for, and when the city suddenly dropped its financial support from half the cost to a mere quarter of it, then it must have seemed impossible for anyone to come up with that kind of money in time.

Ulm had been part of that effort to short the tower and was clearly involved in something, but Gus couldn't see any way Ulm would profit from the kidnapping of Doctor Phand.

Miss Aliyah Gale had initially opposed it, but Phand had seemed very upbeat after their meeting. Had she changed her mind? Why oppose it at all when she stood to make a fortune with a construction project like that?

Even if Phand hadn't hired her firms, that would mean fewer competitors for everything else being built for the Exposition. Perhaps she was so prideful the money wouldn't matter if she'd been snubbed on the deal.

If she was at such odds with Phand as to arrange the complicated kidnapping though, then why had Phand gone from nervous to cheerful after their rendezvous at the Harrison? Gus felt he really needed to meet her to figure out her part in it.

The deadline for Doctor Phand's signature on the Exposition's contract was only six days away. If this were really about that tower, then that gave Gus only five days to find him.

~

"Upon the Book: Caerleon and Geology"

Dr. Edwin Kipps's latest work, *Caerleon and Geology*, first printed just three months ago and already passed into a second edition, has already been discovered by a large section of the reading public. The author's ambition is no ordinary treatise; it is an attempt to harmonize Caerleon's *Compiled History* with the latest discoveries in science and to confirm the order of creation as established in religious tradition.

Modern scientific theories of the world's formation have undoubtedly brought questions upon the veracity of our records upon divine interaction that touch the deepest interests of all men. We will not undertake to determine whether Dr. Kipps has succeeded in his rationale; but if he shall have comforted those of wavering faith, he possibly will not think himself unrewarded for the vast time and labour evidently spent and will have earned the warmest thanks of those who suspect that the science of to-day is fast tending to unsettle their faith.

– *Gemmen Standard*, 13 Tal. 389

~

- CHAPTER 19 -

A temple of the Hidden Moon was hidden in the very heart of Gemmen. Emily and the others gathering there had each separately made their way there through various passages in the sewers, which were icy and particularly treacherous this time of year. Although they followed different paths, they all arrived at the same time, emerging from the various passages that converged upon the temple.

Built beneath an ancient well, the temple was a dome of old stonework decorated with signs and symbols of the faith writ in a silver inlay that reflected dimly in the collective lantern light of the assembling worshippers.

The water around them was deep, but stone tiles rose just above the surface, forcing a somewhat awkward intimacy among the goddess's faithful, who had to stand in close groups to keep from falling in. The underground waterways were cold even in summer, so despite the closeness of her fellows, Emily was still forced to pull her coat tight against the chill.

Fortunately, the ceremony was designed with speed in mind. The temple had been founded when worship of Maladriel was still forbidden by the Triumvirate, so its services were brief and promptly delivered. No sooner had the last stragglers arrived than the three veiled women conducting the ceremony emerged from shadows across the water from their congregation.

Each was cloaked in gray, but the gray was split at the front, and beneath they wore dresses bedecked in silver brocade that vanished into the blackness as the various lanterns around the room were extinguished. There was a soft rustle as every head turned upward, peering at the only light remaining—the starry night sky visible only through the opening of the well beneath which they all stood.

"We live in an era of rapid change." Madame Jande's voice echoed, the room making it seem to come from the darkness all around them. This time, her accent seemed a more southerly Verin. "Factories crank out the future faster and faster each day. Railways speed us through the continent, and great ships let a man see nearly any corner of the world he chooses. A telegraph can deliver messages across the nation faster than a messenger could carry it across the street.

"The world has never moved so fast, yet even the words to describe it aren't fast enough anymore, forcing us to constantly relearn the newest versions of shorthand!"

That brought a round of shared laughter from the group at one of the common blights of the age.

"The whole world is in motion, constantly racing ahead, and at times, it seems away from us. It is easy, in all that, to lose sight of our journey—to see where we are, so far away from where we wish to be, and forget we began so much further away. The future is always beyond our grasp. We cannot ever reach it, but we must always reach for it.

"In those moments where you dwell most in darkness, you need only turn your eyes heavenward."

As she spoke, a soft light began to suffuse the room, barely noticeable at first, as the blackness gloamed into obscura, changing the world from impenetrable darkness into shadowy uncertainty.

"Remember that even when blocked by clouds, the stars still shine. The attention of the queen of gods may seem to wane," she said, and Emily could just barely make out Madame Jande's profile across the water, her arms rising up to reach towards the well shaft overhead. "But for those who hold the faith, her love always waxes, bright and full."

Madame Jande then intoned their communal invocation. The words were in Rejjun, spoken by Caerleon's first faithful as they witnessed the goddess undo the Shadow Negus. Although few Verin understood that language, they all knew the meaning of the words as they closed their eyes and spoke them. "Holy Maladriel, Divine Queen, ruler of the heavens, mistress of hope—your faith is not lost."

Opening her eyes again, Emily found the room transformed.

Above them, the full moon filled the circle of the well, and its reflection shone brilliantly in the pool below. The light danced from the water and caught the silver filigree in the walls, giving the symbols there a luminous glimmer that seemed nothing short of magical.

The three devotees, including Madame Jande, had tossed back their gray cloaks, and the silver brocade worn beneath gave them each a share of that divine radiance. Emily could make out Madame Jande's silver amulet worn atop the brocade, glowing like the moon itself in the reflected light that bathed the room.

The gathered faithful gasped and murmured in wonder. For some, it was their first experience of this seasonal rite, but even though it was Emily's third, she still shared in their awed reverence.

Slowly, the light began to fade once more as the moon continued her trek across the sky, moving beyond the circle of the well above them. Gradually, the lanterns were illuminated once more, and groups began their journeys away down the dismal passages they had followed to reach this hidden temple.

In ancient times, the faithful had to flee quietly, and all in separate directions in the hope of evading discovery by the Triumvirate's orthodoxy, but in modern times, they paused to greet one another and give their thanks to the priestess before being hurried out by the cold of the season.

Emily stepped carefully around the pool; the paving tiles were kept dry, but the water below was still fearsomely frigid should anyone slip. Madame Jande lit her own lantern, bowing her head to each compliment and wishing her congregation well as they gradually slipped back into the night.

The priestess smiled as she saw Emily approach and said, "I always worry we might have clouds, but it seems she blows those dragons aside for us every year!"

Breathless with giddy elation, Emily could not help but gush over the service. "It was … marvelous. It's been such an unpleasant week, and suddenly I feel like she has lifted the weight from my shoulders."

"Those Wardens frustrating you still?"

Emily nodded, frowning a little at the reminder. "The woman … there was this woman who was involved with them, and she wore a black fox stole. At the time, I'd noticed the hook and the loop on it were mismatched, with a silver loop and a copper hook. At the time, I thought it meant she just wasn't quite as rich as she pretended, but then it occurred to me—"

"It must have been leased," finished Madame Jande, following the logic readily enough. No respectable furrier would have made that sort of repair. Any decent odds shop would have had either type of clasp available, which meant that whoever did the repair just happened to have a spare hook or loop on hand but was too hurried to care about the match.

"Exactly!" The import of such a detail could be gossiped over in a social setting by real women of rank, but it would be practically invisible on stage. Theaters would often supplement their ticket sales by lending out disused costume pieces as she had discovered in her prior career and had subsequently made extensive use of in Gus's employ.

Madame Jande nodded and looked interested. The room was growing quite dark once more as the other worshippers slipped away, and bitingly cold. Emily hugged herself and continued, "I asked around, but no one I know recalls ever seeing such a piece at the usual places. Then I went by wardrobes in both Potter and Tanner and turned up nothing."

"Well, what else was she wearing? If she borrowed the fur, perhaps the rest was borrowed as well? What did she look like?"

Emily nodded, replying, "Well, she was a tall blonde," and then held up her hand to show how tall. "Not that you care that she was blonde, I suppose, but the dress was nothing fancy, just blue in a Garren cut."

"That's unusually tall for a woman—did you check Boskin's?" When Emily shook her head no, Madame Jande said, "It's on Chandler Avenue and often leases appropriately tailored feminine attire to a more … masculine clientele. Oh, don't look so shocked! That was an old tradition in theater, going back centuries, and why shouldn't they turn a little coin when such costumes are already in hand?"

Biting back her words, Emily forced a smile and said, "That shall be the very next place I check. Thank you, Madame Jande."

* * *

The man who admitted Emily at Boskin's Theater seemed taken aback by her interest in their wardrobe leasing but nevertheless escorted her down into the basement where they stored such things. He was lanky and tall enough that Emily suspected he took on his current calling after his height made acting roles difficult to find. He also had thin, flat hair that looked nearly as painted on as his eyebrows, which made Emily suspect he often loaned wardrobe to himself.

The Boskin's Theater's wardrobe storage was cool and dry, smelling of stale cedar and dust. As lending was merely a side business of the stage productions, there was no show room or even any effort at lighting their storage space, requiring her to review their stock with only the illumination of a hand-held lantern carried by her host.

Coats and furs were all hung together on one side of the room and packed so tightly that she had to wrestle some of the pieces free in order to pull them into the light of the proprietor's lantern. Black and brown furs looked nearly the same in dim light, and she was close to giving up when her eye caught the uneven gleam of that mismatched clasp.

"This is it!"

Looming behind her and holding up his lamp, the proprietor sniffed incredulously at her choice and said, "Truly? You know, if you keep looking, I know we were just returned a number of others that I think might better suit your color."

"No … ah … well, I wasn't hoping to borrow it myself, I'm afraid." She smiled apologetically, and the man's eyes narrowed in suspicion. "I was rather hoping you could tell me a bit about the person who last rented this."

The proprietor drew back in affront and held his head high as he replied, "Madame, we respect our clientele too much to go about revealing their custom to anyone who might ask. This theater has been lending costume for centuries, and we—"

"It was a tall blonde woman, not a man. She might also have borrowed a blue dress?"

"Oh! Oh, her. Yes, I do believe she borrowed that very piece. Unpleasant woman. She actually bought the blue dress from us, over my objections—it was the perfect thing for the part of Lord Hampsted hiding in the magnar's terem in our upcoming production of *Revolting*."

"Did you happen to catch her name?"

"Oh, I don't think she had one, at least nothing to be interested in. She looked like a factory girl when she came in, and I would have chased her out as a vagrant if that Mister Mors hadn't come in along with her, waving the money."

"Who?"

"He signed to Terry Mors, which now I've had to commit to memory because he's on our list of custom-to-be-refused. We fitted his factory girl for shoes, hat, fur—an entire thing, and he shows up here with just the fur and the shoes, a damaged hat, and no dress at all! He paid for the dress and the hat, but that hardly sews their replacements."

Emily tried not to look too excited over the name and focused her attention on the stole, toying with the mismatched clasp. "I don't know the Mors family, do you?"

"No, and I begin to think I wouldn't care to."

"Any idea where they're from? I've been sent after the woman," she said, and the wardrobe proprietor's eyes narrowed, so she hastily added, "If I find her, I can try to recover that dress for you."

"Well, he was in brown twill when he came to pay for the dress, so I imagine he planned to skip town. Besides, he paid for the thing, so I imagine it was because she ruined the dress."

Emily nodded. A brown twill suit would be an unfashionable choice for anything but travel, which lent itself to Gus's supposition that they'd left town. She checked the spelling on the man's name and bid the wardrobe proprietor farewell. A consummate gentleman, he then escorted her outside and helped her flag down a taxi, which she directed to the Royal Library.

Chandler's Crossing was thankfully near Government District, where the Royal Library stood, so the cab's fare was reasonable. With all their petty cash with Gus in Khanom, Emily was forced to dip into her own savings for the investigation she continued here. Gus never challenged her when she requested reimbursement for expenses, which somehow made her all the more conscious of her spending.

The Royal Library was never the most interesting building, architecturally little more than a giant cube from the outside, but within was a copy of nearly every book ever published in Verin. Within the entrance stood a column bearing the three stars of the Trinity and an inscription in Elven, whose Verin translation just below read, "Knowledge is Illumination."

According to legend, the library had been built atop a temple of the Triumvirate, and buried somewhere in the depths of the building was the lintel of an ancient shrine which read, "Knowledge is Truth."

Emily put little stock in that scandalous tale, for the library was the frequent haunt of the city's inquiry agents, who were all notorious gossips, so such a thing would never remain hidden for long. Those agents frequently gathered at the northwest corner of the third floor for the same reason she headed there now—that was where the library stored its collection of directories.

Every profession, fraternal order and social organization of any decent size maintained books of addresses so that its members might find one another. As such books were written in Verin, copies were sent to the Royal Library. An inquiry agent armed with a name, a city, and a career could very quickly track down an address for nearly anyone of note in the Empire.

Unfortunately, all she had was a name. After an afternoon of searching through professional directories from both Gemmen and Khanom, she had a list of several in each city and very little idea how to narrow it any further. Worse, it occurred to her the man might be from any number of towns surrounding either city or any other place in the Empire, and that was all assuming he wasn't just using a pseudonym.

As she stared at the list she'd already written out, the men gathered at the carrells across from hers broke out into another peal of laughter. If the headache of staring at endless lists of names and addresses weren't bad enough, the cluster of gossipy inquiry agents had not given her a moment of quiet all afternoon.

"… so he says, 'Of course these are genuine. I got the original plates stashed at home!'" The group erupted into laughter again, and Emily rose to go tell them to hold it down. Three she recognized as agents from Drake's, although she wasn't familiar with the fourth of their quartet.

"Ha! Tell me you got witnesses to that!" said one of the man's companions.

"Oh, it was so close. This blonde was sitting at the table next to ours, and she must have heard the whole thing, but after we clapped him, she refused to sign, so we didn't push it."

Another of the group grinned and added, "He's playing up his courage for you—she looked ready for fisticuffs, and when she said no, he backed off like a kicked pup!"

"It's not as if you were chasing her down for it. A dainty miss I might press, but she wasn't that. Innkeep told me she carried her old pa up the stairs on her way in, and I believe it."

Emily took a sharp breath to begin her reprimand as she approached, and then paused in thought. Their eyes all turned to her, and she asked, "Was this a tall blonde? Maybe in blue?"

The first man nodded and said, "Yeah. Came across her in Duros but didn't get the name. You think you might know her? Innkeep said she was travelling alone with her father into Aelfua. If she heard that part about the plates, even just a signed letter to that effect would really help us out."

He was grasping at straws, but then so was she. "Tall blonde, muscular, travelling with an older man with kind of a square beard? And still in that blue dress."

"Yeah. Well, I don't know about her pa. They drove out of town at first light, so I never saw him."

"Drove?"

"There's no rail in Duros!" That was apparently an earlier punch line, and the other three laughed heartily.

Realizing the implication, Emily turned and raced for the stairs, hoping she could make it to the telegraph office before it closed.

~

Carol Thomas, "A Call for Civic Prudence"

Nowhere is the failing morality of our fledgling metropolis more visible than at the literal den of inhumanity that sits in our very heart. In a year's time, when the city bustles with visitors seeking to glimpse the glories of Khanom's future, let us not seek to please their basest instincts with foreign girls in the all-together dancing upon the strings of even lesser creatures.

Though the initial raids by our diligent protectors in the police force has yet failed to find sufficient evidence to secure legal remedy, we may still draw out this poison by denying its entry into the circulation of our commerce until it is forced to withdraw itself. An entertainment club requires patrons, food, and libations, and if we bring ourselves to deny them those, then our civic shame will wither away ere it embarrasses us before the eyes of the entire world.

– *Khanom Daily Converser*, 13 Tal. 389

~

- CHAPTER 20 -

Lost in his own musings, when Gus looked up again, it seemed as if the Viridian had suddenly appeared beside him. The building it sat at the base of lacked any sort of decorative frontispiece, unlike many others along the street, but alongside the doors it bore an elaborately sculpted nameplate in polished bronze atop a backdrop of artificial verdigris.

He was relieved by the green backdrop, although when he stepped inside he discovered it wasn't quite as dim as he'd hoped. There was a stand just inside the door, where the head steward greeted guests before having someone escort them through heavy black curtains that kept even glimpses of the outside world from entering the club without permission.

Gus was critically reviewed when he approached, and the man seemed reluctant to even admit him, but eventually he insistently asked to store Gus's coat and hat, both of which he carried off as if reluctant to touch. Another steward then approached to escort him through the curtains and into the club proper.

The inside of the Viridian was far more lavish than anything Gus had imagined the Aelfuan frontier capable of. Black and white tiled marble floors were polished to an almost mirrored sheen, and the various tables scattered across the floor were far nicer furniture than anything at the sort of places Gus could afford to frequent—black wood carved into elaborate Elven style swirls and topped with stark white tablecloths of the finest linen.

The whole affair was extensively lit by gas sconces that hissed quietly along the walls, their light refracted off the polished floors to make the entire room gleam, even without windows. Above it all, there hung an enormous chandelier with harshly angular sheets of jade green glass alternating with curving sheets of frosted white. Light shone from within that aerial centerpiece, but other more traditional chandeliers hung all around, hissing their constant illumination into the club below.

It was early, and few patrons were seated yet, but still the steward maneuvered him towards the back, where fewer of his customers would have to see. Despite that placement, it would still afford Gus a good view of the stage, albeit a distant one. The stage itself was currently concealed by a heavy curtain, but the sconces on either side of the curtain differed from those in the rest of the room; they were sculpted to look like torches, although they were as clearly gaslight as everything else in the place.

Gus idly wondered what it must cost to keep all those lights on every night, and then it occurred to him that he might not be able to afford a dinner here. The menu provided no indication, just a list of options for each course, so he ordered the courses that looked cheapest along with a strong drink to help him with the bill later on.

As a lover of cheap food and potted meats, he was entirely unprepared for the enormous plate of beef ribs that was brought to his table in the club's opening salvo, so he ordered another strong drink. Before long, the club began to fill with well-dressed men and ladies bedecked in glittering jewels, and Gus wondered if there were other exits he could use later, when he needed to sneak out on the bill.

A band was kept somewhere just out of sight, and their music filtered throughout the Viridian, just loud enough to be heard above the rising din of supper chat, yet shy of overbearing. The music they played was a strange, foreign tune with the sort of snappy baseline that was usually only heard in far more vulgar establishments than this. Gus didn't recognize the song, but the patrons seemed to enjoy it.

Looking around at his fellow diners, Gus was surprised to see the number of women amidst the crowd. Clubs like this were often segregated for their safety and dignity, lest the combination of music and spirits make otherwise sensible people suddenly forget themselves. It was a custom he had never quite understood since neither theaters nor restaurants were segregated, but for some reason it remained common in Gemmen's fancier establishments. Khanom was clearly more liberal in these matters.

A roaming susurration caught his attention, and Gus looked over towards the commotion. The goblin he had met at the Exposition offices was dressed in a well-fitted dinner jacket and wandered about the floor of the club. Salka paused at several tables, and to Gus's astonishment, the swarthy gob was greeted with nearly universal enthusiasm; even the ladies seemed to be concealing any disdain with easy laughter.

Gus could not make out their conversation from the back of the club, but the mellow rumble of Salka's deep voice carried over, even if his words did not. As the gob's circuit of the room drew him towards closer tables, Gus could make out more of the conversation, and he overheard a young woman pleading with him for a song. The gob's olive features looked flattered, but he politely demurred, to the very visible disappointment of the lady at the table as he moved on through the room.

Eventually, he arrived at Gus's table, and his broad ranine face curled up in a grin that might have seemed menacing had the gob not reached over to shake his hand. "Mister Baston! So glad you could make it out. Everyone's been quite excited for the Mazhal dancer."

Bemused, Gus shook the gob's meaty paw and marveled at how disproportionately enormous Salka's hands were to his short stature. The place certainly seemed abuzz, so Gus nodded and said,

"You're quite the celebrity here yourself, it seems. Do you actually own this place?"

Salka laughed and replied, "No, no. Well, the club I own of course, but I just lease the space in the building."

"I'd never have expected people so enthusiastic for a gob club owner. No offense."

"No, it's quite alright. It was a lot of work for me to get to this point," he said, then gestured around the club and added, "When I started as a novelty act, they all jeered when I came out on stage, and the ladies would swoon in terror. The club owners used to make me dress like the savage Rakhas that people expected. Surprising them with sweet music was part of the act, you see."

Gus nodded and was surprised when Salka suddenly bubbled forth into melody. It was not a song he knew, and he quickly realized it was just a wordless alternating scale, but delivered with such sweet puissance that the neighboring tables all paused in conversation and gave a smattering of heartfelt applause when the goblin's trilling had ended.

Impressed, Gus clapped as well, nodded to his host in appreciation, and said, "I can see why they called you Honeyfugler. In the army, we heard goblin songs fighting the tribes in Rakhasin but never anything like that."

Only after the words were out did it occur to Gus that admitting to having served in the army shooting at goblins was probably not the smartest thing he could say to a gob, and so he hastily added, "That was incredible. You've got an amazing talent."

Salka grinned at the attention, giving flattered gestures towards the appreciation all around, then turned back to Gus, "Thank you, thank you. Years of practice. Eventually I bought the club, and now I run it and bring in entertainments like the one you'll see tonight. I found her while reviewing a few novelty acts to replace my own and have since paid quite a bit to import a few more like her over from

Mazhar. If the Exposition brings in as many people as they say, there's quite a fortune to be made running entertainments for fair goers. I might become the next Maurice Sylvester"

"Or Miss Aliyah Gale?"

The gob laughed and said, "One can dream!" Something caught his beady yellow eye, and Salka raised an outsized hand towards a neighboring table in salute then said, "Mister Allen, you must come over."

The man in question was a skinny fellow, his short brown hair kept professionally nondescript, and there was not much else that could be discerned about him in the uniformity of dinner dress. He briefly looked a bit miffed to be called out but rose and ventured over towards the table.

"Mister Baston, this is Eli Allen, and Mister Allen, may I present Gus Baston. I believe you two may share a profession, something to discuss over dinner. I'm afraid I must attend to the entertainment, however. Please excuse me."

Perhaps Salka was just trying to consolidate the seating for dinner since there had been no one else at Allen's table. Gus would have assumed Mister Allen had company coming; otherwise, why had he sat obliquely to the stage rather than facing it? That was odd, and something about Mister Allen seemed imminently familiar, although nothing Gus could quite place.

With that abbreviated introduction, the goblin wandered off to complete his circuit of the room, shaking hands and greeting custom on his way toward the stage. Gus glanced over his dinner companion, trying to place why he seemed so familiar. "Mister Allen, a pleasure. You're not working on Doctor Phand's disappearance, are you?"

Allen shook his head, saying, "You can call me Eli. No, haven't been assigned to that one. Is that why you came to town? Last I heard, Crossing thinks he's still back west someplace."

"Assigned?" The word was a hint, intended or not. Only an organization could assign work, so Allen was part of some group. Khanom's police might employ an inspector or two, given the size of the city, but despite any similarities of technique, Gus doubted many would consider a detecting-inspector as being in the same profession as an inquiry agent. "You're one of Drake's Detectives then? What brings you here?"

The 'detective' chuckled and said, "I'm just here for the hoochie-koochie dance."

Gus puzzled over what that meant, but before he could ask, Salka took to the stage, eliciting a smattering of applause.

"Gentlemen and ladies, we are honored to welcome you tonight to the Viridian!" That simple greeting in the goblin's rumbling bass elicited a surprisingly enthusiastic applause, with several hoots that seemed more suited to the showgirl saloons of lower classes. "Tonight, we transport you to the exotic palaces of Sakloch in distant Mazhar, where the lovely Miss Saneh performs the traditional dance of her ancestors!"

With a wave of his broad hands, the goblin stepped away, and the curtains parted as he left the stage. A breathless hush fell across the room as the music began. The melody taken up by the hidden band was entirely unfamiliar and employed the strange twangs and hoots of foreign instruments that had not sounded at all during the dinner service.

Patent lights washed over the stage, many pouring from behind it to illuminate pale rose fabrics draped above mid-stage, forming a second array of curving curtains with darker stripes of red where they overlapped. The silhouette of a voluptuous woman emerged, tightly dressed from what Gus could discern of her curves through the hanging silks. She raised her arms and began a sinuous twisting of her body to the exotic rhythm of the music.

Gus had been to bawdy entertainments in brothels and saloons and had even first met Emily at the raciest of those—a show where women in bare petticoats and bloomers sang comically naughty lyrics to the admiring howls of their patronage. It had been a warm-up act followed by bidding upon the show's performers for more intimate services to follow.

As he watched that feminine shadow writhe behind silken curtains, those shows seemed utterly tame by comparison. She twisted back and forth, her hips swaying in as brazenly sexual motion has Gus had ever seen beyond the actual act of coitus itself, and though hardly a prudish sort, at first blush it made him vaguely uncomfortable to watch it in such rarefied company.

Public-spirited citizens had shut down shows far less explicit than this for corrupting public morals, yet here in Khanom, the city's upstanding stared rapturously at it.

A cymbal crashed, the music intensified, and the dancer's movements matched pace. The silhouette arms gracefully traced through complex curvatures, but Gus could not pull his eyes from the shadowy echo of the dancer's hips. Again, the cymbal crashed, and in a deft motion, those arms reached through the curtains of silk, and Miss Saneh emerged before them, eliciting gasps and a smattering of applause from her audience.

She wore nothing or as next to nothing as Gus had ever seen a woman not wear. Her costume was far more abbreviated than any woman's actual underthings he had ever seen, and by consequence, what limited modesty it provided seemed entirely immodest. A brasserie of glittering gold covered her chest, and a scaled loincloth of matching sheen hung from her hips, most of her smooth skin bare for all to see. And as she writhed on the stage, her black curls were flagrantly unbound.

Her skin was dark, not the ruddy sun-kissed skin of farm women but a deep bronze that Gus had seldom seen. Gemmen hosted visitors from Mazhar, but he could not recall having ever seen one of their women, and seeing Miss Saneh emerge from that rose-hued silhouette, his breath was stolen away. He wondered if she were so extraordinary there or if the famed harems of her homeland were filled with such women.

Eventually, the music swelled to a crescendo, and with a final crash of cymbals, her body arched back in figurative ecstasy as her dance ended. After an initial smattering of cheers from her audience, she curled upright, bowed her head, and held out her arms in a submissive sort of gesture that was no doubt taken from her homeland, and upon that, the crowd exploded.

Men and women rose to their feet, enthusiastically applauding her performance, and Gus could not help but join in. Her dark eyes peeked up from her bow, and she gave a heartfelt smile at the adulation, which only redoubled the crowd's enthusiasm. The curtains fell closed around her, and as the applause faded, it was replaced by the rumblings of excited conversation at the tables, mixed with renewed calls to service for drink.

Gus lowered himself into his seat, shocked by the unexpected performance. He took a deep draught of his cocktail and wondered what Emily would have thought of all this. The bawdy house he met her in had seemed so risqué at the time but now would always be absurdly tame by comparison.

She might actually be pleased to know that. As far as Gus knew, her newfound religion included no direct prescriptions against such things, but that would probably only last until some new charlatan caught her attention and sold her on the merits of another brand of asceticism hidden just off the margins of Caerleon's holy book.

Gus was so lost in the dazed tumble of his thoughts that he completely forgot about Eli Allen until the man said, "That's really something, huh? I'd heard about it, but this was the first time I saw it."

Annoyed at being pulled from his reverie, Gus looked across the table at Eli and said, "I guess Drake's doesn't pay you well enough to go to these sorts of things very often."

Eli smiled, about to reply, but Gus cut him off saying, "So that means you came here on a case. 'One eye is always open'—that's what it says around that lizard eye in all your ads, right? You're not here about Phand, and you were sitting over there by yourself, in after me but still before most of this crowd and angled where you could watch me—someone's got you looking in to me? Who?"

Had Salka not pushed Eli over here, probably just to consolidate tables and accommodate more guests, Gus might never have spotted him. Eli Allen was good at his job, which Gus hated to see in a competitor.

In response to Gus's accusation, Eli just shrugged, gave a meek smile, and said, "You're pretty sharp. I won't lie, yeah, I'm supposed to keep an eye on you, but clients are strictly confidential. I'm sure you understand."

Rolling over the possibilities in his head, Gus said, "Honestly, I'm not that interesting, and there aren't that many people who'd waste money shadowing me when they could probably just pay me to tell them whatever they wanted. That leaves … Parland? He still thinks I'm holding out on him."

Parland either thought Gus was selling the sword to someone else or thought he had come here to recover it. In either case, that meant the Crossing hadn't tossed his office yet, since the petitioner would no doubt have heard if they'd found that thing just sitting in his desk drawer.

The man from Drake's shook his head and grinned. "Mister Baston, you know I can't tell you anything about that."

"Well, I can assure you his sword isn't here in Khanom. This trip has nothing to do with him," he said. Gus frowned as he watched Allen nod sympathetically without offering any other response— exactly the sort of thing Gus would do if trying to get him to divulge more. He wasn't sure if Parland suspected he was holding out and was paying Drake's to retrieve the sword, or if he just hired them to watch and make sure Gus wasn't selling it to someone else. "Tell you what though, if you're keeping an eye on me, I can make it easier for you if you can do me a simple favor."

"What's that?"

"You guys have agents all over the place, right? I'm looking for a tall blonde woman. Very … strapping. She left Gemmen a few days back in the company of three others. One's an older guy. They're probably travelling under assumed names, but she's tall enough to be distinctive."

"You want me to do your job for you?" The Drake's man grinned, then shook his head before Gus could elaborate and said, "Tell you what, as a courtesy to you, I could ask around, let you know if I hear anything." He ended with a meaningful look, letting Gus know there was a price for this 'courtesy'.

Gus grinned and replied, "And I, of course, will let you know before I leave town or anything. You've been watching me; you know I'm just interviewing people on a case, so you can tell Parland it's all fine. He's been a good friend to me, and I'll get him that sword as soon as I lay hand to it."

Allen started to answer, then paused as a steward approached their table, carrying a large bottle of wine. Coughing softly in apology for having interrupted, he declared in pompous tones, "Sirs, Mister

Salka'tok'tok'ton would like you to accept this bottle of Sarone '89 in toast to your good health." The strange staccato of the goblin name rolled from the steward's lips with unmistakable ease of practice—a clear display of the goblin's unusual social standing. "He hopes that you have enjoyed the show and sends his earnest wishes for success in your endeavor."

Gus looked around the club, but Salka was nowhere to be seen. Was he just that happy to have someone searching for Doctor Phand? It seemed overly generous, but never one to refuse a free drink, Gus replied, "We'd be delighted. Poor us a few glasses, and we'll drink to his health and success."

They did just that, and toasted him again as he took to the stage to introduce another act. The other performances that evening were far tamer musical presentations, and no other dancers took the stage. For the finale, Miss Saneh performed her dance again and was greeted again with tremendous applause and another standing ovation at the conclusion.

While a heavy drinker on most occasions, the Garren wine had a kick Gus did not expect, or perhaps being free, he simply drank more of it. He staggered back to his room at the end of the evening and collapsed into a pleasantly dreamless unconsciousness.

The next morning, he was disturbed by a businesslike rap at the door. Judging by the sun in the windows, it was late in the morning, and when he opened the door, a steward in hotel livery waited in a pose of stiff attention that would have done Gus proud in the army.

He presented a small square of paper, which Gus took before slamming the door back in the man's face, forgetting to tip and only belatedly realizing that was probably ruder than he had intended. Shrugging it off, he looked down at the message: *BLOND & PA BY ROAD, E*

Gus blinked several times, trying to shake off the stupor of sleep as he digested the message. How had Eli Allen managed to wake, find that out, and telegraph him a note after last night? He was so stupefied by that feat of endurance that it took him several moments to grasp the import of the message. If that was the false Alice Phand in disguise, then Doctor Phand wasn't here yet!

~

"Magnar's Widow Confirmed"

The Grand Sultan of Mazhar held a gathering earlier this week for various exiled dignitaries of Tulsmonia. While currently possessing no access to their titled lands, many of Tulsmonia's ousted leaders made their escapes with great personal fortunes, and those have found an eager host in distant Mazhar. The notable highlight of this gathering was the presentation of their exiled queen, Andra Berengar, who spoke to them at some length. Some had doubted that the Sultan's guest was truly the widow of the magnar of Tulsmonia, but the exiled Tuls who emerged from the recent meeting have enthusiastically endorsed her identity.

Tulsmonia's ambassador-in-exile in Mazhar immediately requested the great lady take up quarters within the embassy building to return her to her homeland symbolically until it could be managed in fact. The Sultan, however, has requested she remain a guest of his palace a few more days, so he might welcome her more properly as a visiting sovereign. A great ball is being arranged in her honor, with festivities delayed three days' time, to allow all Tuls refuging in Mazhar opportunity to arrange their attendance.

– Khanom Daily Converser, 14 Tal. 389

~

- CHAPTER 21 -

Anxious for the end of her journey, Dorna woke well before dawn and discovered her route into town was already a bustling thoroughfare of wagons bringing produce into the city. She had arrived with Doctor Phand at the appointed campsite last night and could see the lights of Khanom already visible on the horizon, but the plan had said they must wait until morning, so they did.

Guiding her carriage around slower traffic, she was greeted by several farmers along the way who looked eager to see new faces along their morning route. With two horses and no cargo beyond the two passengers, she easily outpaced the various farmers, which curtailed their efforts at friendly conversation but left her obliged to exchange more frequent good mornings.

It made her feel uncomfortably conspicuous, but if strangers were unusual along this road, she supposed they must seem less sinister in the gloom of early morning than had they arrived at night.

She finally pulled from the shared thoroughfare just outside of town, venturing their carriage along an overgrown trail into the forest. Looking over at her passenger, she saw him slightly stir, and she quickened their pace.

For the Oblivion, she needed Edward Phand half-drugged, cogent enough to walk, and not yet so cogent as to resume the infernal groaning. She had last dosed him per the Master's schedule, but she worried that somehow the Master might not have fully anticipated the vociferousness of the man's stupor.

The trail was bumpy, and Edward Phand groaned softly as they jostled about, but their destination was not far off. Beneath the shadow of the trees, she drew the carriage to a halt near the white stone arch on the side of the mountain that marked their entrance to the Oblivion. To anyone else, it was yet another pale Elven monument—an arc of stone set within a steep embankment of earth.

Dougal was waiting there in his Warden's greens to take charge of the horses and the carriage, and once he did, Dorna gratefully climbed down and stretched her back. The two of them pulled down the drugged Edward Phand, and despite her distaste for Dougal, she was grateful for the help. Here, amidst the sharp smell of pines, she began to feel some of the stress of their journey melting away, despite her growing dread of the much shorter, much more dangerous path still before them.

She took several deep breaths, staring at that white arch, knowing full well the dangers it represented. Dorna knew the Oblivion better than any other mortal soul, and surely this was why the Master had asked her to be the one to brave it with Edward Phand. Feeling an unwelcome surge of adrenaline, she softly recited the Elven words she had been taught, using the wave of their reassurance to steel her nerves for the task ahead.

Popping open a tiny vial, Dougal waved it under Edward Phand's nose, and the man groaned, his face twisting into a grimace. Whatever concoction the Master had provided to Dougal, the scent of it roused their charge to his feet, although his eyes remained closed and his stance woozily unbalanced. Dougal shed his robe and wrapped it around Edward Phand while Dorna retrieved her own robe from the carriage.

Dougal began to fit Edward Phand with a gag, but once he had, the older man began groaning into it. It was a muffled sound, but even that would be far too dangerous, and after looking to her for confirmation, Dougal removed it. Dorna gripped Edward Phand by the shoulder, and under her guidance he staggered forward like a sleepwalker as she performed the ritual which opened the arch to the darkness beyond.

Light from their side of the archway trickled into the labyrinth as they passed through, springing from the white tiles and briefly illuminating the ancient halls. For a moment, Dorna saw sparkling white columns stretching upwards into shadow. Then the way behind her closed, and all light abandoned them.

Kneeling down, she found Edward Phand's feet. She fetched the muffles from the pocket within his robe, and he obligingly raised one foot and then the other at her silent direction as she slid the soft fabric of the muffles over his shoes. She repeated the process for her own shoes, then stood and reached out for the nearest column, feeling a shudder of relief as she found it where she knew it would be.

The Master had taught her the winding paths of the Oblivion when she was a girl, and because of his tutelage, she knew her way through it better than any of the other Wardens. She had, in turn, taught most of the other Wardens, starting them from familiar locations and guiding them through the darkness along a single path, over and over, until they could measure their footsteps without needing sight for guidance.

In oppressive the dark, hearing only the shuffle of their robes and the thundering of their own hearts, many initiate Wardens lost their composure. The newest were always gagged, and the least trustworthy bound, lest their panic cause them to endanger themselves or their fellows as the Oblivion swallowed them. Though she could not see him, Dorna's eyes turned towards where Edward Phand stood, wondering if it would have been better to risk his muffled moans than that he might recover enough to do something louder.

Great danger lurked in these ancient halls, and without the Elven queen to control it, silence and darkness were all that kept trespassers like her safe.

The Master assured them that the guardian the Elves had trapped in the darkness could see no better than they. In her decade of traversing the Oblivion, she had occasionally heard echoes of far-off movement and once swore she had seen a dim and distant light, but other Wardens had stories of hearing it breathe or cowering behind columns watching light stream to either side as it passed.

There were no stories of closer encounters than those, which they all took to mean there were no survivors of closer encounters. Practice kept them hidden, and disciplined silence kept them alive. Still, even well-trained Wardens sometimes vanished in the Oblivion, either lost in the blackness or else discovered. They dared not even whisper here.

Dorna felt the engravings on the column under her left hand but was never certain if they were symbols or figural sculptings. She longed to one day wander these halls with a light in hand and finally see what wonders she shuffled blindly past in darkness and silence. It was one more reason to make sure the Great Restoration finally came to pass.

Taking a long, slow breath, she reached out and gripped Edward Phand's shoulder with her right hand and began guiding him onward. Within the cool air of the labyrinth, every sound echoed loudly into the distance, so Wardens wore robes to reduce the noise of their movements to the softest rustle. If she lost her grip on him here, he might simply be lost forever.

With her left hand, Dorna reached out to reassure herself against familiar landmarks, finding columns each at exactly the number of steps she expected. Normally she could navigate much of this opaque netherworld without needing to check, but pulling along the drugged engineer could throw off the length of her stride and her balance. Any mistake could be fatal here. Even being angled slightly too far to the right could make her lose their way.

Their route would take over five thousand steps, and feeling her nerves fraying after only a few hundred, she tried thinking of her Elven prayer. That had seldom worked, and she found it useless now—she needed to hear the words, even if only whispered. A soft moan from her charge made her tense, heart thundering as she began to second-guess her decision to attempt this without the gag.

She reached out for the next column, and her hand waved through empty air. Dorna's heart thundered in her chest, and to fight her trembling, she forced herself to take slow, deep breaths. Edging slowly forward, her left arm waved back and forth, then she struck solid stone—the next column, just a few feet further than expected.

Dorna shuddered, bowing her head to help quiet her breath of relief. Focusing on her Elven words had thrown off the count of her steps. The Master had faith in her to complete this last leg of the journey with Edward Phand in tow, and she needed to keep her faith in his judgment.

Faith should not require constant reminders. Dougal was likely the second most trusted Warden, after her, and she had never seen him recite the words outside of a meeting. If he needed no affirmation of faith, despite the dark errands he was set upon, then neither should she.

Her hand gripped the column, feeling the sharp corners of engraved detail press at her palm. The Oblivion smelled of nothing but powdered stone—the same honest fragrance her father had always worn when he returned from his work.

She could not see this place, but feeling the stone beneath her hand again, she knew she was not lost. Silently, she scolded her fears; she knew precisely where she was and precisely how many steps into the darkness it took to get from this place to the next one. Nerves steadying again, she pulled Edward Phand along and resumed the count of her steps.

The path they took now was seldom taken, not just because it seldom led to useful points but also because it held larger rooms with longer gaps between the walls or columns. Fewer landmarks meant it would be easier to lose the path. The largest such gap was to occur at her two thousand and fifth step, and she felt a surge of relief as she reached the low, linteled doorway on the other side of that gap, exactly as expected. She ducked her head and reached back to push Edward Phand's head down as well.

Edward Phand moaned softly, and that small sound echoed frightfully all around them. Dorna froze in place, listening intently, but there was nothing louder than the hammering of her heart, and the old man's wheezing breathlessness. Her instinct was to clamp her hand over his mouth, but she worried that would incite more frequent noise, which could be more dangerous than the occasional unmuffled one.

She urged him forwards, stepping lightly, and cringed as he moaned once more. Reaching back, she felt his face with her left hand and discovered his hood had fallen forward, covering his face, and she did her best to push it back out of the way. With that done, he grew quiet again, so she pulled him into motion once more.

They continued like that for some time, the moments and distance hidden by endless black, and the only signifier of the passage of either was the count of her carefully measured steps. Focused on the counting, she sank into the mechanical repetition of her pace, followed by the sweep of her left hand as she sought the next bit of expected masonry.

She might have passed through galleries, halls, small rooms, or enormous corridors, but she knew only the polished stone floor and the count of steps between her guideposts. The landmarks she drew surety from were not even things she could properly describe, merely familiar outcrops of sculpted stone under her hand, where expected.

At her four thousand, six hundred and twenty ninth step, a series of distant clicks yanked her from that placeless reverie. In the endless echoes of the labyrinth, the Master had taught her it was difficult to know where things were by sound alone—a distant echo might be far closer than it seemed.

Dorna gripped tighter to Edward Phand but kept moving. Adrenaline surged, and she felt the instinctual drive to move faster but knew that succumbing to that panic would throw off the count of her steps. She started to move her lips to the Elven words, but left them unvoiced. In silence, the words were no help at all, and eventually Dorna pushed them from her mind to keep focused on her counting.

She struggled against the urge to take longer steps, but she increased her pace until she felt Edward Phand pulling back slightly as he stepped on the hem of his own robe. Grimacing, she slowed again and was relieved to find the next column only a few inches farther than expected—that momentary shuffle had not thrown off her count too badly.

There was a low grinding sound, like heavy bags of sand being pulled along the ground, that seemed only yards away on her right. Whatever it was that slid along the floor, it sounded from the right side in several places at once, which made her realize it must be enormous. It kept going and going, and Dorna's heart thundered in her chest, making her wonder if her heartbeat was loud enough to be heard.

Then the clicking began again—two sets of six taps, some that echoed from ahead, some from behind. Dorna struggled to visualize what could possibly make those sorts of sounds.

Realizing she had frozen in place, Dorna staggered forward, hand waving as she desperately sought out the next landmark even as she knew it was several steps further away, and was terrified that her reaching hand might somehow strike whatever was making that sound.

A shiver of relief rushed through her as she finally gripped the column that marked her route, but the dragging sound continued, echoing from all around them.

She was sweating profusely, and Dorna decided that Oblivion's guardian must not hunt by scent, or surely it would have found them already. The Master said its senses were no sharper than theirs, that the silence and darkness kept them safe. She silently cursed at the trembling of her hands, worried this distraction might make her lose the way.

If she lost her path, she could never find the way home again, and it wouldn't matter whether what lurked here could find them. Steeling herself once more, Dorna pushed further into the black.

The grinding sound continued and seemed neither softer nor louder. Did it follow? Did it just move parallel, biding its time to strike? Or was it simply so large that it occupied the entire distance she'd walked since first hearing it? Thinking back, she guessed that Oblivion's guardian might well be over thirty paces long.

But what was the clicking sound? She could not remember anyone ever describing that in their encounters. Had no one heard that part and lived to tell the tale?

She shook her head, trying to marshal her faith without the Elven words to aid her. The darkness was deceptive. The Master had told her many times that the halls echoed strangely, and the different sounds might mean nothing. Discipline and silence kept them safe. Dorna pushed down the thundering in her chest and moved stubbornly onward.

Her left hand touched upon the next expected corner, which she knew was the beginning of a wall. That wall would leave them cornered if the thing she heard came looking for them, but then, it wasn't as if she could simply flee from her path even if it did. The wall meant one less direction for them to hunted from and a steady guidepost until it ended; it was a luxury she was profoundly grateful for.

Edward Phand continued to stumble along with the languid shuffle of a sleepwalker. In his stupor, he was either indifferent or entirely ignorant of their danger, and Dorna thought that, in some ways, it made him more easily guided than an inexperienced Warden would have been.

Then, once again, he gave a low groggy groan.

Whatever weight was being dragged through the endless black of Oblivion's corridors fell silent.

There was a long pause, and Dorna pulled Phand back against the wall, staring wide-eyed into nothing as if curtains might suddenly part to reveal whatever it was that listened for them. Sometimes there was a light, in the distance, but she could not see it now and for the first time wondered if there might be two guardians. The Master had only ever mentioned it in the singular, but what if—

There were several more clicks, much nearer now, and the dragging sound seemed to draw closer. Gripping Edward Phand tightly, Dorna pulled onward, moving as quickly as she dared and trying to adjust her count for the awkward stride and harried pace. The heavy sound she had already thought so close before felt closer and closer still.

Its presence seemed to echo from behind them now. Did it follow along the same wall they did? The darkness is deceptive, she told herself. It could be on a parallel track. It could just be an echo. The darkness is deceptive. Still, she picked up her pace, using the advantage of travelling along the wall to ease her worries of the exact count.

On and on they plunged, eventually reaching the end of the wall and crossing a gap of ten paces before the next landmark. She

WILLIAM RAY

found it—a narrow jut of stone she always imagined was the end of a perpendicular wall. They pressed through that ancient archway, and she felt an electric thrill of relief as they turned left at the next smooth column of stone, just a few paces further. If it could not see them, then she dared hope that the turn of their path would lose it entirely.

Edward Phand remained blessedly silent for several minutes more, and the sound behind them grew gradually more distant. Dorna staggered onwards, feeling breathless and suddenly desperate for rest, but she was too shaken to stop. Even once those sounds grew so distant she couldn't hear them anymore, her heart continued to thunder, beating so hard that her chest hurt from the exertion.

They reached the final wall. The count of her steps was off again but finally irrelevant as she felt her way along it, searching desperately for the velvety curtain that marked her exit from the Oblivion. She pulled Edward Phand through, pushing him ahead of her, so she could feel behind and make sure it had entirely closed before searching the indented stone behind it for the sigils that would open the portal and make good their escape.

With a soft sliding of stones, the way was cleared, and she pushed Edward Phand through it and the second curtain beyond. After his slow passage, she simply fell inwards behind him, collapsing into the dim light beyond. She lay there panting for a moment, her cheek pressed to the scratchy carpet, then wiped her eyes before she looked up. Other than her charge, who stood a few feet away, the room was empty.

In imagining her return, Dorna had always pictured the Master there to greet her, to congratulate her on a job well done, to honor her as the most faithful with the other Wardens gathered to witness her triumph. Pushing to her feet, she scolded herself for the hubris of that fantasy. Most of the Wardens had jobs to attend at this time of morning, and even the Master had appearances to keep. She was saving the world; she shouldn't need accolades.

Thinking of him reminded her that she could now finally recite the Elven words again, so she opened her mouth to begin them, then stopped.

She had made it without the words. She had brought Edward Phand through as directed, crossing a distance no other Warden could have. The words had been a crutch, and her reliance on them had nearly made her lose her count in the Oblivion. Dougal didn't need the words all the time, and she resolved to use them less as well; she would have faith in her faith.

Edward Phand groaned again, and glaring over at him, Dorna fought the urge to kick the somnambulant engineer in punishment for his earlier noises. Her renewed sense of self-discipline restrained her, so as she was taught, before doing anything else, she adjusted the curtains behind her to make certain that the next time that portal opened, none of the dim light in this antechamber could leak through into the blackness beyond.

Grabbing her dazed charge by the arm, she pulled him none too gently from the antechamber of the Oblivion and into a familiar hallway within the Master's house. He was not waiting for her there either, but shortly after they stumbled in, his maidservant Mathil appeared, taking charge of Edward Phand and leading him away.

Left to her own devices, Dorna felt neither celebratory nor accomplished, simply tired. She found the room set aside for her in his house and collapsed gratefully into her own bed, but despite her best intentions, sleep would not come.

Adrenaline from their close call in the labyrinth still coursed through her, and without a mission to focus upon, Dorna's thoughts tumbled uselessly. Her mission was successful, but much of it still did not sit well with her, despite the desperate necessity for the Great Restoration. She knew she could push those doubts away with the

Elven words the Master had taught her, but having just promised herself to use them less, she stubbornly refused.

Dougal had not needed them, and his path was darker than hers. Thinking of him brought a pang of guilt for the cabman's murder but also shame for her failure to drive the blade home herself. The Master must have seen into her heart; he had known she would fail, that she didn't have the will to do what was necessary to the plan, and that was why Dougal had been sent along as well.

The Great Restoration would bring back a noble people to lead them down a better path, but until it was done, the Wardens were the ones who needed to hold back the evils of mankind. Thanks to the Master's mercy, she had been taught that truth at a young age.

The Wardens were dedicated to a pure cause, but they lacked the power, the majesty, the wisdom, and the experience of the Elves, which meant that they needed to sink to the rest of humanity's level to win. Creatures like Dougal were foul, but surely she had learned by now that her cause justified a certain ruthlessness.

In the end, no doubt more would have to die, and some innocents might suffer, but they were fighting to save the world. There would be sacrifices, and she had to be prepared to accept them. She resolved to steel herself for the cause, to be every bit as ruthless as true devotion required. Next time, she would not need Dougal. Next time, she would drive the knife herself and be willing to endure the guilt for doing it because it was what must be done.

Resolved, she began to relax a bit more and finally drifted off to sleep.

Dorna woke sometime in the afternoon. Judging by the light through her window, it was well before sunset, but still shaken from their encounter in the Oblivion, she lit the lamp anyway.

When she ventured back into the house, the Master's household servants prepared a meal for her, but he still had not returned, so she dined in the kitchen, alone. The house in which he dwelt was opulent, which befitted his station, both true and apparent, but she had never felt comfortable in it.

His servants were too dull to converse with, their minds long since lost. Awash in the magic of his presence, they could converse in no topic but their appointed tasks and took neither umbrage to their duties nor pride in the magnificent dwelling they maintained.

It was unfortunate that they must be so diminished, but as he had long ago explained to her, the risk to the Master was too great for his house to be maintained by mortals of unshackled mind. His true devotees were too rare to be wasted on menial duties.

Watching them bustle about, Dorna felt another twinge of guilt and another longing to recite the comforting Elven words, but she reminded herself of her pledge; she must be ready to face the unpleasant details necessary for their cause.

As the sun set, she took a quick bath to wash away the dust of the road. As she dressed in a clean set of robes to go meet the other Wardens, she felt a renewed sense of her accomplishment. To reach their meeting spot, she must travel through the Oblivion once more, but she pushed down the fluttering of anticipation in her heart and looked to her dressing mirror.

Even without her words, wrapped in the familiar greens she felt strong again. Strong enough to plunge into the labyrinth once more. The route was barely a thousand steps, and despite a metallic taste in her mouth the entire way, nothing occurred, no sounds, no light. Once she emerged through another portal into the back alley that was her destination, she forced herself to laugh at how much that short venture had made her sweat.

Dorna had arrived early and felt conspicuous in her robes, but she could not be seen from the street, and there was no reason for anyone else to venture back here. Gradually, the other Wardens arrived from the street, still dressed in their usual clothes, only donning their own robes once they turned the corner and were out of sight from the rest of the world.

Pride overcoming their usual inclination for secrecy, Dorna stood with her hood thrown back, letting each newcomer take their turn to hail her and laud the success of her mission, and she basked in their adulation. It was unlikely any of them knew the particulars of her assignment, but they all knew she had ushered the Master's plan one important step closer to fruition.

Terry was one of the earliest to arrive, grinning beneath his open hood as if they were old friends. He returned to her the box she had purchased for the Master, explaining he had held on to it to let her be the one to present it. She wanted to hit him with it. Of course it was hers to present—she had bought it! Remembering her sympathy for the Master's household servants though, she tamped down her annoyance; perhaps the Master's presence had taken a similar toll on Terry's mind.

Dougal rejoined them as well, and looking back at him, Dorna felt a chill—his easy smile and placid demeanor concealed a killer, and her growing confidence that she could equal that easy ruthlessness withered at the sight. As he greeted some of the other arriving members, she could not shake the growing impression that he was not more than he seemed but instead far, far less.

His casual friendliness here was no different than what he had offered to the cabbie back in Gemmen. Would he murder any of them with the same ease of conscience? Could Dorna do the same if called to? Looking at him, she felt less certain of it and wondered at the capriciousness of fate that the cause of justice needed someone like him.

Their newest member arrived, robes bundled under his arm. Sandal Ulm seemed like the very emblem of the human regime they hoped to overthrow, but the Master had made her reach out to him all the same. After her awkward attempts to charm Richard Saucier had failed, only the Master had been able to help smooth things over. Sandal Ulm had proven far easier to lure in.

She knew the Master had ways to make sure he remained trustworthy, but men like Ulm were exactly what were wrong with the world. Daily, his workers stripped the forests, and the fires of his factories helped choke the city in soot.

Ulm had earned no share of the sympathy she bore for the Master's other servants or the poor cabbie back in Gemmen, and had he not joined their cause, she would happily have cast him down with the others once the Great Restoration came. Instead, now he would be spared, even though his workers continued to strip the forests and pollute the air. It seemed unfair, and she pursed her lips tight, holding back the Elven words that would let faith smooth over that discomforting inequity.

As she watched Ulm unfurl his robe, another man strolled into view, hands in his pockets and lips pursed as if whistling to himself while strolling between the backsides of the buildings. The newcomer froze as he saw their assemblage in green, seeming startled, and suddenly she recognized him as the idiot inquiry agent she'd hired in Gemmen. How could he be here?

~

"Race Results"

Falmouth Stakes, in which Lord Uster introduced us to Veromatisse, was the principal event of the clay. She is a fine-looking daughter of Wild Oats and Garren Blue and is the first of his present batch of two-year-olds that has yet appeared in public. It did not seem that much was thought of her at home, but for once the public quite neglected Pylian Shot, who actually started at the nice price of 10 to 1, and won easily. Faygar, who was favourite, could only get third, and her seven-pound penalty kept Lovely out of a place.

– Khanom Daily Converser, 14 Tal. 389

~

- CHAPTER 22 -

Rounding the corner, Gus stopped abruptly, staring into an alley crowded with Wardens in matching dark green robes. There were a dozen of them pressed close, chatting amiably and greeting the newly enshrouded Sandal Ulm as he arrived and began to mingle.

Ulm had been easy to follow, and while he had not yet donned his own green robe, he'd carried it casually folded under his arm until he reached his destination—a blind alley that branched off of another alley. The remaining gathered Wardens wore veiled hoods, but their veils were flipped up, exposing their faces as they chatted, and he saw a scattering of unfamiliar men and women.

In general, Gus had found secret societies seldom lived up to the discretion the name implied. They typically left no one fooled but the occasional spouse who had not hired an inquiry agent to be sure her husband was really attending to ancient mysteries rather than younger mistresses.

Towards the back of the alley, one Warden in particular seemed to be the center of attention, and Gus recognized her instantly as the false Alice Phand. Unfortunately, she was also staring back at him with an expression of such astonishment that he knew right away she recognized him as well.

The others all turned to follow her gaze, and as they did, Gus recalled Emily's commentary on green fabrics and began to worry that, as unlikely as it seemed, these might be real Wardens after all. On each belt around each robe was a dagger that seemed markedly less ceremonial than he had assumed when he observed Ulm carrying it to his meeting.

A brutish fellow towards the back pressed his way through the assembled Wardens, his beefy hand going towards that unceremonial knife at his belt. Gus quickly backed away with an amiable smile and a hapless, "Oh, sorry, wrong alley!"

One of the hooded figures chuckled, which felt a little reassuring, but unfortunately it was not enough to keep the rest from advancing as Gus backed around the corner. He limped awkwardly backwards through the garbage-strewn space between buildings that connected the Wardens' meeting spot to the main road. It wasn't far, but backwards was difficult for him, and yet he dared not turn his back on the big man.

The hulking Warden followed around the corner and surged towards him, knife sliding free of its sheathe. Several others behind him followed suit, pulling their own knives to hand as they stepped into place behind the bigger one. Glancing back, Gus realized there was still half a block before this side road's outlet onto Queen's, and the Wardens would easily overtake him before he reached the presumed safety of a public space.

With no other recourse, Gus stuffed his hand into his jacket and pulled out his revolver.

Seeing the pistol, the Wardens froze in place, forming a dark green wall of unfamiliar faces and gleaming knives. Before that wall, however, stood the largest of their number, who bared his teeth and lunged forward across the three steps between them.

On the big man's second step, Gus blazed, catching him square in the chest and eliciting a roar of pain.

The huge Warden dropped his knife and staggered back, blood staining the green of his robe a rusty brown. The other Wardens stared at their wounded fellow in blank-faced shock.

Gus waved his pistol back and forth in case any should recover their momentum, but none did. A pair of whistles sounded from the street behind him, and that was what broke the Wardens' collective daze.

He kept his pistol up, but the fearful gazes of the Wardens were cast over his shoulder. They turned and ran, scampering back into the blind alley they had emerged from. Only one of them stepped forward, loyal enough to grab his injured comrade and help pull him back. The larger Warden staggered, looking woozy as he clutched his hands to his chest to staunch the bleeding, and the two rounded the corner, moving out of sight.

Whistles trilled again, immediately behind him, and the sound of shoes slapping pavement made Gus turn to look as two men in olive green came sprinting down the alley, their uniforms similar enough to their Gemmen counterparts to mark them as the local police. They skidded to a halt when they saw Gus's gun.

One of the policemen gestured menacingly with his truncheon and said, "Hold it right there! You are under arrest!"

Gus grinned at the absurdity of the man's threat, given their comparative armament, but he lowered the revolver. Doing his best to seem non-threatening, Gus held out his hands, releasing the grip of his pistol so that it hung from his finger by the trigger guard, letting the weight turn it upside down to make clear he had no intention of firing it at them. "Constables! I was just attacked by several armed men who ran into that alley!"

The policemen crept uneasily closer, and one reached out for the pistol, tugging it roughly away when Gus did not resist. The other looked down at the blood on the ground and stepped carefully over to the blind alley.

Although Gus could not see around the corner, the constable blanched and took a step back, nodding before turning to Gus. "Alright, we … uh … you're under arrest."

"What?" Gus stepped towards the constable in front and looked around the corner.

The blind alley was empty, aside from a few pages of newspaper cluttering the ground, and there was no sign of the dozen men in green.

Without a dozen bodies crowding it, he could see the alleyway had no doors, just three blank walls from two adjoined buildings, and a cutout constructed around one of those white Elven obelisks, which stood at the end. The trail of blood tapered off down into the middle of the alley, leaving no indication of where they had gone.

The constables looked between each other, the one holding Gus's pistol looked confused, and if the other had witnessed the Wardens' disappearing act, he was clearly unwilling to explain it. After some silent glances back and forth, the policeman holding his pistol said, "Blazing a gun in city limits."

The other constable nodded enthusiastically, so the first continued, "It's illegal. We ourselves heard it and seen the smoking gun right in your hand when we came looking. You're under arrest."

"I was defending myself! They were coming at me with knives!"

The constable who had looked down the alley shook his head and pulled a pair of iron cuffs from his belt. Overwhelmed by adrenaline mixed with outrage, Gus gave the man an indignant shove. It was more an expression of defiance than a serious attempt to knock the constable over, but there was a grim set to the man's jaw as he glanced to his partner over Gus's shoulder and nodded.

* * *

Gus later awoke with a throbbing headache. As he tried to rise from the hard bench he found himself laid across, he discovered several fresh bruises over his body, front and back. The one must have clubbed him from behind, and then they both worked him over before dumping him here.

With a groan, Gus sat up and looked around. He had apparently been deposited into a barred cell, much like the one he had so recently occupied in Gemmen. Summoned by his groaning, a uniformed jailer appeared at the bars separating the cell from the hallway, grinned at his prisoner, and said, "Look who's up! Good. We need a name for your file."

He shook his head in surprise; somehow they hadn't found the calling cards in his pockets before tossing him in here. He could easily have held a knife or keys or who knows what else. Unfortunately for him, he didn't have any of those things.

Being knocked out always left him thirsty, but even still, the dry timbre of his own voice was still a little startling when he croaked out, "Gus Baston. Could I get some water?"

The guard nodded absently, and Gus immediately regretted sharing his real name. His regret was doubled when the guard explained, "You're just in for a twenty peis fine, but since you're here we have to send your name out over the wire, see if there's anyone at the Crossing looking for you."

Gus blanched. If Ollie got word he was here, he'd have them hold Gus for leaving Gemmen until someone from the Crossing could arrive to ship him back. Luckily, Gus knew he had enough for the fine on him and reached into his pocket to pull out his wallet. Opening it, he found it completely empty; while the constabulary hadn't bothered to check his cards, they had taken a moment to relieve him of his cash before tossing him in.

Seeing him come up empty, the guard chuckled amiably and said, "You can go once we get the money. Is there anyone I should contact for you?"

Back home, he could have sent word to Parland, but he doubted his jailer here was willing to loan him a peis to wire his man in Gemmen. Unfortunately, this far out, he had no friends he could call on to spring him. He needed a friend with money or influence or both.

Rain Thomas thought he was a detecting-inspector for the Crossing and was hardly the sort of acquaintance he could call on for bail. That goblin club owner had been supportive, but would be asleep by now. Gus had no idea where to reach him during the day and was less than confident that the police would do business with a gob regardless.

He even briefly pondered trying to contact Dolly Dench, but Gus doubted the man would come within sniffing distance of this place, even if he could be bullied into coughing up the dosh.

As a stranger in town, his best hope was someone with an interest in his work and with enough money and influence that springing him would be an insignificant effort. With few options, he decided to gamble. "Yeah. Could you tell Maurice Sylvester that I'm here? Let him know I found his guy."

There was an awkward pause, and Gus looked back up at the guard, who frowned in a moment of indecision. "Serious? If I bother Mister Sylvester, and he don't know you ...."

Gus grinned, raised his hands, and said, "Just send the message, alright? And maybe get me a drink. My head is killing me."

The guard responded with a nod, then gestured towards the back of the cell before he wandered off. A battered tin cup was there, chained to the wall next to a spigot. Gus filled the cup, wincing as the cold water only redoubled the headache that had come along with his concussion. Instead of drinking more, he just filled the cup again and held it to his head.

After only a couple of hours sitting on the floor by the sink with that cup of water to his head, Gus was surprised to see the dapper figure of Maurice Sylvester being led down the hall to see him.

Sylvester had only to glance at the guard to have the man deferentially bow out, departing with promises to come right away, should his visitor need anything, anything at all.

Sylvester gave a reassuring smile to the departing guard, then turned his attention back to Gus. Looking around the cell, then back to its battered occupant, Sylvester smirked a bit and said, "You've seen better days, Inspector Baston. Why ever are they keeping you in here?"

"Sir! It's good to see you again," Gus replied. He straightened himself up, dumping out the cold water and trying to straighten his rumpled suit. His leg twinged as he rose, making him stagger briefly, and he wondered if he looked as bruised as he felt. "I'd hoped to have a word in better circumstances."

The mine owner's eyes twinkled with an obvious amusement at Gus's straits that would only have seemed suited for a close friend or long-standing enemy, and he said, "You could hardly have hoped for a word in a worse one!" Sylvester chuckled, shook his head, and then added, "It seems like rough treatment for one of their own. Hardly appropriate protocol for a detecting-inspector of the Crossing to be manhandled by our local constabulary."

Clearly Sylvester had realized he was not. Gus wondered whether the man had realized it back in Gemmen or only once summoned to the jail. Hoping Sylvester's tone meant that he was just overly friendly, Gus put on a sheepish grin and said, "Oh, uh, yeah. I *am* an investigator, sir, just not with Chandler's Crossing. I'm privately employed."

Sylvester smiled placidly at the confession, then said, "And I was told you've found your man? Doctor Phand, I assume. How did that land you in here?"

Gus summoned up his most professional tone for reporting and thought Emily would have been proud of his demeanor under the circumstances. "I found the kidnappers here in Khanom, still dressed as Wardens, and they came after me with knives. I discharged my pistol in self-defense, and they fled, but then I was picked up for blazing a gun in the city."

Sylvester nodded thoughtfully as he digested that information, then asked, "And now you know where he is? Tell me."

Gus's instinct was to prevaricate—the closer to a sure thing he seemed, the more likely Sylvester would be to handle his fine to set him back on the trail, but as the city's foremost businessman watched him quizzically, Gus found he had an unusually hard time with it. After a couple of false starts with versions of his story aborted before leaving his lips, Gus sighed and offered a blunter truth than made him entirely comfortable.

"No, but I'm close to finding him. His kidnappers are here in town, so he must be as well, and I know it's some organization bent on stopping that tower from being built. I'm very close to solving it, sir, but they rolled me before they locked me up, so now I can't pay my fine."

For a moment, Sylvester just blinked at him, then laughed, shook his head, and said, "You called me down here, hoping I'd pay your fine? You think I'll pay to set you loose on this ... what, secret society? These elf-less Wardens?"

"I'm very close, I promise." Gus wondered if he should offer up what he knew of Ulm's involvement but hesitated, reluctant to give Sylvester more information for free.

Sylvester wore a thoughtful expression as he considered the request but ultimately shook his head and said, "I'm sorry, Mister Baston, but I can't involve myself in this sort of thing. You're running in the streets, shooting at people the police say weren't there, and you've not actually seen Doctor Phand at all. Even if you're really on to something, it just would be inappropriate for me to be seen setting you loose after all that."

Sylvester offered an apologetic smile and just shook his head to deter the objections Gus was already bubbling forth. Without further farewell, he turned to depart, rapped at the hall door, and quickly greeted by the deferential guard, who was still eager to impress his visitor.

* * *

For time uncounted, Gus lay on the cell's hard bench, staring at the ceiling and trying to forget his various aches and pains. Had anyone asked, he would have told them he was considering the case, but the truth of the matter was he had pushed aside most conscious logic and was simply staring as he tried to stall the dreaded inevitability of sleep.

Once the Crossing responded to the Khanom constable's wire, he would no doubt be held in here for days more until they came to retrieve him. With no reward, Emily would be upset about the money wasted on this trip. Gus felt he was used to being a disappointment and used to lean times, so his biggest regret would be failing to avenge Louis's murder. And perhaps failing to forestall Phand's.

That gloomy reverie was ended as the guard rapped at the barred door with his truncheon, causing a loud ring that struck Gus like a knife to the temple. "Mister Baston?" he called as if his prisoner had not just been rudely rattled at and was due some level of common respect. "You've got another visitor here."

Gus looked up and saw the smirking figure of Drake's detective, Eli Allen. The man wore a light-colored suit and a pale hat as if he were on summer holiday and swinging by to call on an old friend. Doffing the hat, Eli called in, "Gus! You're looking a bit … rough. I was told they just brought you in here for shooting at ghosts."

Pushing back to his feet, Gus tried to brush out his own suit, only now noticing the discolored splotches where it had been stained by whatever awful fluids leaked across the floor of the alley he'd been knocked out in. No wonder Sylvester had decided he was a bad bet. Donning a carefree smile, he replied, "Well, that is how I won my Stars, so I've got to stay in practice."

Eli arched his brow at that and, sounding skeptical, said, "You fought the Lich King?"

"Oh, it wasn't much of a fight. He was dead when we got there."

Eli chuckled at the line and said, "Ghosts don't usually hit back so hard in this part of the world. I guess afterward, you just tripped and fell."

Gus took the hint, nodded his agreement to go along with the story, and said, "Clumsy me. So what brings you here?"

Eli grinned and replied, "I've been told to get you back out. Unless you refuse, my employer has instructed me to pay your fine."

Gus's mind raced, only occasionally tripping over his own thoughts as the sharp pain in his head throbbed. What did Parland's willingness to pay to have him sprung mean? If Ollie Clarke thought he was a serious suspect back in Gemmen, then the Crossing would have tossed his office by now and would have found the thing sitting in his desk drawer, and no doubt Parland would have heard.

Realizing that meant he wasn't going to be arrested when he got home, Gus smiled at him and said, "Much appreciated. Tell your boss I'm very close. Lots of good leads."

The Drake's man nodded and gestured to the guard, who unlocked the door and swung it open.

~

"Tuls Lost in Gedlund"

A formal demand for investigation has been presented to the Marshal of Gedlund by the Workers' Revolutionary Committee regarding the disappearance of several Tuls soldiers stationed along the northern side of the Gryphus range, which divides Tulsmonia from Gedlund. The Marshal has disclosed to reporters that strangers were reportedly seen in the village of Faandyal, along the western edge of the region known as the Valley of War.

According to locals, the spirits residing there rise from their graves each night to continue a battle begun over a thousand years ago. It is the opinion of natives to that region that Tuls soldiers may easily have been mistaken by those spirits as partisans in their eternal conflict. The Verin forces garrisoned in that region refused Tulsmonia's direct request to locate the remains of the missing soldiers, saying that such a recovery mission was both dangerous and impractical.

– Khanom Daily Converser, 14 Tal. 389

~

- CHAPTER 23 -

Dorna and the others waited all night for Dougal to emerge from the Oblivion. The other Wardens had emerged one by one into the Master's sanctuary, but he had not. As soon as the two men who had entered the Oblivion after Dougal remarked upon his absence, Dorna knew that he must be dead.

The antechamber in which they waited was cold and uncomfortable, furnished only by a single gas lamp and two uncomfortable wooden benches. It was never intended as a place to wait, and with murmured apologies to those who remained, one by one the Wardens passed through into the meeting room beyond.

Eventually, only Dorna, Terry, and Marjorie remained. After their weeks on the road together, Terry and Dougal had grown closer, if not close. Marjorie was married but had been having an affair with Dougal for the past two years. Her husband was a horticulturalist who maintained the city's parks, but not a Warden himself, and Dorna wondered what he thought Marjorie was doing on her late nights out.

Dorna knew he must be dead but could not yet bring herself to walk away. She felt the chill emptiness of guilt gnawing at her heart. In the next room, they gathered to celebrate her return, and that moment of her congratulation was the only reason Dougal had met her in the alley instead of here.

Across from her, she could hear Marjorie whispering over and over, and the cadence of her recitations tickled at the back of Dorna's mind. Dorna knew those Elven words so well, and she longed to lean closer, to hear them more clearly and, even more, to recite them. The triumph that had made her reject their easy comfort seemed suddenly hollow.

Stubbornly, Dorna pulled her robe tighter against the chill and leaned back on the bench. If Dougal had just died, why should she feel comfort?

She watched Marjorie's face smooth over, the worry gradually washed away by the comforting words of faith, but it was a momentary thing. The woman's expectant stare gradually grew glum again, and the frown lines gradually deeper as she stared at the black curtain separating them from the entrance of the Oblivion.

It had never occurred to Dorna to imagine a hard man like Dougal being loved and perhaps even in love himself. To the Master, he had merely been one tool of many, and Dorna supposed she had seen him in much the same way. To Marjorie, this plump woman who always smelled of flowers, he had been much more.

Dorna felt a twinge of envy. Dougal, who was so ruthless in their cause, who had murdered and more, had someone faithfully waiting, staring at that black curtain and praying for his safety. If Dorna had vanished in the darkness, her absence would be noticed, but she knew no one would shed the tears for her that now welled in Marjorie's eyes.

Marjorie wiped her eyes on her sleeve, then looked up to Dorna and said, "We should go tell the Master. He ... he sees better than we do. Perhaps he can go find him."

The words struck Dorna with an electric force, and she sat up straighter, feeling all the blood draining from her face. "No!" she said, at first unsure why the idea horrified her so. Marjorie looked confused and perhaps betrayed, and Dorna realized that was exactly the sort of reaction she most feared—just not from Marjorie.

Taking a deep breath, she said, "This is our responsibility. We ... he and Terry and I, we brought that man into this," although, she thought, only at the Master's instruction. Somehow, they had done it wrong. Somehow, she had revealed too much. "This is something we must fix ourselves. Right, Terry?"

She looked over at him, and Terry was a picture of wide-eyed confusion. The intensity of her stare overcame him though, and he replied, "Yes?"

Marjorie frowned at the both of them, then turned her eyes back to the curtain. Sensing an opening, Dorna said, "This way, we get revenge for Dougal. If the Master does this, if he settles it for us, then … then we may not get to play our part."

That seemed to work, and Marjorie slowly nodded and said, "He had a couple of friends I know that would probably help. With five of us, we could, maybe."

Terry shook his head and said, "But he has a gun." Looking to Dorna he added, "You said he was a soldier. You said he got the Queen's Stars for fighting in Gedlund, right? I don't even know where to get a gun!"

Dorna frowned at him, and Terry shrunk back, but she knew he was right; Dougal was their killer, and he was gone. Perhaps Marjorie was right too—the Master would know what to do about this. He would have to find out eventually, but the idea of going to him in failure brought a tight lump in her throat.

What would he do to stop a dangerous man like Baston? When she was in his office, Baston had actually laughed about slaying an immortal, and now her failure had brought him here.

Suddenly, those thoughts clicked together, and she remembered one of the Master's treasures sitting in a room just up the stairs. She could bring Baston to a standstill, and then she could approach the Master with both her failure and a way to triumph over that failure.

Dougal was gone. Now she needed to be the ruthless one.

~

"Traffic Difficulties Move Northward"

Snarled traffic from the southerly districts is expected to move gradually northward and is expected to strike at 1st through 3rd on Queen's over the next week. This latest instance of local improvements is an electrical installation upon a magnificent scale: the street trams to be used for the forthcoming Exposition.

According to the Exposition Council, even our wide Elven roads will be unsuited to the service of the increasing population expected to visit during the Expositions festivities. Much has been said about the extraordinary speed shown during the past twelve months in building; but so far, per the Mayor's promise, no open capital has been raised from the public.

– Khanom Daily Converser, 15 Tal. 389

~

- CHAPTER 24 -

Waking in his own room, Gus eagerly peeled off the rumpled and filthy suit he had fallen asleep in and took few moments to clean himself up. The room had its own water spigot with a basin, so he rinsed himself and freshened his shave before putting on a dark brown tweed that was decent enough that the gentry wouldn't think him a working man but not so nice that a working man might mistake him for gentry.

He never had gotten his gun back from the constables and doubted they would give it to him if he asked for it; chances were it had gone the way of all the money in his wallet.

After luring in the crooks on his first night at Rondel's, Gus had hedged his bet on them and put nearly half of his peis into the hotel safe. Checking his wallet, he confirmed he must have retrieved those funds last night. He might need to skip a few meals, but at least the constables hadn't rendered him destitute in a strange city.

Emily would be upset at the loss either way, but train stations were usually filled with poor saps who had been robbed and hadn't the money to get back home. Thinking back on it, he hadn't seen anyone like that loitering around Khanom's pristine main hub, and he doubted that was due to an unusually strong spirit of generosity. Beggars were probably relegated to the hubs down below, and Gus made a mental note to take a careful look at a rail map later for the best one in which to beg his fare, just in case.

Going through his pockets after changing, he found a rumpled note stuffed into his dirty jacket, and fishing it out, it appeared to be on the hotel's stationary. Although he had no recollection of receiving it, it was balled up to fit his hand, so he suspected the front desk must have handed it to him on his way in last night.

Flattening it out, he recognized Dench's sharp scribble and could easily imagine the message in the man's petulant voice. *Girl may be Dorna Michts. Grew up in KMC dormitories, south. Ask there. – A.D.*

Dorna Michts. Was that really the false Alice Phand? If he'd known the name just a bit sooner, he could have tried it out to watch her react.

He wondered if she was also the D.M. from the letter he had found in Saucier's house. Although not completely certain, Gus thought KMC probably meant the Khanom Mineral Company. How could a girl from the mines be mixed in with the likes of Ulm? If she were the D.M. from Saucier's letter, who had entrusted her with sending such an expensive bauble as that elfsteel buckle?

Pondering these questions as he left the hotel, Gus paused to wink at the desk clerk on duty, the same man who had given him the slotted key. Keeping the resident thieves wary should keep the contents of his room relatively safe while he was out in the town, although he supposed now all that was left to be stolen were his shaving kit, his clothes, and a few bullets.

There were no cabs waiting outside, so he wandered south along Queen's and began watching traffic for one. It was the weekend at last, and the daytime streets seemed less bustling than they had the day before. Judging by the sun, his recovery from the evening out had let things slip to midday, and he wondered if the Drake's detective was any better off. Gus's recollections were fuzzy, but he had no memory of triumphantly drinking the man under the table.

He wanted to comb over the alleyway the Wardens had vanished in, but if he wanted to talk to people who might know this Dorna Michts, his best chance would be today. As much as Detecting-

Inspector Clarke liked to brag about physical evidence, Gus knew the answers to most mysteries came from people.

The alley would be just as there tomorrow, but the miners would be harder to reach. They would be returning from temple just now, assuming they went, and from there, like all good people, they would go out for a drink. Gus didn't know enough about mining to know when they started their workday, so he wasn't sure when they would leave the public houses and head home, which meant he needed to head there before it got too late in the day.

With most offices closed, the cabs were sparse, and the few he spotted had passengers already. Hoping to have better luck on a busier street, Gus made his way down to Queen's. His leg was stiff, so he paused there to stare across the street at Miss Aliyah Gale's building.

As he loitered, a black carriage with lace curtains pulled to the front of the building and waited there. Realizing who that must belong to, Gus began fording the avenue, thankful that the day's traffic was slow enough that he could manage it without being run down.

When he reached the opposite corner, Gus saw Miss Aliyah Gale emerge from the building in a dress of shimmering green. She boarded the carriage, and it began rolling northwards, past the corner on which Gus stood.

He ran as best he could, in order to keep up as the carriage pulled past, then leapt onto the step below the door and grinned through the window at the carriage's lone passenger. As much as he hoped to impress upon her that he was not some sort of urban highwayman, the smile he gave her was as much to hide the grimace of pain from the jolt that jump gave his leg.

Her driver reacted quickly, shouting indignantly, and sparing the horses the lash of his buggy whip as he awkwardly swatted back at

Gus with it instead. Wincing between swats of the driver's whip, Gus called out, "Miss Aliyah Gale! I'm ... oww! I'm Gus Baston! I've been trying to ... oww! Stop it! Trying to reach you to talk about Doctor Phand!"

When her surprise at his sudden appearance in her window wore off, Miss Aliyah Gale gave a languid sigh and nodded in acquiescence. Looking towards the driver, she pronounced, "That's enough. Let him come in."

Although she spoke with a conversational softness that was barely audible over the clatter of carriage and hooves, the driver instantly pulled his whip away. Gus and the driver exchanged glares, but then Gus opened the carriage door and slipped inside. He sank into a plush seat opposite hers as the door swung closed behind him and was surprised how quiet it was in the velvet interior.

Looking unamused, Miss Aliyah Gale said, "I'm on my way to a meeting with the mayor. What is it you want from me, Mister Baston?"

Her voice had an elegant burr to it that seemed vaguely foreign, but her accent was unplaceable. Dark curls were piled high on her head in an old-fashioned style, and she wore a glimmering green silk dress covered in Easternist dragon motifs. The dress was form-fitting enough to border on indiscrete, especially without the usual bedecking of ribbons and lace that Verin women typically wore.

As entranced as he had been with her figure when he first saw her in Gemmen, now Gus could only stare enraptured into her eyes, for the first time noticing their color as their emerald sparkle was set off by the same shade in her dress. She seemed perfectly poised and composed as if strangers routinely leapt into her carriage on her trips through town.

She sat patiently as he stared as if his awkward delay were similarly routine. Finally, he said, "I'd love to know what you were meeting with Doctor Phand about back in Gemmen."

She arched an elegant eyebrow and replied, "An interesting line of inquiry, Mister Baston. Very few people knew about that meeting. I was there to sign a contract. The details were worked out by wire, so we merely needed to meet to sign the papers, which we did. You think that relates to his disappearance."

He nodded, feeling awkward and uncomfortable despite the luxuriant seating—something in her sharp consideration withered confidence. Gus wondered what Emily would have thought of her. "What was the contract for? Something about the tower?"

Miss Aliyah Gale gave a small nod and said, "It was. After certain political setbacks, he needed financing to complete it, so I agreed to back his project."

Gus blinked at that, more pieces falling together. "As I understand it, he needed quite a bit. Millions. You loaned him that much?"

She chuckled and waved a manicured hand dismissively, and for the first time, Gus noticed the intricate jewels that adorned her hand. It was some exotic combination of rings and bracelets connected into a single elaborate piece by a fine golden mesh; the sort of absurd jewelry one might see displayed but never worn, and she had donned it for a meeting with a local politician. "Not a loan, Mister Baston, an investment. I purchased a large share of the tower's future revenue. The project would also benefit the city immensely, which in turn would further enrich me and grow other investments I own here."

It seemed like an impossible sum, but having already seen so many displays of Miss Aliyah Gale's wealth, Gus began to rethink his skepticism. "What sort of collateral do you get for all that money?"

She shook her head, "It's an investment, Mister Baston. The money won't change hands until the contract is approved. Doctor Phand personally owns the patent on the tower's design, even though he's been developing the project through his firm. Without him, the deal won't go forward. That would mean a considerable diminishment of profit for me, so I'm hoping he's found soon."

Gus briefly wondered how much money you had to have before not owing someone a million peis would be considered a loss, but the carriage pulled to a halt, and the driver hopped down to open the door. She gestured for Gus to exit first, which he did, though a struggle against the stiffness in his leg left him embarrassed in the process.

Miss Aliyah Gale made a far more elegant exit, smoothly rising out of the doorway and descending gracefully down the stairs as if weightless. Her hand lightly rested on the proffered hand of the driver, but it seemed to be more of a polite gesture than a matter of necessity.

Taking advantage of the delay her descent provided, Gus turned and asked, "But you'd voted against the tower originally. You wanted a park. Why the change of heart?"

Her eyes seemed to spark at that, although Gus supposed it could have just been a trick of the light. Smirking, she replied, "No change of heart, merely of mind. When Doctor Phand presented his construction plan, I saw I might profit from it after all."

She bowed her head in farewell, and then turned towards the city's civic center. A well-dressed man waited eagerly by the door, standing ready to open it as soon as she approached.

Gus briefly wondered if Miss Aliyah Gale had ever been down into the basement to meet with Secretary Ryerson and look over the model cities there. He supposed she must have at some point, as a member of the Exposition's council, but somehow a visit to that cluttered space seemed too far beneath her station.

Another question came to mind, and Gus called after her, "What would happen if he died?"

The waiting man had already opened the door for her, but Miss Aliyah Gale paused in the entrance and looked back at Gus, considering for a moment before she replied, "The patent would be disposed of in his will, I imagine. It would go to his wife, or his firm, or whomever he's designated."

Gus turned that over in his mind as she disappeared inside.

If Doctor Phand died, someone else could build the tower. Miss Aliyah Gale might want to stop the tower to get out of her investment, but her contract was with him, so surely his death would have gotten her off the hook and been far easier to arrange than a strange kidnapping that already involved murder. If someone were just trying to stop construction of the tower though, then killing Phand would have just moved the rights to someone else, who could move forward with construction.

To be sure he was neither dead nor available, they had to hold him until the Exposition's deadline had passed. In just four days though, they would almost certainly need to dispose of him to avoid being exposed afterward. Why would they need to stop the tower from going up?

~

"Royal Visit to Zutruss"

Yesterday, the frontier fortress in Zutruss was visited by her highness, the Princess of Whitby. In honor of the occasion, both Verin and Garren border detachments turned out in full dress. With relatively few local settlers in the area, the gathered military forces featured more performers than admirers, but by all reports, the Princess was an enthusiastic witness to their maneuvers.

Banners for the local regiments were unfurled above the fortress, and within, the walls were hung with a display of the seven Elven banners taken by Verin forces during the war. The collection also included the tattered remains of a Warden flag, which they surrendered to the Imperial forces upon being abandoned by their masters.

– *Khanom Daily Converser*, 15 Tal. 389

~

- CHAPTER 25 -

Resuming his search for a taxi, Gus began to wander back over towards Queen's. The ride to the city's civic center had taken him in the opposite direction of KMC's dormitories, and he was now on the north end of Palace Park. His mind tumbled through the variables as he stared down the length of the park that ran along Queen's.

As he continued to stroll along the street, he reached the end of Embassy Park and the beginning of Palace, where his eyes caught on one of the city's ubiquitous white obelisks. Staring across at the manicured lawn and scattered plantings surrounded in those strangely one-side trees, Gus suddenly noticed a curious difference between Embassy Park and the park on the other side of 10th avenue. Palace Park had several monuments spaced around it, but unlike most blocks in the upper city, Embassy Park had none.

Any other day, he'd have seriously considered turning back to ask Secretary Ryerson why that might be, but unless Ryerson was meeting with Miss Aliyah Gale, his office would almost certainly be closed today. As he contemplated going back to check anyway, Gus saw an empty taxi meandering south alongside the park.

Relieved, Gus flagged it down and, remembering his experience visiting Mister Thomas down below, he waited until he was inside before he asked to be taken to the dormitories of the Khanom Mineral Company. The cabbie seemed disappointed by the destination but begrudgingly drove them south, towards the mountain.

As the parks rolled past the window, Gus thought back on Ulm's words about Phand's proposed tower. It was 'inappropriate' because it was going up where the queen's palace once stood, except the tower wasn't going up there at all. The tower was planned to occupy Embassy Park, directly across the street. It was a strange error for someone on the Exposition Council to make, but Gus had no idea what that might mean.

The road south took them beyond the tall buildings of the city's center, and Gus was finally able to see the homes of Khanom's well-to-do. Large houses akin to those in Gemmen's Old Park lined the southern rim of the plateau, and he could see that others, just a trifle smaller, were along the slopes just beyond.

Eventually the taxi reached the southeastern edge of the plateau, and Gus saw his destination. Sylvester's workers were kept in a small valley between the plateau of the upper city and the steeped slope of the mountain. The strange ring of wind that created Khanom's sooty kirtle was more diffuse here and became nothing more than a thin gray cloud that kept well above the KMC dormitories.

Like the other corporate dormitories he had seen, these were large utilitarian edifices, utterly lacking the decorative whorls that festooned the city above. With no work today, miner's coveralls hung from poles that extended through every window, mixed with a smattering of other laundry items, all waving like flags.

He paid the cabman and looked around the empty lane to which he had been delivered, wondering how far he would have to hike to find a ride back.

The dormitories were hemmed on all sides by the wealthier sections of southern Khanom. Gus was certain KMC's miners had someplace to drink and socialize that didn't require them to cross through the entire city at every recess. There were few people outside, so he decided to peek inside the first dormitory he came to and ask after the likely local watering holes.

The entrance opened to a long, whitewashed hallway, adorned only by the stenciled numbers painted upon the uniformly spaced doors. The first two doors Gus rapped at gave no response, but beyond the third he could hear loud conversation and raucous laughter, so he turned the handle and looked inside without bothering to knock.

At first, he took it to be a party, but as he looked over the room, he realized that no one lived here. Cheap household furniture, probably company issued to each room, had been rearranged, sometimes torn apart, and supplemented with other bits of junk to create a makeshift public house for the dorm dwellers to gather in.

Community public houses, unlike fancy social clubs, were places men and women frequently comingled, and this was no exception. Beer was being passed around with little wooden chits trading hands in exchange, often passing through several hands before reaching the bartender.

When Gus stepped inside, several of the patrons stared at him in obvious surprise, although the man standing behind the overturned bed frame that served as their makeshift bar gave a welcoming grin, likely happy to see a customer that would pay in cash rather than mining company scrip.

Settling onto an old barrel that served as a chair, Gus looked around at the furniture and realized it was all much less temporary than he would have first guessed. Despite the improvised arrangements, the wear on nearly everything marked its consistent use in the makeshift pub for a decade or more. He wondered if Maurice Sylvester even knew this was here or if the barkeep had simply set it up in secret.

As Gus approached the bar, the regulars greeted him with smiles and murmured welcomes, although conversation did seem to quiet down a bit at his presence. Gus always preferred something with a bit more bite than the three-penny beer the patrons here looked to be drinking. Counting out half a peis, he slid a small stack of pennies across the sideboard and asked, "You have anything back there other than beer?"

The bartender grinned and scooped up the cash with one hand as the other set down a small, empty jar. With a flourish, he produced a clay jug and poured from it a light-yellow, clear liquid that looked like urine and smelled like turpentine.

A hush fell around the room as Gus looked down at the drink, and unsure what else to do, he lifted his glass in toast to the bartender and then tossed it back.

It burned his throat, and he had to fight back the urge to sneeze as the fumes of the stuff tickled his nose. Clearing his now sore throat, Gus set the jar down and panted as it burned at his gullet. The room erupted into a merry cheer, and several people clapped him on the back in congratulations; whatever that stuff was, it had clearly been a test he had passed.

Without any demand for more coin, the bartender pushed across a mug of the beer, which tasted awful but at least seemed to soothe some of the burning in Gus's throat. The bartender grinned over as Gus gulped it down and asked, "So what brings you down here, stranger?"

His throat was still rough, and Gus coughed a few more times before he managed to reply, "Trying to find someone whose father used to work down here. Dorna Michts?"

The bartender shook his head, but an older woman seated nearby answered, "Oh, I remember her! Little straw-haired thing." Gus nodded, and she turned to the bartender and said, "Her father was Edmund Michts—they moved out here when her mother died. He worked the seam with us and even helped organize meetings back when there was still union talk."

Noting that her father 'was', Gus asked, "What happened to him?"

The old woman sighed and said, "Oh, well, he was a good worker, got promoted to gold, and you know how it is. The copper's dangerous too, of course, but the seam's more recent—newer tunnels, better built. The gold mine's running on forty years now. They have a lot more accidents."

Gus didn't really know anything about mining but didn't think he needed to, so he just nodded, and she resumed her story. "His poor little girl was left an orphan, but then some rich uncle or something took her in. He sent for her with his own carriage and everything. It was before these new buildings went up, so it must have been about twenty years ago."

"Did you know the uncle?" The old woman shook her head, so he asked the room, "Anyone here work the gold mine?"

The bartender snorted, and the woman cackled, and a few of the other patrons grinned and shook their heads. The woman grinned at what was apparently Gus's gaffe and replied, "No, no, they get their own dorm near the mine. It's lots nicer, from all I hear. They make more money too, though that may change soon with all the electrical!"

"Electrical uses copper?" he asked, and the woman nodded enthusiastically. Gus smiled amiably at her assumption of impending good fortune from the rise in copper, but one of the details in her story niggled him, so he asked, "If the gold mine has its own dorms, why was Dorna still here to be picked up by her uncle?"

"Poor man didn't last but a day. He hadn't even been moved out yet when he died. Then the uncle came in, swept her away."

Thinking back to his conversation with Miss Aliyah Gale's valet, he asked, "That uncle wasn't Cornelius Zephyr, was it?"

She laughed again, apparently already a bit tipsy, and said, "No! I'd remember if he came down here!" With a girlish giggle, she poked at one of her neighbors at the bar and said, "Remember those suits he wore? And the hats? He was always so fancy! You know, my sister worked as one of his maids for a week, but she was fired when she worried about the ghosts."

The bartender rolled his eyes, clearly too young to have known much about Zephyr, so Gus asked, "Ghosts?"

Eyes widening, the old woman nodded earnestly and said, "She said at all hours, there was this voice in the walls, a deep rumble in a language she didn't know. Probably elfish."

"Really?" He thought back to his visit to Miss Aliyah Gale's office and the strange rumble he had heard there, felt nearly as much as heard. Could it have been a voice? Gus was not a believer in most ghost stories, but he had lived through enough of them not to discount the possibility. The old woman nodded again, so he added, "She was smart to get out of there then. Did she know Miss Aliyah Gale?"

The bartender chuckled and said, "Nobody did."

At that, the old woman nodded. "He's right. She was named in his will, and a young girl rode into town the very day after he died and moved right into his office."

"Does she live there?" They shook their heads, so he asked, "Where does she live?" No one knew. "What about Miss Dorna Michts? Where is she these days?"

The old woman shrugged, but a man spoke up from the back of the room and said, "She still lives in the city someplace. She came by here for the Hearth Festival with a bunch of others from the Upper. Wasn't dressed like one from there, but she was helping give out food. She even remembered me."

"Blonde?" Gus asked, then held up his hand and added, "And about so tall?"

The man nodded, and Gus finally felt certain he had the name of his false Alice Phand. And probably the D.M. from Saucier's letter. Grateful, he laid down a peis to refill everyone else's beers. Despite the enthusiastic gratitude, they knew little else about Dorna Michts, so he pressed for more about her father, but he had died so long ago few remembered him.

Edmund Michts had died unusually quickly, but it seemed like most only worked there a year or two, even though they reputedly lived in far grander style among their fellow gold miners for as long as they stayed. A few were said to have struck it rich and left the city, but no one in the makeshift pub knew any of those personally.

The mortality rate at Sylvester's gold mine seemed disturbingly high, but despite that, none of the miners seemed concerned by it. Eventually, they all toasted to someday making the climb up there and striking it rich.

The miners' world was strangely cloistered; they dwelt in company dormitories and bought their necessities from the company store. They all paid for drinks with wooden chits, and Gus wondered if any of them had any real money or if they were slaves to company scrip. Gemmen's factories weren't exactly models of fair pay for fair work, but at least their pennies were actually paid.

As he began his long hike back to the upper city, Gus was a little disappointed to come away with little more than a name, but it was more than he'd had before. Dorna Michts. First, she had gone after Saucier, trying to lure him in with the promise of elfsteel trinkets, and then she had been involved in Phand's kidnapping.

The elfsteel buckle sent to Saucier was an extravagant gift, and how could a poor miner's daughter possibly have an uncle rich enough for such a thing? And who would consider stopping Phand's tower worth expending that kind of treasure merely as bait?

~

"Tuls Government-In-Exile Formed"

Tuls aristocrats gathering in Sakloch have presented their exiled queen with a request to reform the Tuls government, in preparation to retake their homeland. The Sultan allowed the magnar's widow use of his throne room for the occasion and honored her with a dais only slightly lower than his own as he observed the gathering.

By all accounts, despite her difficult situation, the queen received the petition with grace and dignity. She confirmed her intention to grant their request, but noted that in the absence of her deceased husband, formal steps could only be taken if the Duke of Maustoya or the Duke of Errapol could lead a reformed Congress in the magnar's absence. As both men are reported dead, the Tuls aristocracy will be forced to nominate replacements once a sufficient quorum of exiled lords can be achieved.

– Khanom Daily Converser, 15 Tal. 389

~

- CHAPTER 26 -

The Master's grand parlor had been cleared, and the curtains closed. The large room was furnished for entertaining, littered with plush chairs and elegant couches in rich reds and deep blues. Dorna had lit only two of the gas lamps along the wall, which hissed softly and on their own could only dimly light the large space they had gathered in.

The artworks hung here were more mundane than those he kept elsewhere, traditional landscapes mixed with human portraiture that so little resembled the Master's human guise, Dorna wondered how anyone was fooled by them. It seemed ironic to her that amid such bland décor, few ever took notice of the stone sarcophagus, a rectangular box of pale granite, polished smooth, but covered with graven sigils no man could read. It was one of the Master's most puissant treasures, yet she had seen countless visitors resting drinks upon it like a table.

Marjorie had brought the two men she promised, and Dorna stood three paces from the foot of the box, watching as the two men wedged prybars beneath the tightly fitted stone lid. They all wore their Wardens' robes, although Dorna felt a twinge of guilt at that since they had come together for a task the Master had not planned for them. She did not know what Marjorie had told Dougal's two friends they were doing, and she did not ask.

A small brazier burned beside her, and in the chill of early spring, she cherished its warmth. Indoors and wrapped in her thick green robes, she should have been warm enough, but somehow the cold had overtaken her as if it radiated from her very bones. Ever since having seen the Master open the stone box as a girl, she felt that way whenever she was near it.

Looking at the angular script chiseled into the stone, she imagined they were dire words of warning from whoever had crafted it. They covered every inch as if to be absolutely certain whoever came across it would heed their words, forgetting that eventually their language would be lost to the ages.

In her hands, she held another box, a small wooden rectangle with no visible opening. It was covered in similar script to the sarcophagus, but the pale pine surface of the wooden case had been polished nearly smooth in the centuries that had passed since it was made.

The men wedging back the stone lid had little notion of what lay within, and had Dougal emerged from the labyrinth, perhaps it could finally have remained forever sealed as its makers had intended. The Master's paragon of ruthless obedience to the cause was gone though, and it had been her fault.

She thought she had followed his instructions so perfectly, but somehow she had gone awry. However Baston had managed to follow her, he was out there still, no doubt still hunting them, and he was a threat Dorna had brought upon the Great Restoration. She needed leverage that would stop him quickly.

Staring across at the stone box, she wondered if Dougal would have gone this far. Perhaps it was simply too dangerous for mortals. Perhaps they would open it and all be killed. It had not been opened in years, but she was sure she remembered the necessary steps. The danger to her cause was too great, and if releasing this monster would fix her mistakes, then she must be ruthless enough to do it. She would be the servant the Master needed.

It was no longer simply a matter of being as good as Dougal. It was her failure that led to his death, so she must fulfill his role in their cause as well as her own. He was the one for hard-hearted tasks and dark doings, and this was the darkest, hardest course of action she could think of.

Marjorie's two Wardens gathered around the stone box, grunting as they slowly wedged their pry bars beneath the lid. The stone was already chipped, but the lid was heavy and very tightly fitted. Stone ground against stone as they pried it free, and when it came loose, there was a sharp hiss as the stale air within finally escaped the box after years of compression. Dorna had warned them it would happen, but both men still jerked back nervously.

Stepping between them, Terry counted out, and on three they pulled at the stone lid, groaning in effort as they worked together to gently lower it to the floor. In the dimly lit room, Dorna could see only shadow inside, and at the silence that greeted them, she worried something had gone wrong or that the box was somehow empty. Now that the box was open, however, she dared not step away from her place by the brazier.

Panting and brushing stone-dusted hands on his jacket, Terry leaned forward to peek inside. As soon as he did, he paled and stepped quickly away, his fearful expression and eager retreat told her that it was definitely not empty.

Dorna gripped the wooden case tightly, hoping that a tighter grip would hide the trembling in her hands as a wintry breeze leeched the last warmth from the room. The lights guttered, but even in the sudden chill, their gas lamps were not so easily extinguished. Her eyes darted nervously to the brazier, but its coals still burned.

It rose, not as a man might rise from bed or even climb from a box; instead, it simply lifted upright in one motion, like an idle marionette whose strings were pulled upward. Pale, knobby limbs crudely parodied the shape of man. It was hairless and cloaked only in a gray linen robe of rotting fabric that had long since faded to translucency.

It stretched out; bones crackled as old joints began to move once more, and its ancient sinew creaked like stretching leather.

The thing's skin was smooth and unblemished, uniformly unnaturally parchment pale, but as the loosed immortal slowly turned in the air to settle upon its feet, its yellow eyes settled upon her, the sole Warden stationed before it. It snarled, a lipless mouth parting open over a jagged maw, its open jaw spreading inhumanly wide as it stalked towards her.

Dorna held up the wooden case, and the beast stopped in its tracks, cursing at her in an ancient tongue long since passed from the world. The thing raised its talons and reached towards her, and though still several steps away, she knew it could cross that distance in the blink of an eye.

In the sternest voice she could muster, Dorna said, "No." She swung the box over the brazier, holding over the flames with one hand. The monster froze in place, yellow eyes fixed upon the smoke that curled around the box.

The thing sneered and cursed again, drawing itself up in outrage, so she turned her hand, precariously dangling the box from two fingers pinched around its corner. The immortal hissed at her again as smoke began to smudge the lower edges of the box with a dark stain of soot. She wondered if it was fast enough to grab the box before it fell in the fire and how quickly the box would burn, along with whatever it contained.

Yellow eyes darted between her and the small case, clearly pondering the same questions, so she demanded of it, "We will speak in Verin."

She held herself as stiffly as she could, terrified to let it see her trembling. The demand for Verin was absurd and desperate; the Master had spoken to it in Elven, a language as old as time, and one the creature surely knew. Dorna's Elven was limited to recitation by rote; she had never understood more than a few words in that sacred tongue, which was not enough to explain what she needed. She had to hope the monster could speak her language.

Those pale-yellow eyes bored into her, and she could feel her heart thundering in her chest, and each breath was a struggle to draw under that dread scrutiny. Finally, in a dry, raspy voice, it hissed, "Barbarian."

It glared about the room, and though she dared not look away from it, from the corner of her eye, she could see the other Wardens flinching back fearfully. "You will obey me," she commanded. "You will do as I say. I have an errand you must do."

The beast raised its boney hands as if to grasp the wooden box from several paces away, and though its yellow eyes remained focused on the box, it snarled at her, "Foolish slave, I will not serve you! Where is your master?"

Yellow eyes turned back to Dorna, their gaze boring into her with an unsettling intensity that made her want to shrink back. With a sudden burst of adrenaline, Dorna realized the thing now loomed within arm's reach. Somehow, though she had not noticed it move, it had crept closer, close enough now to grab at the case.

She quickly raised her other hand, and at that signal, Marjorie opened the drapes behind Dorna.

Sunlight poured in, the window flooding the room with dazzling white light. The immortal shrieked, a horrific, inhuman sound that made Dorna flinch, and wherever it was graced by the sun, its skin softened and began to flow like melting wax.

It crumpled to the floor, forced to kneel at her feet in the only hiding place it could reach—Dorna's shadow. The immortal terror mewled in pain, and Dorna felt a surge of triumph.

She snapped her fingers, and Terry hurried over bearing a map, which he displayed for the immortal in trembling hands. His obvious fear of the creature just made her feel all the more powerful for facing it down, and as she towered over the monster, she commanded, "You will make all haste to the city of Gemmen. In this building," she gestured to the map, and Terry helpfully put his finger on the specific block, "on the fourth floor, a woman spends her days. Find her and bring her to me as quickly as possible."

It sneered up at her as defiantly as it could manage from its abject pose on the floor, "Fool woman! You would loose me simply to murder your romantic rivals?"

As the monster cowered at her feet, her first impulse was to kick it, but fearful common sense checked that reckless notion. "Bring her to me alive! She must be brought here unharmed."

The immortal rapped its talons against the floor, and an inhuman rattle sounded in its throat, an impatient growl. "Killing is faster and more certain. Send me against your real foe, foolish mortal."

It was tempting, but having seen the medals on Baston's wall, she dared not risk one of the Master's prize possessions to fix her own mistake. "No! He fought the Lich King and has slain your kind before. Just do as I say and bring me that woman. Alive!"

It growled at her from its awkward place at her feet, and she waggled the ancient wooden box above the fire, feeling whatever mysterious leverage it contained sliding about inside. At that motion, the immortal froze in place again, inhuman yellow eyes fixed once more upon the case in her hand. The monster sneered but thankfully dared nothing further.

"Do that, then return to your slumber, and I will not set this ablaze." Looming over the immortal, she pronounced, "*Saloda*?"

Its yellow eyes darted between the box in her hand and her face, and Dorna stiffened her shoulders to fight her nervous trembling as it weighed her bargain. Waggling the box again, she repeated, "*Saloda?*"

It snarled at her, but then begrudgingly repeated her crude Elven.

Dorna raised her free hand, and Marjorie drew the curtains shut, plunging the room into dim gaslight that now seemed even darker than it had before. The beast glared up at her from its place on the floor, then burst apart into wisps of black smoke that were quickly scattered by an unfelt draft, like ethereal serpents slithering into nonexistence.

Around the room, one of Marjorie's Wardens gasped, and Marjorie pressed herself fearfully back against the wall, but Dorna sighed in relief. Slowly, she lowered her arm from above the brazier.

Saloda, it had said. The deal was struck.

When she had witnessed this before, the Master had assured that terrified young girl that the immortal was bound to his word. She did not know why, or how, but she knew that for the sake of whatever was kept in that wooden case, it would do her bidding and then return itself to its stone prison once done.

Dorna scratched at the sooty black that now stained one corner of the wooden case, only then noticing the pain in her hand from having had held it above the fire too long. It was red, and she rubbed at it tenderly, hoping she wouldn't blister.

Marjorie took a deep breath and began to softly recite the Elven chant they all knew so well. The others took it up with her, and Dorna's lips parted, instinctively drawn to join in, but then she shook her head and closed her mouth.

There was a risk that this, tampering with the Master's secret arts without him, would disappoint him even more than just leading

Baston to them would. The words could make her feel better, but they would not lessen the risk she had just undertaken.

When the monster returned, she could seek the Master's help with her plan and perhaps confess herself to him then. The Great Restoration was all that mattered. If this worked, then surely he would forgive her.

~

"Rakhasin Rail Expansion Planned"

The story of the Royal Rakhasin Railway Company during the first year of its existence is a remarkable one, and the effect of what is being done is exciting the notice of both Verinde and Garren, for northeastern Rakhasin has virgin farmlands enough to meet the ever-expanding requirements of Verinde, and we may expect to hear little more of Garren grain "corners."

In the just completed first year, the company built and acquired 783 miles of road. The company has let contracts for the construction of an additional 150 miles before the wet season commences. By the fall, therefore, there should be over 1,000 miles in operation. Of the land on either side of the line not reserved for other purposes, about 750,000 acres have been sold during the past six months, chiefly in lots of 160 acres, and to Verin immigrants.

– Khanom Daily Converser, 16 Tal. 389

~

- CHAPTER 27 -

Well lubricated on the bathtub hooch the miners drank, Gus slept well and woke the next morning feeling refreshed. The signature deadline on the tower project was three days away; these imitation Wardens probably wouldn't risk Phand turning up dead before then, but based on his brief encounter, they seemed like an anxious lot, which meant they might do something stupid.

Whatever mastermind had plotted the kidnapping was smart, but Gus had seen nervous underlings take down savvy criminals before. A panicked flunky might act without orders, which might get Phand killed early, so Gus skipped lunch and went out to examine the alleyway he had caught them in.

Traffic was typically light at the start of the week but better than the day before, so he had little trouble finding a cab to take him six blocks up Queen's. When he stepped off the main road towards the alleyway, he paused to recall the Wardens' disappearance as it had happened.

He moved to where he had been standing when the police approached, and from there he could see a brownish stain of blood from the Warden he had shot. A trail of dark droplets led into the side alley just beyond. Nearly a dozen men had been in that alley when he arrived, and not a minute later, it was empty.

The bloodstains were easy to follow around the corner and into the side alley, but from there they vanished. The alley stood in a perpetual gloom cast by the tall buildings surrounding it, but even hunched down, he could track droplets no further than the center of the narrow space.

One of the fellow cultists might have helped stopper their fellow's wound, but a delay to do so would have left them with even less time to disappear. Gus paced back and forth, poking at the bare walls and kicking aside drifts of garbage that had settled into the strange niche between buildings. There were doorways in the alley that stood directly off Queen's, but there was nothing else that connected to this strange alcove for the Elven obelisk.

Looking up, he wondered if they might have ascended somehow, but there were no windows overhead, just a dozen or so stories of flat wall. Had they gone for the roof, he liked to think he would have noticed the gang of them still clambering up the wall while he stood below with the police. The only feature of note was the white obelisk at the end of the alcove, stark against the gray cement of the back walls.

The two buildings that formed the alcove shared a wall that extended to 10th, but they split on either side of the obelisk before reaching the alleyway off Queen's. Like the others he had seen in Khanom, it was a white pylon with a semicircular concavity that faced the alleyway. Wedging himself between the wall and the Elven artifact, he peered around it to look behind it for a hidden opening in either building but found nothing there.

Stepping into the arc of the obelisk, Gus looked over the various glyphs graven across the smooth white stone. There was nothing familiar there, although he did not know Elven, so that was not very surprising. If the glyphs were symbolic, their meaning was too abstract for him to decipher by shape alone. He kicked it a few times but succeeded only in hurting his foot; it did not seem hollow, nor did it budge at his efforts.

After a few more minutes examining the alleyway, he gave up on it. Not sure where to go next, he returned to Queen's and strolled south along the park. The city did seem strangely quiet for what was traditionally a working day back home, but he supposed even in Gemmen, many businesses unofficially idled the day after Temple.

As he neared the intersection with 10th, he could smell baking bread, and a sudden hunger for it made his stomach clench. A half-block down, a small café on 10th was selling baguettes with cream for three bits, a price just shy of outrageous, but he gave in to hunger's demand and purchased one. He claimed a seat outside and ate slowly while reading through the café's newspaper.

According to the paper, it was the Queen Mother's birthday again. Some sort of naval action between pirates and a flotilla of mercantile concerns had resolved. There was also something about another railway expansion planned in Rakhasin. It was a decade late for him to care about that, but it did remind him that the fifth member of the Exposition's council, Mister Beck, was supposedly traveling there, although he wasn't mentioned in the article.

As he assuaged the rumbling from his belly, Gus's thoughts began returning to the false Alice Phand who had gotten him tangled in all this. Who was Dorna Michts? It was probably the next question he needed to answer, but he wasn't sure where to find her. He considered a visit to the KMC's gold mine, but Dorna's father was only there a single day twenty years ago, and Gus had no reason to think she had ever been there.

Dorna Michts was taken in by an unknown wealthy uncle. It was also around twenty years ago that Cornelius Zephyr had died and Miss Aliyah Gale suddenly appeared. In Gus's experience, the wealthiest families tended to have well known genealogies, and it would have been a strange year indeed when two young girls were both so unexpectedly elevated.

With the various false fronts in the kidnapping, it seemed unlikely Dorna Michts was the end of it, regardless. From what Gus could recall, she was dressed no differently than her fellow Wardens, and with other secret societies he had encountered, the leaders were always bedecked in symbols of office, a particularly important step in a group that usually hid their faces.

If Dorna Michts wasn't their leader, then maybe it was her 'uncle', but given Khanom's surprising affluence, Gus felt he wasn't anywhere near to narrowing down the uncle's identity. It might not even really be a man; if Miss Aliyah Gale had sent her new valet in her personal coach to collect Dorna Michts, he could easily have been mistaken for a wealthy uncle.

Gus wasn't sure how any of that would lead Dorna Michts to the Wardens or why anyone would be a Warden with no Elves. He could almost chalk that up as just a club with poor taste, but the layers of misdirection in Phand's kidnapping pointed to someone with experience evading the law or access to that experience, neither of which came easily to the sort usually indulged in secret societies.

The real Wardens went out of business nearly forty years ago, but if the Warden robes were merely misdirection from a criminal enterprise, then wearing the robes in Khanom made no sense. At a loss, he returned to Rondel's, hoping perhaps a bath and another drink might help him sort his thoughts.

The desk clerk greeted him cheerfully as he entered, which was off-putting until he realized it was not the same gentleman who had arranged the slotted key earlier. Pausing there a moment, Gus asked, "Do you know the Michts family?"

The clerk shook his head and replied, "No, sir. They expected as guests here? If you like, I could pass along your card."

Gus sighed and shook his head, but rather than explain himself to the clerk, he just said, "If they do, just tell them Gus Baston is looking for them."

"Oh! Mister Baston? A gentleman just dropped off a note for you."

Gus hoped it would be from Eli Allen or even another hint dug up by Dolly Dench, but as the clerk passed him the note, the feminine script of Gus's name on the outside of the folded sheet brought another pair of suspicious characters immediately to mind—the letters *D* and *M.* Inside, the note read:

There is an important meeting tonight at sunset in the warehouse on Derrick & Southland.

It was unsigned and the paper of decent stock but unadorned. Did she expect him to imagine some anonymous benefactor? There seemed very little chance this was not some sort of trap, but it was the best chance he had to learn more about these Wardens and what they had done with Phand.

On a whim, he sniffed at it, but it only smelt of paper and ink, and he was not sure how he could have told anything about who wrote it by scent even had he detected more. The clerk chuckled at that, so Gus gave the man a stern frown and demanded, "Where is Southland and Derrick?"

A street map was quickly fetched from below the clerk desk, and it showed Southland was within the lower city, on the edge of town closer to the mountains. Cab fare would be a nuisance, and Gus felt a little uncomfortable going in unarmed since the police had stolen his pistol after the last strange meeting he dropped in on.

"Any idea where I could buy a pistol around here?"

The clerk stammered over that one a bit, saying something about restrictions on weapons within the city, so Gus bid his farewell.

The promise of a revealing trap left Gus feeling re-energized about his investigation, but with several hours before sunset, he decided to forgo his bath and instead go confirm Mister Beck really was travelling abroad. Most of the city seemed to slumber the day after

Temple, but Gus felt confident a rail company would still have someone in the office.

A bit of luck got him an enclosed cab shortly after stepping outside the hotel, and with traffic so thin, Gus decided to hire him for the day. The driver's name was Errol. He was youngish, unmarried, and their brief exchange of pleasantries upon his hiring revealed a disappointing disinterest in music.

Errol did, however, know where the rail offices were, although that hardly seemed impressive since Gus had already spotted those on his way into town. The Eastern Rail Company was back at the northern edge of the plateau, adjacent to the main hub.

Staring at passengers loitering around the neighboring platform, Gus contemplated buying a ticket for Doctor Phand. He needed to get the man home to be sure of collecting his reward, but if Gus were rolled again, by the police or otherwise, they'd be less likely to steal a ticket to Gemmen than they would the cash to pay for it. In a tight spot though, still having the thirty peis for a third-class ticket in hand would more useful than an extra ticket.

Deciding to hold on to his money for now, Gus proceeded into the rail office. A brief meeting with Beck's secretary and a glance at the shuttered office over the man's shoulder, supported the story of wintering in Rakhasin. A bit of flimflam got Gus the home address, and Errol drove him all the way across town and into the hills to double check that alibi at Beck's residence.

The railway man's house would not have looked out of place in Old Park but for the series of telegraph poles erected across the yard connecting a wire to one corner of the house. Unlike Saucier's home, Beck's appeared to be thoroughly out of service with all the windows shuttered. Dead leaves clustered in some of the eaves, which meant the shutters were not only closed but also had not been opened for several months.

As Errol waited on the street, Gus took the time to circle Beck's estate, but there was no sign of any human presence, nor that there had been any time recently. It looked as if Beck really was wintering in Gambai.

Gus had passed through the Rakhasin colonial capital of Ganbai a few times while in the army, but at the time, it had just been a port and a decent whore house. He wondered if Beck's presence there meant that Rakhasin had finally been civilized.

If Beck was really on the other side of the world, then he probably wasn't the man behind the Wardens. Ulm had been the best lead at finding them, and Gus decided his next move would be to go shake him down for more information. First though, he needed to survive whatever trap Dorna Michts was luring him into.

~

"Jeune Divorce Case"

The hearing on this much talked-of and long-expected case commenced yesterday in Gemmen, in the Court of Divorce before Lord Palvasher and a specially convened jury. The matter has been so frequently mentioned that it is almost unnecessary to say that the question which now came on for trial was not the guilt or innocence of Lady Jeune in respect of the charges of adultery, but of her sanity and capacity to plead an answer to the charges.

As detailed yesterday, Lord Jeune's team of petitioners had presented their arguments across the petitioner of Lord Hartwell, acting as guardian for the accused, his daughter. At yesterday's hearing, evidence and argument was presented by Lord Hartwell's petitioners that the Lady Jeune's thoroughly well-proven infidelity was symptomatic of a persistent unsoundness of mind of unknown causation from which she is said to suffer still. If held so by the jury, then Lord Jeune shall be obliged to her continued maintenance as his wife.

– Khanom Daily Converser, 16 Tal. 389

~

- CHAPTER 28 -

Errol assured Gus that no place atop the plateau would sell him a pistol any day of the week, so they passed through the ring of soot into the town below. It seemed honest advice, but the closest he came to success was finding a shop with a new Simpson revolver on display in the window, and all Gus could do was gaze upon it longingly—the day after Temple, the shop was as closed as everything else.

With the sun getting lower and no other likely options for armament, Gus finally had Errol drive him down to Southland. Gus guessed he had a bit over an hour before the sun set, giving him time to look the place over before stepping into whatever trap these Wardens were arranging.

There were other warehouses in the area, but only one stood at Southland and Derrick; across from that were what appeared to be a doctor's office and some sort of boarded-up shop. It seemed the old white roads were spread further apart down below; Southland was Elven, and starkly contrasted by Derrick's black surface. Where they intersected, the human-laid tar lapped sloppily over the edges of the ancient Elven tiles.

When they arrived at their destination, Gus quickly discovered that Errol had absolutely no knack for discreet observation—the man parked directly across from the entrance, then turned in his perch to stare directly at it. Missing Louis terribly, Gus quickly debarked and told Errol to drive around the block and wait for him on the corner two blocks down Southland.

The warehouse was a large square building with narrow windows along the roofline that would provide light inside but no view. The sign on the doors read *Gotha Aelfua* in a fancy script, which meant nothing to Gus.

Circling the building, he found all the doors chained shut and heavily locked, but for one in the front. There was no indication of what was stored there, but that was hardly unusual since an independent storage company would rent space to whoever needed it.

As he looked around, he kept an eye out for anything he might use as a weapon. In the alley between Southland and Marjorie, he came across a discarded tangle of plumbing. It was wet and covered in some sort of grease, but he managed to wipe that off with a bit of newspaper he found nearby. The pipes were rusty, but a decent length of the inch-thick cast iron would make a serviceable club.

Gripping at a section of it, he managed to tear off a one-foot piece of it, although the twist to free that part from the rest left it jaggedly torn at one end. He tucked it into his jacket, jagged point up to avoid tearing his pocket and then returned to the front door of the warehouse. It swung quietly open, and he stepped inside.

Crates were stacked on pallets atop a well-pounded earthen floor but clustered in shipping groups rather than neat rows, which left the interior something of a maze. The boxes smelled of fresh-cut pine, having been recently manufactured somewhere nearby and filled with local goods soon to be loaded into cars at the nearest rail hub come tomorrow morning.

The light from the windows was dim, but he saw no signs of movement nor heard any reaction to his entry. If his assumption of ambush was right, it seemed they weren't here yet. Going back outside, he tried to find a subtle vantage from which to watch the one unlocked door.

Without a paper, he had a hard time looking inconspicuous, but in the full hour ahead of the 'important meeting', no one came in or out of the warehouse, and he began to wish he'd brought a paper just to distract himself. Down the block, he could see Errol had one and was reading it as he sat idle on his perch.

A few people passed further down the street, none seeming to notice him as they turned off down other lanes or entered other buildings. When the lamplighter began making his rounds, Gus did one last circuit of the warehouse. Everything was still locked, with no sign the other doors had been disturbed.

Shortly after the sun settled on the horizon, a light sprung on inside, and Gus cursed at having missed his glimpse of whoever must have stepped inside while he checked the other doors. Placing one hand on the broken pipe in his pocket to reassure himself it was there, Gus entered the warehouse once more.

The lights were in the back, so he crept quietly that way through the maze of pallets until he could see the lanterns illuminating a space at the end of a corridor of boxes. They spotted him almost immediately, and Gus began walking slowly forward. As this was to be an ambush, he expected someone to close in behind him, but strangely that never happened.

Altogether, there were six Wardens gathered in a semicircle in that light, their green hoods drawn up to render them a menacing sameness, punctuated only by angry eyes peering out at him through triangular holes cut into the veils that covered their faces. It was a decent number for an ambush, but it would have made far more sense for one of them to close off his escape route, and he wondered briefly at the degree of that incongruity with the planning of Phand's kidnapping.

At the center of the group, one of the Wardens reached forward to remove the hood of another Warden standing at the front of the group. Gus recognized Emily immediately; she looked disheveled, and the Wardens had tied a gag beneath the hood. She kept her hands behind her, and he realized they must have tied them.

"Emily!" he exclaimed, and her bright green eyes perked up with an intense fury. Clearly, she did not appreciate her involvement in this caper, and Gus wondered how they had gotten her all the way to Khanom. She tried to say something, but her words were lost behind the gag.

The Warden that had unmasked Emily gripped her shoulder, and when she spoke up, Gus immediately recognized the voice of the false Alice Phand. "We will no longer accept your interference, Mister Baston! You've made an enemy of the Wardens!"

Glancing at the group, Gus noticed that even though Dorna was talking and holding Emily hostage, the other Wardens still seemed tense. Someone who felt in control of the situation, someone trying to project menace to keep things calm, would stand tall and try to seem authoritative. Instead, even in their robes he could tell they leaned slightly forward, and their eyes were fixed on him. Judging by those stiff postures, the four other Wardens still expected to spring on him and were just awaiting the signal.

From the attacker's perspective, Gus knew that a fearful-looking man seemed like an easier target than an angry one, so he scowled and stepped forward, not wanting to look cowed by their numbers. If they all piled on at once, the broken piece of pipe in his pocket wouldn't amount to much, but few men would want to be first into a fight, knowing they'd be sure to be hit before their numbers overwhelmed him. So long as he didn't look too vulnerable, they'd wait for their signal, whatever that was.

"I *was* out of your way! You came to me! You involved me in this mess, then you killed my friend, and now—now you're kidnapping my receptionist?" Gus gave it all the incredulous indignation he could muster, hoping that bluster might yet carry the day. If they had gone to the trouble of kidnapping Emily, then they must not want him dead.

The Wardens remained tense, but Dorna didn't yet give them whatever order they were waiting on. "You mean the cabbie?" she replied, and he could hear a fatigue behind her words. "You … you killed my friend too, you know. The one you shot. He was the one who … who took care of the cabbie back in Gemmen. You've already had your revenge."

In the army, Gus had fired on a few men but, as far as he knew, had never actually hit one, not a living one anyway. He'd been in some tight scrapes since but never had a death laid at his feet. The news rocked him a bit, and he struggled to maintain his composure. "What about Phand?"

"No, he must stay with us. That's just money to you though, right? We'll give you your girl back, and you'll go away."

She seemed to be looking for an excuse to let him go, and while he had no intention of abandoning the case, he nodded slowly in agreement. Seeming satisfied with that, Dorna pushed Emily forward a step.

The other Wardens watched quietly, but their tense readiness remained even as Emily crossed the few steps between them. They were still planning to jump him, still waiting on the signal.

Emily repeated something into her gag as she walked slowly forward, the intense outrage in her eyes seeming increasingly out of place as she moved away from her captors. Another step, and she repeated herself again. Gus wondered for a moment if it was supposed to be some sort of warning; she seemed pretty upset about it.

Then he realized the fearful expression of an imperiled victim was entirely absent from her face. She stalked forward with a stiff intensity that screamed out warning to him more clearly than whatever it was that she kept urgently reciting into her gag. When her unbound hands swung out from behind her back, Gus was in motion even before she raised the knife that was clutched in her fist.

He sprang backwards, the blade grazing a shallow cut across his belly that would have eviscerated him had he not pulled away. Without thinking, he swung a right cross that caught Emily on the side of the head, and she fell limp from the blow. He was immediately sorry for it, and lunged forward to catch her, fighting a sharp stab of pain in his leg.

Hooded green heads turned towards Dorna, who shouted at Emily, "No, not yet!" Then, turning to the other Wardens, she said, "Well … go! Get him! Get him!" and the Wardens all drew their knives.

Gus tried to shift his weight to his uninjured leg, leaning Emily against his shoulder while he reached for the only weapon he had. A burr on the jagged end of the pipe caught on the waist of his jacket as he pulled the pipe from his pocket, and it tangled in the fabric as he tried to wrest it free with one hand.

Seeing the blunt end of it emerge, half-covered in cloth, one of the Wardens recoiled and shouted, "He's got a gun!"

That shout brought the others to a wary halt, and quick to take advantage, Gus stopped trying to pull it free and instead pointed the blunt end of pipe at them from under the tangle of his jacket. "Get back! All of you, stay back!"

They eagerly obliged, and one towards the back even fled between crates. Dorna shouted at one of her hooded allies, "You said they took his gun!"

After a moment's hesitation, Dorna's gang of Wardens took to their heels, scattering amid the boxes, fleeing towards some back corner of the warehouse. Dorna cursed and yelled at them to grab the gun instead, but they ignored her, and one even tossed aside his knife as he scrambled to escape. A heartbeat later, Dorna turned to join them in flight.

Gus laid Emily gently to the floor as he watched them. They hardly seemed the sort of expert criminals one would expect to find associated with Phand's carefully planned kidnapping. Dorna Michts had essentially confirmed Phand was still alive when she said he had to stay with them, but Gus still had no idea where they were holding Doctor Phand, so he needed to pursue them and find out more.

Reluctantly leaving Emily unconscious on the floor, Gus carefully followed their flight towards the back corner of the warehouse. There was no door to the street back there, and since he didn't hear anything going on there as he approached, Gus worried this might be a more elaborate trap. By the time he crept around the last stack of boxes to peer into that back corner, they were gone.

The tightly stacked crates afforded no hiding place the Wardens could have slipped into, and the only oddity was the column of white stone that had been used by the builder as a plinth to support that corner of the warehouse. There, the concave side of the Elven monument faced inward, creating a shadowed alcove of ancient runes.

Gus stepped forward to pushed at the column and found it every bit as immobile as the other he had tried. The walls around it felt firm, and none of the nearby boxes moved easily. He looked over the column again and felt the answer must be there somehow, but he was too worried over Emily to figure it out now.

He returned to where she lay quietly on the cold clay floor and saw her face was still relaxed in unconsciousness. Gus tried to wrap his mind around what could have driven her to attack him like that. Had she met these people at temple and been won over to their cause?

It would have taken one hell of a speech to turn her on him, and the more he thought about it, the harder it was to understand. After all these years, he liked to think they meant more to each other than that. If these really were Wardens, they didn't just hate him; they hated all of human civilization, and that certainly didn't sound like her. And why gag her if she was on their side?

The possibility that she had been convinced to turn on him like that tapped a deep well of emotion that felt like ice in his chest. He pushed that down and slipped his arms under her, unwilling to abandon her, even after she tried to kill him.

~

"Royal Birthday"

The fourteenth anniversary of the birthday of the Princess of Whitby, His Imperial Majesty's eldest, was honoured by festivities throughout eastern Aelfua yesterday. The mounting of the Royal Guard by the 1st Regiment took place, and the band of the Grenadier Guards played in the newly constructed Calwright Theater in Jinnai.

By the Princess's desire, Marshal Kilgrave gave his drawing-room entertainment at the mayor's home in the afternoon; and a pair of Rakhasin goblin minstrels, entertainers trained by Khanom's own resident of the breed, provided song and merriment through the evening.

– *Khanom Daily Converser*, 16 Tal. 389

~

- CHAPTER 29 -

Errol helped Gus unload Emily from the cab outside Rondel's, and despite his tight finances, Gus gave him as healthy a gratuity as he dared. The crooked clerk was back on duty at the front desk, and his eyes lit up with dozens of questions on seeing Gus returning with an unconscious woman in his arms. Hoping to get a closer look, the clerk even went so far as to help them into the elevator, but a stern look sent the man back to his station without further inquiry.

Staggering down the hall with Emily in his arms, Gus made it to his room and dumped her onto the bed. After checking to make sure she was still breathing, he removed his jacket, and it stuck briefly to the ruined shirt beneath. The jacket had been open when Emily lunged for him with the knife, so it was only slightly torn, but the shirt beneath it was clearly ruined.

He peeled the shirt off to look at the cut beneath, which was an ugly mess but didn't seem too deep despite how much it hurt. Ripping the ruined shirt apart, he used the remains of it to wrap around his belly, drawing it tight to stop the bleeding.

Feeling an unusual surge of modesty, he pulled out his spare shirt and buttoned himself back up. While certain that Emily had seen him naked when they first met, that had been years ago now, Gus had been quite drunk at the time, and his memories of it were hazy. There was a mirror in the room, and looking over at his reflection, he wondered if he should wear a girdle; the little bit of slimming from his bandage made him look a little more fit and maybe even a little younger.

Staring down at Emily, still tangled in the green robe, he had a hard time trying to piece together why she would have turned against

him like that. It was so unreal that, between breaths, he could almost
imagine he dreamed it; the slice across his belly gave sharp
confirmation of her attack with each inhale.

He felt a cauldron of rage rising to a boil inside him. Gus knew
he probably wasn't the best boss—he seldom paid on time, he mocked
her religion, and he always underestimated her connections—but he
had thought they were still close enough that she wouldn't just set him
up as a patsy for some elf cult. He might even have imagined
something more romantic could grow between them if he weren't a
cripple and a former soldier.

He had no idea what other weapons she might be carrying in
that green robe, so he rolled her out of it to check. Beneath the
Warden's robe she still wore the same sort of blouse and skirt she
wore to work, which surprised him since she seldom dressed that way
anywhere other than his office.

Stranger still, he discovered thick wool socks had been slid
over each of her shoes. The oddity of it made him clamp down on his
emotional turmoil. He needed answers, and those were easier to get
with a cool head or, at the very least, the appearance of a cool head.

She groaned softly, and Gus hurriedly bound her hands to the
headboard with a remaining strip of his ruined shirt. Out of an
abundance of caution, he took the belt from her robe and used that to
tie her ankles together as well. She mumbled something, and he leaned
over her, trying to make out the words. It sounded like something
foreign and familiar, although he couldn't yet place the language.

Emily's eyes fluttered open, she stared up at him a moment in
obvious confusion and then let out a bestial shriek. She thrashed atop
the bed, trying to strike at him with her hands, and when that didn't
quite work, she swung her feet, flopping atop the sheets like a fish out
of water and snarling in frustration.

She gnashed her teeth and lost any last vestige of order to her
hair as her bucking about finally made her usually careful bun spill

free of its moorings. Staring up at him, she chanted aggressively in the same foreign tongue she'd mumbled with when coming to, and Gus suddenly realized what it sounded like.

"Since when do you speak Gedlunder?"

She spat at him and then rasped out, "You will not stop the Great Restoration!"

Composed. He needed to look composed and in control. Taking a deep breath, Gus forced a confident smile and replied, "That's alright. I hadn't been planning to. What's the Great Restoration?"

Emily thrashed about again, then scowled at him as if searching for the right curse to scream out. He actually looked forward to hearing it—in all the time he had known her, he had never heard Emily use a swear word. Even when she worked the bawdy house, she had always seemed too composed for any verbal vulgarity. If she had ever looked ready to say something truly severe, this was that moment.

Instead, after bleary-eyed hesitation, she defiantly announced, "You cannot stop it!"

"If that's true, why try to kill me?"

That seemed to offend her further, and she began to chant again. He listened carefully, but of the few words from Gedlund he still remembered, none were part of her recitation, but that only ruled out 'fish', 'roof' and 'give'. Still, something else about it tickled at his memory.

Emily seemed to grow a little uncertain about whatever she was saying, stumbling over parts of it and frowning in concentration as she tried to get it right. He'd seen men who never quite recovered their wits after a blow to the head, and for a moment, Gus worried he had done something similar to her when he hit her in the warehouse. He shook his head, trying to chase that worry away—she had been trying to kill him.

There was something familiar in the rhythm of her chant though. Emily stubbornly pushed her way through it a couple of times, and on the third he asked, "What's this thing you keep saying?"

She seemed to forget her anger a moment and with a distracted frown answered, "It's the Elven prayer the Master taught me, for when things seem confusing. He said he would help me learn it, but there wasn't much time. I need to remember it, but I can't quite get it right."

Emily took a deep breath and tried again, carefully sounding out the unfamiliar syllables and trying to match that eerily familiar rhythm as best she could remember. Seeing her weird struggle brought a pang of pity, and in a gentle tone he said, "He's the one who told you about the Great Restoration?"

She nodded, still trying to focus on the prayer. Her rabid anger was fading, and she wore a childlike expression of single-minded intensity. In that moment, she didn't seem herself at all, and suddenly Gus realized where he had heard that same rhythm before. It followed the same beat as the wyrd tune he had heard in Aelfua a decade ago, in a haunted village on the coast.

The eerie sound of the mesmerized villagers humming it as they limped along to the fiddler's tune still haunted his dreams. He had witnessed people maiming themselves in their desperation to obey whatever strange mission the music gave them, then crawl eagerly onward to their next task. Some nights, the image of that desperate obedience was more terrifying than Lady Paasil descending from the sky.

On a hunch, Gus began to whistle bits of that fiddler's tune; Emily's eyes turned sharply to him at the sound, but she just pouted at the distraction and kept trying to focus on her own words. It was difficult, and the song's strange nature kept lulling his own thoughts away, but Gus stubbornly continued to whistle as much of it as he could and picked up at the beginning again whenever the song made the task slip from his mind.

Looking dazed, Emily blinked and wrinkled her nose as if there were a foul odor in the room. Finally, she gave up trying to finish her chant and petulantly demanded, "What are you whistling?"

She still didn't seem all there, but her tone certainly sounded more like the Emily he knew. Thinking back to Claude's attempted lyrics, Gus grinned and replied, "Ogria Girls."

She shook her head at the unfamiliar name, so Gus sang to her, "Love knows no nation's borders, though war may be the norm, and often patriots grow hateful. Our Verin girls are lovely, the Tuls will keep you warm, but the Ogria girls are grateful."

With a look of shock, Emily exclaimed, "What? That's horrible!"

That idiot's intensity had faded from her eyes, and while she still looked worse for wear, Gus felt a swell of both relief and triumph. He chuckled at her reaction and said, "Oh, it's a soldier's song—the kind of thing men off fighting goblins find amusing. It's a catchy tune though, right?"

He hummed a few more bars of it, and she nodded, the fiddler's infectious music caught in her thoughts and perhaps disrupting the rhythm of whatever prayer she'd been given by this 'Master'. Over the years, he had tried hard to forget as much as he could about his last trip through Aelfua, but for once, he was glad couldn't.

Emily nodded but then frowned and glanced down as if trying to remember something, so Gus quickly added, "Here, I'll teach it to you."

She was resistant at first, and Claude's incomplete lyrics only grew more offensive as the song went on, but the wyrd tune made it difficult to resist. Over the next hour, he kept pushing her, teaching her the lyrics line by line and pestering her until she repeated them back.

By the end, she looked exhausted, but then they sang the first few bits of the song together, and she even laughed as they both tapered off into the muddled uncertainty the fiddler's music instilled in mortal minds. Shaking her head and looking bemused, she said, "That's a terrible song."

Gus grinned and replied, "Well, that's why they don't allow women in the army."

Emily nodded, then looked wounded. After a pensive moment, she said, "I'm sorry about the knife."

The cringing look on her face was as unfamiliar to him as the bloodthirsty attacks that had come earlier, but it brought a surge of such profound relief that it made him shiver. If this chant really were some sort of wyrding, like the fiddler's music, it might not yet be safe to set her loose, but mesmerism could be beaten more easily than a poisoned heart.

Back in Gemmen, Emily had suggested these Wardens were real, and he had scoffed at the idea because there would be no point to Wardens unless an elf was still around and somehow involved in the modern world. Now that seemed disturbingly plausible.

Gus rose to his feet, fetched a cup by the room's basin, and filled it with water. "Yeah. What was that about? Who's this master you mentioned?" He lifted the cup to her lips and helped her take a few sips before giving her answer.

She looked away, her eyes refusing to meet his as she stared off into the corner, deep in thought as he set the water aside. When she finally answered, she murmured, "I'm not sure. He was all … pointy." A look of alarm crossed her face, and she added, "Maybe he was

Elven? That doesn't make sense. It's hard to think. He taught me a prayer, though, that's supposed to help …."

"No, it won't help, just forget that." He watched her carefully, trying to decide if she was truly as addled as she seemed or merely taking her time to construct believable lies. He wanted to believe, but she had always been a canny liar. "When did you get to Khanom?"

The look of shock on her face was better acting than he expected. "Khanom? Is that where we are?" She sat up straighter and glanced around the room as if somehow that might contradict him, then sighed and said, "I had just left our office and was going home. I was cutting through the alley, and no one was there, but then someone grabbed me! And … and then this cold, cold wind. It was so cold, I couldn't breathe, and I must have blacked out. When I came to, there was a woman there. I think it was Missus Phand—the false one who hired us!"

Gus nodded and offered her another sip of water, which she eagerly drank down as she worked to order her story in her own head. It felt true. "I couldn't see, but she was talking to the Master. It's like a dream now; it just keeps fading. I'm not sure how much of it really happened."

"It's alright. Just tell me what you think happened."

"Then he came in to see me, and we spoke, and at the time it seemed to make so much sense. The world is in danger from … something, but we can help him save it. Something inappropriate on the queen's palace? Does that make sense?"

Gus nodded, even though it didn't make a lot of sense. Everything suggested this was about Phand's tower, which wouldn't be on top of Palace Park. According to the Exposition office's map, nothing was happening in Palace Park. Her choice of words reminded him of Ulm's odd repetitions though, and he doubted that was a coincidence.

Emily shrugged in confusion and looked frustrated. "That's most of it, I think. He told me a prayer to say and made me practice it a few times and then he left. The false Alice Phand came back in, and we must have talked some, but I don't remember it."

He nodded again and waited for her to continue, and after a moment, she did. "We got all dressed up and went somewhere strange. I remember we walked in total darkness for such a long time, it felt like hours, but then suddenly we were at that warehouse. When they said you were an enemy, I suddenly ... I wanted ...."

She started to sob. With a swell of pity, Gus wanted to embrace her, but that seemed odd with her arms tied up, so instead he just leaned down, resting his forehead against hers. After a bit, she gathered herself again and then coughed softly to let him know. He leaned back again, and in a quiet voice, she asked, "Does any of it make sense to you?"

"Some of it. They want to stop Phand's tower, and Ulm said it was about the palace too, but it's not even going up where the palace was, so why say that? Did they say what they're trying to restore?" Emily shook her head, uncertain, so he said, "Plus walking for hours in the dark. With all the street lamps, it's not dark anywhere in this town. I need to go check some things out."

"Hey!" she called indignantly as he began to walk away and wiggled her bound hands.

He grinned but still did not trust her enough to let her loose, "Don't worry. I'll be right back. If you start wondering about that Elven prayer again, just be sure to sing a little bit of 'Ogria Girls' first." She shouted his name a few times as he left the room, and while he felt a twinge of guilt for leaving her tied up, it was entirely counterbalanced by the giddy relief that she seemed to be recovering.

Once out of Rondel's, he began walking down the street towards the alley where Ulm had met with the other Wardens. He was exhausted, and his leg hurt, but taking six blocks of night air to work off the coursing adrenaline seem like a good idea. He passed several other Elven columns along the way and wondered what exactly he had gotten himself mixed up in.

He did not know what to make of the Wardens or Elves or the end of the world, so he focused on the job he had come to do, which was to get justice for Louis and find Doctor Phand. Dorna claimed Louis's actual killer was dead, but whoever or whatever had put the killer up to it was still out there. Whatever they were up to, it didn't seem to have anything to do with the Elven queen's palace, so he doubted they were saving the world either.

There were copious patent lamps throughout the upper city; in some places it almost seemed like daytime as the light reflected from the white tiles of the Elven road. Wherever Emily had gone in total darkness, it couldn't have been through the upper city.

The alleyway was darker, but enough light spilled through from the main road for Gus to see that the Warden's blood still stained the ground. He crouched down to follow that trail in the darkness of the blind alley, and it did seem headed towards the Elven monument before it tapered off.

Approaching the monument, he tapped at it again, listening for any indication that it might be hollow, but heard no echo. He pushed at the flat base, trying to rotate or slide it, but nothing happened. He felt sure this was connected to however the Wardens were traveling unseen, but he could not see any way to operate it. If there really was an elf, that probably meant magic was involved, but the Wardens were humans, and they could operate it.

He suspected the writing probably held some explanation, but the runes scrawled across the inner face, a geometric language of arcs and angles, were meaningless to him. His old friend Gilmot could probably have solved this in a moment, but Gus didn't know anyone else who knew so much as a word of Elven; with the Elves gone, no one bothered to learn it anymore.

Finally, he stepped up onto the base and stood within the curve of the crescent-shaped column to study the writing more closely. Humans were bad at magic, which he hoped meant this was somehow less mystical than it appeared, so he searched again for any joins or crevices that might indicate a button or a latch of some kind.

His fingers probed at the characters, trying to find a spot where the letters themselves might hide a button or a latch, but most of the symbols were open ended, which left fewer possibilities. There were no seams, and the chiseled surface showed no signs of having ever been anything less than a single solid block of milky white stone. He ran his hand over the surface, perfectly smooth but for the chiseled divots of the runes. He felt no give to any of them.

Suddenly, the ground vanished beneath his feet, and his elbows crashed hard onto the pavement around the Elven obelisk. The base of the column had vanished, leaving him dangling over a steeply slanted chute that disappeared into darkness below the city. Even as he realized his predicament, the white stone was sliding into place from under the column. He barely pulled his legs out of the gap before the stone base quietly resealed the opening.

The column once again looked completely solid and utterly seamless.

He stood back and prodded at the runes but could not get it to open again. Now that he knew that it did, however, he knew they travelled underground. The columns were everywhere in Khanom, but if there was any hope to track Phand's kidnappers, it was down there.

All he needed to do was explore whatever city-wide system of tunnels they were using and then rescue Phand before the Exposition deadline passed.

That sounded daunting enough, so he set aside the possibility that an elf would be waiting for him at the end of those tunnels—an elf with powerful wyrding and an army of knife-wielding Wardens.

On his return to Rondel's, Gus paused at the bar for a belt of something stiff before going up to the room. When he arrived back at his room, he found that Emily was unrestrained, sitting on the bed and sipping water.

His heart stopped a moment, but she didn't go for her knife and instead just gave him a sharp look that said she still took being left tied up a bit personally. Rather than mention it though, she only asked, "Did you find what you were looking for?"

"I did! Looks like the Wardens are literally underground. That's how they move through the city without being seen. That's why it was so dark when they took you. In the morning, I'll go buy a lamp and make my way down there."

She nodded as if that made sense and then said, "You should take someone with you, just to be safe." At his skeptical look, she hurriedly added, "Not me! Do you know anyone here who knows about tunnels?"

With a grin, he replied, "I'll have you know the owner of the Khanom Mineral Company and I are well acquainted."

A quick derisive snort that fell just short of outright laughter was her response, and she said, "I doubt he actually digs the mines himself."

"No, probably not, but I think I know just who to ask."

"An actual miner?"

"No, even better! A nightclub owner."

~

"Curse Threatened Upon Garren"

An edict from the Longying Emperor has formally decreed that a curse will be placed upon Garren and all its peoples, unless control of the island of Hemdou is returned to his kingdom by the next full moon. While the people of Longying have long claimed that their Emperor is a dragon and possessed of the vast magical power such a curse would require, very little evidence has emerged in recent years to support that belief.

As readers will recall, after the Longying courts of trade forbade all further importation of goods from western nations, an assault upon their ports was commenced by two Garren commercial interests: the Maraes Ferma and the Societa Commerce Ogrien. The two companies have offered to cede control of seized territories to Garren in exchange for military support from their home nation, but so far, their merchant ships have readily rebuffed Longying's military attempts to retake Hemdou.

– Khanom Daily Converser, 17 Tal. 389

~

- CHAPTER 30 -

Despite the exhausting day, Gus spent the night awake. He left Emily on the bed and used a spare blanket to make himself a pallet on the floor. Unfortunately, when laid face down, the cut on his belly was too uncomfortable to let him sleep. Face up was little better—his fall in the alleyway had bruised his elbows, and combined with the constant ache in his leg, it was too much to let him sleep soundly.

Emily did sleep, but she spent the night tossing and turning, apparently in the grip of the same sort of dream that had haunted Gus since the war. In the wee hours before dawn, Gus decided he had lain still long enough and finally gave up on sleep. Emily was still asleep when he rose, dressed again, and slipped out of the room as quietly as he could manage.

At the front desk, he paused to demand the loan of a lantern, which the sleepy clerk managed to produce after a bit of cajoling. At a better hour, the clerk might have questioned him, but he lacked the wherewithal to deny an insistent customer this early on.

Lantern in hand, Gus made his way to the Viridian. The club showed every sign of being closed when he arrived, but he knew some of the elaborate dinners he had seen on offer the other night required a full day's preparation, and he doubted Salka'tok'tok'ton would leave all that preparation to chance. He guessed the gob would be there to usher in the morning shift of bakers and chefs before retreating to his diurnal slumber.

He was right. When Gus arrived, Salka's mouth split into a wide grin, and in his deep voice he rumbled, "Good morning, Mister Baston! What brings you out my way at this hour?"

Gus grinned back and said, "I have a lead on Doctor Phand! You're invested in the Exposition and struck me as the adventurous sort, so I thought you might want to help me rescue him from his kidnappers."

Goblins' broad mouths always gave them impressively expressive frowns, and Salka's managed to make him look both wary and thoughtful. "You might be better served calling upon the police, Mister Baston. I'm not sure what I can do for you. Despite the reputation for savagery that some of my tribal brethren have built, I am really not much help with fisticuffs, and human guns are hardly scaled for Rakhas hands."

He held up his oversized paw, and Gus was surprised in all his time fighting in Rakhasin that it had never occurred to him that their rifles would have been exceedingly difficult for the natives to wield. It was probably why they relied upon spears and clumsy sorcery.

Changing his tone to be a bit more pleading, Gus said, "Please, it's nothing dangerous for you. I've found some old tunnels under the city. I could use some expert guidance to find my way through them. You're my only hope, and I'm Doctor Phand's only hope."

Salka seemed moved by that, and the idea of tunnels clearly sparked the gob's curiosity, for he said, "Under the city? What sort of tunnels?"

"Elven, I guess? There's an entrance only three blocks from here. If it's too threatening, you can just back out." Gus doubted he would. Anyone that travelled across the world to settle in a city full of strangers had to have at least some sense of adventure, and to be the only goblin in a human city, Gus bet Salka had more of that than most.

Salka looked back at his bustling crew as if weighing how poorly they might fare without his morning supervision. With the sun steadily rising, he had probably not planned on staying out too much longer regardless, so eventually adventure won out. He nodded his broad head and said, "Very well, I'll take a look."

As they made their way to the alleyway, Salka was the object of veiled stares by the morning pedestrians, who made every effort not to be caught gawking at the unusual pedestrian pressing through their morning commute. They passed another Elven obelisk along the way, but Gus had no idea if they all worked the same, so he led Salka to the one he was sure the Wardens had travelled through.

They stepped off of Queen's, and Salka suspiciously eyed the dark stains where the Warden that Gus had shot—supposedly the one who had murdered Louis—bled onto the ground. Gus tried to feel some satisfaction in that bit of revenge, but it only left him sad and empty.

Pulling at Salka's shoulder, Gus urged him around the corner and towards the white column. Gesturing over the symbols on its inner face, he said, "This is how they do it. It opens somehow, and there's a tunnel below." The goblin looked skeptical, so Gus began tapping at the script. "I did it accidentally before, which is how I know it works. You've got to hit the right words in Elvish or something."

Salka smiled up at him and said, with just a hint of smugness, "That could take you awhile then. The columns aren't Elven. They're Duer."

"What the hell is 'Duer'? Like those little dolls people make out in the country? The little mountain spirits they give booze?" He prodded at more of the words on the column and wished he had been more methodical in his earlier effort.

The goblin shrugged and stepped closer into the arc of the column to examine the words. "I don't know anything about that. They were an old people who lived underground, like the Rakhas do. They left many ruins in Rakhasin, supposedly cursed, but we'd sneak out to play in them when I was young."

"But this was an Elven city! Why would they have Duer monuments everywhere?"

Salka chuckled and said, "I don't know, but if they were Elven, why did they get left behind when the Elves took everything else with them?"

Gus was stumped by that, and as he considered it, he remembered passing by an old temple in Aelfua while he was in the army. Gilmot could read Elven, but he hadn't understood several foreign symbols on that one. "Some expert you are. Maybe I should have brought an archaeologist."

The goblin ignored him and then pointed out one of the chiseled characters and said, "That one means 'down,' I think."

It was lower than Gus remembered pushing at before, so with a skeptical frown, he reached past the gob and pushed against the word. In the blink of an eye, the base of the column on which Salka stood gave way, seeming to vanish entirely.

For someone with such a deep voice, the high-pitched screech that sounded as Salka slid away into darkness was a bit of a shock. Remembering how fast the opening closed before, Gus hugged the Rondel's lantern protectively, took a deep breath, and leapt down after him.

Gus fell onto his back in a tight chute of polished stone, which briefly knocked the breath from him as he slid rapidly downward. The light overhead vanished, plunging him into total darkness as he plummeted into the depths.

The chute was obviously designed for someone of narrower frame, and his bruised elbows banged at the sides as he rapidly banked through a series of sharp turns in the stone chute. Just as he was about to recover his breath, Salka's screaming fell silent, and an instant later the chute was suddenly gone. Gus hung suspended in the air for a brief moment that felt far longer than it was and then dropped hard atop his companion, who responded with a pained whimper.

It was still pitch black. Salka recovered from the fall first, squirming beneath him a moment until Gus recovered and they awkwardly disentangled. Gus's elbows ached, and the chute had hit them in just the wrong way, leaving his fingers with a tingling numbness. He could hear the goblin move about in the dark, grunting a little as he worked out whatever bruises had been earned in the fall and then in Gus's subsequent crash atop him.

Trapped in featureless black, Gus sat on the cool stone floor and sucked in strangled gasps of cool air as he tried to get his wind back. He put the lantern in his lap and then wriggled his fingers, trying to restore feeling to his hands. His eyes darted around, but there wasn't even the faintest glimmer of light, and he couldn't pick a single shadow from any other. He raised a hand to his face, and while he could feel it brush his nose, to his eyes there was nothing but empty black.

He had no notion of how deep they had fallen, nor how far sideways that chute might have directed them as they fell, and absolutely no notion of how to get back. Submerged into darkness beyond any he had ever known, Gus's panicked thoughts turned to the descriptions of hell that had been hurled at him while sitting among impassioned congregations as a boy.

He inspected the hotel's lantern with his fingers, and it seemed to be unbroken. Nervous he might lose a piece of it in the dark, Gus opened it very carefully and began fumbling around with the matches he carried in his pocket.

Salka paced around him and murmured in a soft, reverent voice, "This is amazing."

Gus's only matches were safety matches, and it proved frustratingly difficult to strike one without being able to see the surface it was supposed to rub against. Irritated and uneasy in the darkness, he called out, "Don't wander off!"

Salka gave no reply, but after a moment more, Gus finally got the match to ignite. As light blossomed around his fingers, he felt an enormous surge of relief and carefully paired it to the wick of the lantern. Lit, the lantern provided no more light than the match had until he slid the glass chimney over it and closed it up. With a soft sigh at the return of sight, Gus glanced around, first spotting his guide's back and then raising the lantern higher for a better look at where the chute had dropped them.

They stood on one side of a wide corridor, the opposite side of it only dimly in view, and both ends stretched well beyond his small island of illumination. Everything was made of polished white stone, decorated in sharp geometric patterns, dotted with occasional runic chiselings. The floor was laid in the same tiles as the Elven roads.

Unlike the pale white stones along the floor, however, here the walls were streaked in color. Slogans in Duer script were painted large across the walls in reds, yellows, browns and blues. To one side he saw a crude drawing that appeared to depict a large man urinating on a symbol painted in a different color. None of that graffiti extended higher than six feet, above which the white stone remained as clean as it was on the surface.

Gus saw the chute they had fallen down, which emerged from the nearby wall, and it was not nearly as far from the floor as he had imagined. Beside it sat a white column similar to the one somewhere overhead which, hopefully, would be their way out again. "Salka, you know the word for 'up,' right?"

The gob nodded and walked over, pointing to a circle overlapped with triangles and three wavy lines that indicated direction in no way Gus could discern. To Gus, the Duer script just looked like a series of boxes, and he had trouble telling the characters apart, so he sighed and resolved not to lose track of his guide.

He had hoped the Warden's blood trail would extend down here, but there was no sign of it at the base of the chute. After staring around at the floor in the immediate area gave him no leads, Gus began walking further down the corridor, only to be stopped by a purposeful cough.

"That way is a dead end."

Gus turned back to face Salka, who raised a large hand to shade his eyes from the lantern. "Fine. You're supposed to be my tunnel guide. Which way?"

Salka harrumphed as if offended at either the appellation or Gus's demanding tone. He was still the better dressed of the two of them, and for a moment, Gus felt a little ridiculous for talking down to him; even if he were just a gob, Salka had led a career as a successful entertainer, owned the most popular club in town, and was even involved in the planning of a multimillion-peis exposition.

That thought took but a single bleak moment, and then Gus reassured himself that, while exceptional for his breed, Salka was not human and never could be. There was some comfort in that, and the gob seemed to realize it too, for his arch expression relented, and he replied, "Very well. This way, Mister Baston."

They ventured further along the corridor, which ended in a doorway just slightly higher than his head, and Gus was amazed as they left the large corridor and stepped into what was an even larger room of some sort. Columns of white stone stretched off into the distance, and the far wall was farther away than his light could reach. The ceiling arched far overhead, the top vanishing into a dim pool of shadow.

They walked through that vast chamber, steps echoing sharply on the polished tiles of the stone floor. "This is incredible. Did you know any of this was down here?"

"I don't think anyone knows," replied the gob. He walked about thirty feet ahead with his back to the lantern light. "I've lived here for over a decade, and this is the first I've seen or heard of it. Look at it all! It must extend beneath the entire city!"

"Someone must know. The Wardens know about it," his voice echoed loudly, and at the mention of Wardens, Gus began to worry that with all these echoes they might hear him coming. It was as silent down here as it was dark, and he realized he didn't need to speak quite so loudly to be heard. Lowering his voice, he remarked, "Miss Aliyah Gale must surely know. She owns the companies that dig out the sewers and the gas lines."

Salka lowered his own voice and said, "And the buildings. We're much deeper than most of those things reach, but," he said, pausing and pointing upwards, "these ceilings are quite high at their peak. Someone must have encountered them in all the construction over the years."

They continued further forward for a time, keeping mostly quiet as they explored the Duer cavern. He had never heard any suggestion that the mountain spirits placated by high-country rubes had once been anything real, which made him think they must have left long before the Elves did.

"It is quite old, isn't it?" Gus asked and rapped his shoe against a column as he passed it. That tapping echoed louder than he expected, and there was a distant clatter afterwards, like stones spilling on some distant portion of the floor.

Realizing how far sound must carry down here, Gus recalled the socks the Wardens had pulled over Emily's shoes and supposed they must have been used to muffle her footsteps down here. Wondering why the Wardens would need to be so carefully quiet in their own secret tunnels, he asked, "You don't suppose it's unstable do you?"

He got no answer and wasn't sure which that meant but didn't want to risk asking louder if the answer was yes.

As they walked on, most of the room extended beyond his light, and there was little to see beyond the floor and the white columns that would occasionally emerge from the darkness. Gus's attention drifted from his guide, and he peered into the darkness as he wondered again at how far away the walls were. The echo suggested immensity, but only the goblin knew for sure.

Salka halted and scrambled backward so quickly that Gus stumbled into him while distracted by the designs painted around the base of a nearby column. The gob hissed something too soft to be heard, and as Salka continued to pull backwards towards him, Gus could feel him trembling.

Holding the lantern higher, Gus could not see whatever distant object had caught Salka's attention, but then the goblin repeated himself in a terrified falsetto, "Douse the lantern! Quickly!"

Looking around at his small island of visibility in a sea of endless darkness, Gus had absolutely no intention of extinguishing the only light. He opened his mouth to make that point, but then, in the distance, he heard another clatter of stones atop tiles, followed by a soft grinding sound, like someone were dragging a heavy sack across the floor.

The clattering he had worried indicated instability echoed again and took on a rhythmic intensity that stole away his illusion of stones falling randomly to the floor. The dragging sounded more steadily, and the combination reminded him of a train picking up steam. For a brief instant, there was a distant flicker of light, and he asked, "What is that?"

The goblin's answer was a choked squeal, and he covered his eyes as he rapidly turned, circled around behind Gus, and began to flee, only then thinking to shout behind him, "Run! Run!"

Whatever the horror was that had shaken his guide, Gus could hear it rapidly approaching, so he took to his heels.

Even with the gob's shorter legs, Gus had trouble matching pace to Salka's panicked flight back the way they came, and in moments the goblin had fled past the range of his light. Gus could only try to follow the echoes of Salka's feet slapping against the tiled floor. Whatever pursued them sounded like it was drawing nearer, and Gus risked turning his head to glance back, trying to spot whatever Salka was so terrified of.

That's when Gus's foot hit against something unexpected, and the world spun wildly around him as he tumbled to the floor. The lantern slipped from his hand as he hit the floor, and its glass chimney shattered, sending shards skittering everywhere. Thankfully, the wick stayed lit, or he might never have found it again – but without the glass chimney, the flame was little brighter than a lit match.

The shadows weighed heavily, and Gus pushed unsteadily back to his feet, realizing the chamber had fallen eerily silent. The sounds of his own breathing and the thunder of his heart threatened to overwhelm him, but he forced himself to breathe slowly and lifted the lantern to look around. A large lump lay at his feet, and bending down with the dimmed lantern to see what he had tripped over, he recognized the green cloak of the Wardens.

"Where did it go?" hissed Salka from behind him, giving Gus such a start that he nearly yelped in alarm.

"I don't know! You're the only one that can see!" Gus hissed back, keeping his voice down, even though the echoing hall probably made that pointless.

Salka shielded his eyes from the dim flame of the broken lantern and peered down at the body Gus had tripped over, "Who is this? It looks like he's been shot."

"He killed a friend of mine. I shot him, so he fled down here. I guess we're even now." Looking down at the body, Gus wanted to feel some surge of vindication for having avenged Louis, but it never came, so he gave the body a petulant kick.

"Well, if you're quite done with him then, the place we came in is over that way," grumbled the goblin, gesturing off to one side.

Gus started to retort with something about how the gob had abandoned him in the dark, but then he heard it again, the stoney clatter and rumbling weight rapidly approaching. He looked to Salka who was simply staring back at him impatiently, not having heard it yet. When he did, his head jerked up, looking frantically off into the dark, and stumbled a step or two back, already half out of Gus's tiny realm of light.

Like a storm, it was upon them—the heavy rumble suddenly seemed to come from every direction at once. Salka made a frightened squeal, turned in a circle, and then fell to the floor, curling into a ball with his face down and his arms over his head. A light twinkled in the darkness, just for a moment, closer now, although Gus couldn't tell how close.

Shadows moved. Nothing close enough to make out in the dim light of his broken lantern, but just beyond the point he could see, the darkness took on strange, shifting patterns and extended all around them in an unsettling wall of sinuous motion.

Light flickered again above the moving shadows but drawing lower, nearer, and slowly widening. It became a dull orange glow sketching a jagged row of shadowy knives. There was a deep rumbling, and just above that light, he could see a yellow glimmer reflecting the light of his lamp. As it neared, it resolved into a great yellow eye.

That terrible eye was larger than a dinner plate, and once Gus recognized its yellow shimmer as an eye, the jagged shadows below it became teeth, and the fire behind them a curious horror he had no name for.

There was a deep rumble, a sound he felt in his bones more than he heard it—strange, foreign sounds that, after a moment, he realized must be words, for amid them he heard a pair of syllables he thought might be his own surname. He quaked at the sound, frozen in place. The yellow eye narrowed, half-concealed by some dark eyelid on the face he could not quite see. It snorted, and flame blossomed from between those teeth, roiling out in an infernal cloud of heat that made Gus falter back a step.

An incongruous sound caught his attention: a soft, purposeful cough, just to the right of the fiery jaws. As he looked towards the strange sound, he was stunned to see Miss Aliyah Gale stepping confidently into his narrow circle of illumination.

Despite the surroundings, Miss Aliyah Gale was once again dressed in shimmering silks, this time a dark green upon which was painted a mesh of silver and gold lines to create a hint of serpentine scales. Surging adrenaline made it hard to think clearly, but as he glanced between her and the glowing maw of the thing that surrounded them, Gus suspected this would be bewildering regardless.

The voice of the monster that coiled around them rumbled again, but Miss Gale seemed to ignore it. Her eyes fixed upon Gus, she said, "I asked you a question. What are you doing here, Mister Baston?"

Feeling helpless and too overwhelmed to conjure a believable lie, Gus decided to go with the truth: "We, uh, were looking for Phand. The kidnappers came this way." He nudged Dougal's corpse with his foot and said, "So I thought he might be down here?"

Gus's nerves made the statement come out like a question, and he clenched his teeth, trying to overcome the panic. Thoughts racing, Gus forced himself to take slower, deeper breaths and tried to think of how to get out of this alive.

Miss Aliyah Gale looked down at the corpse at his feet. That deep voice began to rumble behind her, and as it did she said, "These thieves in green—do you know who they are?"

Despite the surreal circumstances, Gus recognized that as a real question. Whatever else was happening here and now, Miss Aliyah Gale and her monster were not behind the kidnapping. Whatever she was, she wasn't the elf he was up against. That realization helped steady his nerves. If she was asking questions, then maybe he could talk his way to survival.

"They call themselves Wardens," he struggled to keep his gaze on her, and she simply stared back, her attention focused entirely on him as if the beast behind her wasn't even there. It remained silent as she did, watchful, listening, waiting for him to elaborate. That was when he realized she had only ever spoken when it did. "What are you?"

The monster's jaws widened, brightening the room as more light shone between its enormous teeth, but in the sudden contrast of light and darkness, he could see the beast no more clearly than he before; only Miss Aliyah Gale seemed clearer, a bemused smile upon her lips.

The deep voice rumbled behind her again, and then she spoke, "We were the first children of the gods, the first shape given to shapeless things. It is from our strength that oceans learned power, from our flights that wind learned speed, and from our appetites that fire learned … hunger." From the woman, the last word seemed almost sexual, but the lingering snarl behind her gave it a different meaning entirely.

Gus looked back and forth, between the unblinking stare of the great yellow eye and the piercing green of Miss Aliyah Gale's, not sure which to focus on now that he understood the two voices were really one. Strange foreign syllables sounded again in that deep voice, and then Miss Aliyah Gale said, "How do these Wardens enter? How did you find this place?"

The creature's voice fell silent just before her question ended— Miss Aliyah Gale was the echo.

He stood as straight as he could, trying to sound confident and knowledgeable. If he knew things she did not, he was useful, and useful things were less likely to be eaten. "They use the Duer columns in the city. I'm told an elf leads them, so I guess the Elves must have known about these tunnels as well."

The gargantuan behind her snorted, sending forth a gout of flame as it did. Gus jerked back from the heat, but Miss Aliyah Gale ignored it. She chuckled and slowly nodded as the voice rumbled behind her a fraction of a second before she spoke.

The sound of his name in that deep rumble was unsettling, but then Miss Aliyah Gale spoke over it, echoing in Verin, "The Elves are gone, Mister Baston. These lands were all ours. We watched as the Duer built this place, and we allowed it. Then the Elves came and stole the Duer kingdoms, one by one. The affairs of Elves and Duer were so insignificant then, and in the folly of youth, it became our habit to simply ignore them. Now that at last the Elves have left and with men spilling over every corner of the world, I decided to move my collection here, thinking it would be safe."

Gus nodded as if all that made perfect sense, as if it corresponded to everything he had expected when coming down here. He willed himself to look both useful and agreeable.

The terrible eye and great fiery maw rose upward, no longer resting at his eye-level but instead rising well above his head. A second golden eye glimmered above that glowing maw as that monstrous head turned in the dark to face him directly, its deep rumble growing louder in a great snarl of reptilian fury.

Miss Aliyah Gale's human countenance struck him as equally fearsome when she ignored the thunderous creature behind her and spoke in a furious hiss, barely audible over the roar that still echoed behind her, "And yet there are still thieves! Precious keepsakes stolen away in my moments of quiet repose! Missing trinkets here or there, but in mere decades, so much has gone missing—where are they, Mister Baston? Where do they hide?"

Gus held up his hands, pushing down instinctive terror and trying to seem calm and reasonable as he replied, "That's what I'm here to find out. I'm tracking them." He paused, a small tug at his pant leg briefly called his attention back down to his companion. Salka still cowered on the floor but was peering up now. "We, I mean. We are tracking them down. As soon as we find anything, we'll let you know. I promise."

The yellow eyes and glowing maw rotated around them, staring down from the heights, rumbling softly. While the other face was inhumanly inscrutable, the face of Miss Aliyah Gale seemed to be weighing the risks of letting them live, now that they had found their way down here. Never one to gamble without trying to tip the odds, Gus smiled a bit and added, "Is there any reward for recovery of the stolen treasures?"

Salka hissed in indignation, tugging at Gus's pant leg, and Miss Aliyah Gale seemed taken aback by his blatant cupidity. Gus, however, put on his blandest smile and waited. It would be one thing to kill a trespasser and, for some ancient and terrible power like this, probably little different than squashing an insect found skittering through the larder. An employee, however, was something she would have an interest in preserving.

The woman's eyes narrowed, and she frowned. But then the beast rumbled behind her, and she echoed, "Yes. I will arrange for something appropriate to the value of whatever you manage to recover."

Gus felt a giddy swell of relief that he would not be eaten. Grinning like an idiot, he said, "Don't worry, you're in good—"

An enormous claw closed around Miss Aliyah Gale, and her face showed not the slightest bit of concern as she was yanked backwards and out of sight. The glowing maw vanished into the black and the shadows all around them lurched into motion as the monster rapidly receded into the darkness.

~

"Territorial Justice"

With law enforcement stretched thin across the unsettled territories in Rakhasin by the recent unpleasantness, it is unsurprising that some residents of Keat's Field have been required to take the law into their own hands.

Recently, a goblin working upon a licensed claim was caught digging into a neighboring claim to his own benefit. The goblin confessed to the deed when attempting to sell the stones found there but asserted the purchase of a license from an entrepreneur of local renown. The subsequent confirmation of that story was not widely believed, and an angry mob saw to it that the gob was hanged. Members of the township have expressed concern that this may further strain relations with the indigenes.

– *Khanom Daily Converser*, 17 Tal. 389

~

- CHAPTER 31 -

"You've gone mad!" hissed the goblin as Gus shone his diminished lantern over the body on the floor, trying to figure out which way the Warden had been going. "What happens if you don't find these stolen trinkets?"

"Well, then I guess we don't get the reward." The trail of blood leading up to the body at least told them what direction the Warden had been going, but there was no sign of any sort of light he might have carried, and Gus worried the man might have been totally lost.

"If we're lucky!" Salka stared nervously into the darkness, and in that deep, melodious voice, he groused, "Whatever that thing was, I don't relish the prospect of being eaten and then cooked any more than I'd like it the other way around. You shouldn't have promised anything!"

"All I promised was that we'd tell her if we found anything. If I hadn't, we'd probably be dead already. You're the one who can see down here; help me look around! Where was he going?"

The gob gave a melodramatic sigh and took a few steps out of Gus's dim circle of light. He walked around just beyond sight but never so far Gus couldn't hear his footsteps echo nearby. After a few moments, he returned and said, "This place is a maze! If all those columns lead down here, then it's as big as the city, and he could have been going anywhere. If he came in where we did though, then it looks like he was going towards the mountain along that row but then began to veer this direction."

Gus couldn't see any sort of row and had no idea how Salka knew which way the mountain was, but he just nodded and said,

"Well, lead on then—towards the mountain. That's our best chance of finding them, saving Phand, and maybe recovering some of Miss Aliyah Gale's stolen whatevers."

Salka did not seem entirely satisfied with that, and after his harrumph, they journeyed in relative quiet for a time. The light from the broken lantern was too dim to show much—walls would emerge from the gloom then turn away, but Salka led them ever onwards as if guided by some internal compass. Gus had always imagined goblins living crammed together in muddy little holes, but now he began to wonder if their homes were far more extensive than he ever would have guessed.

With little to see, Gus listened intently but heard only the sounds of their own footsteps echoing on the white stones of the floor until Salka paused just ahead of him and, in a tone of surprise, said, "Huh. Watch out for the stumps."

"Stumps? We're underground. How can there be stumps?" That's when his foot hit one.

Yelping in surprise more than pain, Gus had to stop walking, and Salka looked back at him in annoyance as Gus took a moment to look down at his nemesis underfoot. It was no natural tree stump and instead was a roughly broken projection of wood emerging from a perfectly square hole in the floor.

Holding the dim lantern higher, he could see another such projection not far off. "They're every few yards," noted his companion, "Laid out in squares. I think they were like buildings once, although the lumber's all gone now."

Gus nodded and said, "Maybe so. You're pretty good at this; ever considered giving up the glamorous life of a big city club owner to become a private inquiry agent? It pays less, but I'm sure I could find work for you doing all sorts of grubby odd jobs."

"No, I couldn't say that it's occurred to me. If my career in archaeology doesn't work out once the club winds down, I'll keep your offer in mind."

Gus chuckled, but his reply was interrupted as Salka gasped and commented, "Look at that!"

"You'll have to take me closer, I'm afraid."

Impatiently, the goblin grabbed his hand and tugged him off to the side along a cleared path between the rows of stumps that must have once formed a narrow avenue between the underground wooden structures.

A pillar emerged from the gloom, and as the light neared it, he saw it was a statue. The enormous man atop it stood eight feet tall and was nearly five feet across. His broad nose and close-set eyes were difficult to see clearly in the gloom, but Gus could make out the bushy beard and saw a pickaxe carried across the statue's broad shoulders.

"Do you suppose that's what they looked like?" Salka hissed in reverent awe as they stared up at him.

"He's got the bogey beard and everything, so I suppose so. I had no idea they were so large."

"Don't be foolish. How often do your people make statues the same size as the man? Besides, most of the doors we've passed down here are much smaller." The goblin paused and then added, "Although I suppose you haven't been able to see them. If I had to guess, I'd say the Duer were closer to my size than yours."

"Huh. Well, he's no elf lord, so unless you've changed your mind on being eaten, we should keep looking." Salka frowned at him, seeming to welcome neither the reminder of what they had just encountered nor what Gus had obliged them to search for. Grinning back at him, Gus said, "Maybe if you find some of her missing keepsakes, Miss Aliyah Gale will give you a tour of her lair down here."

The goblin shuddered at the suggestion and led Gus back across the wide gallery of square stumps, angling along some route that only Salka could see. Gus felt impatient at the goblin's short stride but could hardly find his way alone, so he tried to content himself with the limited scenery visible within his tiny circle of light. They hiked for what felt like hours, but the blackness beyond his lantern gave no indication of the time above, and Gus regretted having never replaced his lost watch.

They passed into a narrower corridor and then out again into what, judging by the echoes, seemed like another open area. He could just dimly make out Salka at the edge of his light, and without the corridor walls to stare at, Gus turned his contemplation to the white tile floor that seemed to roll into being from the shadows beneath the goblin's heels. It was a dreary, monochromatic contemplation, and he was weighing the practical and entertainment value of counting the goblin's footsteps when a surprising spark of color caught his eye.

"Wait!" he cried out, staring down at a small reddish footprint that marred the white stone tile between them. "That's not yours, is it? No, definitely not. That's a man's boot."

Wondering if they might just be travelling in circles, Gus lifted up his own shoe to make certain there was no mud on it, but he hadn't encountered any red mud like that since coming to Khanom. The floors had been notably pristine everywhere else though, which made Gus confident this print had not lain here for centuries.

He raised his dim lantern, scanning the floor nearby for more prints as he turned in a slow circle, then saw another just a bit further off to the left. Whomever it was, they had crossed his path, although Gus could not see far enough to determine where he had come from or where he was going.

"There's another. Do you see it? It's not us, and it's definitely not Miss Aliyah Gale in those shoes. We need to follow him." Salka nodded, then turned to follow the prints, but Gus caught his shoulder and said, "No, the mud's coming off his left boot as he walks, so that trail will end wherever it stops rubbing off the bottom of his shoe—probably just in the middle of another hallway. If we go the other way, we can follow him all the way back to the mud and see where he came from!"

Salka looked skeptical but turned back, tracking the heel towards another print just a little further off. After a few more steps, he murmured, "You may be on to something."

The bootprints became more frequent, and soon a second boot joined the first, leaving a clear trail backwards through a narrow corridor. They ducked under a short doorway and into a series of small rooms, the last of which Gus knew they had reached when the goblin turned the corner and murmured in surprise, "Well, look at that."

Holding forth his lantern, Gus stepped forward and saw a wall had been broken inwards, and fragments of white stone were scattered on the floor around it. Beyond that crude aperture lay a rough-hewn tunnel supported by wooden beams. "Well, mister archaeologist, this doesn't look much like the work of the Duer."

Salka grinned at him, and Gus could see a glint of intrepid curiosity in the goblin's eyes as he replied, "I must concur, Mister Baston. It is decidedly suspicious. Shall we?"

Gus smiled and gestured for the goblin to proceed. For the moment, the excitement of discovery overwhelming the discomforts of more sensible fears. Salka stepped over the broken wall and into the tunnel, and Gus followed close behind.

The tunnel was small enough that Gus had to hunch down his head to walk inside, and it slanted steadily upwards. Unlike the very dry Duer kingdom it invaded, moisture seeped into the rough-hewn tunnel, and after only a few steps inside, their feet squished in damp red earth.

Salka paused again, making a strange gesture with his hand at the blackness ahead, and then excitedly whispered back, "It's curtains!"

"What do you mean 'it's curtains'? Does the tunnel stop?"

"No, no, it is quite literally curtains. Come see."

Gus crept upwards, pushing in beside the goblin, and with his light drawn closer, he could see that what had seemed merely more shadows were, on close inspection, heavy black curtains hung across the support beams. He pushed them slowly aside, and his lantern illuminated a small space with another set of heavy curtains beyond.

Across the top of the second set of curtains, Gus could see a slim sliver of light, and he heard the sounds of someone hammering at something in the space beyond. Turning back to Salka he whispered, "We may have found them. Better stay behind me."

"You've brought a pistol, I trust?" Salka asked as he moved back down the tunnel to place himself behind Gus.

Gus offered a reassuring grin and replied, "I don't think we'll need it."

The goblin looked no more reassured by that than Gus felt about it, but before Salka could question him further, Gus pushed through the curtains and into the lit space beyond.

The tunnel widened into a larger chamber as they moved forward but was still roughly hewn by comparison to the Duer halls behind them. The ceilings arched upward from the curtains in a way that suggested this was once a natural cavern that the tunnelers had connected to the ancient labyrinth. The natural walls had been widened in places and shored up with wooden beams as needed.

A great hearth burned on one side of the chamber, tended by a large man in a leather apron who kept it burning with the large cord of wood stacked nearby; there was a chimney leading most of the smoke away, but it still made the chamber feel hot and grimy. Judging by the different layers of soot on the wooden columns, this hearth had been in operation on and off for years, if not decades. A tunnel on the other side of the chamber sloped upwards and, Gus presumed, outwards.

Another man worked at an anvil nearby, chuckling to himself with simple-minded amusement as he gleefully pounded away with his hammer. Those things Gus noticed first because they were bright and noisy, but then his attention caught on something else entirely.

Across the room was a stacked pile of shimmering gold.

Gus stared at it in shock, having never seen anywhere near so much in one place. Small crates appeared to be stacked with coins, and piled about those were crowns, scepters, some sort of picture frame, and various figurines depicting men, women, or dragons.

He quickly realized these must be Miss Aliyah Gale's stolen treasures. If someone had been stealing in amounts like this for decades, then the wealth stolen from Miss Aliyah Gale's 'collection' would be enough to make anyone fantastically rich.

Lost in speculation, Gus's reverie was cut short when Salka hissed, "That's Saucier!"

Turning back, Gus saw the goblin pointed to the grinning idiot at the anvil. Taking a more careful look, Gus saw the man wore his dinner clothes, but they were filthy and ragged, having already fallen to tatters in the weeks since his disappearance. Watching the operation more closely, Gus saw the man at the fire push a gold figurine into the furnace, and a few moments later, he pulled the sagging soft metal from the fire and placed it upon the anvil.

Saucier, renowned patron of the arts, giggled to himself and then hammered the statuette into a shapeless lump of metal, which he then tossed into a barrel behind him. It was the same sort of manic devotion to a mindless task he had seen in Aelfua once before; it was only missing the music.

Gus stepped further into the chamber, but when neither of the two men acknowledged his presence, he said, "Richard Saucier? Sir?"

Saucier looked up at him, smiling broadly as if he had just bumped into an old friend while on holiday. The man working the fire seemed less amused and busied himself with working the bellows and checking the flume. The fire tender began to chant a series of foreign syllables, and after the first few, Saucier smiled and joined in.

Salka watched, dumbfounded, but Gus recognized the sound right away. It was the same prayer Emily had been struggling with as she recovered. Grabbing Salka's arm, Gus pulled the goblin towards the tunnel across the chamber and said, "Don't listen! Do not listen to it! Hum something else to keep it out of your head!"

He hurried them further up the tunnel until he could no longer hear the chanting below. His bad leg ached from the exertion, and he paused to rest and stretch it out. Bewildered and clearly exhausted, Salka asked, "What happened to him? What were they saying? It sounded ...."

At Salka's question, Gus could feel the memory of the chant tickling at his mind, and upon catching himself trying to sound out that first syllable, he shook his head and whistled the first few bars of the fiddler's tune to his dumbfounded companion. The gob was clearly frustrated at that baffling response but followed Gus as he continued along the upward-sloping stone corridor.

Crude stone stairs were supplemented in places by wooden ones as the caves and connecting tunnels extended onward and further upward. Eventually they reached an open room that had been cut into the earth, the exit to which gave them their first glimpse of sunlight.

Between them and the outside world, the room held a row of chairs, in which sat a half-dozen men dressed as miners, holding picks and shovels across their laps as they waited out their day. The miners bore dazed, dreamy-eyed expressions on their faces, and Gus doubted they would be any more helpful with his questions than Saucier, but he instantly recognized their uniforms.

They all wore matching coveralls, each embroidered with the logo of the Khanom Mineral Company.

Gus led Salka past them and to the tunnel entrance that lay just beyond. Across a small valley to the north, he could see the city of Khanom atop its plateau. A large building stood near the entrance to the 'mine', which he assumed was the dormitory for the gold miners so envied by those working the copper seam. The other miners had said the gold mine was dangerous, but thinking back to the men sitting idle, those dangers now seemed far less accidental.

A two-rail funicular sat idle on the slope, leading down to a small utilitarian building that probably served as storage. A very large house sat adjacent to that building, and pointing it out to Salka, he said, "That's Maurice Sylvester's place, isn't it?"

The goblin shaded his eyes and peered down at it uncertainly, and Gus suddenly recalled his friend was not only many hours beyond his usual diurnal slumber, he probably couldn't see much in the bright light of early afternoon.

Gus gave Salka a friendly pat on the shoulder and then said, "Thanks for all your help. I think we've found our kidnapper and our thief. I'm betting Doctor Phand will be there too. This is probably the dangerous part, so you should head back the way we came. If you see Miss Aliyah Gayle on the way, remind her she owes us that reward."

"What about you?"

With a sigh, Gus looked down at the imposing edifice below and said, "I have to try to rescue Doctor Phand before that elf decides his time has run out."

~

"Investment News"

For some time, the complaint has been made that, in managing portions of the civic fund, the city does not select Khanom Mineral Company Annuities in preference to the other stocks and thus affect a saving of public money due to the lower price of the security. It has been answered that the Khanom Mineral Company Annuities are so limited in amount, that they would rise to the level of the other stocks directly once an operation of any magnitude was commenced; therefore, it is incorrect to suppose the whole difference in price would be saved. To-day, however, Khanom's broker has, for the first time, employed civic funds in the purchase of Khanom Mineral Company Annuities.

– *Khanom Daily Converser*, 17 Tal. 389

~

- CHAPTER 32 -

The funicular was driven by weight, so to descend the mountain, all Gus had to do to was step aboard and release the brake. Looking down at the houses on this side of the valley, Gus could see Mister Beck's house was not that far away from Sylvester's, and he shook his head ruefully at how close he had come yesterday, totally unaware that Doctor Phand's kidnapper was just a few doors down.

Though far from the main attractions, electrical lines for the tram system were already strung through most of the area. The trams would not be running until they could receive a dramatic unveiling for the Exposition. Once in service, Khanom's trams would provide easy mass transit options for the handful of wealthy residents living here in opulence, although Gus supposed such large houses also had staff who might be permitted to ride them in to work.

Exiting the funicular, Gus stepped through the construction detritus surrounding the final tram stop, which would be conveniently located right at Sylvester's doorstep. Having spent the entire day hiking through the Duer underworld, Gus's legs were aching, so he paused to rest at the future tram terminus. Leaning against one of the new electrical junctions, he massaged his left calf and studied Sylvester's abode.

It was a large blue and gray edifice with three floors, towering gables, and a scale siding that gave it a decidedly piscine aspect. Two wires were strung from the junction he leaned against, draped inelegantly across the yard before being joined to the house. The second wire seemed like an oddity, and Gus wondered if that meant Sylvester owned a personal telegraph.

Approaching the house, Gus hesitated at the door, not sure if he should knock or just step inside. After their failure to murder him at the warehouse, he had no idea what to expect of the Wardens inside— the kidnapping had been so carefully orchestrated, but everything else had been strangely clumsy.

His best guess now was that he faced a sharp criminal mind working with duller tools, but he also knew a hammer could kill a man as dead as a knife if it were swung hard enough. This was the part where he could really use a plan, but looking around the grounds, nothing sprang to mind.

If Doctor Phand was to get out alive, however, someone had to go in after him. After a deep breath to steady his nerves, Gus gripped the handle and opened the door.

Beyond the threshold, the foyer opened into a main hall where thick eastern rugs covered the dark wood of the floors. Despite the wire from the tram, Sylvester's house appeared to still be lit mostly with softly hissing gas lamps rather than electricity. Side tables lined the walls, topped with vases, statuettes, and other odds and ends, and were spaced apart only by large works of art similar to the depictions of Elven cities in the Exposition offices.

To his right, Gus saw a large parlor filled with portraiture and elegant furnishings in keeping with the main hall's opulence, made strange only by the presence of a large stone box. Nothing seemed to indicate this was anything other than the residence of a wealthy man of business with a slightly eclectic interest in antique art.

Concealed doorways marked the entrances to servants' passages in all the usual places, although strangely no footman or other domestic appeared and took notice of the stranger creeping inside. Gus supposed that meant attention was elsewhere, and they weren't expecting any other visitors. A wide staircase swept upwards to the second level, and there he heard voices.

Creeping up the stairs, he nosed around the upper level until he found a side passage through which the voices came. The side passage was an interior space with no windows and was hung with various ornaments of ostentatiously Elven origin. There were paintings, strange wooden masks, and other odds and ends. Glints of elfsteel marked the collection as legitimately antique rather than simply the Elven-styled work of Modernists.

Moving quietly towards the voices led him around the corner to a small chamber with no furniture and at least two dozen Wardens standing in a broad cluster, chatting amongst themselves in collegial tones despite their covered faces. Pulling back against the wall, he peeked around the corner and scanned over the robed figures for one wide enough to be the round-bodied engineer. None of them quite matched his proportions.

There was a shiver, like a sudden draft of cold air that Gus felt within himself rather than against his skin. It seemed to strike everyone at once. All conversation halted, and in eerie unison, the Wardens all turned to face away from him towards the front of the room. In a wave from front to back, the Wardens fell to their knees, save for two towards the front.

Those two Wardens grabbed a pair of wooden sculptures and pressed them together into a sort of throne, and then they too fell to their knees. Although he saw no one, Gus could hear the tapping of footsteps from the room ahead, and all the gathered Wardens pressed their hooded heads to the floor in obeisance. Stepping from some hidden alcove towards the front of the room, their Elven lord emerged, facing the hallway Gus peered in from.

The elf was slender beyond healthy human proportions and moved through the room with unearthly grace. Gus could see the elf's face was very angular, his chin coming to a definite point that gave him a vulpine cast as he gazed out over his gathered servants. His pale gray eyes were downcast, with a twinkle of satisfaction as he admired the servility of his kneeling followers, and his thin lips curled into a self-satisfied smirk.

The green silks the elf wore were cut in similar style to his Wardens, but the opulent fabrics used seemed to mock the congregation abasing themselves in rougher woolens upon the hard marble floor. As the elf walked softly between the rows of his followers, Gus caught a glimpse of the slippers peeking beneath his robe and realized the tapping footsteps he had heard before must have belonged to someone else still hidden from view.

Gus surveyed the dozens on the floor, wondering if there was any way he might slip past them to see who lurked in whatever hidden passage the elf had emerged from, but no solution came to mind. Then his hopes of remaining unnoticed were dashed as the elf's sharp, reedy voice called out, "Mister Baston! What a pleasant surprise it is to see you here after so much effort has been put in to seek you out."

That last part seemed like a barb aimed at someone else, so Gus merely smiled and stepped fully into the hall and stood in the doorway of the Wardens' meeting chamber. The elf's voice was different, more strained and higher pitched, but its cadence and tone were unmistakable to someone who knew to listen for them, so Gus replied, "Sorry to have put you to the trouble then, Mister Sylvester."

There was a soft gasp from someone amid the kneeling wardens, apparently unaware of his host's true identity. The elf grinned, his sharp jaw making the smile look predatory as he stepped between his followers and towards the doorway. Although the proportions of his face were inhuman, his features resembled those of his human guise—like the distorted reflection of a fun house mirror.

"You seem strangely intent on spilling all my secrets," he said and then slightly twitched the fingers of his right hand. It was clearly a signal to someone, although as far as Gus could tell, he was the only one who could see it.

The kneeling Wardens, faces still to the floor, began to chant softly as if in prayer. The foreign words were meaningless, but Gus could feel the rhythm of the syllables tugging for his attention. Like a good song, the chanting filled him with an urge to just hum along until he could mimic the words himself. It tickled the mind like something once known and recently forgotten.

Gus took a sharp breath to break his focus on the quiet prayer, and said, "You know Verin girls are lovely."

The elf lord tilted his head in curiosity and said, over the chanting, "You are an odd one, Mister Baston. You're being quite troublesome."

"That's how I make my living. I'm just here for Doctor Phand though; if you release him, then I'll be on my way."

Sylvester chuckled, and the chanting stopped as his mild laugh echoed around the room in the throats of his kneeling followers. They all instantly hushed just as he spoke, "He's here of his own accord, Mister Baston."

The elf snapped his long, slender fingers, and Doctor Phand stepped out of the same hidden alcove from which Sylvester had emerged. Phand was still wearing the dinner jacket he had been in when he was kidnapped. He looked rumpled and dazed but physically unharmed. His eyes, however, were unfocused, and his voice stilted as he intoned, "I need to stay, Mister Baston. Just two more days would be most appropriate."

Gus nodded; after seeing Emily and then Saucier, he had expected nothing less. The elf had arranged Louis's murder, had set Gus to take the blame for that and the kidnapping, and then somehow abducted Emily from Khanom. There needed to be some sort of justice for all that, but Gus looked around at the room full of mesmerized

Wardens, each one with a knife on their belt, and he did not like his chances.

"So he'll stay just long enough to miss that signing deadline, right? I don't care about your local politics, Sylvester, or your grand restorative or whatever else. The reward on him doesn't say anything about getting him home before your deadline."

It was true enough, and the words made Sylvester's inhuman grin sharper with a glint of triumph in his eyes. All that remained was for Gus to make some sort of threat of disclosure that might get him out alive, which would hopefully leave him with custody of Phand in a couple of days. While he paused to think over how to phrase it, there was a deep, low rumbling, like a distant storm or perhaps a small earthquake.

The others didn't seem to notice it, but it came from somewhere deep below the house, and hearing it, Gus grinned back at Sylvester and was pleased by the flicker of surprise in the elf's eyes. "Unfortunately, though, you messed with me and mine, and I'm afraid that I can't have. That cabbie in Gemmen you had them kill was a friend of mine."

The elf shrugged and nodded in unconcerned confession to the murder. Gus smiled and waited for something to come of that rumbling, but it just stopped. He began to worry he might have overplayed his hand. Sylvester opened his mouth to respond, so Gus quickly added, "And then you kidnapped Emily, and tried to—"

"Emily?" the elf interrupted, not seeming to recognize the name. He glanced down at one of the robed figures bowing at his feet, and Gus guessed that one must be Dorna. She seemed to shrink down a bit, cringing beneath her master's questioning gaze, even though with her face to the floor, she couldn't possibly see it.

Sylvester sighed, shook his head, and then said, "Is that who that was? My apologies, Mister Baston, I was told she related to the search for Doctor Phand, but my plans for you ended in Gemmen. It seems the subsequent attempts to curtail your further involvement may have been handled … inappropriately. I do dislike loose ends."

The figure Gus took for Dorna flinched at the words. There was another rumble, deep below, but nothing more, so to drag things out a bit longer, Gus said, "I know what this is about. Your first vote for the tower was just a dodge—you've been trying to stop it all along."

Sylvester nodded again and said, "You know, despite your reputation, you're actually somewhat good at this, Mister Baston. It is about Phand's tower. Those meddling mortals seek to build an iron tower atop the Elven queen's palace—"

"No. That was across the street. They're building it on the old Embassy building."

The elf frowned when Gus brought up the Embassy building, and Gus knew he must be hitting close to the mark. Realizing that, the pieces began to fall together in his mind: the Elves accepted no foreign embassy at the queen's summer court, but the Elven city of Khanom had sat atop another, older city. The Embassy building wasn't there for ambassadors visiting the Elven court; it was for ambassadors visiting from the Elven court.

Grinning at Sylvester, he said, "The old Duer embassy connected the Elves to the city below. You're worried they'll dig out the foundation for the tower and find the tunnels."

Sylvester laughed, and again that laugh was eerily echoed by other voices as the Wardens mirrored his good humor. "Very clever," he said, eyes fixed on Gus.

Raising his voice slightly, Sylvester adopted a tone that made it clear he addressed the entire room as he said, "When my people left, we knew it was only a matter of time. Humans are short-lived and thus short-sighted. We would bide our time until humanity was on the verge of collapse as you've been so many times in your history.

"Thus, the Great Restoration—we would return, ushering in the renewal of true civilization, sweeping aside the old order to bring about an age of peace. Alas, some guidance is required in the interim, so I have remained to gather followers and make ready."

Sylvester's monologue was a sales pitch, but Gus recognized right away it wasn't aimed at him, and he bet that meant at least some of the Wardens were not entirely under Sylvester's spell. That seemed promising, but Gus wasn't sure what to do about it.

The rumbling below had not resumed, and he wondered how much longer he could stall. Forcing a bit of cocky swagger, Gus said, "This thing with the tower isn't about the Elves at all though, it's just about the treasure hidden down in those Duer tunnels."

The elf stiffened at the mention of treasure but kept his sharp smile, and in a light tone as if it didn't matter to him at all, he replied, "There are treasures there, left hidden for me in the ruins below— something we might use to capitalize upon humanity's endless greed. Unfortunately, it seems that in their greed, your rulers were cleverer than expected; their 'treasure trove' law claims any Elven riches discovered in Aelfua are prizes of war to be seized by your government."

Whether it was a lie or a mistake, the elf's answer was certainly not for the soon-to-be-murdered investigator, Gus was sure. As much as they seemed under his control, there was no reason to give a speech explaining himself unless some of his followers could break free. Gus glanced around the kneeling Wardens, searching for any sign that they might recognize their master's duplicity.

Sylvester sighed and went on, "That meant I could not sell them directly of course, and thus many great works of art have had to be rendered down into base metals in order to realize their value—

truly a loss for the ages and another tragedy brought about by the greed of men."

The elf's fingers twitched his signal, just as they had before, and the kneeling Wardens all rose to their feet, chanting the same soft words in Elven. Gus felt it tug at him, the way a good song would drive men to tap their toes in time with the beat.

The first few syllables seemed strikingly familiar, and one was almost like the Gedlunder word for 'give'. The other words weren't anything like 'fish' or 'roof', and they tickled at the back of his mind like something familiar but forgotten. He paused, listening to the second repetition, trying to remember the words.

Fighting against it, Gus shook his head and then hummed a bit of the fiddler's song, focusing on Claude's incomplete lyrics. Verin girls are lovely. The Tuls will keep you warm.

Sylvester watched him, a bemused smile stretched across thin lips. "You seem unusually resistant, Mister Baston," he said, his voice only slightly louder than the chants of his followers. "Not by blood, I think. What's holding you back from joining us, hmm?"

Gus gritted his teeth and grinned at the elf as he replied, "Ogria Girls."

Sylvester simply chuckled and said, "They were Verin girls before. Which is it? I suppose I'll just have to ask this 'Emily' about it." He made a minute gesture with his hand, and the Wardens all reached down, drawing daggers from their belts in a single synchronized hiss of metal.

Their chant continued, beating at Gus, and the rhythm of it began to throw off the pacing of Claude's lyrics. The fiddler's tune was difficult to keep going in the best of circumstances, and trying to hold on to it amid Sylvester's wyrd distraction began making Gus dizzy.

Moving as one, the Wardens all turned to face him, drawn blades gleaming in the gaslight.

"I do have a bit of news you might be interested in," Gus managed, and Sylvester tilted his head curiously, somehow subtly signaling the Wardens, who instantly fell still and silent. It felt as if a sudden pressure had been removed, and Gus sighed in relief, holding up a finger to request a moment while he caught his breath. As he did, he heard a lighter pair of footsteps from the direction of the hidden alcove, which made him grin a bit as he said, "It's a bit of a good news, bad news sort of thing."

"And what is that, Mister Baston?"

"Well, you don't have to worry about the treasure trove law because the stuff you found wasn't left by the Elves. It belonged to someone else."

The elf's thin lips curled up as his inhuman grin broadened. "Really, Mister Baston? That is good news!"

Towards the back of the room, the Warden that Gus earlier guessed to be Dorna turned her head sharply, looking at Sylvester in seeming surprise. The rest of the Wardens kept their collective gaze fixed upon Gus, knives still in hand as their master continued, "I'll have to consult with my attorneys on how best to capitalize it, of course. And your bad news?"

Really hoping he wasn't overplaying his hand again, Gus said, "That's also the bad news, I'm afraid."

The elf looked confused, and as he started to ask for more, Miss Aliyah Gale emerged from the alcove and said, "They belong to me."

Sylvester turned from Gus to face her, and the eyes of his mesmerized Wardens followed suit. She stepped confidently into the room, still dressed in the elegant fashions that had adorned her in the Duer city below, and Gus briefly wondered if she dressed herself or was just some doll bedecked by the monster. She looked utterly unconcerned by the cultists and their drawn knives as she walked towards the center of the room, her eyes focused on the various decorative objects hung upon Sylvester's walls. "I am pleased to see not everything was destroyed."

Because he was listening for it, Gus heard the deep rumble far below, and it seemed to be growing louder. Unsure what might happen in a clash between the elf and Miss Aliyah Gale, Gus decided to focus on his own mission. The Wardens were all facing the center of the room, so he circled to the edge, and when not one head turned to follow his movement, he hugged the wall and made his way back towards Phand.

"The irony is, I might never have seen them again if you hadn't been trying so hard to stop the tower," she continued. "After I lost the initial vote, Doctor Phand hired one of my surveyor teams to examine the park, so I was able to examine his plans. It won't expose my secrets. In fact, it's quite a bit safer than anything else that might go there. An empty park would always be filled eventually. Now, it will be a monument to the city's strength and remain long after the exposition."

Sylvester's smile was fading, the elf uncertain, and at some unseen cue his followers took up the Elven prayer once more. Gus felt it creeping in to the corners of his consciousness, and Doctor Phand began mumbling through it as well, although he seemed unsure of the words. Gus grabbed the engineer's arm and tried to pull Phand away from the others, but the mesmerized engineer resisted.

Their knives were still out, although the Wardens were just standing in place as Miss Aliyah Gale strolled through their midst towards the room's entrance. Peering out and into the hallway, she said, "I've been looking through my collection recently, trying to determine what all had been taken. Some of the missing items were quite old, like these Elven trinkets you've kept for yourself."

She seemed entirely unmoved by the chanting, and Sylvester frowned slightly, clearly having expected some sort of reaction from her. The rumbling below that accompanied her conversation seemed steadily louder. Miss Aliyah Gale was important within the city for her wealth and business acumen, and judging by Sylvester's expression, Gus doubted anyone knew of the thing she actually represented.

Donning his smile again, the elf replied, "Perhaps we could reach some sort of agreement? The treasure was under an Elven city, so I'm hardly to blame for the confusion, and what's done is done, after all."

Miss Aliyah Gale continued as if Sylvester had never spoken, "Others were quite a bit older. Some of those missing keepsakes were acquired before the rise of your queen."

Sylvester glanced uneasily downward at the rumbling beneath their feet, and some of the chanting faltered when a few of the Wardens were distracted by it as well.

"A few missing odds and ends were even made before the Elves first awoke on these shores—older than the forests that cover these mountains, crafted by artisans in times and styles lost forever to the ages." Her words were delivered in a cool voice, like a teacher lecturing students. The second voice resounded clearly now, an angry snarl that rose from the depths.

Gus dragged Doctor Phand back, away from the group, relieved to discover that as the chanting faltered, the man was far more easily led. The elf and his knife-wielding Wardens stood between them and the hallway, but moving to the back of the room, Gus could see into the hidden alcove and the dark hall that lay beyond it. The hallway led to stairs going downward, but he couldn't be sure of finding an exit above ground if they went that way.

Then monstrous voice below them spoke much more clearly, the sound of the words distinct even if their meaning was not. Strangely, Miss Aliyah Gale said nothing.

Gus looked back at her and saw that she glowered at Sylvester, but the elf stepped backwards as if he had understood whatever had been left untranslated. Whatever he had heard, the remaining entranced Wardens had stopped chanting and looked around at each other in clear confusion.

Sylvester turned to his followers and shouted, "Kill her! Kill her now!"

The newly uncertain Wardens began to close in on Miss Aliyah Gale but then halted as she convulsed. She made a retching sound, and her mouth opened wide, water burbling out as if she had just taken a drink. Even Sylvester looked momentarily confused as her mouth opened wider still, with more and more water pouring out, pooling at their feet and rolling across the marble floor in a spreading pool.

She leaned forward, and the water kept pouring from her open lips and onto the floor—more water than she could ever have contained. In a panicky voice, Sylvester shouted again, "Kill her!"

A loud rumble below shook the house, and the angry voice continued below them. The room rocked from side to side, and the Wardens stumbled, a few even slipping in the water on the floor as they tried to keep their feet. Gus grabbed Phand and yanked him back into the alcove.

Behind them, the marble floors cracked, buckling upwards as something shoved through them from below. The floor exploded, great chunks of marble knocking green-cloaked Wardens in every direction as a terrible head emerged. A great scaled maw large enough to swallow men whole rose from the floor. It looked as much like a wolf as a lizard, with great black teeth and a raging inferno behind them.

Daring to look no longer, Gus pulled Phand and ran, half-dragging the fat man behind him as he pulled desperately toward the stair. Men and women screamed behind them, their desperate cries nearly drowned out by the horrible roar of what had come for them.

Gus was relieved to discover that although the stairway continued further downward, there was a doorway on the ground floor leading from the stair and into a servants' passage.

Everything around them shook, and Phand stumbled. As Gus paused to pull him back to his feet, an enormous serpentine coil crashed through the wall, and a gargantuan clawed limb anchored itself on the floor ahead of them, pushing the reptilian form further upward. In the process, it tore through the wall, exposing the parlor Gus had passed through on his way in.

Gus tugged Phand through the new opening just as marble tiles from the floor above them began raining down into the collapsing passageway behind them. The house creaked and groaned, artwork falling from the walls as the building around them cracked and twisted. He rushed Phand through the foyer, shoved him out the front door, and then dragged him all the way to the curb before turning to look at the chaos behind.

The walls crumbled, and pipes burst from the ground, spilling a spray of water across the lawn. Scattered blue flames began cropping up inside from broken gas lines as Sylvester's house collapsed, slowly joined by orange and red as the wooden frame caught alight. One of the electrical lines snapped from the frame and fell to the ground nearby, sparking fitfully.

The earth shook as the house rocked back and forth, collapsing inwards on itself. A gas pipe burst up from the ground in the front yard and sent up a steady gout of blue flame in a fountain of light. Gus pulled Doctor Phand a little further down the street, towards the jumble of tram-line construction, but was unable to take his eyes from the scene. Even as the house crumpled, the wreckage undulated as the great beast destroyed the entire structure from within.

A figure in green emerged from the shifting wreckage and fled, some panicked Warden who discarded his hood and robes as he ran down the street and away from the scene. Gus watched warily as another began crawling free and was caught entirely off guard when the elf's thin, reedy voice piped up behind him, "That was entirely unexpected. Is that who you've really been working for all this time?"

~

"Fraud Unmasked in Mazhar"

In a shocking turn of events, the supposed queen of Tulsmonia residing in Mazhar has been unmasked as a fraud. The exiled Duke of Errapol arrived in Sakloch to great pomp from other exiled Tuls aristocrats gathered in Sakloch. His Grace, a long-time confidant of the magnar, was personally acquainted with the magnar's royal physician and immediately recognized that the man identified to him as Doctor Gleb Nichols was not who he claimed to be.

After questioning by the Sultan's security personnel, the charlatan confessed to his deception, and he will have been beheaded by the time this report sees print. His true identity has not been established to our sources in Mazhar, but despite official silence on the topic, it is well known that his female accomplice fled the palace with several items of value that had been presented to her by admirers taken in by the deceit.

– Khanom Daily Converser, 17 Tal. 389

~

- CHAPTER 33 -

The terrible beast spat out the flaming corpse of one of Dorna's fellow Wardens and then lunged for another. She looked for the Master, but he had vanished, and for a terrible moment, she feared he had already been consumed.

The floor tilted wildly, and with a loud crash, it vanished from beneath her feet. Tumbling down, she desperately tried to grab for anything, but everything within reach just came crashing down with her.

The breath was knocked from her lungs as she hit the ground floor, and on pure adrenaline she managed to clamber down the corridor as more of the level above began collapsing behind her.

She pushed off her hood to get a better look around and saw another Warden trapped under a fallen beam behind her, so she rushed to his aid. Working together, she managed to free him but felt a pang of heartbreak to see the smudged face of the Elven queen lay beneath him. The rest of the tapestry was pinned under marble tiles she knew she hadn't the strength to move.

Dorna pondered trying to slide the tapestry out, but as she paused, the wall beside her cracked, and a broken pipe began spitting fire. Singed but not alight, she sprang back, but then serpentine coils tore through everything, and there was no time to save any of the Master's treasures. The other Warden turned and fled the house, and despairing, Dorna followed.

Once outside, she turned to look at the wreckage behind them, wondering if any others made it out. Surely the Master had escaped, but Marjorie, Terry, all the others ….

She glanced over at the Warden she had rescued and was shocked to see him tearing off his robes and casting them aside. Dorna felt a bitter pang upon discovering the Warden she had saved was Sandal Ulm, of all people. He glanced at her only briefly, not even uttering a word of thanks for his rescue before turning to run away.

Looking around as she tried to catch her breath, Dorna saw that a few of the Master's neighbors had stepped outside and were watching the destruction of his house with bewildered horror. With an enormous surge of relief, she saw that there, in the street, stood the Master. He had lost his robes but not yet taken on his human guise.

Across from him stood Baston—her mistake.

She had tried so hard to follow the Master's plan, but somehow that man had ruined all of it, and somehow, with so many precious things destroyed in his wake, Baston had escaped with Phand.

For the first time in her life, the Master seemed suddenly fragile. He did not age, but despite all their power, Elves could still be killed, and now he faced a true killer and stood unarmed. She headed towards them, but battered and still breathless, she feared she wouldn't make it in time. She wished the Master had some sort of weapon, and as if in answer, a pistol suddenly appeared in his hand.

With a surge of relief, Dorna watched as he took charge of the situation. She stepped behind him, to stand at the Master's shoulder and be the silent support he needed in this dark hour.

Dorna felt her confidence rewarded by the Master's fearlessness. He would make everything as it should be. That was his mission.

The Master's features softened and broadened, rolling back like wax melting from a candle. His elf's body widened and swelled, taking on more human proportions until once again he donned his familiar disguise as Maurice Sylvester, captain of industry.

Sylvester stretched a little and rolled his wider jaw as he settled into the new shape. He kept his gaze on Baston and, even his voice made human, he said, "Truly? Amazing how far you people will go for so little money. You've certainly made shambles of my work here. I'll have to change faces again and start over someplace else, likely with considerably less capital on hand."

In the distance, the fire bell began ringing. Dorna glanced around to see if any of the neighbors had noticed the Master's transformation, but their eyes all seemed fixed upon the fiery destruction of his house.

Sylvester smiled and waved the pistol casually toward Baston as he said, "Well, after all this, I can't just let you go. Step away from Doctor Phand if you please."

Instead, Baston pulled Phand a little farther back, putting the doctor directly behind him. She had no idea what had become of Baston's pistol, but as he glanced around at the ground, it was obvious he was unarmed and looking for a weapon. There was some scattered detritus from the tram line's construction, but they had already finished installing the junction box. The only thing left behind that might be dangerous to the Master was a discarded iron bar, so Dorna angled herself to intercept Baston if he went after it.

With a cocky grin that seemed entirely out of place in his circumstances, Baston said, "Before you shoot me though, just tell me, all that Great Restoration stuff—that was a scam, right? I mean, obviously no one left you any treasure, and you've been as sharp at crime as a career criminal."

The remark about treasure bit at Dorna. Had the Elven queen truly left nothing for her Master? That ill-fitted the tales of her generosity and foresight, and it seemed unlike the Master to make that sort of mistake.

Then Sylvester chuckled and said, "You know, I only came to Khanom because I thought they might have forgotten something here. I never expected to find vast vaults of gold below the city. I knew they were watched by something, of course, but in so vast a space, it was easy enough to be quiet and avoid being caught."

That struck her like a blow to the chest. He had known! He had known nothing was left for him and had hoped that the perfect queen had just … forgotten something?

Baston glanced at her and then added, "So you're not some Elven agent at all then. Why are you still here?"

Dorna took a breath to angrily refute that insolence, but before she could, the Master laughed and replied, "No idea! No one bothered to consult me on it at all!"

She felt dizzy, her world seeming to melt into alien new shapes, just as the Master's face had done moments before. As terrible as that confession was, he continued blithely on, and she realized he had no idea she was standing behind him. "I was a prisoner, actually. It was the strangest jailbreak of all time—I went to sleep in my cell and awoke in an empty field with no idea what had happened."

Baston laughed with him and said, "Magic, huh?" He glanced her way again, and Dorna felt like she might be sick.

The Master went on, unaware of her and thus entirely heedless of her distress. "Indeed! You know, the funny thing is, before they all left, the handful of charms and such that I knew were nearly useless. The ley lines were tapped by an entire civilization, but now that I'm the only one drawing on them, it's amazing what I can do. It's a different world, but you'd hardly notice since humans have always been more resistant to magical energies."

His voice was full of a breezy confidence he only occasionally used in her presence. She'd always considered it a sign of her status as a trusted companion. Now Baston took her place, seeming to mock her as he replied, "Oh?"

Sylvester, seemingly pleased to have someone to confess it to, nodded as he said, "Iron in the blood or something. It makes some minds more difficult to entrance than others."

Baston glanced at her again and then asked, "Like Dorna's father? I've seen your supposed gold mine, so I know there was no chance of a cave in or whatever you said killed him."

As he said that, something clicked together in her mind, two pieces of information she had always had yet held intractably separate for years: her father had died because of corrupt mine owners, and he had worked in Sylvester's mines. How had she not realized that before? Had that been his magic too?

Too cruel just to leave it with that, Baston added, "You wanted him out of the way to keep the copper mine from unionizing."

Dorna looked back at Baston, shocked. She had no idea how he knew her father was involved in that, but the Master had always said he supported ….

"Oh, yes, I couldn't have that!" Sylvester replied, seeming amused at the very notion. "Pulling him out of the real mine extinguished the union talk, but unfortunately, once we had him up here, he was just too resistant to sit quietly. It was a shame to get rid of him, but I couldn't have him running around once he'd seen so much."

An incandescent rage blossomed in Dorna's chest. The world narrowed to the man standing in front of her, blithely confessing to the murder of her father. He had killed her father out of pure greed. Despite that though, the Master had still taken her in, and he had raised her ….

"The girl was an unexpected bonus—you see, too many charms rots the human brain over time, but then I thought that if I started with a young one that was a little resistant by blood and just trained her to use the spells on herself—"

There was a sudden scream, and from the soreness of her throat, Dorna realized it was hers. Her arms thrust forward, shoving Sylvester and nearly knocking him from his feet. She was shocked by it for only a moment because once the floodgates of that outrage had burst, every bit of her fury felt undeniably righteousness.

Sylvester staggered forward, and as he turned to face her, she swept up the iron bar she had been guarding. She swung it, catching him hard on his left shoulder, but as he staggered back from the blow, he shot his pistol.

At first, she thought he had missed, but an instant later there was a terrible burning at the back of her right shoulder. She tried to swing the iron bar again, but her arm didn't raise like it should. Looking down, she saw the bullet had torn through her shoulder, and it was all she could do not to drop her weapon.

Rubbing at his own injured shoulder, Sylvester sighed and in a voice of strained patience began a recitation in Elven. A panicked expression crossed Dorna's face as she recognized the sound. It was a chant he used on his enemies.

She'd seen him use it on Baston's girl and knew it was powerful, but he had never turned it on her. Looking over, she saw Doctor Phand already swaying to the words, and everything became blurry as the Master's Elven prayer seemed to infuse her with a numb warmth. Sleepily, she noticed that even Baston was no match and was also beginning to gently sway to the rhythm of the Master's chant.

They were no match for it. The Elves were the true rulers of mankind as it had always been meant to be. Time seemed to slow as she drifted away, but then a strange, discordant tweet caught her attention.

There was another and another after that. She could turn her head, and when she did, she discovered that Baston was the source of the noise.

The world snapped into focus.

Baston was whistling something, and Sylvester was staring at him curiously, his head cocked at the sound as if recognizing it.

Dorna's shoulder throbbed with momentarily forgotten pain, but she felt the iron bar still in her hand. She surged forward, crying out to marshal her strength as she gripped the iron bar in both hands. Sylvester turned back to her as she drove her weapon deep into his chest.

The Master had always seemed to know everything, and the shocked look on his face was utterly alien to her. He screamed and blazed his pistol wildly several times, and she felt a hard blow to her stomach that knocked her from her feet.

Blood pooled around her, hers she supposed, and with a triumphant snarl, Sylvester turned his back on her to face Baston. The iron bar had gone all the way through Sylvester's chest, and she could see part of it protruding from his back. His inhuman grace faltered, but he kept his feet and his grip on the pistol.

Sylvester ignored her, and as she felt the warmth leaving her body through a hole in her lower back, Dorna wondered if that inattention meant she was already dead. He looked down at the iron bar she had buried in his chest and then back to Baston and panted out, "So ... as you can see ... resistance is ... troublesome. You ... you've proven quite resistant ... yourself ... Mister Baston."

Troublesome was all she had managed. She tried to move, and it was agonizing, but despite that agony, her legs responded. Clenching her teeth, Dorna turned onto her side and pushed herself up to her knees.

Still faced with the pistol, Baston raised his hands and said, "It was a trick I learned in army, when we fought the Lich King."

Sylvester coughed up a bit of blood and then paused to wipe it from his lips. She had hurt him after all. Either because he was giddy from the blood loss or simply arrogant, rather than shoot, Sylvester asked Baston, "Oh? Did the Lich King use … use this kind of magic?"

Baston smirked a moment and then replied, "I don't know; he was dead when we got there."

Sylvester grinned at that, then his shoulders shook, his eyes twinkling as he laughed at the stupid line, having to pause to cough. "He was dead when—" he began and then laughed and coughed again, struggling for breath.

Rekindling her anger, Dorna pressed back to her feet, ignoring her own pain as she charged forward with vengeful ire that would not be twice refused. Gripping at the iron spike in his back, she roared and shoved at Sylvester with all her might.

He gasped in surprise and gripped at the pole as she swept him from his feet. With a scream that mixed pain with rage, she turned him and rammed into the tram line's newly installed junction box. The iron bar pierced the box, and it exploded in a shower of sparks.

Dorna was thrown back several yards, landing hard on her back, but Sylvester remained there, impaled. Lifting her head, she saw his body danced about, limbs jerking in a spasmodic dance for a moment and only slowly falling limp as he began to smolder.

Behind him, Baston was dragging Phand away as quickly as he could manage.

Turning her head, she saw that the movement within the house had stopped, and now it looked as if the entire edifice were slowly crumbling into the Oblivion. It grew hazy and dim as she watched, and someone ran towards her. For a moment, she dimly hoped it might be Terry, but as it drew closer, she saw the helmet and realized it was someone from the fire brigade.

He shouted something, but she was too tired to make sense of it. Closing her eyes, she wanted to pray, but she refused to utter the only words that came to mind.

~

"Fire Reported"

A catastrophic fire has been reported at the home of Maurice Sylvester. At the time of publication, Mister Sylvester has not been found, but surviving retainers report he was home when the great inferno commenced. While there is still some reason to hope he is merely convalescing in private, the destruction of his beautiful home and his renowned collection of art contained within it is a heartbreaking loss to our community.

Bodies have been recovered from the ruin, and formal death notices will be published in our Temple Day issue. No significant damage to neighboring homes was noted.

– Khanom Daily Converser, 18 Tal. 389

~

- CHAPTER 34 -

Gus awoke with a start, brought wide awake by the sight of a green-robed figure sitting in a chair across from his bed. Blinking a few times, he felt enormous relief to discover it was merely the unconscious Doctor Phand, sleeping in a chair, using Emily's discarded Warden robe as a blanket.

Judging by the light seeping through the drawn curtains, it appeared to be early morning. Turning his head, he saw that Emily shared the bed with him, fully clothed. Looking down at himself, he recalled that he had fallen asleep in that state himself. Their modesty in the eyes of whatever was left of Phand had been preserved.

Though his panic at the sight of the Warden greens had been unjustified, in recovery from that shock, Gus found his heart was still beating too fast to go back to sleep. He sat up in the bed and turned sideways to begin stretching out his left leg as he pondered what to do. One return ticket to Gemmen was in his jacket, but they needed three.

Digging into his pants, he counted out forty-six peis. A third-class ticket home for Phand would cost thirty, but that didn't leave him enough to pay Emily's fare. Sixteen peis wouldn't even be enough to stay here the three nights it would take for him to get home and have a bank wire back a pay order.

As he recounted, Emily stirred beside him and said, "How late is it?"

"Still early. Any chance you brought much money with you for the trip out here?"

Sitting up beside him, she frowned and said, "They didn't give me time to get more money. I've only got eight peis three."

"This part would be much easier if kidnappers would ply their trade in the mornings. We're still six shy of fare, and no meals on the way." Slipping out of bed, Gus walked over and began patting down Phand's pockets until he found a likely wallet. The man had been abducted on his way home, so it was predictably light—only three peis eight. "Well, two and a half shy of fare, and no meals."

"Dining car porridge is five pennies. We could get by on a peis and a half for meals."

Gus looked skeptically down at Phand and said, "You think he'd eat that? And only two meals a day? Two peis ten, at least."

Emily rose from the bed and began throwing his loose things into the carpet bag. When he looked at her skeptically, she handed him his mandolin and said, "Well, we can't stay here, regardless, and I'm already packed."

They roused Phand, who mumbled sleepily but managed to get to his feet and into the elevator. He still seemed out of his wits, but at least he was easy enough to direct. Gus had never followed up with Bridgton after the war and was not sure if the man would ever recover from the elf's magic. Fortunately, the reward offer had made no mention of the man's condition upon return.

When the doors opened, Gus let Emily lead out Doctor Phand while he managed the luggage. He approached the desk to ask after anything he might still have left in their safe, and as he did, the clerk looked up at him with an expression of alarm, hurriedly gesturing to one of his footmen. It wasn't the crooked one, so Gus was not sure what to make of the man.

"Sir! I'm so sorry; I didn't see you come down. She's in the lounge sir."

"Who is?"

"Miss Aliyah Gale! She's been waiting several minutes, I'm afraid." The man stepped from around the desk to personally escort him to the sitting area just across the lobby. Miss Aliyah Gale was seated there in an overstuffed chair, surrounded by a trio of very attentive gentlemen in business attire. The trio appeared to be explaining something to her, but her gaze was fixed on Gus.

"How deep was her voice?" he asked and received only a puzzled look in reply, so he added, "Was there like, a rumbling sound when she talked, like an earthquake or something?"

The clerk shook his head, replying slowly, "No, sir? Shall I have the lobby boy bring you some tea?"

Gus absently replied, "How about coffee?"

Phand was walking at a ponderous shuffle, and Emily was still guiding him from the elevator towards the front door. Gus gestured for her to take a seat with Phand somewhere near the front desk and then crossed the lobby towards Miss Aliyah Gale.

She wore an elegant Easternist frock of red silk that shimmered in the morning light filtering through the windows, and it was perhaps a bit more tightly fitted than the Gemmen social scene would typically find acceptable. Miss Aliyah Gale's eyes turned to Doctor Phand, and at that subtle gesture alone, the three men around her immediately ceased their chatter and hurried over towards where Emily and Phand had settled.

Gus recognized the impatient intensity of petitioners when he saw it. Emily could manage them for a bit, but his guess was that they were after custody of Phand.

He approached Miss Aliyah Gale, who was settled in her chair as if upon a throne, and said, "So sorry to keep you waiting!" She smiled patiently as if such an apology were really due, and the lobby boy hurried over to deliver his coffee. "You brought a lot of friends just to deliver the bounty on your art thief."

Miss Aliyah Gale smirked at that and said, "I never promised you a bounty. I promised a reward based on things recovered, and yet there wasn't anything you actually returned to me."

Gus did his best to look offended by that, but in truth he was so relieved not to hear the deep rumbling of her true voice somewhere nearby that he didn't manage a very convincing performance. If she was here to take Phand though, then he wouldn't get his reward for returning the man home. Feeling cornered, he sipped his coffee and then blanched at the bitter taste, spitting it back into the cup.

The melodious laughter across from him eased his tension a bit, and Miss Aliyah Gale said, "Is the coffee here so bad? I drank some earlier, but I'm sure you'll understand that the experience of it is a bit attenuated for me."

"It's the worst I've had since my days with the army, back in Gedlund."

"I didn't realize you had fought against the Lich King."

"Well," he replied, in his best air of wry humility, "He was already dead when we got there."

Nothing. She just looked at him as if waiting for more. When it was clear he was done, she produced an envelope, which she held out to him. "I'll be taking Doctor Phand, to complete his signatures. As this will interfere with your recovery of Missus Phand's proffered reward, I devised an amount I thought suitable, based upon that, and also what I will likely be able to recover from Maurice Sylvester."

Gus accepted the envelope but decided opening it then might be bad form. For the moment, he only heard her human voice, but he did not doubt the other one was speaking, no matter where it might really be.

Glancing back at Emily and Phand, he saw Miss Aliyah Gale's petitioners had been expecting the envelope as their signal, and one was trying to balk Emily while the other two led off Doctor Phand.

Gus waved at her to signal it was alright, and she frowned but let them herd off her charge.

When he turned back, he saw Miss Aliyah Gale had stood— clearly, she considered their morning's business concluded. She took a few steps and then turned back to him, as if a new idea had just occurred to her, and said, "I was impressed with your work here, Mister Baston. I'd be interested in engaging you as one of my agents."

The seemingly impromptu offer made him wonder if her expressions were real in any way or simply chosen for her. Thinking back to Salka's line about being eaten and then cooked, the safest option seemed like a polite demurrer. "Retainer work? I've done that for a few businesses over the years. It's not usually my favorite line, I'm afraid."

Emily stepped up alongside and gave him a reproachful look for turning down the business. Smiling at Miss Aliyah Gale, Emily asked, "What exactly do you need?"

Miss Aliyah Gale smiled as if that response had answered her question. Gus resolved then and there if she did anything even slightly out of the ordinary, he would just grab Emily and run.

Instead, she said, "So you did not learn all my secrets. Among my various interests, I own an investigative agency, Mister Baston. Originally, it was just to cut the costs of tracking down stolen pieces of my collection, but it's done quite well for me and now turns a considerable profit. I'd like you to join it."

He rolled the idea around a moment. Then the details clicked together, and he laughed. "Drake's? And with the lizard eye and the motto! Oh, you should be ashamed or at least laugh at more of my jokes. Eli Allen was working for you all along! That's why he bailed me out. You bailed me out so that I would find Doctor Phand."

Miss Aliyah Gale only responded with a mild smile and awaited his answer.

The idea of joining his rivals as a franchisee was a notion he had never considered as a possibility, and as much as he enjoyed his independence, it was tempting, at least until he remembered what he was really talking to. "What about Emily?"

Miss Aliyah Gale glanced over at Emily and said, "Her?" From the tone, it seemed she was little impressed by what she had seen. "We already have a specially trained staff at our offices in Gemmen, but I suppose you could bring her along if that's important to you."

What was important was arranging a polite refusal for a phenomenally dangerous employer, and she was making it difficult. Gus glanced over at Emily, who looked unhelpfully intrigued by the proposition. Both women watched him expectantly.

"Tell me, this Miss Aliyah Gale, the body I mean, where did she come from? Did you just make her from clay, or was she someone once?"

Miss Aliyah Gale tilted her head quizzically at the change of direction but then gave an indifferent shrug and replied, "Some farmer's daughter, I think. She was born in Aelfua but suffered an injury. Her mind was gone, but I was able to repair the body and make use of it."

Emily's eyes widened at that revelation, and Gus said, "That doesn't really sound like the life for me. I've seen your boys before—very clean-cut, law-and-order types for the most part. I'd imagine they're very reliable, show up to work on time, honest day's work, and all that. I rather enjoy the unsavory cases, and I like having the freedom to fix things my own way."

The patient smile faded, and Gus tensed to grab Emily and run if needed, but Miss Aliyah Gale just nodded and said, "Very well then, Mister Baston. I am disappointed, but no one can have everything. If you change your mind, I'm sure you will let me know."

"Wait, what's going to happen to Doctor Phand?"

Miss Aliyah Gale sighed and lifted the pendant necklace from her décolletage. Given her nature, Gus briefly tensed in expectation of some sort of magic and was only slightly disappointed when he realized it was a small watch she used to check the time. It seemed such a natural gesture, but knowing that everything she did was staged by a distant puppeteer, he recognized it as a blunt signal of impatience.

Still, he pressed on. "Obviously you need him to sign the city's agreement for the tower, but after you make him do that?"

"He'll be sent home, Mister Baston. I'm not that sort of monster." Turning to leave, she paused and then said, "Mister Salka'tok'tok'ton was also sent home. Whatever his share of your expedition was, it is also in that envelope."

The hotel's clerk hurried to personally open the door for Miss Aliyah Gale as she made her way out, and Emily opened the envelope to peer inside as soon as her back was turned. Emily's lips moved with her counting as she thumbed through the rail certificates inside, and then she said, "I don't know what all that business about her body was, but her money seems good. How much of this belongs to Mister Salcat … tot … whatever?"

Gus watched the doors close behind Miss Aliyah Gale, then turned to Emily and replied, "Oh, probably none of it. I mean, he was very clear he wanted no part of that deal. If it's any consolation, he owns a very expensive nightclub here in town, and we could spend a great deal of money there tonight, now that we're flush."

"Certainly not! I've spent more than enough time out here on the fringes. We'll go out on the next train." She turned and headed toward the door, refusing his forthcoming effort to convince her to spend time enjoying Khanom before their return home.

With a sigh, Gus walked to the front desk to check the safe, then collect his carpet bag and mandolin. Limping out with them, he found Emily had already flagged down a taxi. The cabman tossed his things onto the roof as she climbed inside, and Gus felt a renewed pang of melancholy over Louis's death. Even seeing Sylvester's house collapsing, the avengement did nothing to assuage the loss.

Emily reached down to help him into the taxi, and as he pulled inside, he glanced down at the envelope and said, "Some of that is for Louis, though. His family, I mean."

She nodded in agreement, and as the cab began rolling forward, she stared out the window, looking a little melancholy herself. After an awkward moment of silence, he finally asked, "Are you alright? After the elf and all that …?"

Emily shook her head but held up a hand as if to ward off the very topic. "For now, I'd just rather not think on it."

It was a sentiment he could understand.

Thinking of her recovery, he wondered if Dorna Michts had survived. If she did, would she revive the Wardens and try to find a better elf? What else would she do if she gave all that up? She was an admirably stubborn woman or had been anyway.

They arrived at Khanom's main hub and saw the westbound already pulling in to the station. Emily hurried to the ticket office to exchange one of the rail certificates for coin and ticket while Gus wrangled his luggage and paid for the taxi out of his thinning wallet. Noticing their hurry and Gus's limp, the driver helped him all the way to the platform, and feeling generous based upon whatever was in Miss Aliyah Gale's wallet, he tipped the man a whole three peis.

Emily met him there with no luggage beyond the envelope and her ticket. She grinned at him as they waited for the arriving passengers to finish off-loading, and when he raised a curious eyebrow at her suddenly cheery demeanor, she replied, "I'm looking forward to traveling first class."

"First class? My return's only for third!"

Waggling the envelope at him, she said, "Then I suppose you'll be riding back alone."

Astonished by her sudden spendthrift, he said, "How much is in there?"

"Plenty. We could both use a weekend in the country. Maybe you should take some of the extra cash and go get the cure."

"Cure for what?"

"All your drinking! If you weren't always so hung over, you could make it to work on time in the mornings. Mister Hallin's been calling about his divorce for weeks."

"There's nothing wrong with my drinking! I do it as well as three regular men put together. Besides which, if you recall, Hallin's wife wasn't actually cheating on him. What am I supposed to do?"

Emily smirked, looked him up and down, and then said, "I'm sure you could be charming if you cleaned up a bit. When we get home, I'll tell Mister Hallin to bring along reliable witnesses."

~ ~

The AUTHOR'S NOTE

Thank you, dear reader, for joining me here once again!

While writing *Gedlund*, I was struck by the convergence of so many great tales that had emerged from the latter nineteenth century. The same period that held Alan Quartermain and Gunga Din also played host to Sherlock Holmes and the Lone Ranger. Epic adventures of great variety abounded in a world of ever-expanding possibilities.

As a result, this was a very different book than the last! The mystery story was invented after the Road Hill House murder in the 1860s, so for this second story, I have tried to bring some of that into my world of fantasy.

Unwilling to simply mirror Sherlock Holmes and other giants of the era, however, I researched the actual private investigators of the day and was rather surprised by much of what I found. If you're curious, I recommend Alan Pinkerton's books on the subject, but overall, there were two primary lessons learned and applied here. First, until Pinkerton's famous agency came along, private investigators were often regarded as freelance criminals, and in many ways, they were. It was a career generally only adopted by very questionable people, and Sherlock Holmes' veneer of the genteel consultant was always a bit incredible.

Second, I was astonished by the era's industry of crime. I'd always imagined Victorian pickpockets as the starving scamps from Oliver Twist, but in point of fact, 'petty' theft could be a very lucrative career. With no credit cards, no interstate banks, and few inter-city organizations, people carried a lot more cash, at all times, than I'd ever really considered. As Gus elucidates, travelers had to carry every penny they might possibly need to spend on a trip, and an amazing array of scams arose to relieve them of all that. The hotel safe, which often seems superfluous to modern sensibilities, suddenly made sense as a tradition arising from desperate necessity.

Their world was barbaric in all sorts of unexpected ways, and a large part of the appeal of writing these stories, for me, has been drawing a fantasy world wherein the past was less idealized than the future. Instead of gazing upon our heroes gazing fondly at their own past, we would watch them try to set it behind them. I think the damaged Gus Baston from this story has embodied that idea very well. I've enjoyed writing him and love writing Emily as well, so I may have to revisit them very soon—possibly in short story form.

The next major project, however, is a different sort of story altogether. I've done a military adventure and now a mystery. For the next, I intend to write a western—a story that returns to Rakhasin in the town of Keat's Field, where Sheriff Glynn Sorley struggles to keep law and order amid the rush for buried treasure. If you've been reading the newspaper clips at the start of each chapter, you've seen hints of it already.

Older, stranger things than Miss Aliyah Gale still lurk in forgotten corners of the world. I look forward to sharing them with you.

Sincerely,

William Ray

ACKNOWLEDGEMENTS

My sincere thanks to my editor at Writer's Ally, Harrison Demchick, who once again thoroughly eviscerated my initial draft. Additionally, special thanks to Ramona Marc for her patience with me in creating the look I needed for my cover.

Acknowledgement must also be made of my great friends Pete Cornell and Christy Ozeroglu. Many years ago, Pete provided the initial kernel of inspiration that has blossomed into all this, as well as graciously providing me with names for the gods.

Christy's helpful and patient review of every draft from the earliest and clumsiest to this final iteration has helped me immeasurably in assembling this book. Her generous attention with my writing at its worst is immeasurably important, and the book would never have happened without her help.

Many thanks to all my friends and family who have given me their support and encouragement over the years, but my greatest debt of gratitude is to my wife, Amelia, without whose love, patience, and generosity I would be utterly lost.

Made in the USA
Coppell, TX
22 September 2020